How Come I Always Get Blamed For The Things I Do?

A Pickles Collection by Brian Crane

Also by Brian Crane

Pickles

Pickles, Too

Still Pickled After All These Years

Let's Get Pickled

Oh, Sure! Blame It on the Dog!

25 Years of Pickles

Grampa, Will You Tell Me a Story?

How Come I Always Get Blamed For The Things I Do?

A Pickles Collection by Brian Crane

BAOBAB PRESS

RENO, NV

Published in 2010 by Baobab Press
The publishing imprint of Baobab Books, Inc.
Reno, Nevada
www.baobabpress.com

Pickles is syndicated by the Washington Post Writers Group.

First Edition

21 22 23   10 9 8 7 6
ISBN-13: 978-1-936097-01-2
ISBN-10: 1-936097-01-X

Printed and bound in the U.S.A

MIX
Paper from responsible sources
FSC® C011935
FSC www.fsc.org

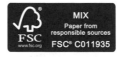

DEDICATION

This book is dedicated to my wonderful parents, Ray and Helen Crane, who bought me my first set of drawing pens and India ink. They encouraged me in so many ways to be one of those guys who writes and draws comic strips for a living and doesn't sponge off his mom and dad.

This book is also dedicated to my parents-in-law, Bud and Ardella Long, who provided me with countless ideas for my comic strip over the years without even knowing it. They also provided me with my adorable wife, Diana, who is both my chief cheerleader and critic.

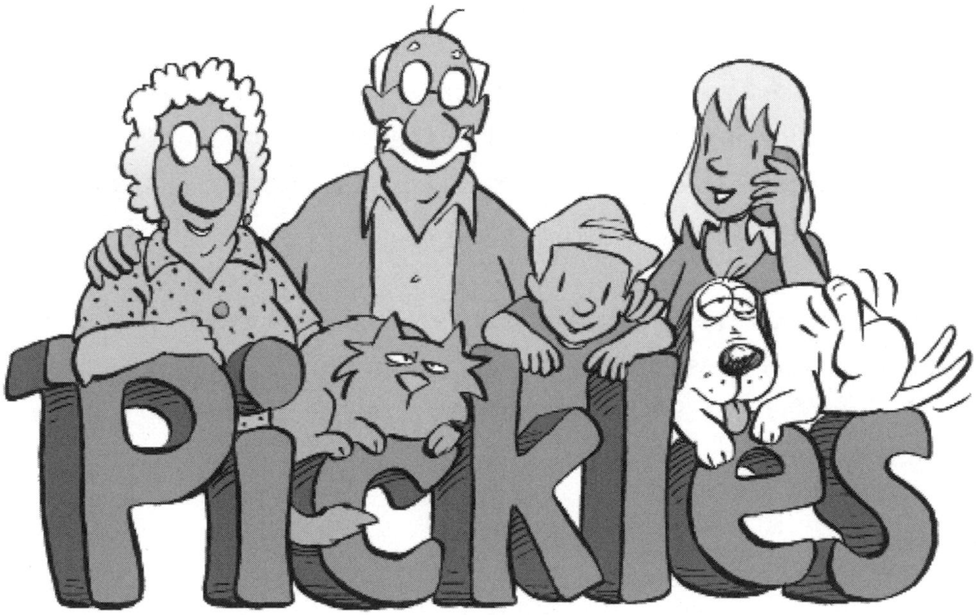
Pickles

INTRODUCTION

by Amy Lago

It is April 2, 1990. Duke and UNLV are preparing for tipoff in Denver tonight for the men's NCAA Division I Basketball championship. Home mortgage rates hover around 10 percent. A personal computer costs just over $1,000. Alannah Myles' "Black Velvet" is the No. 1 song on the Billboard chart, and if the stereo in the new car you're looking to buy has anything besides AM and FM, it is likely a cassette tape player. President George H.W. Bush is setting a trend for choosing moderately priced restaurants, and expensive restaurants are noticing a slump. The Soviet Union has just sent more armor to rebelling Lithuania. The trade relationship between the U.S. and Japan is testy, with an imbalance of $49 billion in 1989, and the U.S. is threatening to impose a tariff on Japanese goods come June.

"It is my belief, you cannot deal with the most serious things in the world unless you understand the most amusing." — Winston Churchill

You turn the page and find Snoopy preparing for a Beagle Scout hike, Mr. Dithers yelling at Dagwood for leaving a coffee ring stain on the Becker contract, and Calvin, dressed as Stupendous Man, getting ready to torment his baby sitter, Rosalyn. And in 20-some newspapers, a gentleman from the O'Reilly Seed and Bulb Company stands upon Opal Pickles' stoop to ask her, after 16 years of requesting the company's catalog, "When the heck are you going to buy some seeds?"

MRS. OPAL PICKLES OF 478 CRABTREE LANE?
© 1990, Washington Post Writers Group
I'M CLARENCE O'REILLY OF O'REILLY SEED AND BULB COMPANY, INC.
OUR RECORDS SHOW THAT YOU'VE BEEN REQUESTING OUR FREE CATALOG EVERY YEAR FOR THE PAST 16 YEARS. AND WE WERE JUST WONDERING...
4/2
... WHEN THE HECK ARE YOU GOING TO BUY SOME SEEDS?
BRIAN CRANE

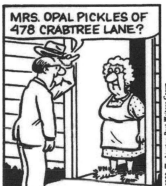

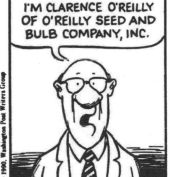

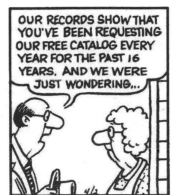

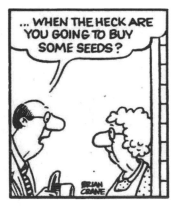

The first *Pickles* strip, April 2, 1990

So it is with the news. Humans cannot abide the incessantly serious. On any newscast, in any newspaper, on any news website, you will find at least a little something to amuse and lighten the burdens of the day. And since that humble day 20 years ago, many a reader has returned to Earl and Opal Pickles' house for that amusement.

"I never blame myself when I'm not hitting. I just blame the bat."
— Yogi Berra

The cartoonist behind *Pickles*, Brian Crane, is an unassuming, genial family man, married for 38 years and a father of seven. So most readers wouldn't suspect that he could easily be a covert operative for the CIA or FBI. His mind is a recorder, storing observations for use another day. But not every overheard conversation suits Earl and Opal Pickles. They are a unique couple, bound by 50 years of marriage, during which time each has pecked and heckled and elbowed the other. But they don't know what they'd do without each other. Brian has said that he based the Pickles on his in-laws, Bud and Ardella Long. If that is so, then readers might conclude that either he must have a lot more in-laws, or he is, indeed, a government spy, because not a day passes without a *Pickles* fan writing Brian to accuse him of having planted a camera in his or her house.

Because of how devoted Brian is to his creation, putting in six days of work each week, you can't believe the camera hypothesis for a minute. And the multiple in-laws theory is absurd because of

Brian's 38 years of devotion to his loving, supportive spouse, Diana. So that leaves only one explanation: Brian is a natural in the comics field, with an ear for dialogue as soothing and comfortable as your favorite slippers- until you discover the dog has left a "present" in them. Brian also has a keen eye for funny pictures, drawing Opal to conjure Sheriff Andy's Aunt Bee mixed with a little Hazel (and, perhaps a pinch of Rosie, the Jetsons' maid), and producing Earl out of a Wilford Brimley-Walter Brennan cross.

Finally, Brian is a master of storytelling, exposing foibles that are so common to human experience, they can be traced back to man's very beginnings. Surely the caveman insisted on fixing his own spear, no doubt cutting his hand and slicing his deerskin shirt, cursing and blaming the spear, until the caveman's wife shyly suggested that a visit to the local spear-maker might be in order (before the caveman ruined anything else). So it is with Earl and Opal. Except the spear is a plunger, the spear-maker is a plumber, and Opal pointedly told Earl to call a plumber before he attempted the repair job himself.

It is no small feat that, as of this writing, *Pickles* has accumulated 700 newspapers and will undoubtedly be closing in on 800, or more, by the time you read this introduction. That feat is testament to his syndicate's unwavering belief in his talent, his wife's stalwart encouragement and faith in her husband, and an editor's sense of when to shut up.

Amy Lago is Brian Crane's editor at The Washington Post Writers Group.
She has been a comics editor for more than 20 years, shutting up for the likes of Scott Adams, Darrin Bell, Berkeley Breathed,
Lynn Johnston, Stephan Pastis and Charles M. Schulz.

Sunday Pickles

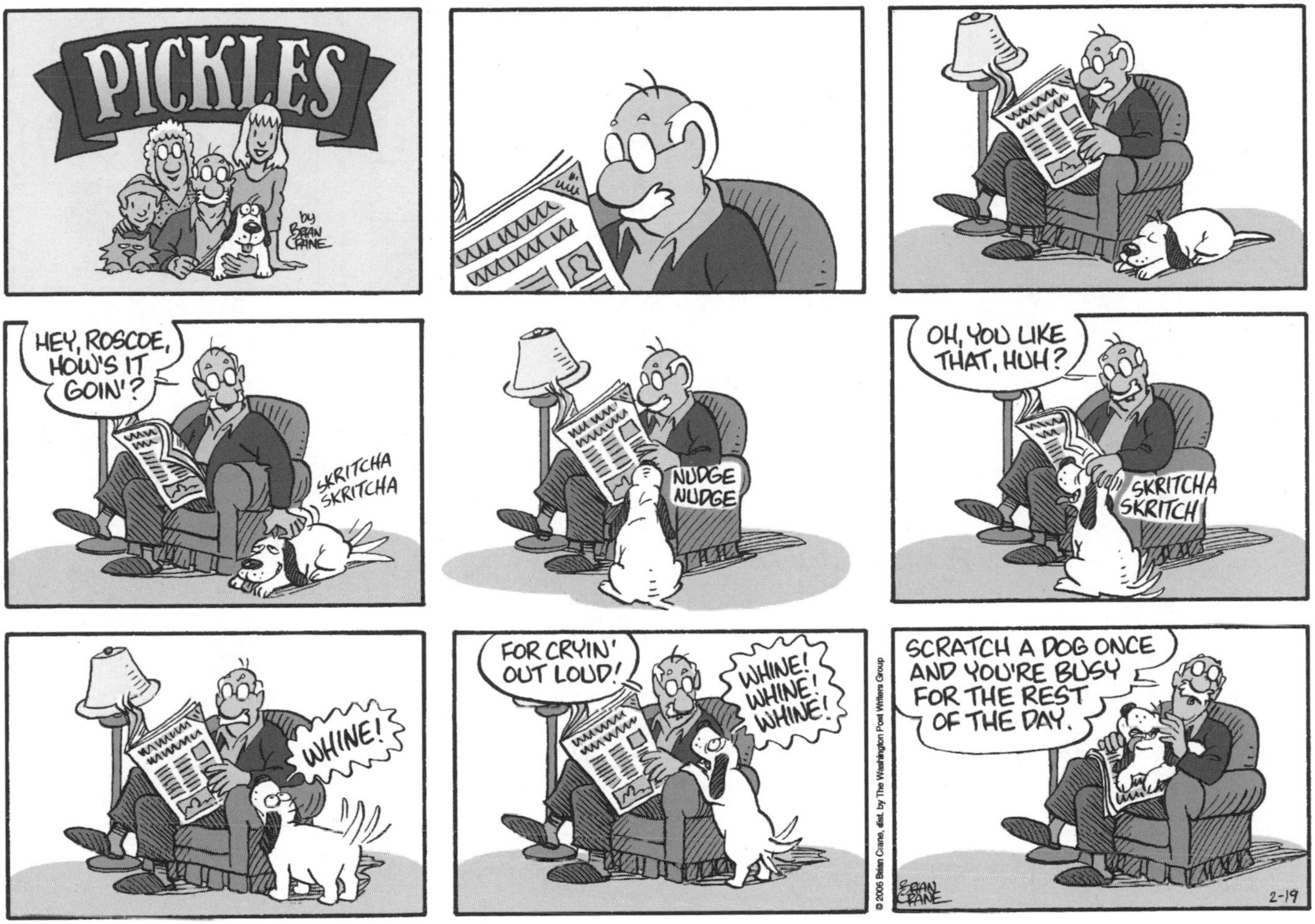
PICKLES
by Brian Crane
HEY, ROSCOE, HOW'S IT GOIN'?
SKRITCHA SKRITCHA
NUDGE NUDGE
OH, YOU LIKE THAT, HUH?
SKRITCHA SKRITCH
WHINE!
FOR CRYIN' OUT LOUD!
WHINE! WHINE! WHINE!
SCRATCH A DOG ONCE AND YOU'RE BUSY FOR THE REST OF THE DAY.
© 2006 Brian Crane, dist. by The Washington Post Writers Group
BRIAN CRANE
2-19

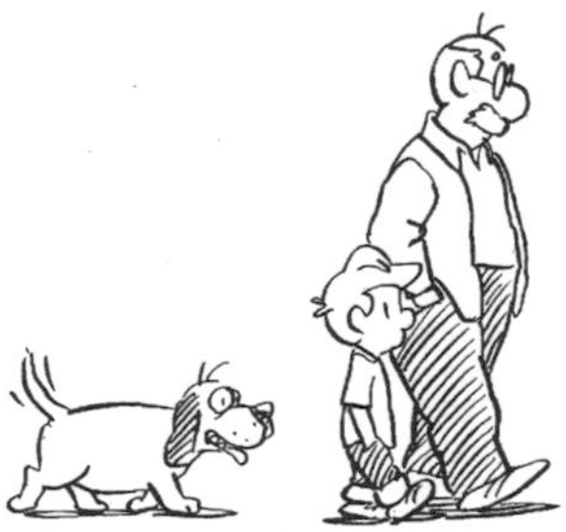

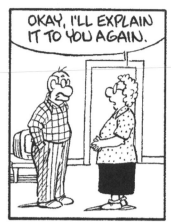

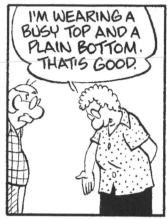

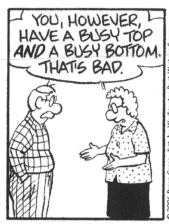

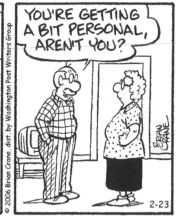

OKAY, I'LL EXPLAIN IT TO YOU AGAIN.
I'M WEARING A BUSY TOP AND A PLAIN BOTTOM. THAT'S GOOD.
YOU, HOWEVER, HAVE A BUSY TOP AND A BUSY BOTTOM. THAT'S BAD.
© 2006 Brian Crane, dist. by Washington Post Writers Group
YOU'RE GETTING A BIT PERSONAL, AREN'T YOU?
BRIAN CRANE
2-23

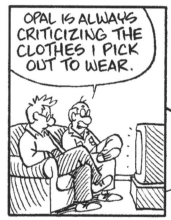

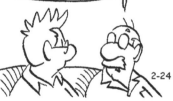

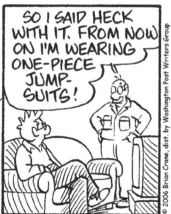

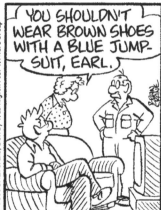

OPAL IS ALWAYS CRITICIZING THE CLOTHES I PICK OUT TO WEAR.
SHE HAS THIS RULE THAT YOU CAN WEAR A BUSY WITH A PLAIN, OR A PLAIN WITH A PLAIN, BUT NOT A BUSY WITH A BUSY.
2-24
SO I SAID HECK WITH IT. FROM NOW ON I'M WEARING ONE-PIECE JUMP-SUITS!
© 2006 Brian Crane, dist. by Washington Post Writers Group
YOU SHOULDN'T WEAR BROWN SHOES WITH A BLUE JUMP-SUIT, EARL.
BRIAN CRANE

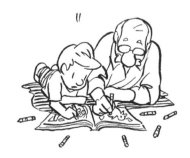

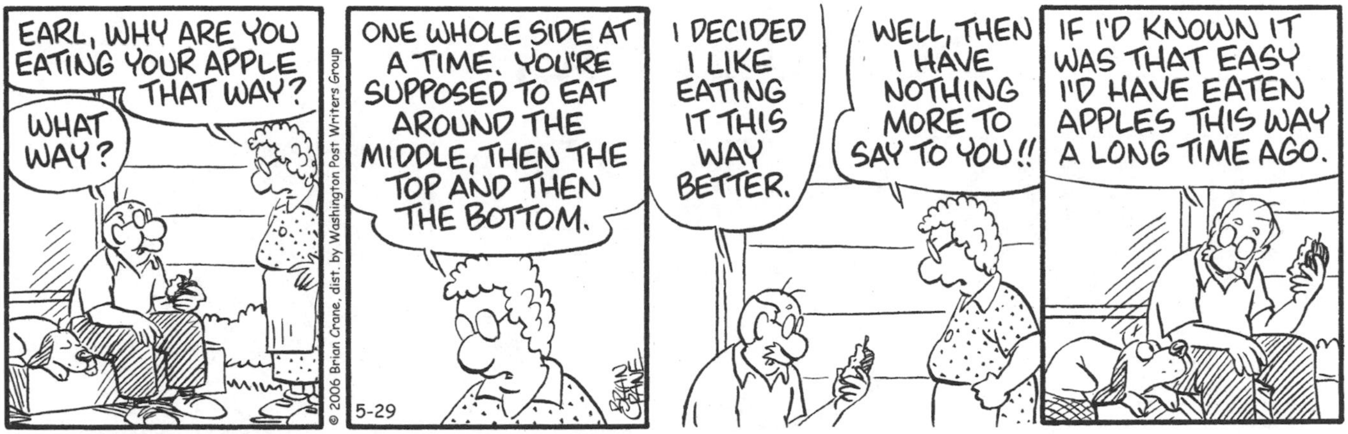
EARL, WHY ARE YOU EATING YOUR APPLE THAT WAY?
WHAT WAY?
© 2006 Brian Crane, dist. by Washington Post Writers Group
ONE WHOLE SIDE AT A TIME. YOU'RE SUPPOSED TO EAT AROUND THE MIDDLE, THEN THE TOP AND THEN THE BOTTOM.
5-29
BRIAN CRANE
I DECIDED I LIKE EATING IT THIS WAY BETTER.
WELL, THEN I HAVE NOTHING MORE TO SAY TO YOU!!
IF I'D KNOWN IT WAS THAT EASY I'D HAVE EATEN APPLES THIS WAY A LONG TIME AGO.

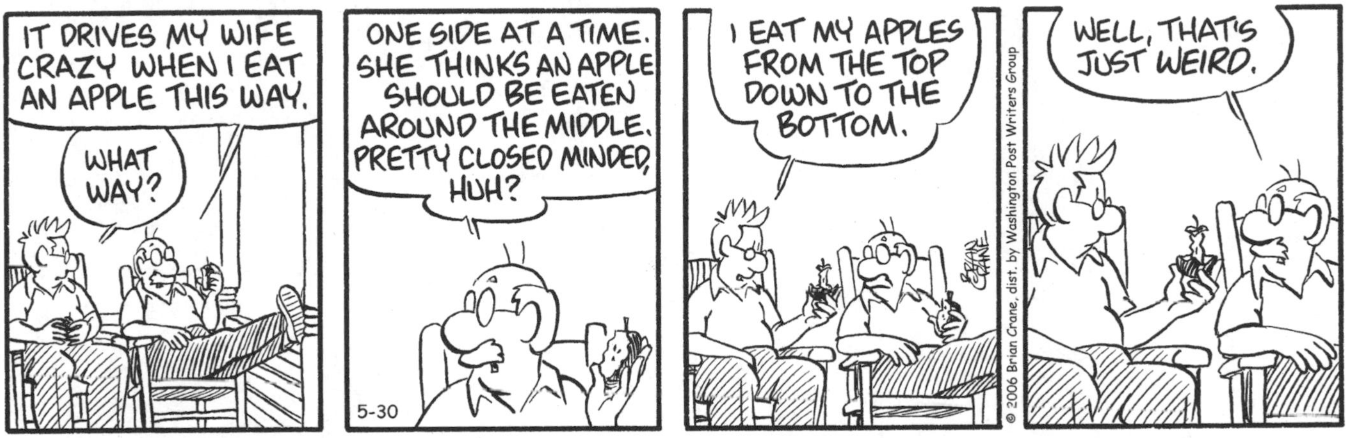
IT DRIVES MY WIFE CRAZY WHEN I EAT AN APPLE THIS WAY.
WHAT WAY?
ONE SIDE AT A TIME. SHE THINKS AN APPLE SHOULD BE EATEN AROUND THE MIDDLE. PRETTY CLOSED MINDED, HUH?
5-30
I EAT MY APPLES FROM THE TOP DOWN TO THE BOTTOM.
BRIAN CRANE
© 2006 Brian Crane, dist. by Washington Post Writers Group
WELL, THAT'S JUST WEIRD.

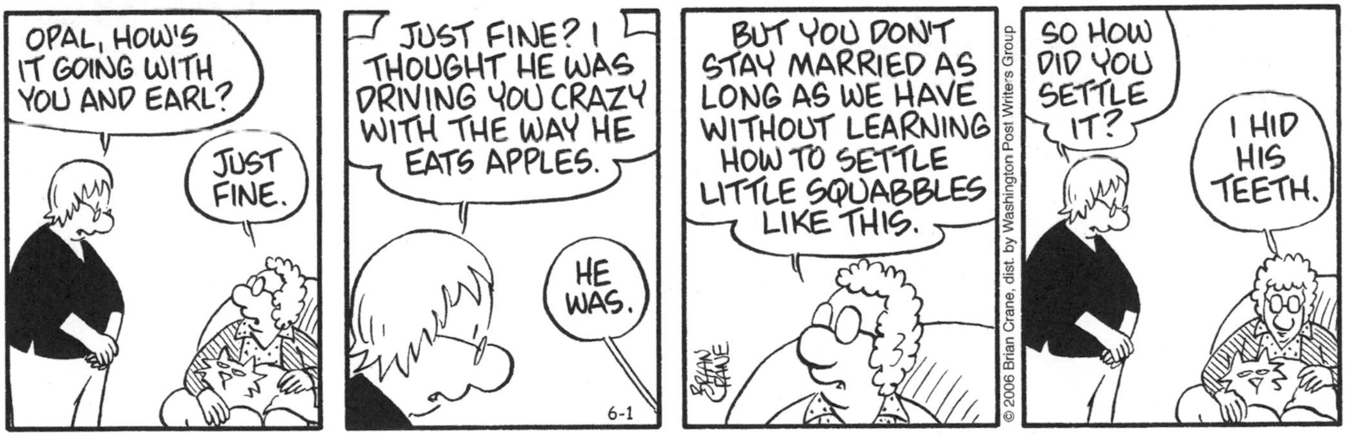
OPAL, HOW'S IT GOING WITH YOU AND EARL?
JUST FINE.
JUST FINE? I THOUGHT HE WAS DRIVING YOU CRAZY WITH THE WAY HE EATS APPLES.
HE WAS.
6-1
BUT YOU DON'T STAY MARRIED AS LONG AS WE HAVE WITHOUT LEARNING HOW TO SETTLE LITTLE SQUABBLES LIKE THIS.
BRIAN CRANE
© 2006 Brian Crane, dist. by Washington Post Writers Group
SO HOW DID YOU SETTLE IT?
I HID HIS TEETH.

Sunday Pickles

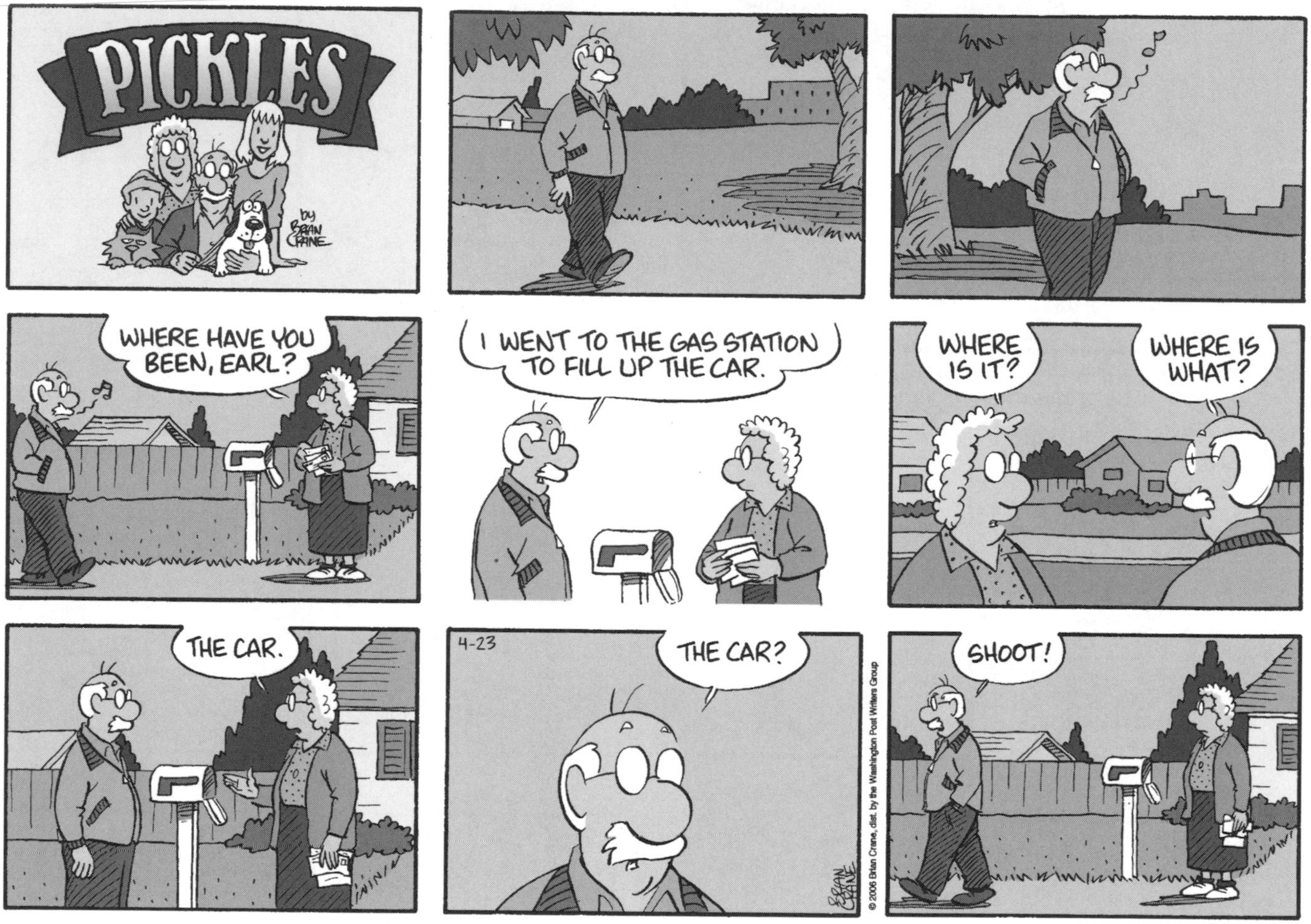
PICKLES
by Brian Crane
WHERE HAVE YOU BEEN, EARL?
I WENT TO THE GAS STATION TO FILL UP THE CAR.
WHERE IS IT?
WHERE IS WHAT?
THE CAR.
4-23
THE CAR?
© 2006 Brian Crane, dist. by the Washington Post Writers Group
SHOOT!

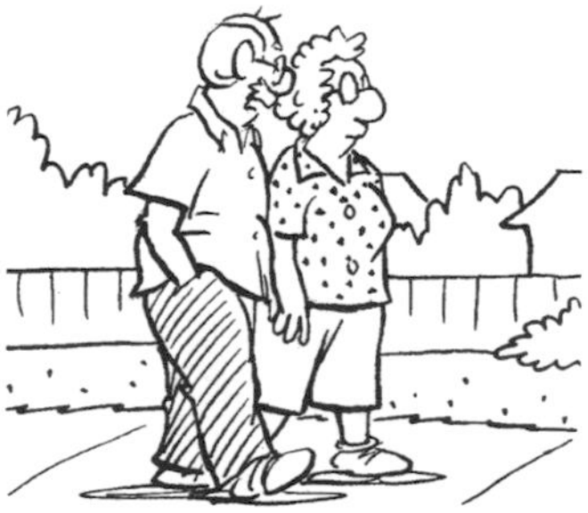

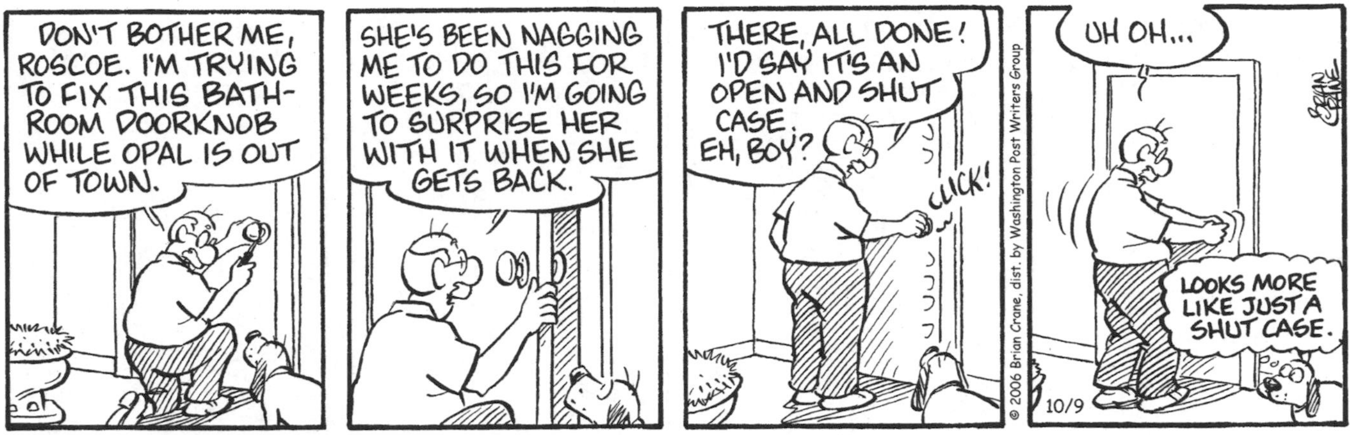
DON'T BOTHER ME, ROSCOE. I'M TRYING TO FIX THIS BATHROOM DOORKNOB WHILE OPAL IS OUT OF TOWN.
SHE'S BEEN NAGGING ME TO DO THIS FOR WEEKS, SO I'M GOING TO SURPRISE HER WITH IT WHEN SHE GETS BACK.
THERE, ALL DONE! I'D SAY IT'S AN OPEN AND SHUT CASE. EH, BOY?
CLICK!
© 2006 Brian Crane, dist. by Washington Post Writers Group
UH OH...
LOOKS MORE LIKE JUST A SHUT CASE.
10/9

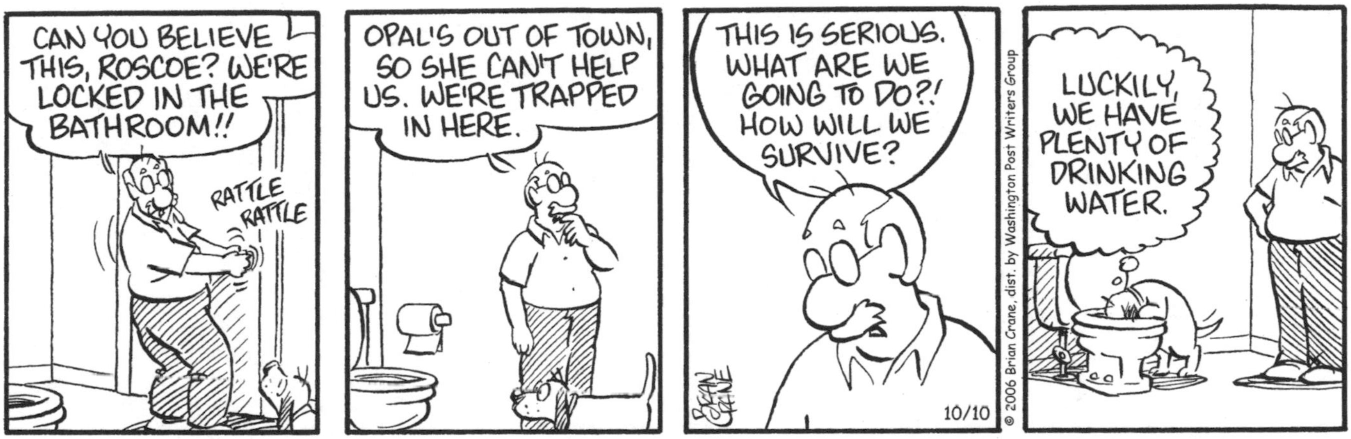
CAN YOU BELIEVE THIS, ROSCOE? WE'RE LOCKED IN THE BATHROOM!!
RATTLE RATTLE
OPAL'S OUT OF TOWN, SO SHE CAN'T HELP US. WE'RE TRAPPED IN HERE.
THIS IS SERIOUS. WHAT ARE WE GOING TO DO?! HOW WILL WE SURVIVE?
10/10
© 2006 Brian Crane, dist. by Washington Post Writers Group
LUCKILY, WE HAVE PLENTY OF DRINKING WATER.

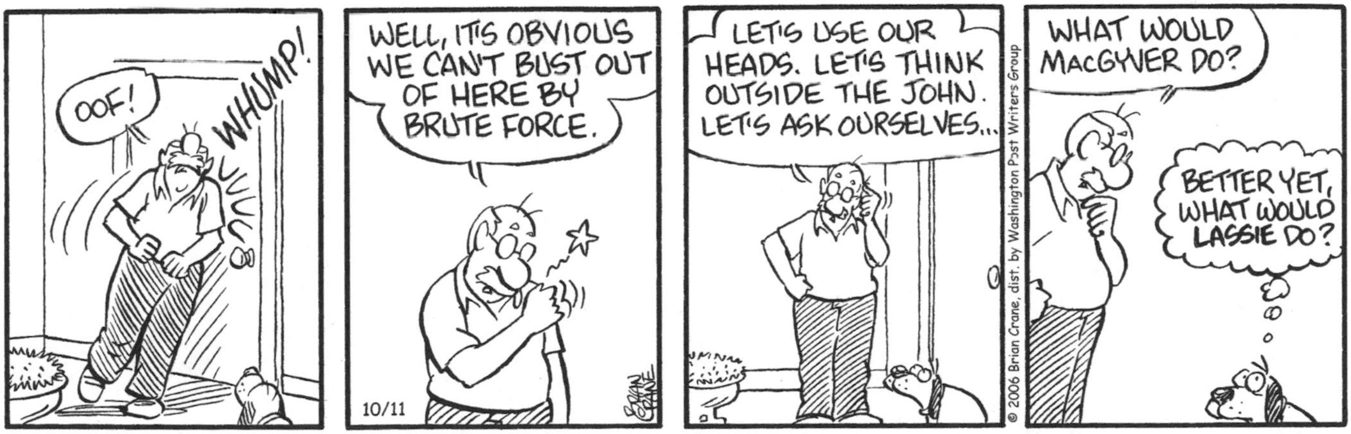
OOF!
WHUMP!
WELL, IT'S OBVIOUS WE CAN'T BUST OUT OF HERE BY BRUTE FORCE.
10/11
LET'S USE OUR HEADS. LET'S THINK OUTSIDE THE JOHN. LET'S ASK OURSELVES...
© 2006 Brian Crane, dist. by Washington Post Writers Group
WHAT WOULD MACGYVER DO?
BETTER YET, WHAT WOULD LASSIE DO?

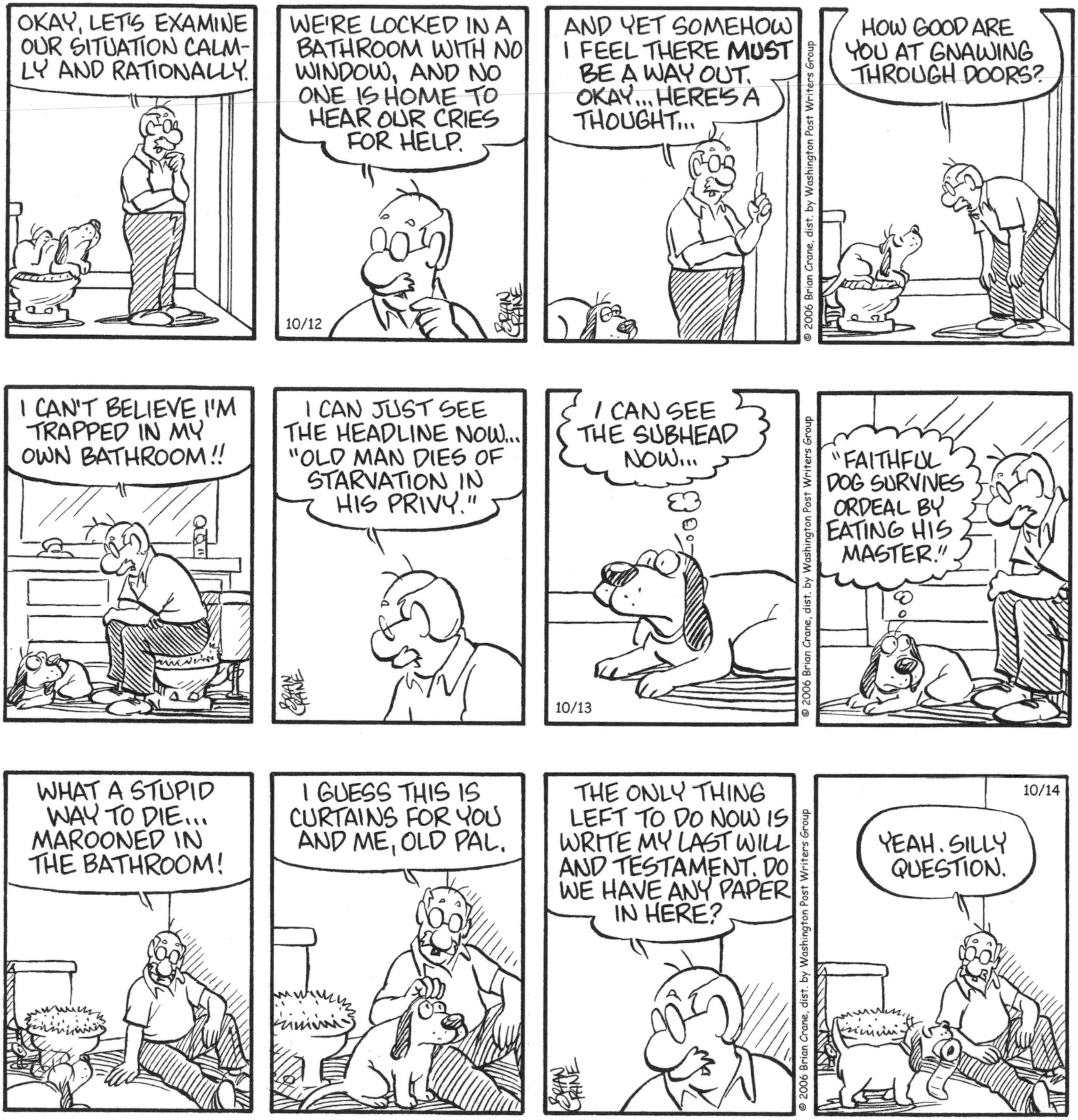
OKAY, LET'S EXAMINE OUR SITUATION CALMLY AND RATIONALLY.
WE'RE LOCKED IN A BATHROOM WITH NO WINDOW, AND NO ONE IS HOME TO HEAR OUR CRIES FOR HELP.
10/12
AND YET SOMEHOW I FEEL THERE MUST BE A WAY OUT. OKAY... HERE'S A THOUGHT...
© 2006 Brian Crane, dist. by Washington Post Writers Group
HOW GOOD ARE YOU AT GNAWING THROUGH DOORS?
I CAN'T BELIEVE I'M TRAPPED IN MY OWN BATHROOM!!
I CAN JUST SEE THE HEADLINE NOW... "OLD MAN DIES OF STARVATION IN HIS PRIVY."
I CAN SEE THE SUBHEAD NOW...
10/13
© 2006 Brian Crane, dist. by Washington Post Writers Group
"FAITHFUL DOG SURVIVES ORDEAL BY EATING HIS MASTER."
WHAT A STUPID WAY TO DIE... MAROONED IN THE BATHROOM!
I GUESS THIS IS CURTAINS FOR YOU AND ME, OLD PAL.
THE ONLY THING LEFT TO DO NOW IS WRITE MY LAST WILL AND TESTAMENT. DO WE HAVE ANY PAPER IN HERE?
© 2006 Brian Crane, dist. by Washington Post Writers Group
10/14
YEAH. SILLY QUESTION.

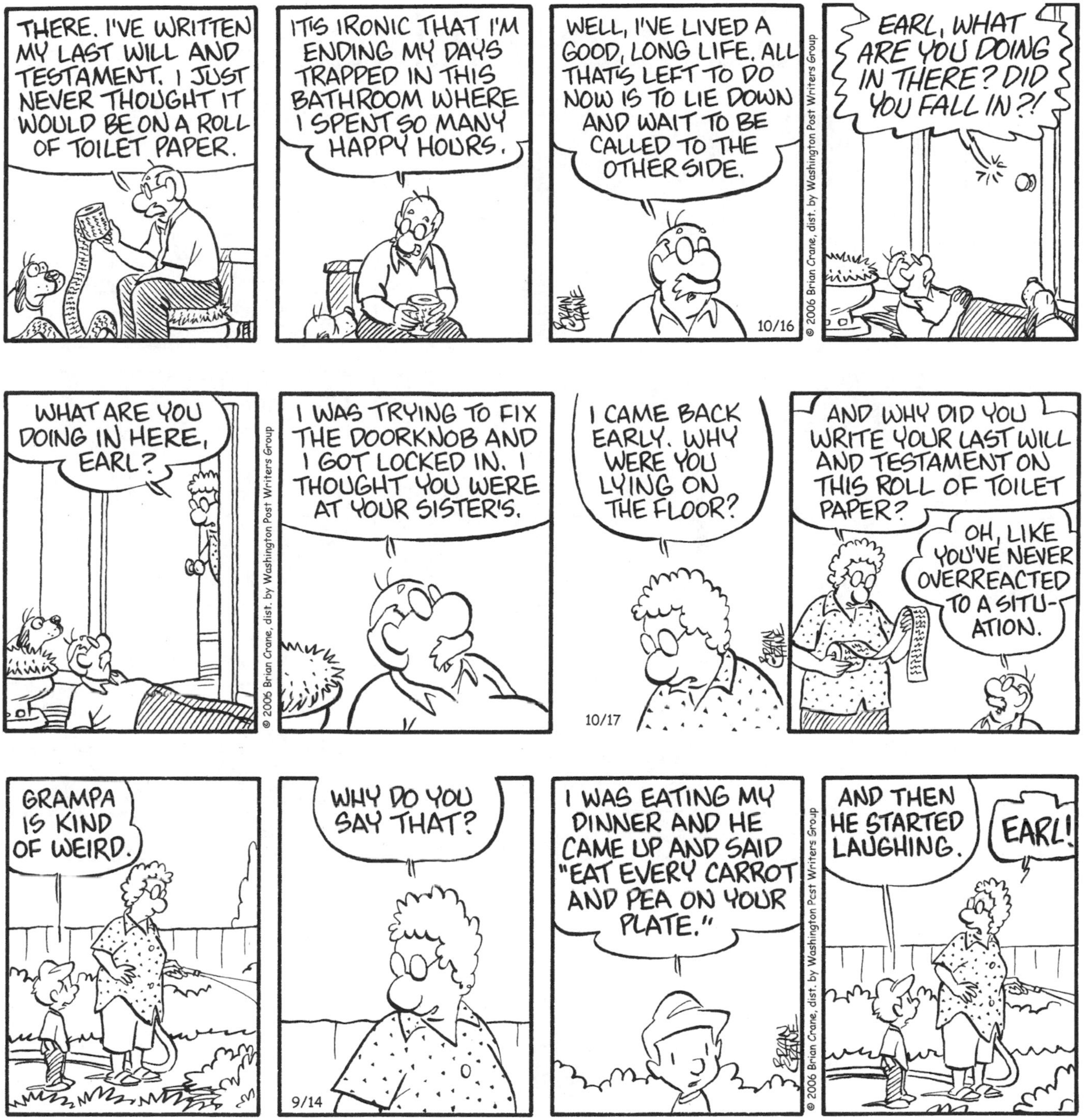
THERE. I'VE WRITTEN MY LAST WILL AND TESTAMENT. I JUST NEVER THOUGHT IT WOULD BE ON A ROLL OF TOILET PAPER.
IT'S IRONIC THAT I'M ENDING MY DAYS TRAPPED IN THIS BATHROOM WHERE I SPENT SO MANY HAPPY HOURS.
WELL, I'VE LIVED A GOOD, LONG LIFE. ALL THAT'S LEFT TO DO NOW IS TO LIE DOWN AND WAIT TO BE CALLED TO THE OTHER SIDE.
10/16
© 2006 Brian Crane, dist. by Washington Post Writers Group
EARL, WHAT ARE YOU DOING IN THERE? DID YOU FALL IN?!
WHAT ARE YOU DOING IN HERE, EARL?
© 2006 Brian Crane, dist. by Washington Post Writers Group
I WAS TRYING TO FIX THE DOORKNOB AND I GOT LOCKED IN. I THOUGHT YOU WERE AT YOUR SISTER'S.
I CAME BACK EARLY. WHY WERE YOU LYING ON THE FLOOR?
10/17
AND WHY DID YOU WRITE YOUR LAST WILL AND TESTAMENT ON THIS ROLL OF TOILET PAPER?
OH, LIKE YOU'VE NEVER OVERREACTED TO A SITU-ATION.
GRAMPA IS KIND OF WEIRD.
WHY DO YOU SAY THAT?
9/14
I WAS EATING MY DINNER AND HE CAME UP AND SAID "EAT EVERY CARROT AND PEA ON YOUR PLATE."
© 2006 Brian Crane, dist. by Washington Post Writers Group
AND THEN HE STARTED LAUGHING.
EARL!

SundayPickles

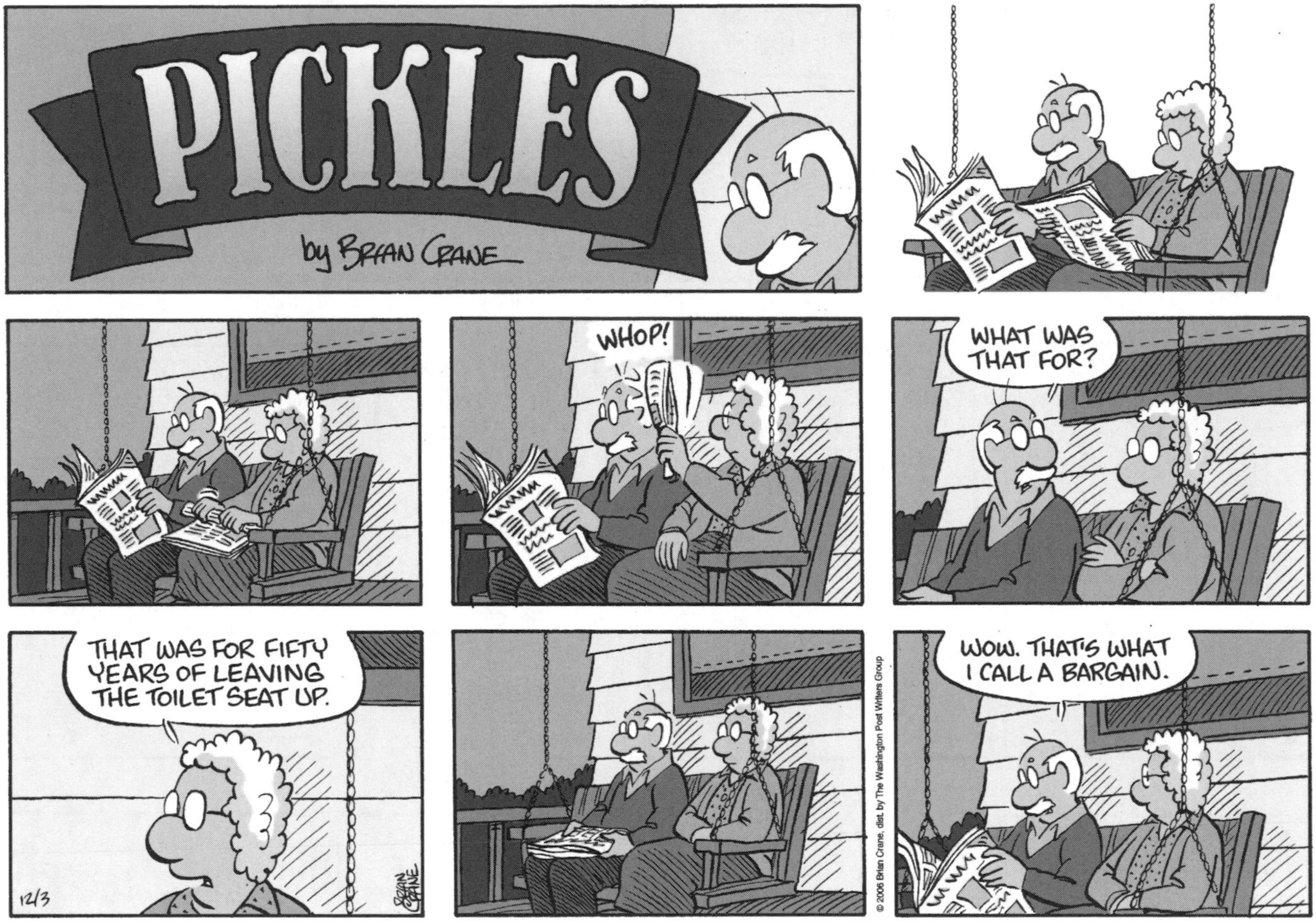
PICKLES
by BRIAN CRANE
WHOP!
WHAT WAS THAT FOR?
THAT WAS FOR FIFTY YEARS OF LEAVING THE TOILET SEAT UP.
12/3
BRIAN CRANE
WOW. THAT'S WHAT I CALL A BARGAIN.
© 2006 Brian Crane, dist. by The Washington Post Writers Group

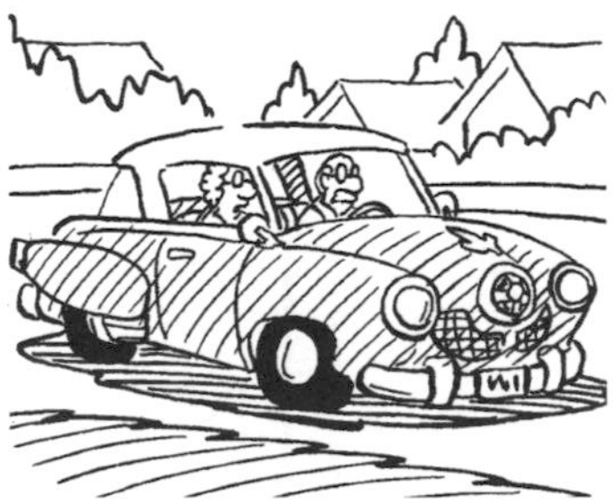

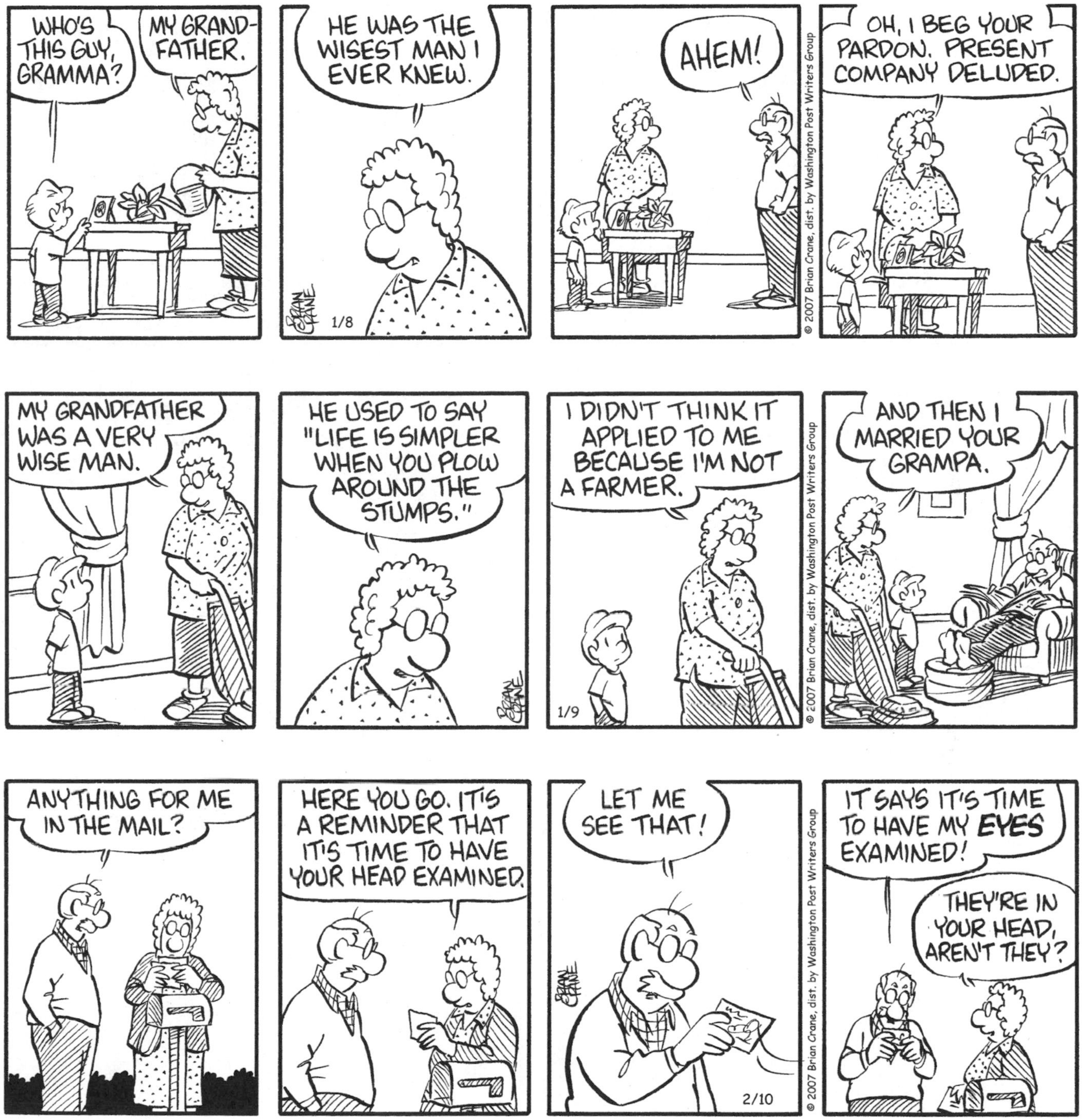
WHO'S THIS GUY, GRAMMA?
MY GRANDFATHER.
HE WAS THE WISEST MAN I EVER KNEW.
1/8
AHEM!
© 2007 Brian Crane, dist. by Washington Post Writers Group
OH, I BEG YOUR PARDON. PRESENT COMPANY DELUDED.
MY GRANDFATHER WAS A VERY WISE MAN.
HE USED TO SAY "LIFE IS SIMPLER WHEN YOU PLOW AROUND THE STUMPS."
I DIDN'T THINK IT APPLIED TO ME BECAUSE I'M NOT A FARMER.
1/9
© 2007 Brian Crane, dist. by Washington Post Writers Group
AND THEN I MARRIED YOUR GRAMPA.
ANYTHING FOR ME IN THE MAIL?
HERE YOU GO. IT'S A REMINDER THAT IT'S TIME TO HAVE YOUR HEAD EXAMINED.
LET ME SEE THAT!
2/10
© 2007 Brian Crane, dist. by Washington Post Writers Group
IT SAYS IT'S TIME TO HAVE MY EYES EXAMINED!
THEY'RE IN YOUR HEAD, AREN'T THEY?

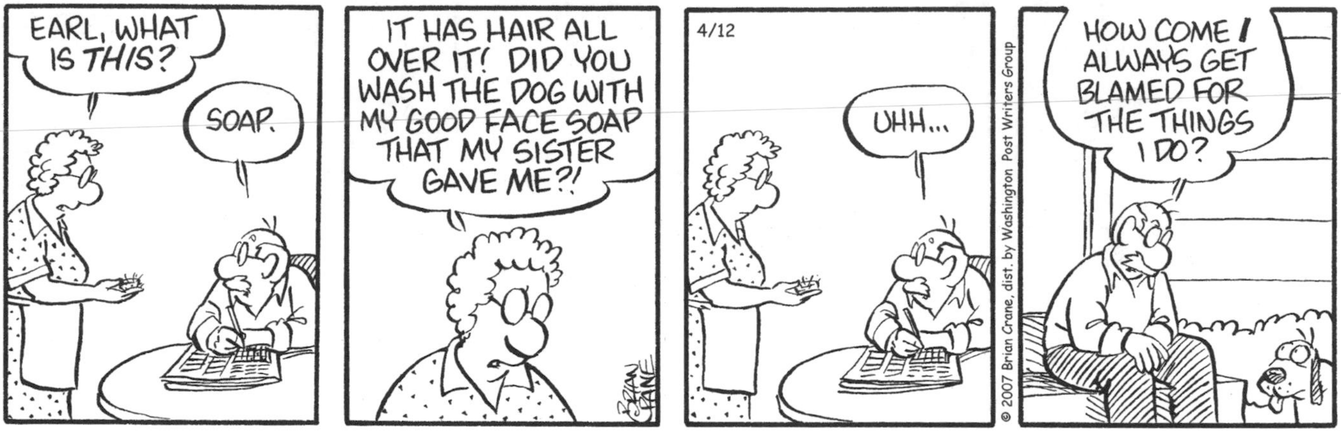
EARL, WHAT IS THIS?
SOAP.
IT HAS HAIR ALL OVER IT! DID YOU WASH THE DOG WITH MY GOOD FACE SOAP THAT MY SISTER GAVE ME?!
BRIAN CRANE
4/12
UHH...
© 2007 Brian Crane, dist. by Washington Post Writers Group
HOW COME I ALWAYS GET BLAMED FOR THE THINGS I DO?

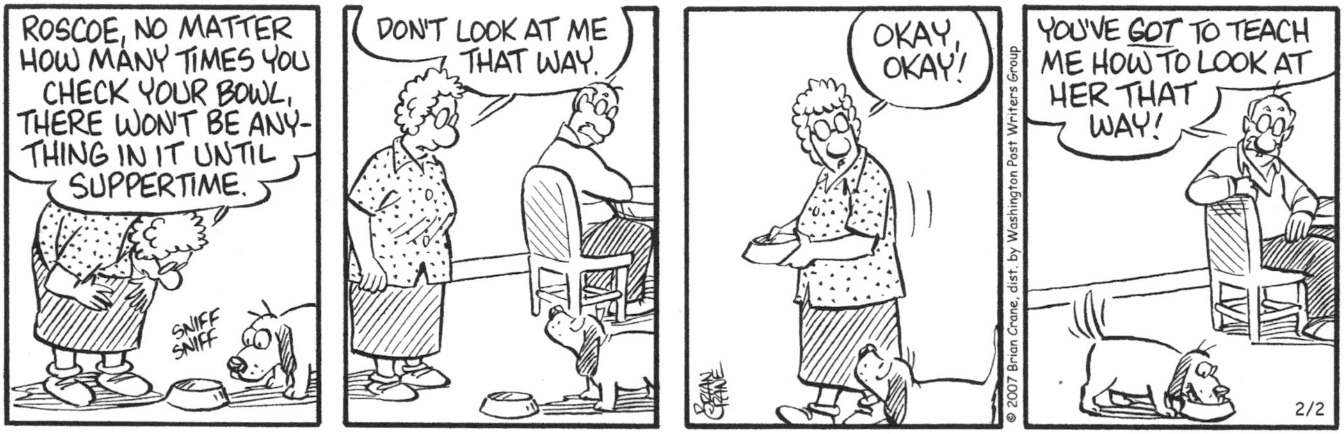
ROSCOE, NO MATTER HOW MANY TIMES YOU CHECK YOUR BOWL, THERE WON'T BE ANYTHING IN IT UNTIL SUPPERTIME.
SNIFF SNIFF
DON'T LOOK AT ME THAT WAY.
BRIAN CRANE
OKAY, OKAY!
© 2007 Brian Crane, dist. by Washington Post Writers Group
YOU'VE GOT TO TEACH ME HOW TO LOOK AT HER THAT WAY!
2/2

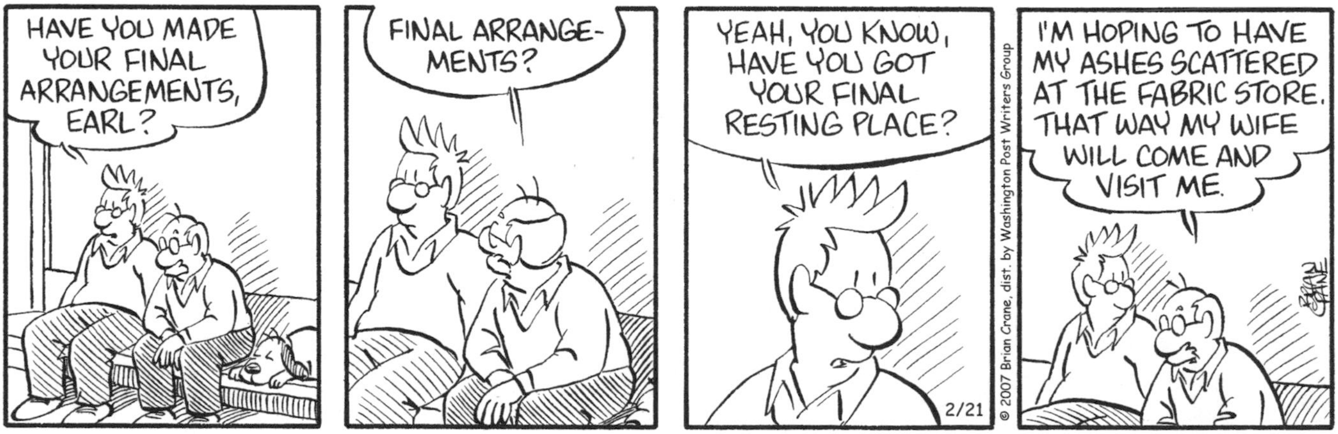
HAVE YOU MADE YOUR FINAL ARRANGEMENTS, EARL?
FINAL ARRANGEMENTS?
YEAH, YOU KNOW, HAVE YOU GOT YOUR FINAL RESTING PLACE?
2/21
© 2007 Brian Crane, dist. by Washington Post Writers Group
I'M HOPING TO HAVE MY ASHES SCATTERED AT THE FABRIC STORE. THAT WAY MY WIFE WILL COME AND VISIT ME.
BRIAN CRANE

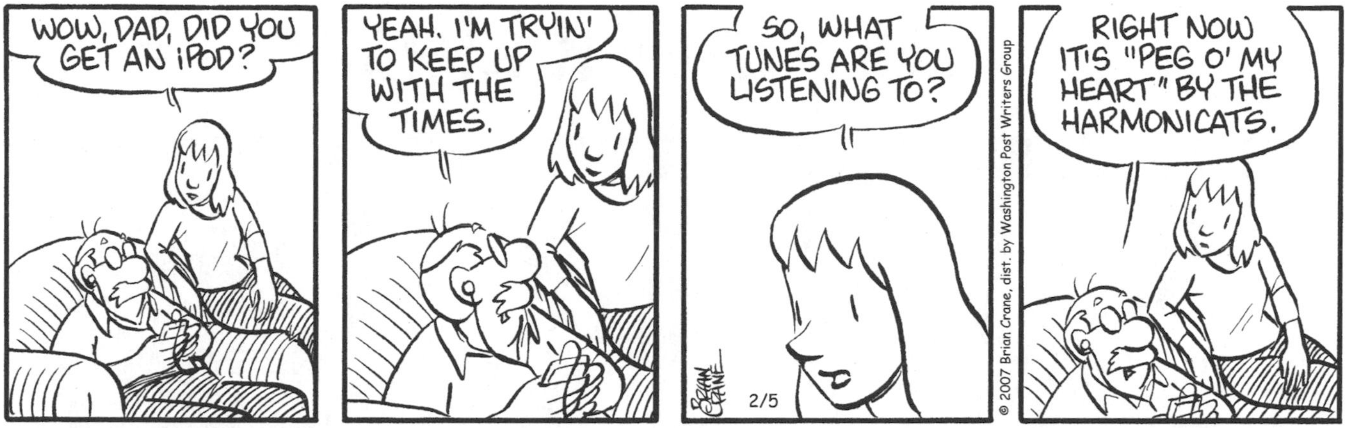
WOW, DAD, DID YOU GET AN iPOD?
YEAH. I'M TRYIN' TO KEEP UP WITH THE TIMES.
SO, WHAT TUNES ARE YOU LISTENING TO?
2/5
RIGHT NOW IT'S "PEG O' MY HEART" BY THE HARMONICATS.

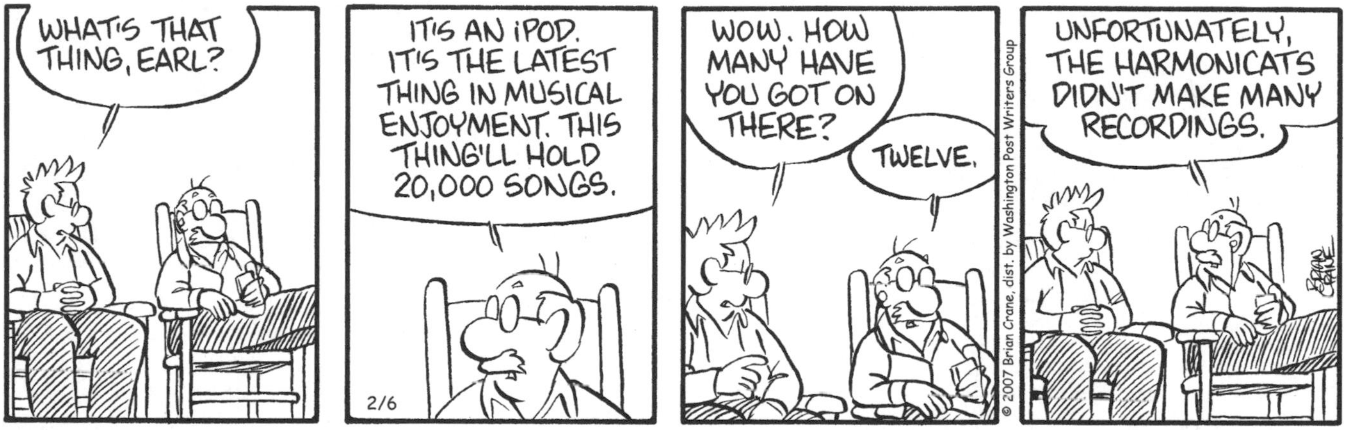
WHAT'S THAT THING, EARL?
IT'S AN iPOD. IT'S THE LATEST THING IN MUSICAL ENJOYMENT. THIS THING'LL HOLD 20,000 SONGS.
2/6
WOW. HOW MANY HAVE YOU GOT ON THERE?
TWELVE.
UNFORTUNATELY, THE HARMONICATS DIDN'T MAKE MANY RECORDINGS.

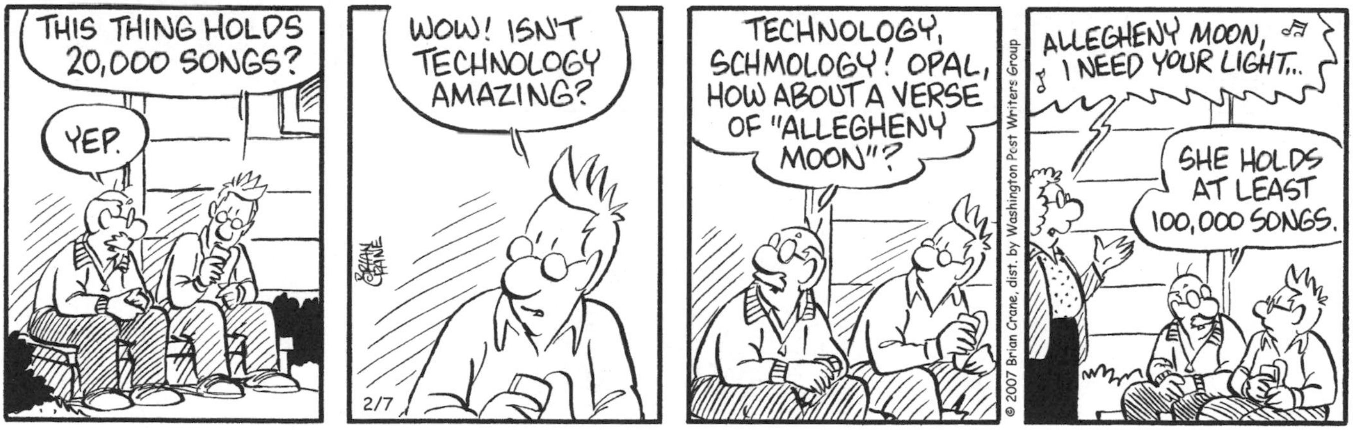
THIS THING HOLDS 20,000 SONGS?
YEP.
WOW! ISN'T TECHNOLOGY AMAZING?
2/7
TECHNOLOGY, SCHMOLOGY! OPAL, HOW ABOUT A VERSE OF "ALLEGHENY MOON"?
ALLEGHENY MOON, I NEED YOUR LIGHT...
SHE HOLDS AT LEAST 100,000 SONGS.

SundayPickles

PICKLES
by BRIAN CRANE
HEY, CLYDE!
HEY, EARL. WHAT'S UP?
NOT MUCH. MY WIFE BEAT ME UP THIS MORNING.
OPAL BEAT YOU UP?
YEAH. SHE HADN'T DONE IT FOR A LONG TIME, BUT SHE USED TO BEAT ME UP ALMOST EVERY DAY.
DON'T YOU THINK YOU SHOULD GET SOME HELP? YOU KNOW, REPORT IT TO THE AUTHORITIES?
1/14
© 2007 Brian Crane, dist. by The Washington Post Writers Group
WHY? I LIKE IT WHEN SHE GETS UP BEFORE I DO.

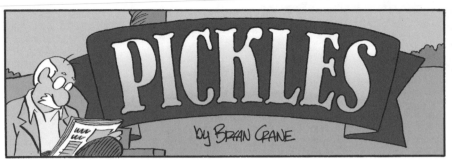

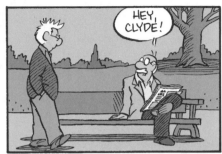

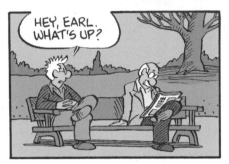

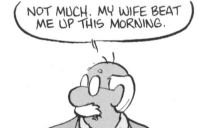

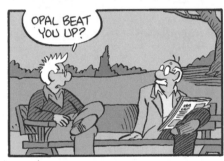

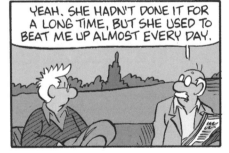

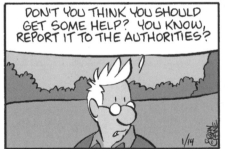

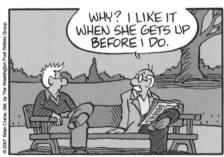

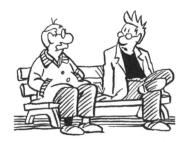

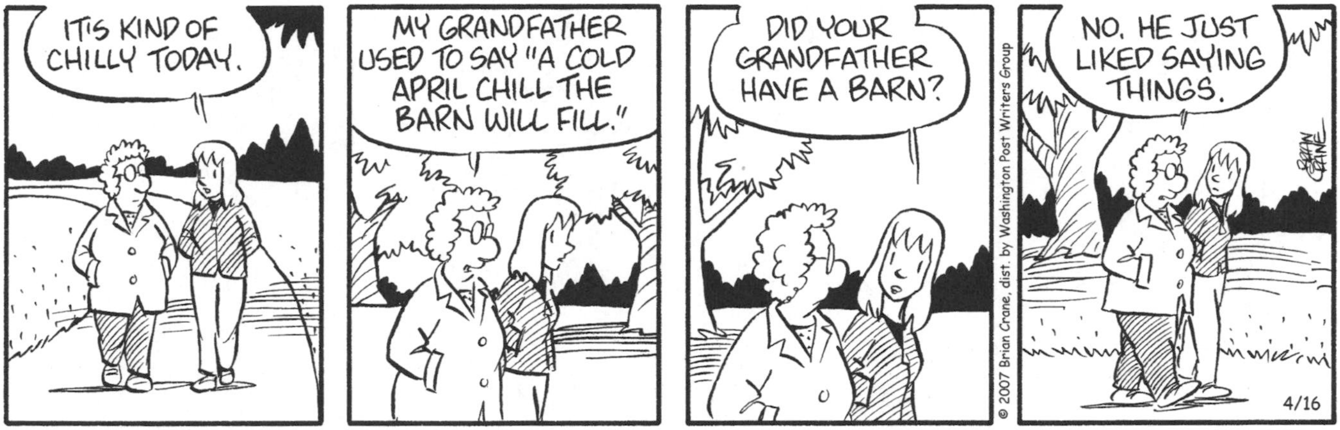
IT'S KIND OF CHILLY TODAY.
MY GRANDFATHER USED TO SAY "A COLD APRIL CHILL THE BARN WILL FILL."
DID YOUR GRANDFATHER HAVE A BARN?
© 2007 Brian Crane, dist. by Washington Post Writers Group
NO. HE JUST LIKED SAYING THINGS.
4/16

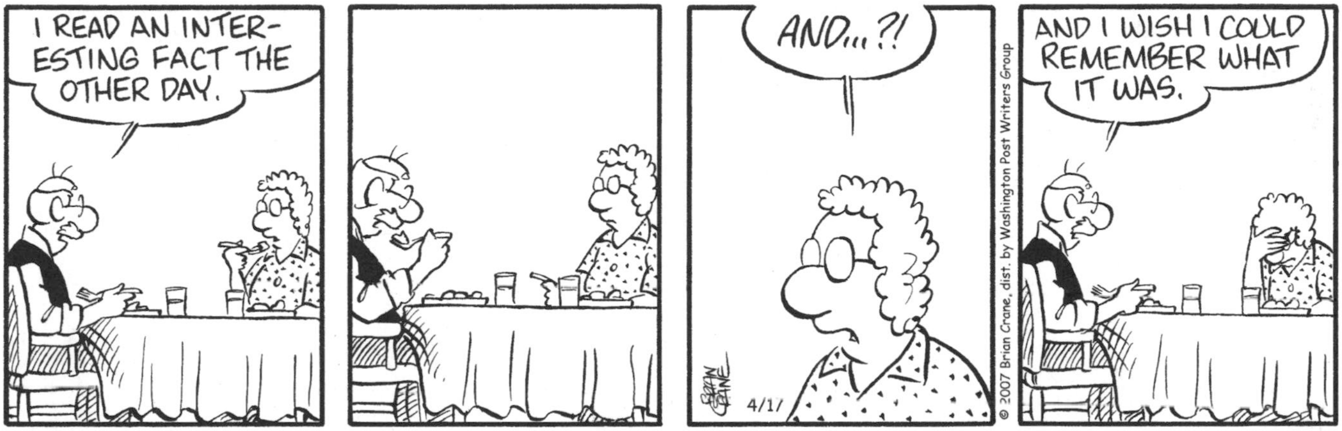
I READ AN INTERESTING FACT THE OTHER DAY.
AND...?!
4/17
© 2007 Brian Crane, dist. by Washington Post Writers Group
AND I WISH I COULD REMEMBER WHAT IT WAS.

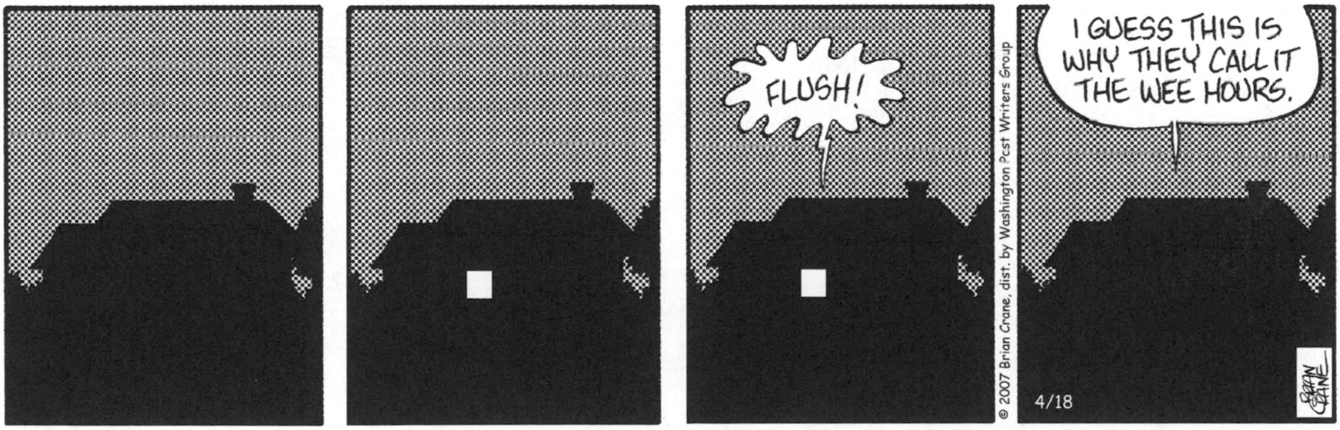
FLUSH!
© 2007 Brian Crane, dist. by Washington Post Writers Group
I GUESS THIS IS WHY THEY CALL IT THE WEE HOURS.
4/18

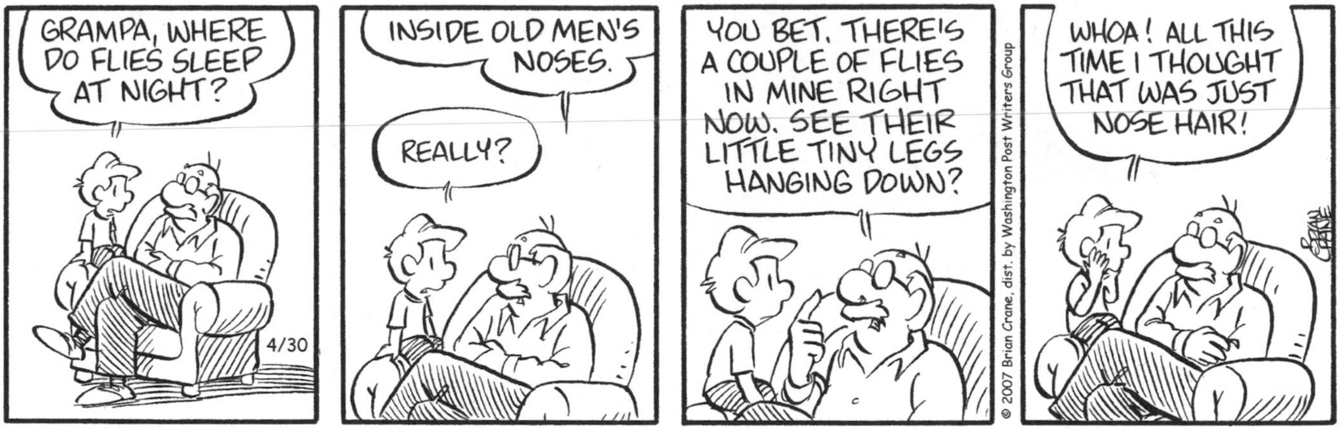
GRAMPA, WHERE DO FLIES SLEEP AT NIGHT?
4/30
INSIDE OLD MEN'S NOSES.
REALLY?
YOU BET. THERE'S A COUPLE OF FLIES IN MINE RIGHT NOW. SEE THEIR LITTLE TINY LEGS HANGING DOWN?
© 2007 Brian Crane, dist. by Washington Post Writers Group
WHOA! ALL THIS TIME I THOUGHT THAT WAS JUST NOSE HAIR!
BRIAN CRANE

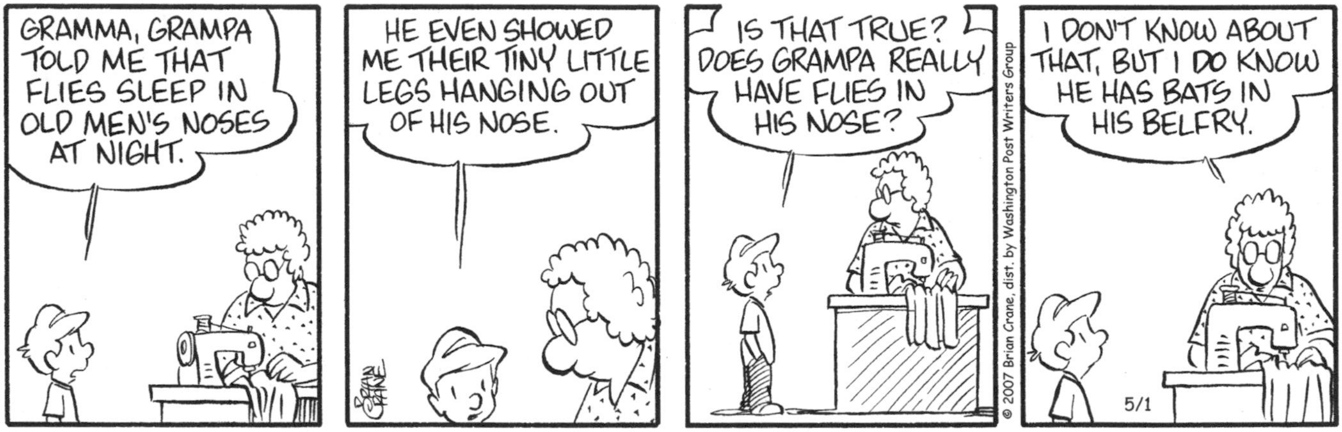
GRAMMA, GRAMPA TOLD ME THAT FLIES SLEEP IN OLD MEN'S NOSES AT NIGHT.
HE EVEN SHOWED ME THEIR TINY LITTLE LEGS HANGING OUT OF HIS NOSE.
BRIAN CRANE
IS THAT TRUE? DOES GRAMPA REALLY HAVE FLIES IN HIS NOSE?
© 2007 Brian Crane, dist. by Washington Post Writers Group
I DON'T KNOW ABOUT THAT, BUT I DO KNOW HE HAS BATS IN HIS BELFRY.
5/1

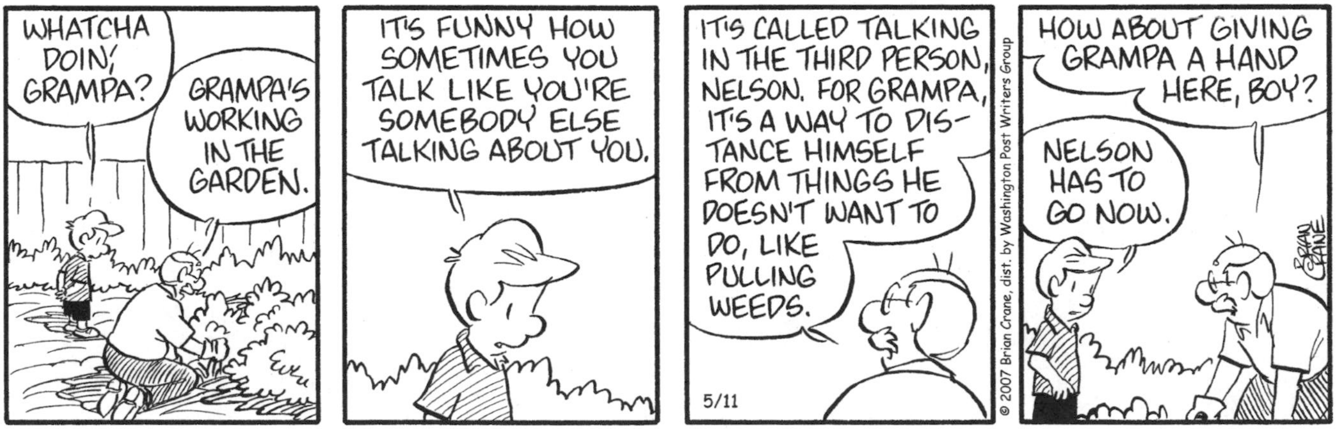
WHATCHA DOIN', GRAMPA?
GRAMPA'S WORKING IN THE GARDEN.
IT'S FUNNY HOW SOMETIMES YOU TALK LIKE YOU'RE SOMEBODY ELSE TALKING ABOUT YOU.
IT'S CALLED TALKING IN THE THIRD PERSON, NELSON. FOR GRAMPA, IT'S A WAY TO DISTANCE HIMSELF FROM THINGS HE DOESN'T WANT TO DO, LIKE PULLING WEEDS.
5/11
© 2007 Brian Crane, dist. by Washington Post Writers Group
HOW ABOUT GIVING GRAMPA A HAND HERE, BOY?
NELSON HAS TO GO NOW.
BRIAN CRANE

Sunday Pickles

PICKLES
by BRIAN CRANE
HEY!
WHO KEEPS CHANGING THE CHANNEL?
NOT ME.
I THINK YOU'RE SITTING ON THE REMOTE.
I AM?
OH, YEAH. I GUESS I AM!
HEY, LOOK. I CAN CHANGE CHANNELS WITH MY KEISTER!
I CAN TURN UP THE VOLUME TOO! PRETTY COOL, HUH?
© 2007 Brian Crane, dist. by The Washington Post Writers Group
I ALWAYS THOUGHT YOU MUST HAVE A HIDDEN TALENT. I JUST NEVER SUSPECTED YOU WERE SITTING ON IT.
LOOK... I CAN MUTE!

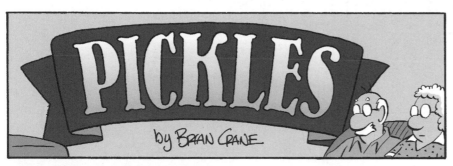

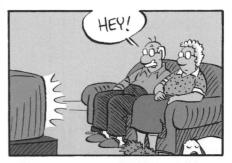

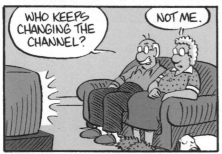

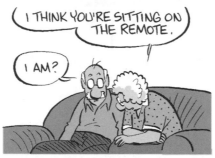

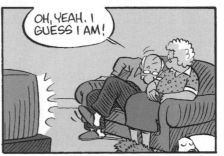

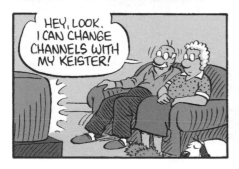

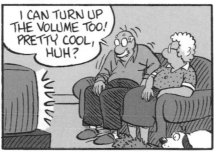

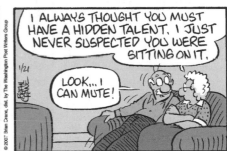

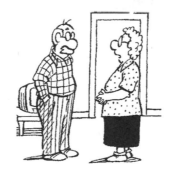

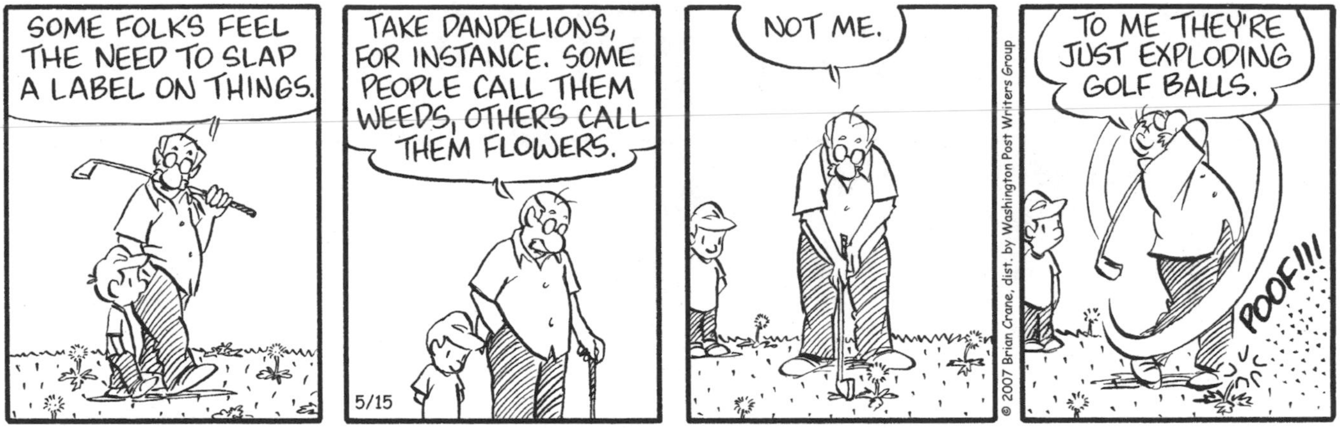
SOME FOLKS FEEL THE NEED TO SLAP A LABEL ON THINGS.
TAKE DANDELIONS, FOR INSTANCE. SOME PEOPLE CALL THEM WEEDS, OTHERS CALL THEM FLOWERS.
5/15
NOT ME.
© 2007 Brian Crane, dist. by Washington Post Writers Group
TO ME THEY'RE JUST EXPLODING GOLF BALLS.
POOF!!!

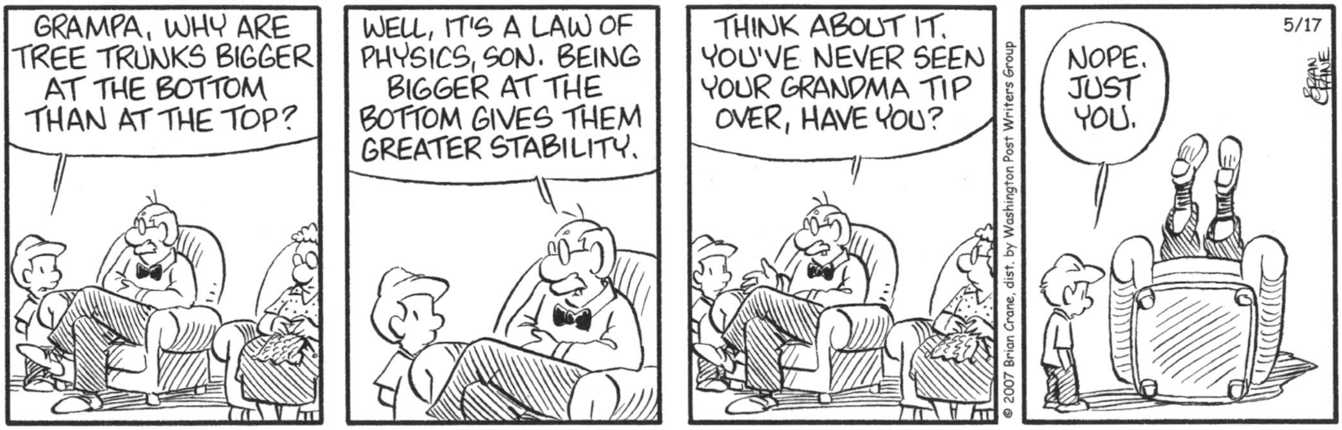
GRAMPA, WHY ARE TREE TRUNKS BIGGER AT THE BOTTOM THAN AT THE TOP?
WELL, IT'S A LAW OF PHYSICS, SON. BEING BIGGER AT THE BOTTOM GIVES THEM GREATER STABILITY.
THINK ABOUT IT. YOU'VE NEVER SEEN YOUR GRANDMA TIP OVER, HAVE YOU?
© 2007 Brian Crane, dist. by Washington Post Writers Group
5/17
NOPE. JUST YOU.

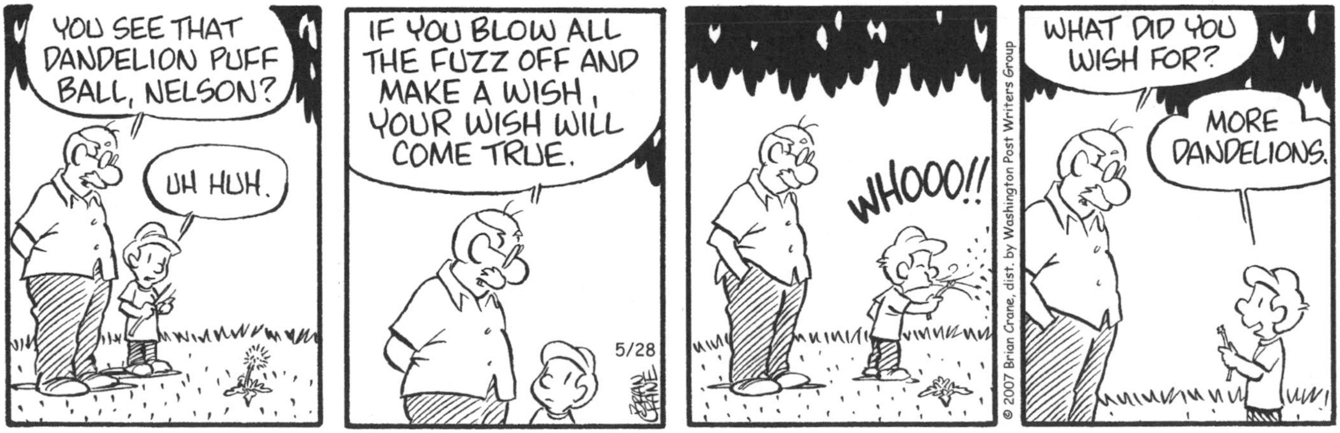
YOU SEE THAT DANDELION PUFF BALL, NELSON?
UH HUH.
IF YOU BLOW ALL THE FUZZ OFF AND MAKE A WISH, YOUR WISH WILL COME TRUE.
5/28
WHOOO!!
© 2007 Brian Crane, dist. by Washington Post Writers Group
WHAT DID YOU WISH FOR?
MORE DANDELIONS.

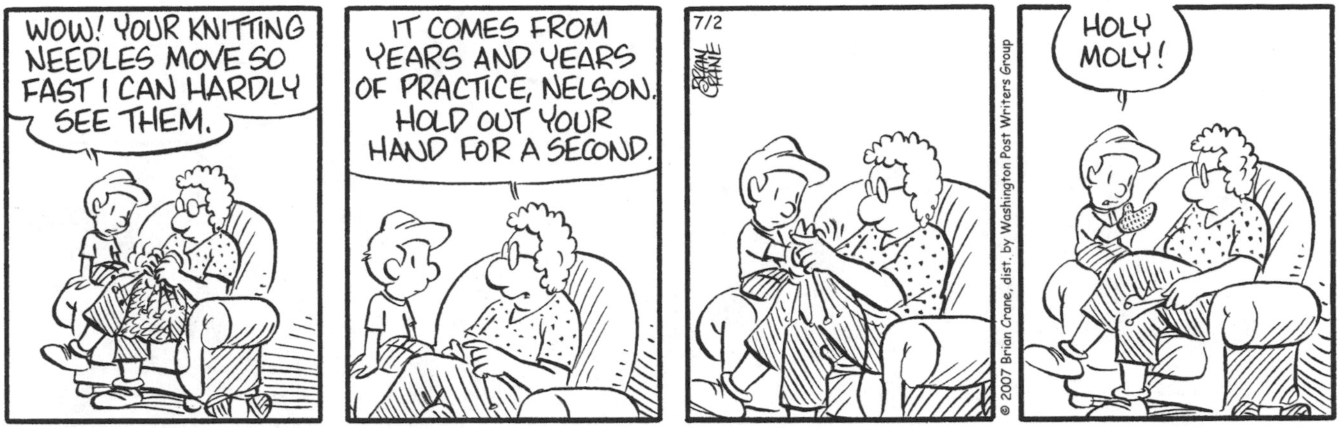
WOW! YOUR KNITTING NEEDLES MOVE SO FAST I CAN HARDLY SEE THEM.
IT COMES FROM YEARS AND YEARS OF PRACTICE, NELSON. HOLD OUT YOUR HAND FOR A SECOND.
7/2
HOLY MOLY!
© 2007 Brian Crane, dist. by Washington Post Writers Group

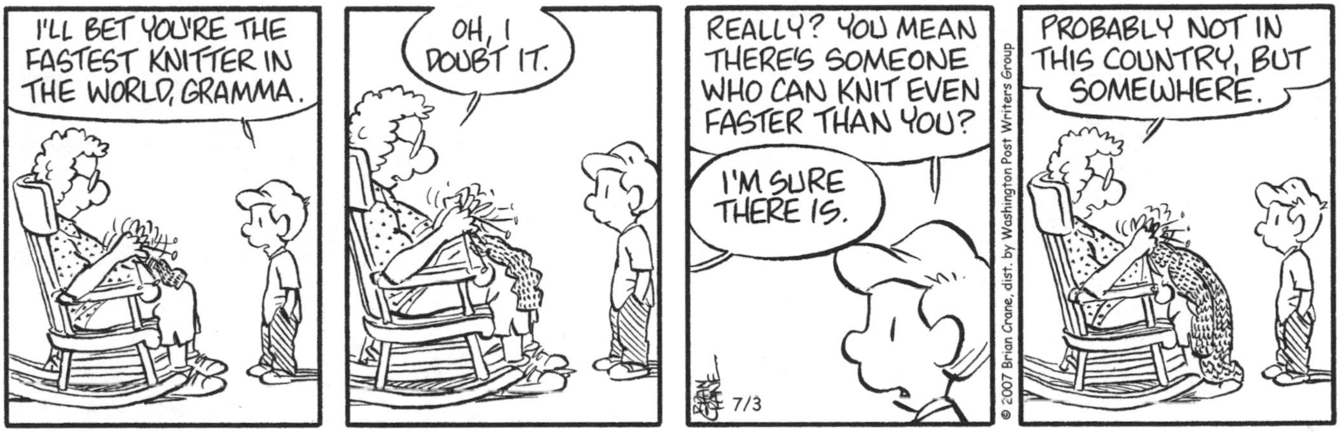
I'LL BET YOU'RE THE FASTEST KNITTER IN THE WORLD, GRAMMA.
OH, I DOUBT IT.
REALLY? YOU MEAN THERE'S SOMEONE WHO CAN KNIT EVEN FASTER THAN YOU?
I'M SURE THERE IS.
7/3
PROBABLY NOT IN THIS COUNTRY, BUT SOMEWHERE.
© 2007 Brian Crane, dist. by Washington Post Writers Group

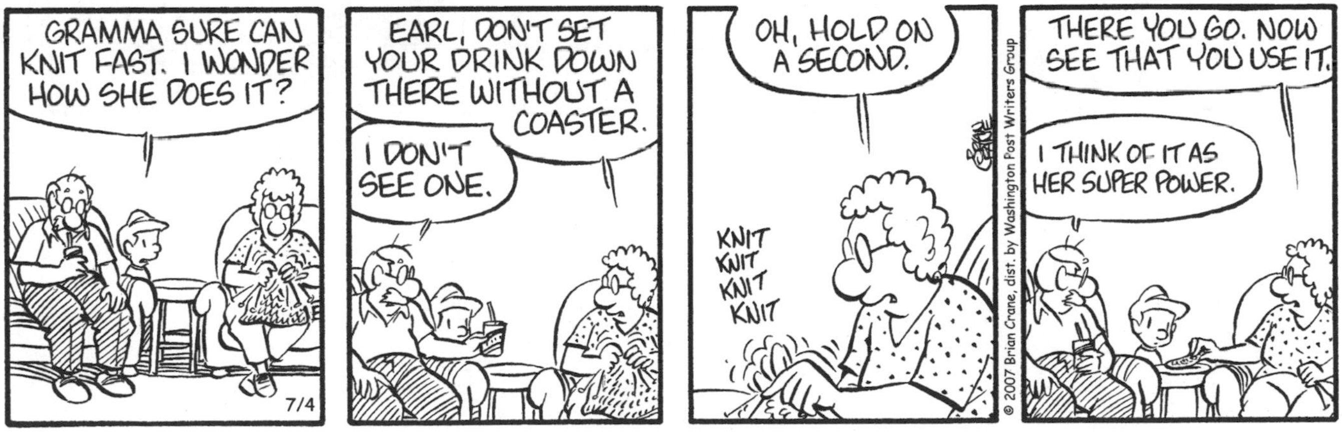
GRAMMA SURE CAN KNIT FAST. I WONDER HOW SHE DOES IT?
7/4
EARL, DON'T SET YOUR DRINK DOWN THERE WITHOUT A COASTER.
I DON'T SEE ONE.
OH, HOLD ON A SECOND.
KNIT KNIT KNIT KNIT
THERE YOU GO. NOW SEE THAT YOU USE IT.
I THINK OF IT AS HER SUPER POWER.
© 2007 Brian Crane, dist. by Washington Post Writers Group

SundayPickles

PICKLES
by Brian Crane
PRRR...
UHHH... DO YOU MIND?!
PURRR..
WHAT'S YOUR FAVORITE PET, GRAMPA, A DOG OR A CAT?
HMM. GIVEN THOSE CHOICES, I'D HAVE TO SAY A DOG.
BUT TRUTHFULLY, MY FAVORITE PET OF ALL IS A GRANDSON.
GRANDSONS AREN'T PETS!
YEAH. I GUESS YOU'RE RIGHT. I'M SORRY.
3/11
GO FETCH ME THE REMOTE, WILL YOU, NELSON?
OKAY.
© 2007 Brian Crane, dist. By Washington Post Writers Group

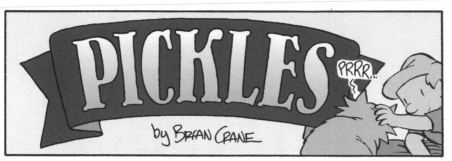

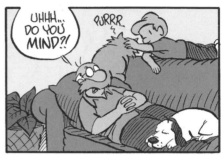

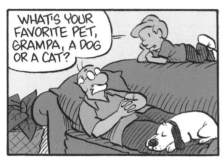

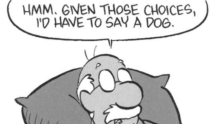

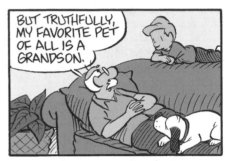

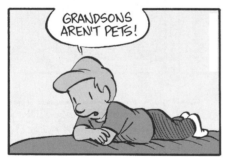

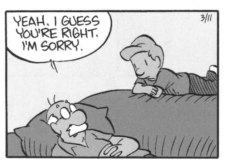

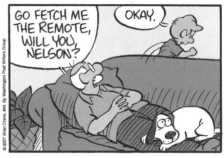

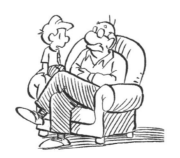

YOU WANT TO KNOW WHAT'S REALLY AMAZING ABOUT GRAMMA'S KNITTING?

NOT ONLY DOES SHE KNIT EXTREMELY FAST, BUT SHE CAN DO IT WITHOUT LOOKING.

IT'S LIKE HER FINGERS WORK INDEPENDENTLY OF HER BRAIN.

7/5

THAT'S TRUE. JUST LIKE GRAMPA'S MOUTH WORKS INDEPENDENTLY OF HIS BRAIN.

WHAT ARE YOU DOING THERE, OPAL?

I'M PUTTING STICKERS ON ALL MY BELONGINGS SAYING WHOM I WANT THEM TO GO TO AFTER I'M GONE.

7/16

AH... GOOD IDEA. ARE YOU GOING TO PUT ONE ON ME TOO? HA HA HA!

© 2007 Brian Crane, dist. by Washington Post Writers Group

WHEN'S THE LAST TIME YOU CHECKED THE BACK OF YOUR HEAD?

DO ME A FAVOR, SYLVIA. LOOK AT THE BACK OF MY HEAD AND TELL ME IF YOU SEE A STICKER.

A STICKER?

YEAH. OPAL'S BEEN PUTTING STICKERS ON ALL HER BELONGINGS SAYING WHO SHE WANTS TO INHERIT THEM AFTER SHE DIES.

7/17

I THINK SHE MIGHT HAVE PUT ONE ON THE BACK OF MY HEAD JUST TO BE CUTE.

OH, I THINK I SEE IT.

© 2007 Brian Crane, dist. by Washington Post Writers Group

IT LOOKS LIKE YOU'RE BEING DONATED TO THE HUMANE SOCIETY.

PICKLES
by BRIAN CRANE

LOOK AT YOUR GRANDMA GO. SHE'S A REAL SEWER, YOU KNOW.

IN FACT, PEOPLE OFTEN COMMENT ON WHAT A GREAT SEWER SHE IS.

IT'S PRONOUNCED "SOWER," NOT "SOO-ER," IF YOU DON'T MIND!!

BETTER YET, JUST SAY "SEAMSTRESS."

OR BETTER STILL, JUST GO AWAY.

YOUR GRANDMA'S A WONDERFUL SEWER, BUT SHE CAN'T TAKE A COMPLIMENT.

© 2007 Brian Crane, dist. By Washington Post Writers Group

6/24

SMOOCH!

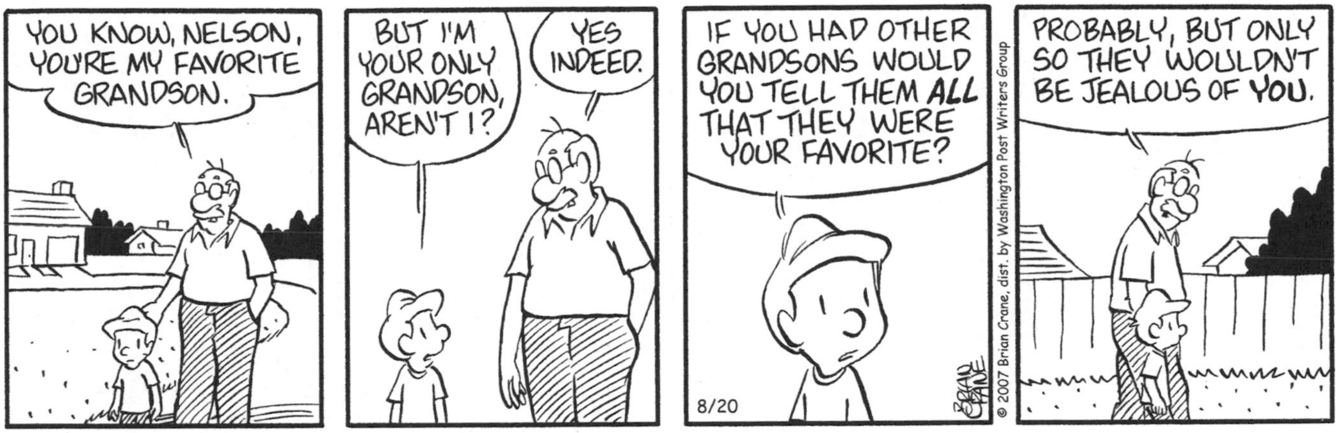
YOU KNOW, NELSON, YOU'RE MY FAVORITE GRANDSON.
BUT I'M YOUR ONLY GRANDSON, AREN'T I?
YES INDEED.
IF YOU HAD OTHER GRANDSONS WOULD YOU TELL THEM **ALL** THAT THEY WERE YOUR FAVORITE?
8/20
© 2007 Brian Crane, dist. by Washington Post Writers Group
PROBABLY, BUT ONLY SO THEY WOULDN'T BE JEALOUS OF **YOU**.

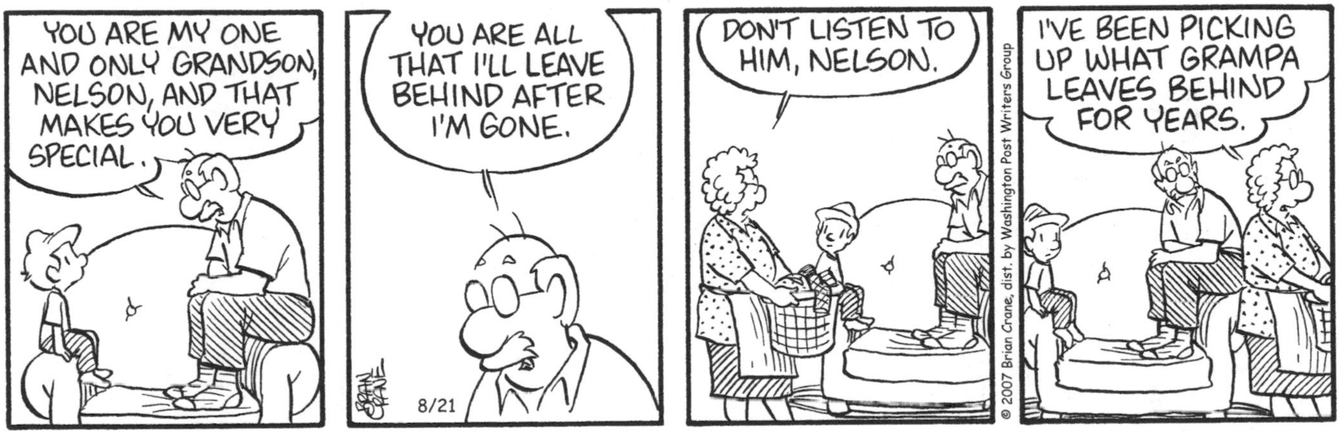
YOU ARE MY ONE AND ONLY GRANDSON, NELSON, AND THAT MAKES YOU VERY SPECIAL.
YOU ARE ALL THAT I'LL LEAVE BEHIND AFTER I'M GONE.
8/21
DON'T LISTEN TO HIM, NELSON.
© 2007 Brian Crane, dist. by Washington Post Writers Group
I'VE BEEN PICKING UP WHAT GRAMPA LEAVES BEHIND FOR YEARS.

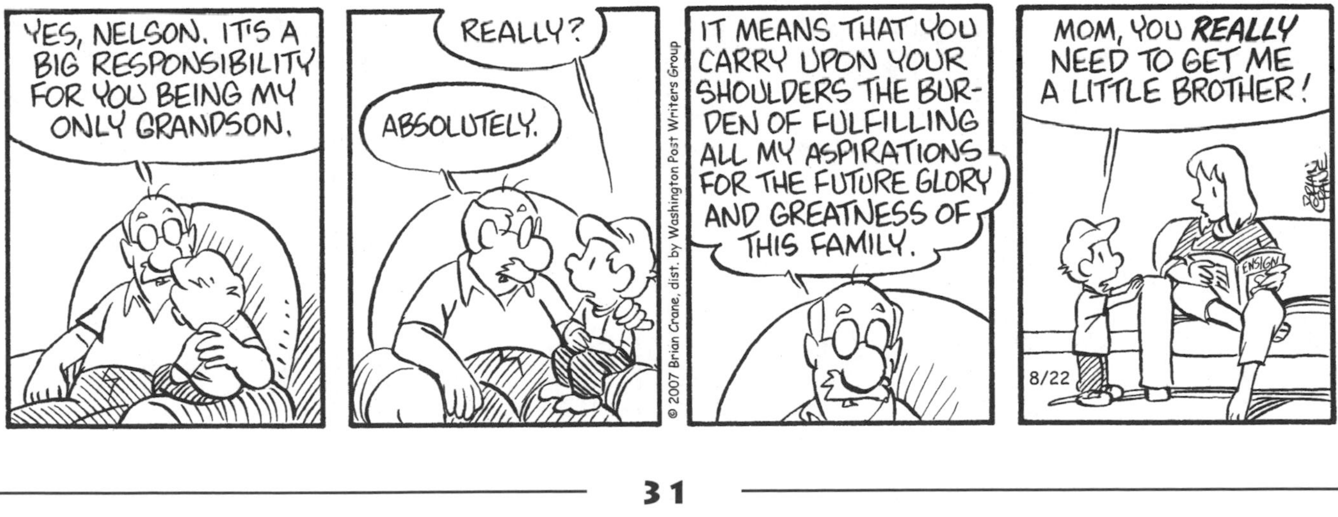
YES, NELSON. IT'S A BIG RESPONSIBILITY FOR YOU BEING MY ONLY GRANDSON.
REALLY?
ABSOLUTELY.
© 2007 Brian Crane, dist. by Washington Post Writers Group
IT MEANS THAT YOU CARRY UPON YOUR SHOULDERS THE BURDEN OF FULFILLING ALL MY ASPIRATIONS FOR THE FUTURE GLORY AND GREATNESS OF THIS FAMILY.
MOM, YOU ***REALLY*** NEED TO GET ME A LITTLE BROTHER!
ENSIGN
8/22

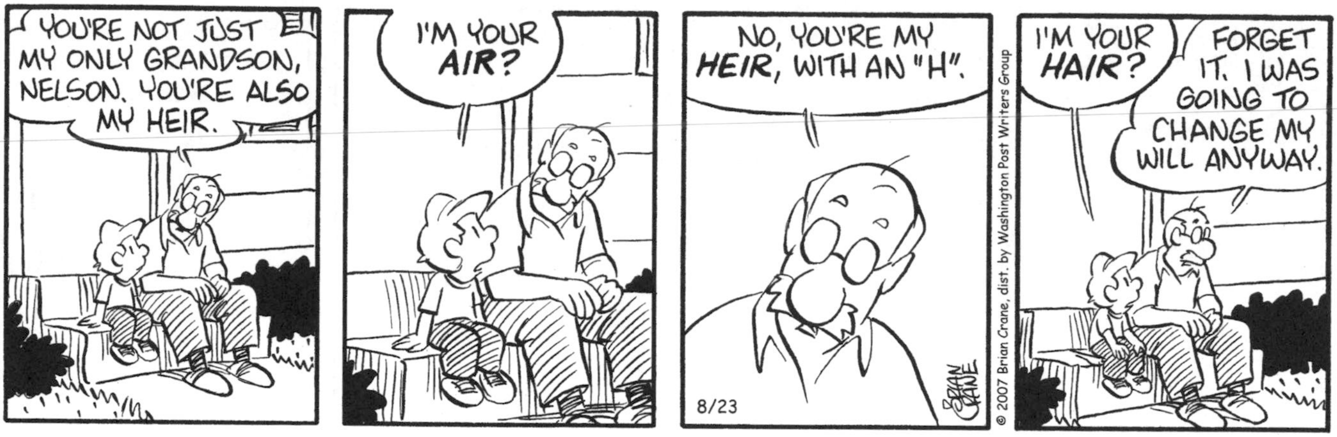
YOU'RE NOT JUST MY ONLY GRANDSON, NELSON. YOU'RE ALSO MY HEIR.
I'M YOUR **AIR**?
NO, YOU'RE MY **HEIR**, WITH AN "H".
8/23
© 2007 Brian Crane, dist. by Washington Post Writers Group
I'M YOUR **HAIR**?
FORGET IT. I WAS GOING TO CHANGE MY WILL ANYWAY.

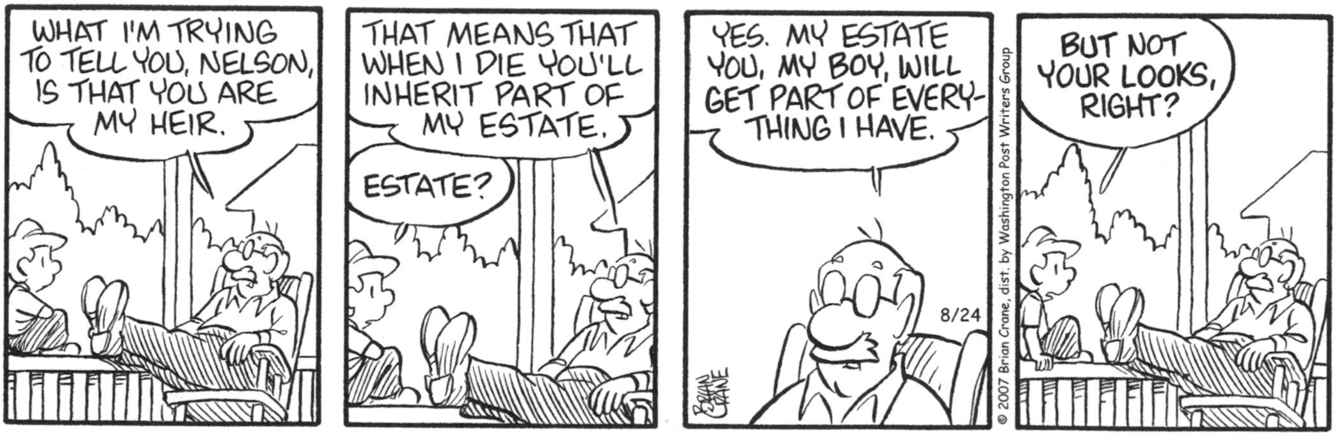
WHAT I'M TRYING TO TELL YOU, NELSON, IS THAT YOU ARE MY HEIR.
THAT MEANS THAT WHEN I DIE YOU'LL INHERIT PART OF MY ESTATE.
ESTATE?
YES. MY ESTATE YOU, MY BOY, WILL GET PART OF EVERYTHING I HAVE.
8/24
© 2007 Brian Crane, dist. by Washington Post Writers Group
BUT NOT YOUR LOOKS, RIGHT?

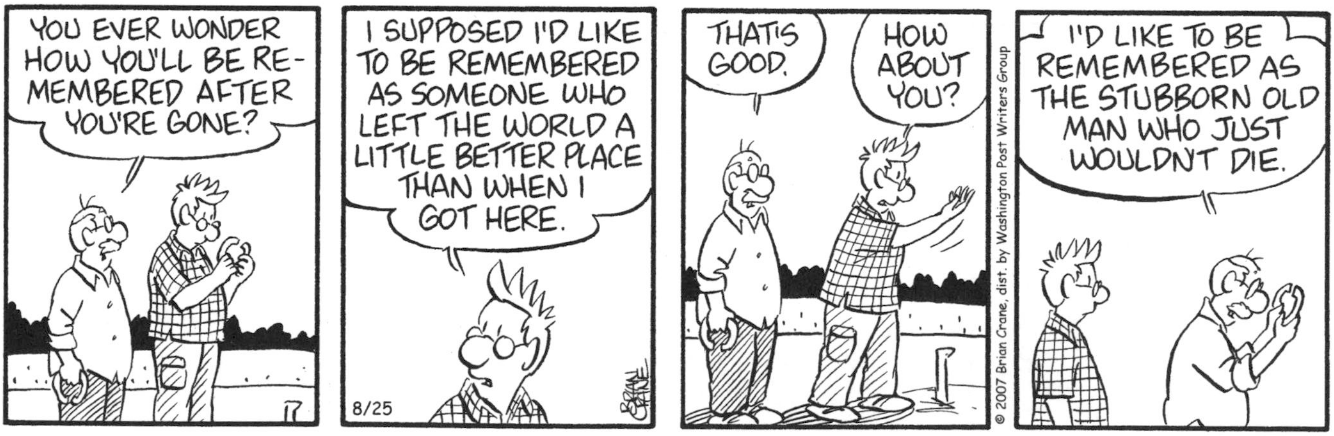
YOU EVER WONDER HOW YOU'LL BE REMEMBERED AFTER YOU'RE GONE?
I SUPPOSED I'D LIKE TO BE REMEMBERED AS SOMEONE WHO LEFT THE WORLD A LITTLE BETTER PLACE THAN WHEN I GOT HERE.
8/25
THAT'S GOOD.
HOW ABOUT YOU?
© 2007 Brian Crane, dist. by Washington Post Writers Group
I'D LIKE TO BE REMEMBERED AS THE STUBBORN OLD MAN WHO JUST WOULDN'T DIE.

SundayPickles

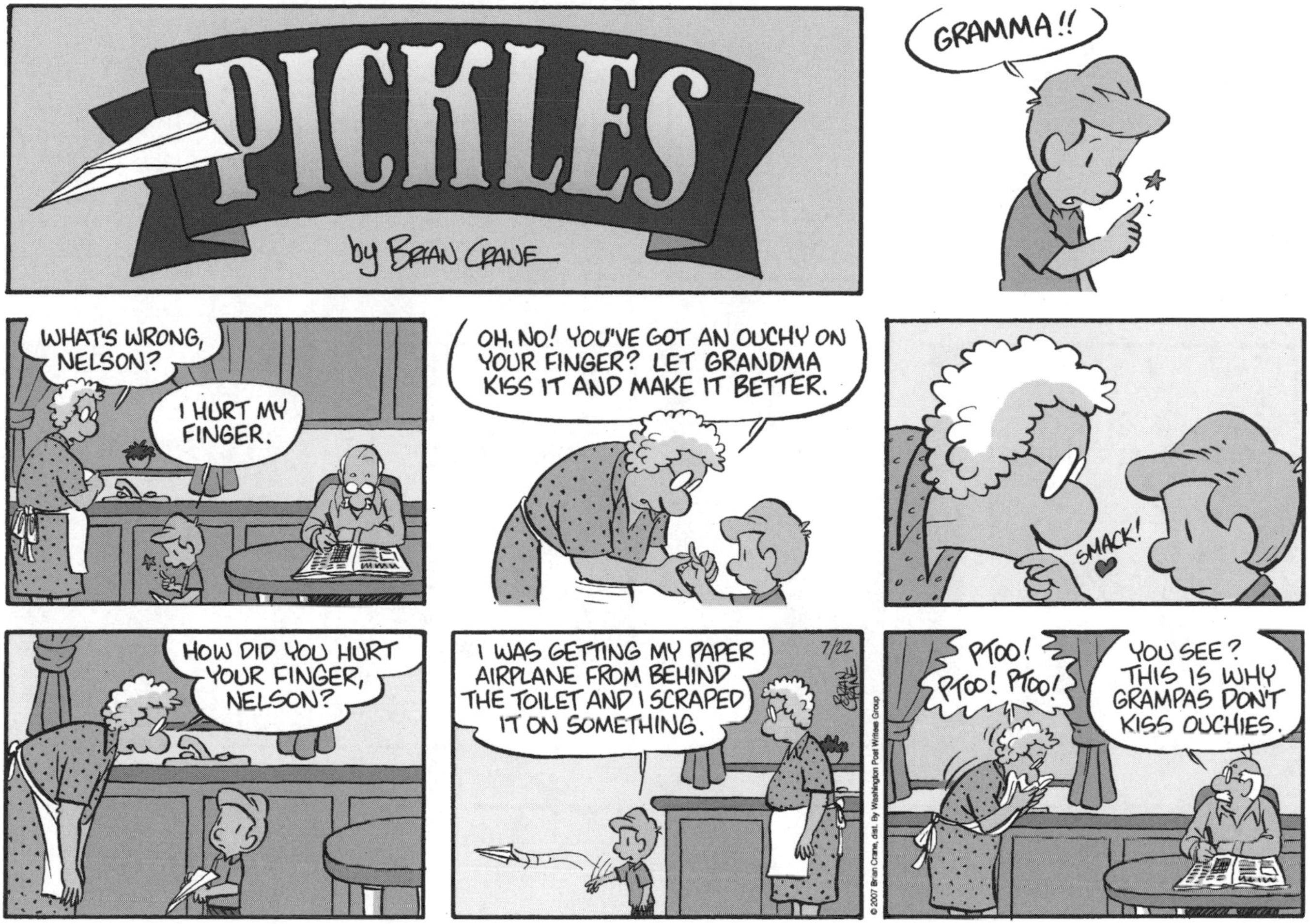
PICKLES
by Brian Crane
GRAMMA!!
WHAT'S WRONG, NELSON?
I HURT MY FINGER.
OH, NO! YOU'VE GOT AN OUCHY ON YOUR FINGER? LET GRANDMA KISS IT AND MAKE IT BETTER.
SMACK!
HOW DID YOU HURT YOUR FINGER, NELSON?
I WAS GETTING MY PAPER AIRPLANE FROM BEHIND THE TOILET AND I SCRAPED IT ON SOMETHING.
7/22
© 2007 Brian Crane, dist. By Washington Post Writers Group
PTOO! PTOO! PTOO!
YOU SEE? THIS IS WHY GRAMPAS DON'T KISS OUCHIES.

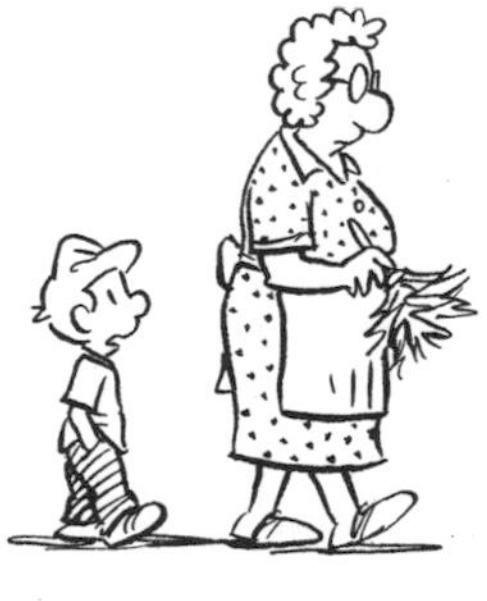

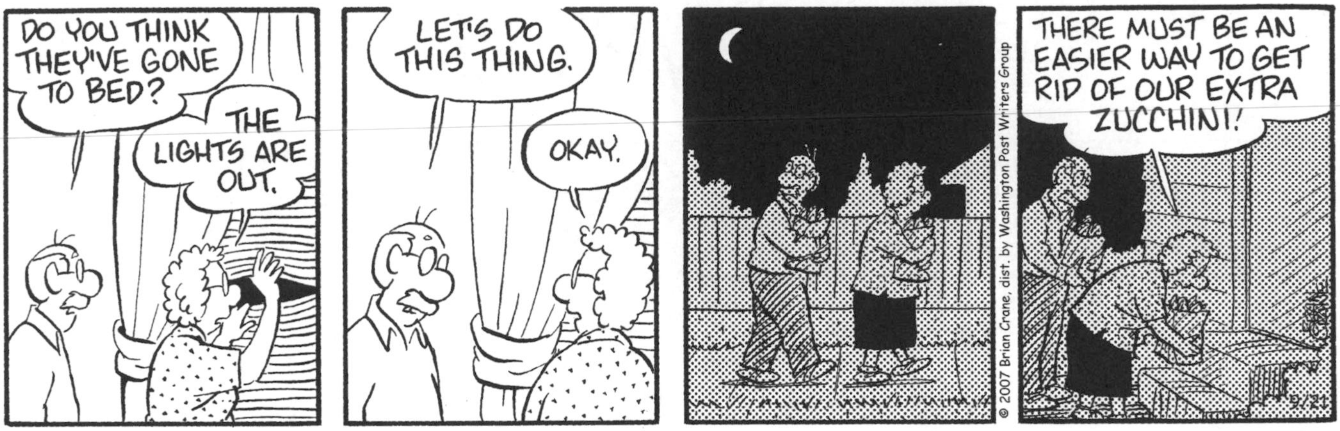
DO YOU THINK THEY'VE GONE TO BED?
THE LIGHTS ARE OUT.
LET'S DO THIS THING.
OKAY.
THERE MUST BE AN EASIER WAY TO GET RID OF OUR EXTRA ZUCCHINI!
© 2007 Brian Crane, dist. by Washington Post Writers Group
9/21

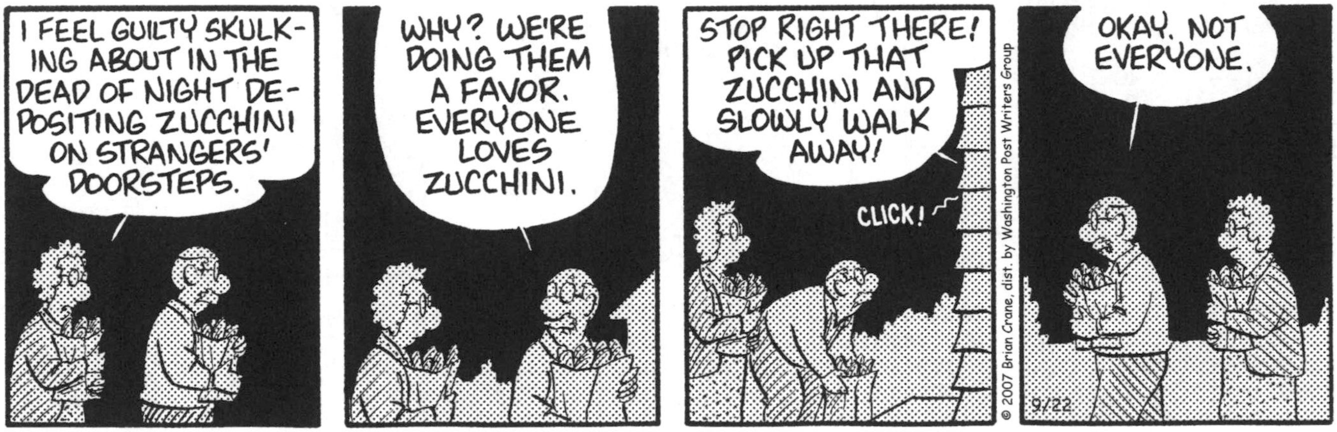
I FEEL GUILTY SKULK-ING ABOUT IN THE DEAD OF NIGHT DE-POSITING ZUCCHINI ON STRANGERS' DOORSTEPS.
WHY? WE'RE DOING THEM A FAVOR. EVERYONE LOVES ZUCCHINI.
STOP RIGHT THERE! PICK UP THAT ZUCCHINI AND SLOWLY WALK AWAY!
CLICK!
OKAY. NOT EVERYONE.
© 2007 Brian Crane, dist. by Washington Post Writers Group
9/22

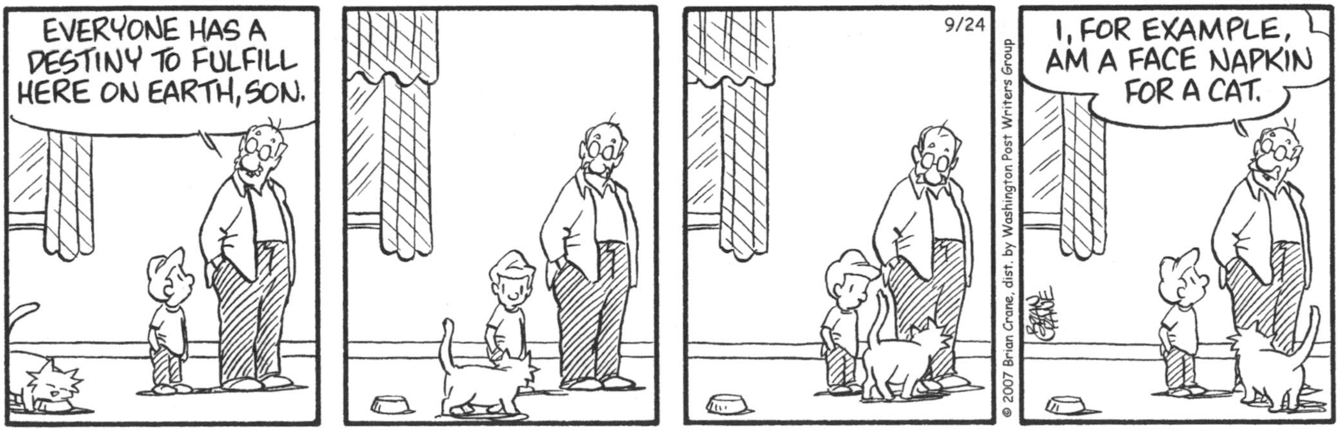
EVERYONE HAS A DESTINY TO FULFILL HERE ON EARTH, SON.
9/24
I, FOR EXAMPLE, AM A FACE NAPKIN FOR A CAT.
© 2007 Brian Crane, dist. by Washington Post Writers Group

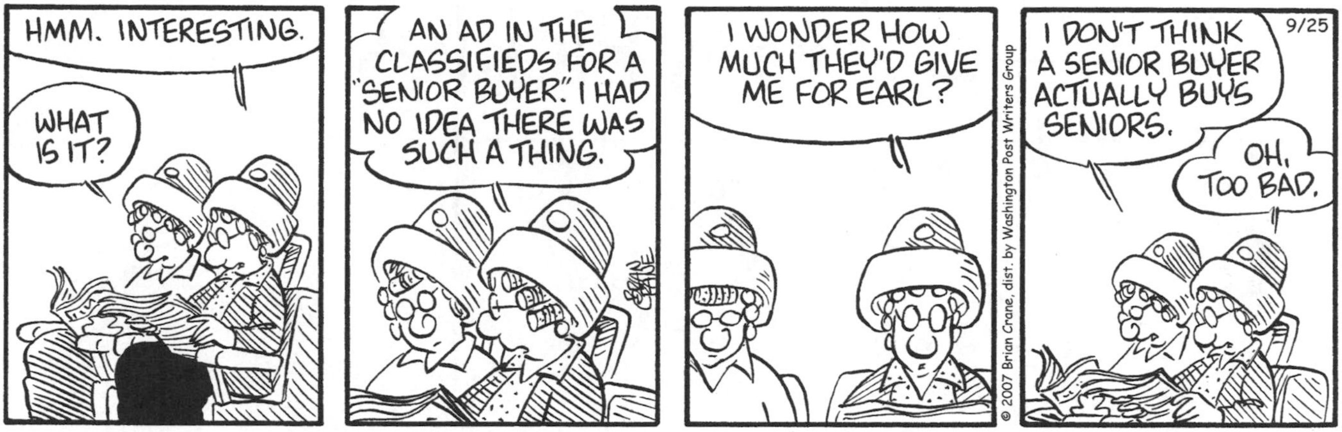
HMM. INTERESTING.
WHAT IS IT?
AN AD IN THE CLASSIFIEDS FOR A "SENIOR BUYER." I HAD NO IDEA THERE WAS SUCH A THING.
I WONDER HOW MUCH THEY'D GIVE ME FOR EARL?
© 2007 Brian Crane, dist. by Washington Post Writers Group
9/25
I DON'T THINK A SENIOR BUYER ACTUALLY BUYS SENIORS.
OH, TOO BAD.

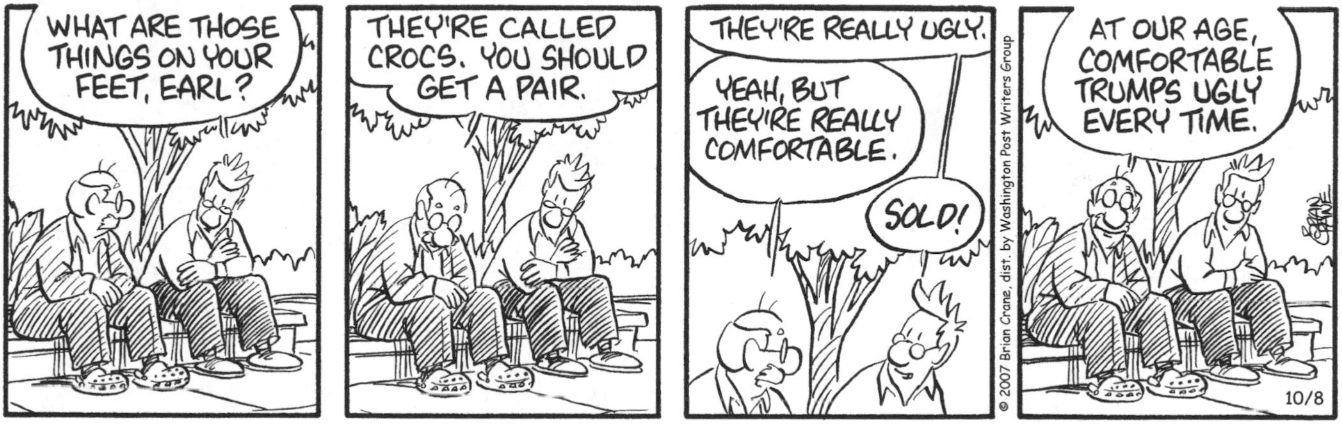
WHAT ARE THOSE THINGS ON YOUR FEET, EARL?
THEY'RE CALLED CROCS. YOU SHOULD GET A PAIR.
THEY'RE REALLY UGLY.
YEAH, BUT THEY'RE REALLY COMFORTABLE.
SOLD!
© 2007 Brian Crane, dist. by Washington Post Writers Group
AT OUR AGE, COMFORTABLE TRUMPS UGLY EVERY TIME.
10/8

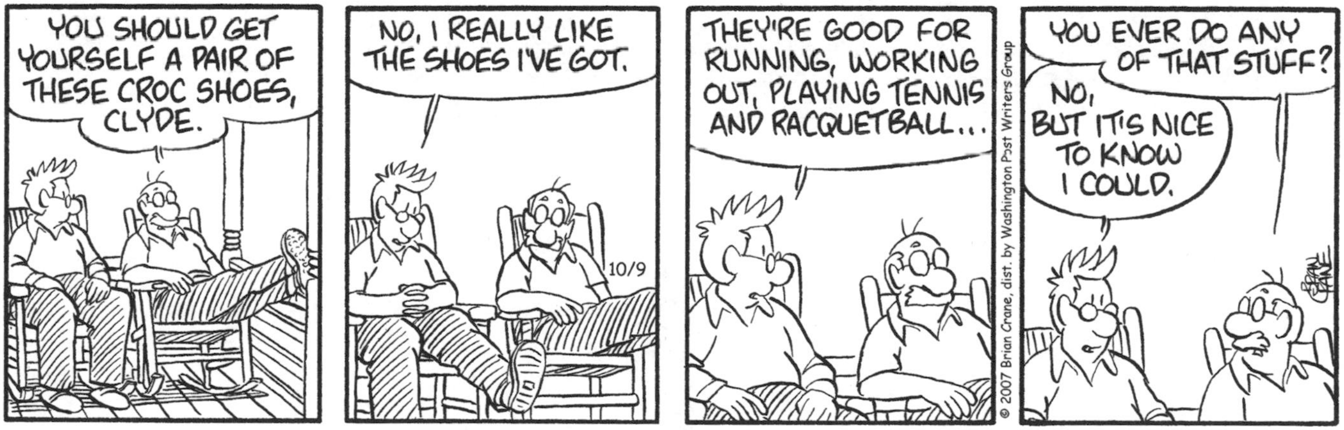
YOU SHOULD GET YOURSELF A PAIR OF THESE CROC SHOES, CLYDE.
NO, I REALLY LIKE THE SHOES I'VE GOT.
10/9
THEY'RE GOOD FOR RUNNING, WORKING OUT, PLAYING TENNIS AND RACQUETBALL...
© 2007 Brian Crane, dist. by Washington Post Writers Group
YOU EVER DO ANY OF THAT STUFF?
NO, BUT IT'S NICE TO KNOW I COULD.

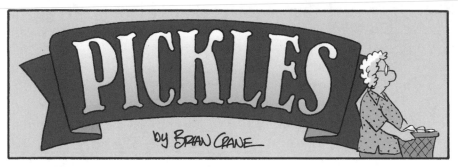

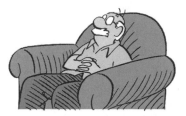

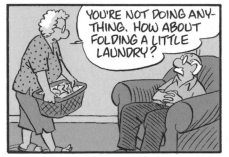

PICKLES
by BRIAN CRANE
YOU'RE NOT DOING ANYTHING. HOW ABOUT FOLDING A LITTLE LAUNDRY?
picklescomic@sbcglobal.net
SPROING!
© 2007 Brian Crane · dist. By Washington Post Writers Group
I JUST REMEMBERED I NEED TO GO ROTATE MY TIRES OR SOMETHING.
9/23
BRIAN CRANE

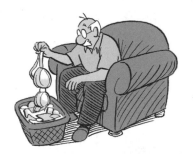

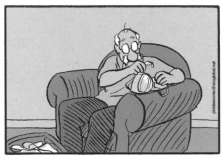

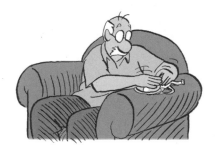

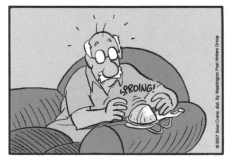

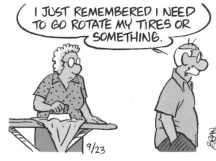

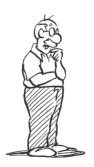

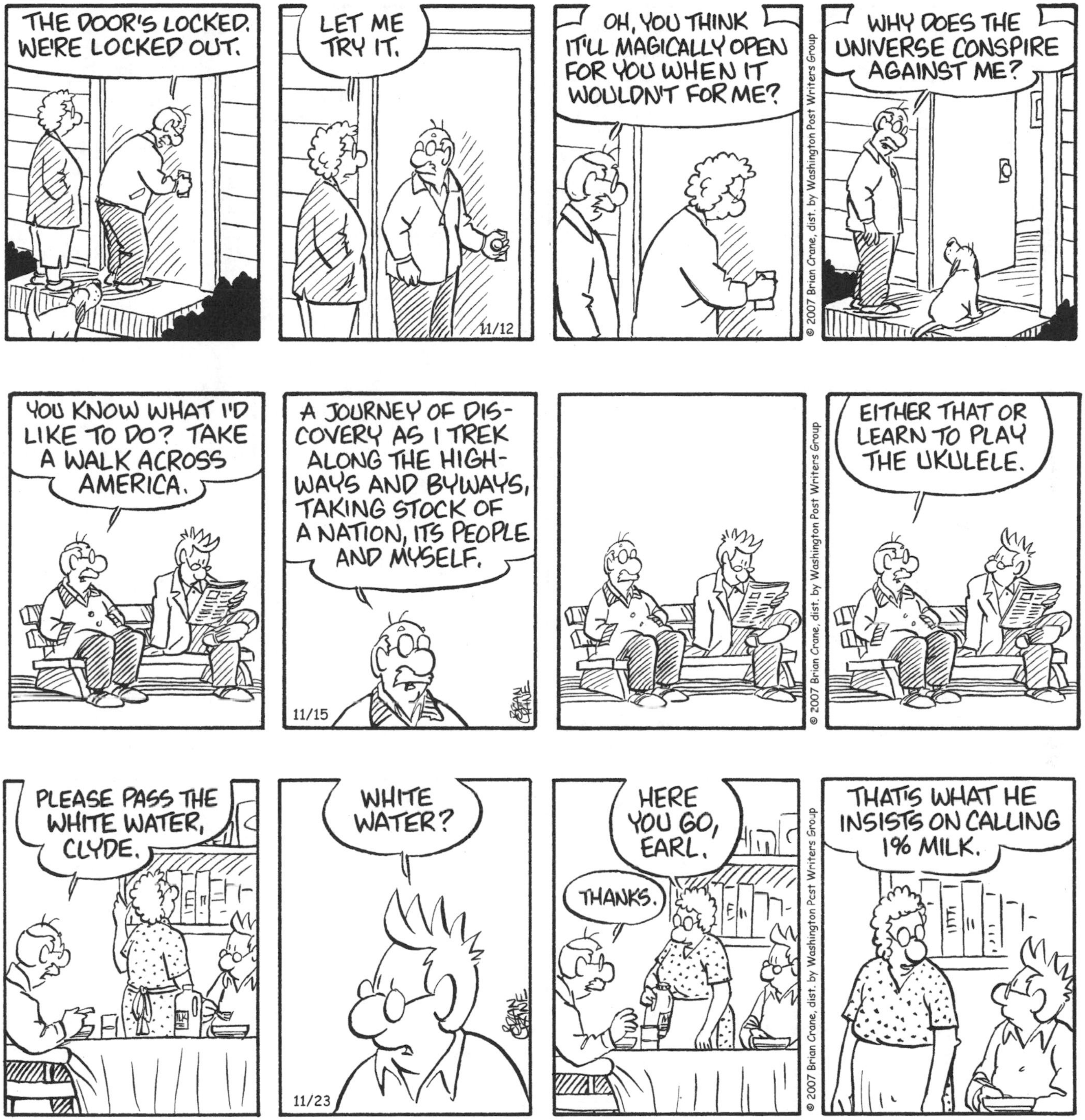
THE DOOR'S LOCKED. WE'RE LOCKED OUT.
LET ME TRY IT.
11/12
OH, YOU THINK IT'LL MAGICALLY OPEN FOR YOU WHEN IT WOULDN'T FOR ME?
© 2007 Brian Crane, dist. by Washington Post Writers Group
WHY DOES THE UNIVERSE CONSPIRE AGAINST ME?
YOU KNOW WHAT I'D LIKE TO DO? TAKE A WALK ACROSS AMERICA.
A JOURNEY OF DISCOVERY AS I TREK ALONG THE HIGHWAYS AND BYWAYS, TAKING STOCK OF A NATION, ITS PEOPLE AND MYSELF.
11/15
BRIAN CRANE
© 2007 Brian Crane, dist. by Washington Post Writers Group
EITHER THAT OR LEARN TO PLAY THE UKULELE.
PLEASE PASS THE WHITE WATER, CLYDE.
WHITE WATER?
BRIAN CRANE
11/23
HERE YOU GO, EARL.
THANKS.
© 2007 Brian Crane, dist. by Washington Post Writers Group
THAT'S WHAT HE INSISTS ON CALLING 1% MILK.

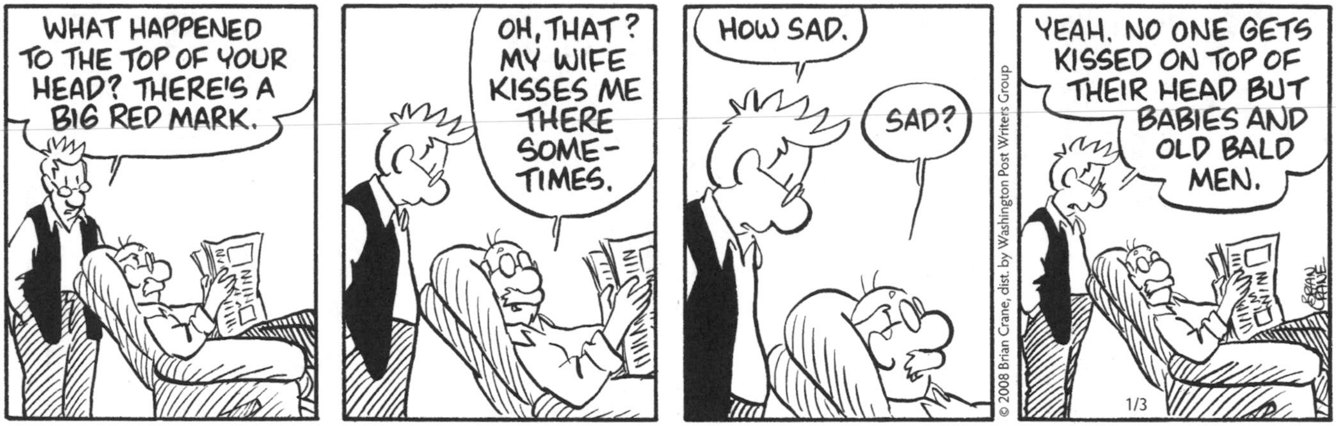
WHAT HAPPENED TO THE TOP OF YOUR HEAD? THERE'S A BIG RED MARK.
OH, THAT? MY WIFE KISSES ME THERE SOME-TIMES.
HOW SAD.
SAD?
YEAH. NO ONE GETS KISSED ON TOP OF THEIR HEAD BUT BABIES AND OLD BALD MEN.
1/3
© 2008 Brian Crane, dist. by Washington Post Writers Group

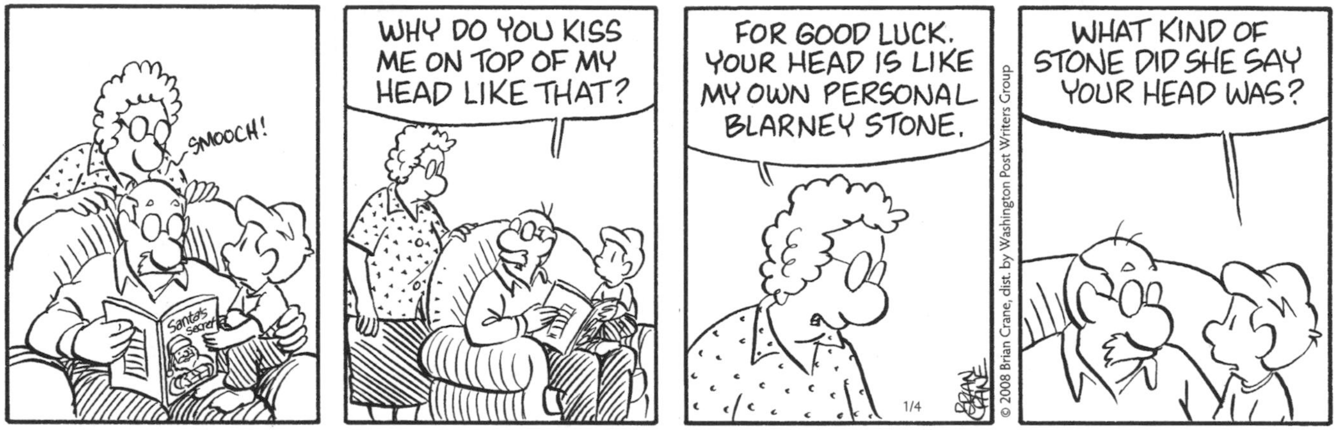
SMOOCH!
WHY DO YOU KISS ME ON TOP OF MY HEAD LIKE THAT?
FOR GOOD LUCK. YOUR HEAD IS LIKE MY OWN PERSONAL BLARNEY STONE.
1/4
© 2008 Brian Crane, dist. by Washington Post Writers Group
WHAT KIND OF STONE DID SHE SAY YOUR HEAD WAS?

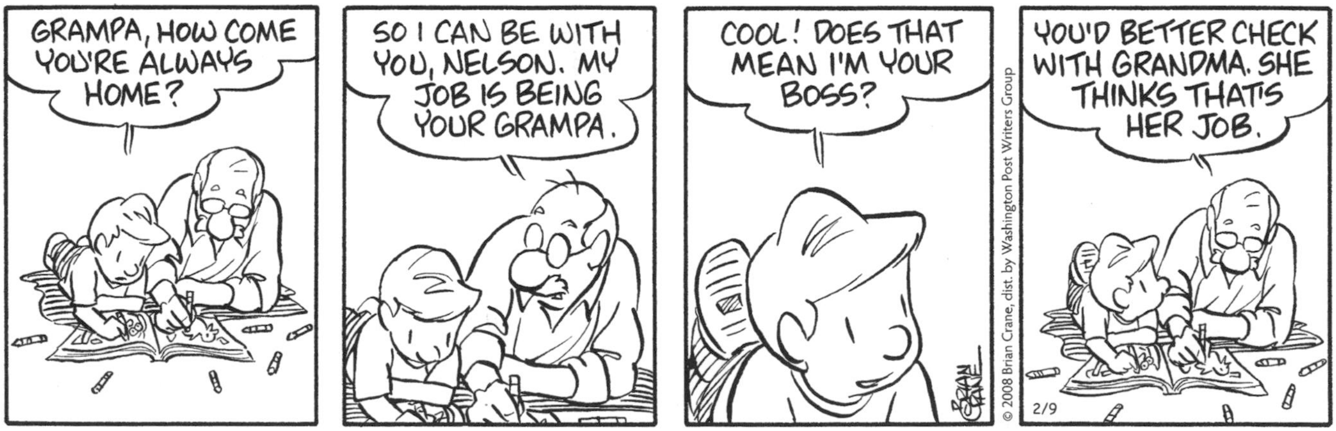
GRAMPA, HOW COME YOU'RE ALWAYS HOME?
SO I CAN BE WITH YOU, NELSON. MY JOB IS BEING YOUR GRAMPA.
COOL! DOES THAT MEAN I'M YOUR BOSS?
© 2008 Brian Crane, dist. by Washington Post Writers Group
YOU'D BETTER CHECK WITH GRANDMA. SHE THINKS THAT'S HER JOB.
2/9

SundayPickles

PICKLES
by BRIAN CRANE
SNIFF SNAFF
SNIFF SNEEF
SNORF SNARF
DO YOU SMELL THAT?
UH HUH!
OOH! CINNAMON ROLLS!
THEY'RE FOR THE CHURCH SOCIAL.
DON'T TOUCH THOSE CINNAMON ROLLS! GOD IS WATCHING!
HEY, LOOK... A PIE! SHALL WE HAVE SOME?
WON'T WE GET IN TROUBLE?
© 2007 Brian Crane, dist. By Washington Post Writers Group
DON'T WORRY. GOD'S WATCHING THE CINNAMON ROLLS.
10/14

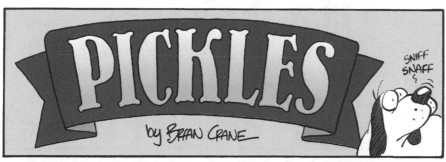

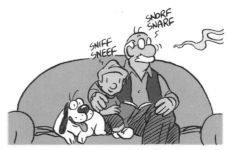

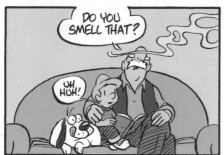

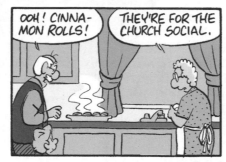

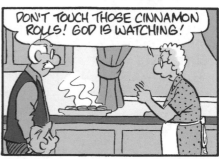

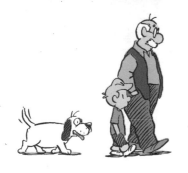

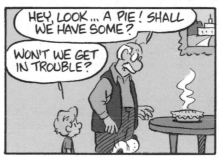

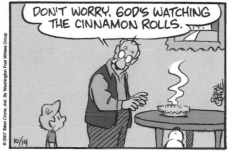

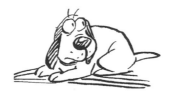

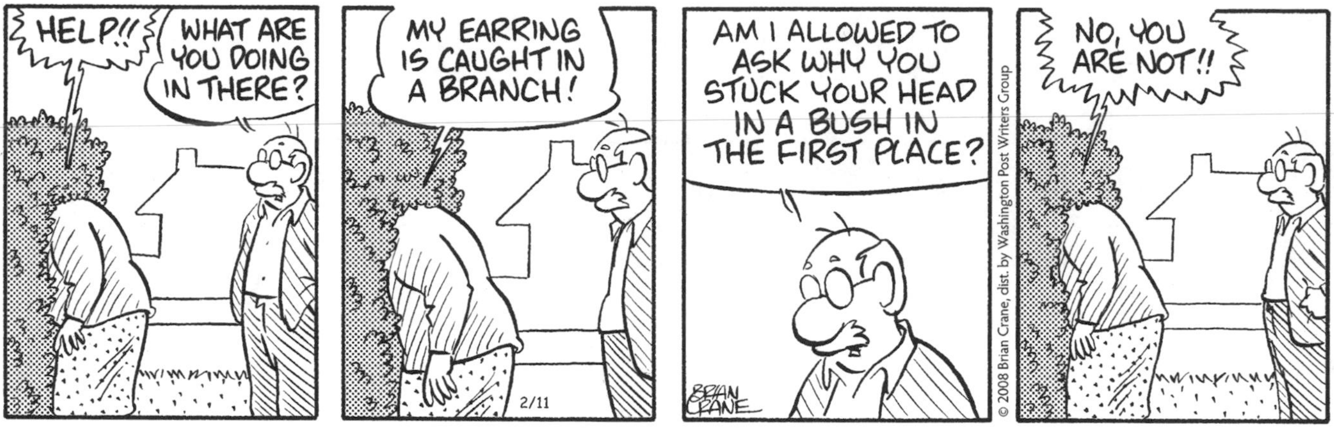
HELP!!
WHAT ARE YOU DOING IN THERE?
MY EARRING IS CAUGHT IN A BRANCH!
2/11
AM I ALLOWED TO ASK WHY YOU STUCK YOUR HEAD IN A BUSH IN THE FIRST PLACE?
BRIAN CRANE
© 2008 Brian Crane, dist. by Washington Post Writers Group
NO, YOU ARE NOT!!

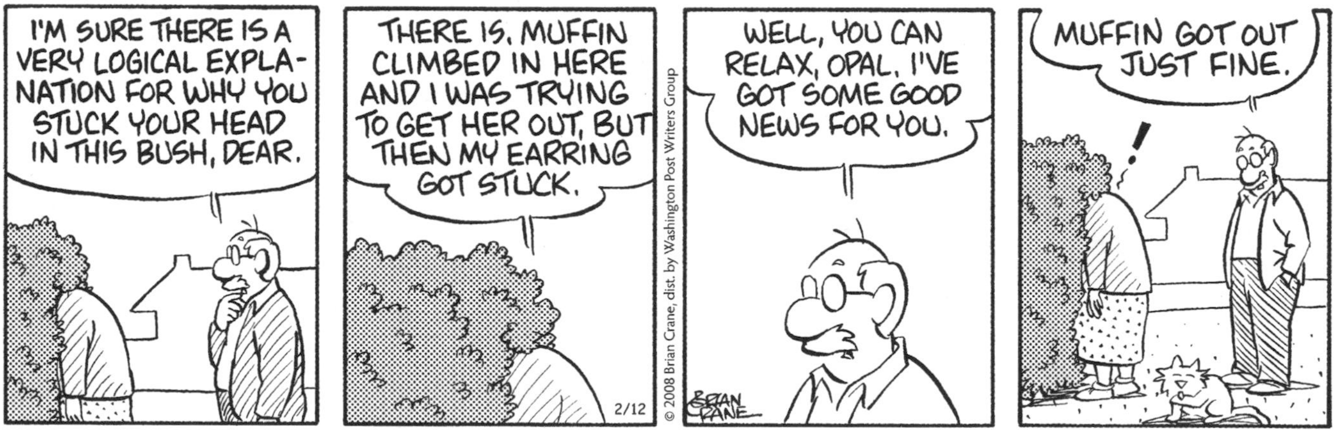
I'M SURE THERE IS A VERY LOGICAL EXPLANATION FOR WHY YOU STUCK YOUR HEAD IN THIS BUSH, DEAR.
THERE IS. MUFFIN CLIMBED IN HERE AND I WAS TRYING TO GET HER OUT, BUT THEN MY EARRING GOT STUCK.
2/12
© 2008 Brian Crane, dist. by Washington Post Writers Group
WELL, YOU CAN RELAX, OPAL. I'VE GOT SOME GOOD NEWS FOR YOU.
BRIAN CRANE
MUFFIN GOT OUT JUST FINE.
!

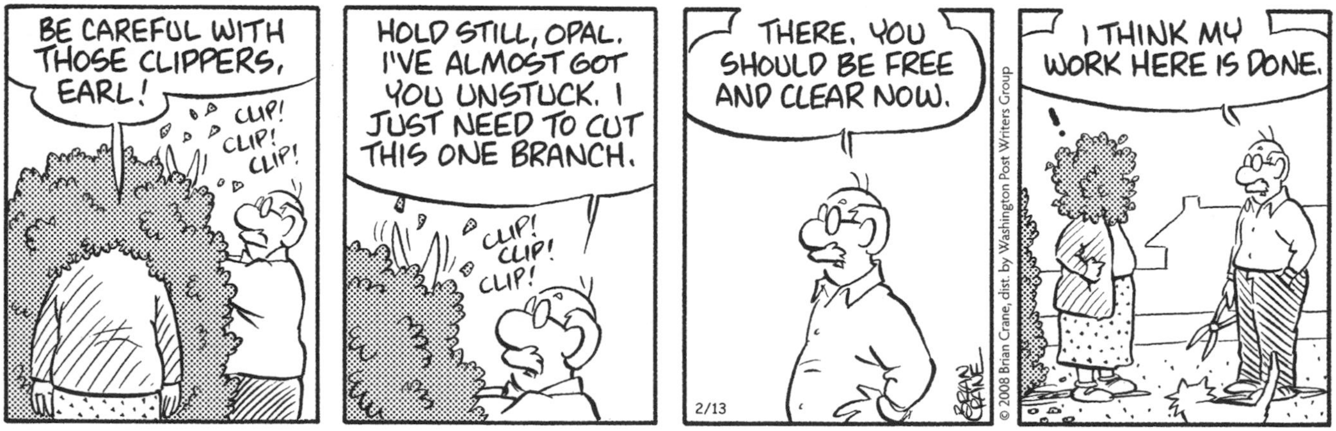
BE CAREFUL WITH THOSE CLIPPERS, EARL!
CLIP! CLIP! CLIP!
HOLD STILL, OPAL. I'VE ALMOST GOT YOU UNSTUCK. I JUST NEED TO CUT THIS ONE BRANCH.
CLIP! CLIP! CLIP!
THERE. YOU SHOULD BE FREE AND CLEAR NOW.
2/13
BRIAN CRANE
© 2008 Brian Crane, dist. by Washington Post Writers Group
I THINK MY WORK HERE IS DONE.
!

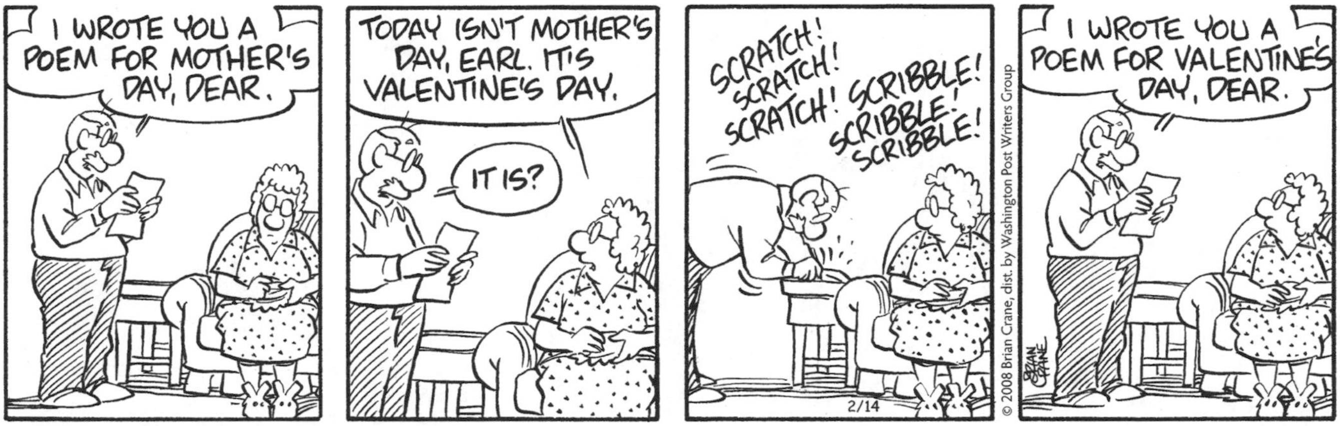
I WROTE YOU A POEM FOR MOTHER'S DAY, DEAR.
TODAY ISN'T MOTHER'S DAY, EARL. IT'S VALENTINE'S DAY.
IT IS?
SCRATCH! SCRATCH! SCRATCH! SCRIBBLE! SCRIBBLE! SCRIBBLE!
2/14
© 2008 Brian Crane, dist. by Washington Post Writers Group
I WROTE YOU A POEM FOR VALENTINE'S DAY, DEAR.

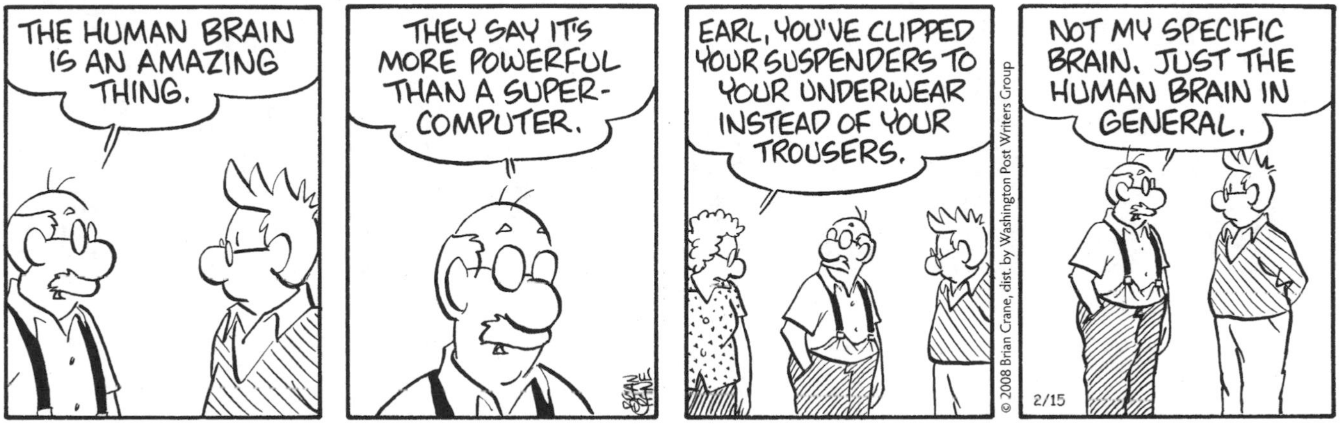
THE HUMAN BRAIN IS AN AMAZING THING.
THEY SAY IT'S MORE POWERFUL THAN A SUPER-COMPUTER.
EARL, YOU'VE CLIPPED YOUR SUSPENDERS TO YOUR UNDERWEAR INSTEAD OF YOUR TROUSERS.
© 2008 Brian Crane, dist. by Washington Post Writers Group
NOT MY SPECIFIC BRAIN. JUST THE HUMAN BRAIN IN GENERAL.
2/15

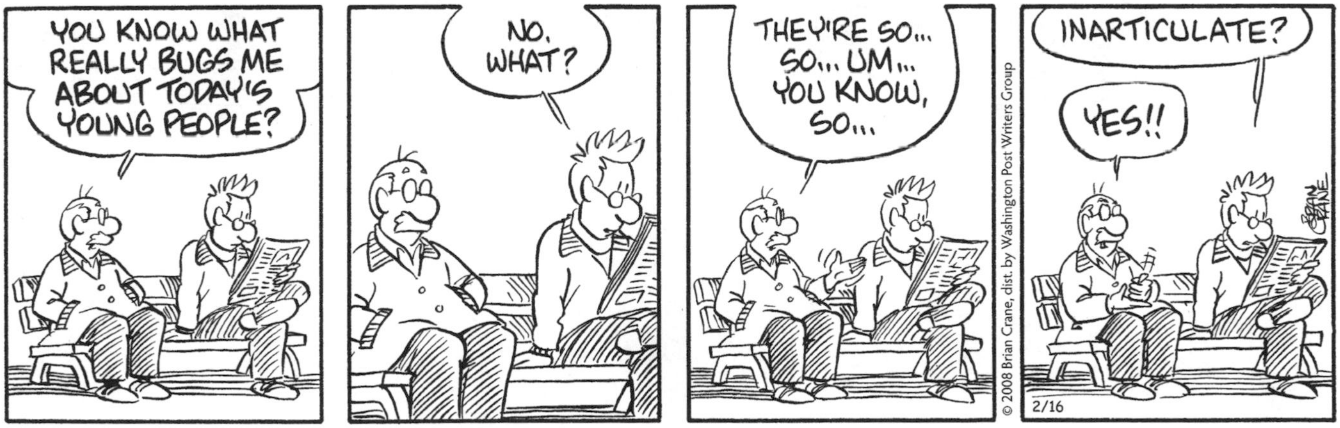
YOU KNOW WHAT REALLY BUGS ME ABOUT TODAY'S YOUNG PEOPLE?
NO. WHAT?
THEY'RE SO... SO... UM... YOU KNOW, SO...
© 2008 Brian Crane, dist. by Washington Post Writers Group
INARTICULATE?
YES!!
2/16

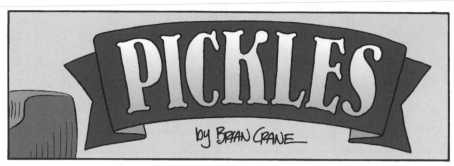

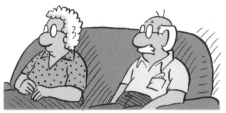

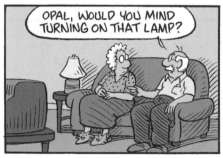

SundayPickles

PICKLES
by BRIAN CRANE
OPAL, WOULD YOU MIND TURNING ON THAT LAMP?
WHY?
I HAVE A HARD TIME HEARING WHEN IT'S DARK.
CLICK!
I KNOW WHAT YOU MEAN.
YOU DO?
11/11
© 2007 Brian Crane, dist. By Washington Post Writers Group
YEAH. I CAN'T HEAR VERY WELL WHEN I'M NOT WEARING MY GLASSES.
BRIAN CRANE

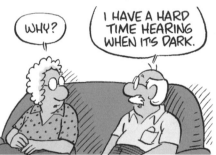

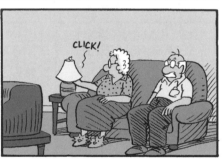

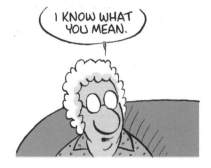

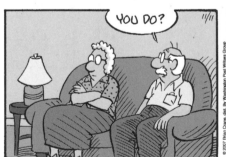

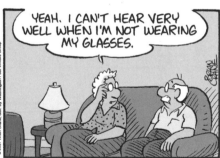

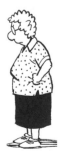

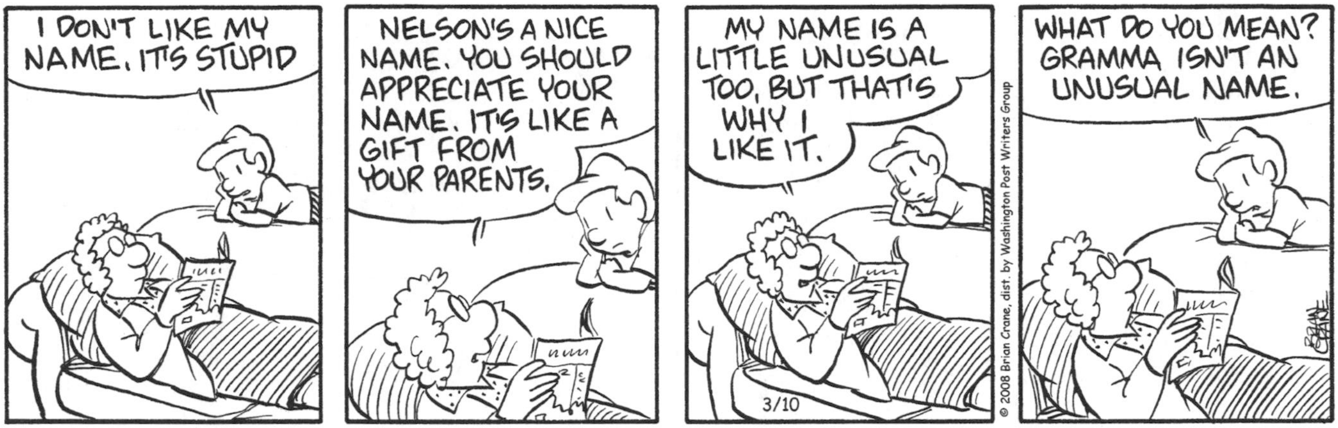
I DON'T LIKE MY NAME. IT'S STUPID
NELSON'S A NICE NAME. YOU SHOULD APPRECIATE YOUR NAME. IT'S LIKE A GIFT FROM YOUR PARENTS.
MY NAME IS A LITTLE UNUSUAL TOO, BUT THAT'S WHY I LIKE IT.
3/10
WHAT DO YOU MEAN? GRAMMA ISN'T AN UNUSUAL NAME.
© 2008 Brian Crane, dist. by Washington Post Writers Group

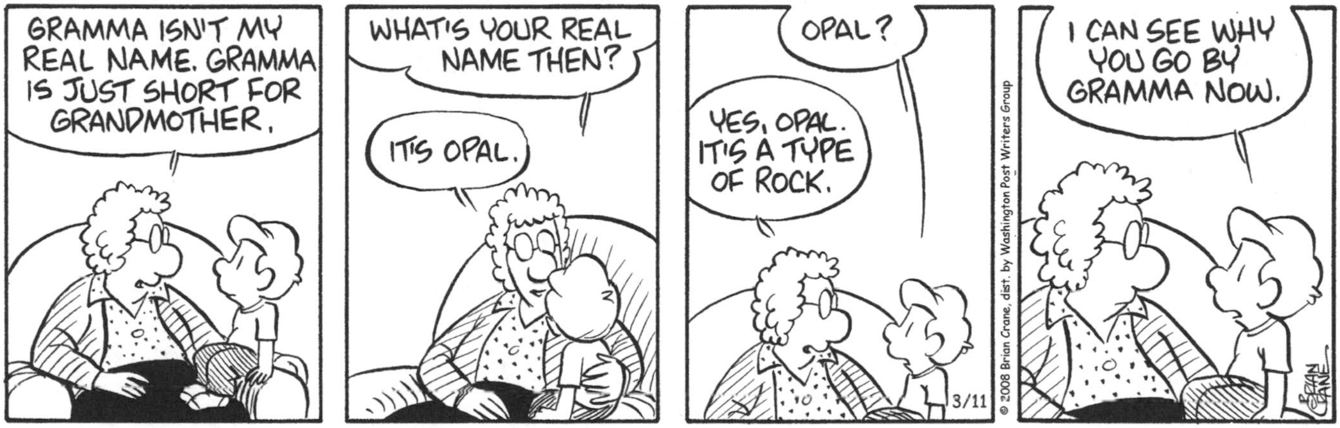
GRAMMA ISN'T MY REAL NAME. GRAMMA IS JUST SHORT FOR GRANDMOTHER.
WHAT'S YOUR REAL NAME THEN?
IT'S OPAL.
OPAL?
YES, OPAL. IT'S A TYPE OF ROCK.
3/11
I CAN SEE WHY YOU GO BY GRAMMA NOW.
© 2008 Brian Crane, dist. by Washington Post Writers Group

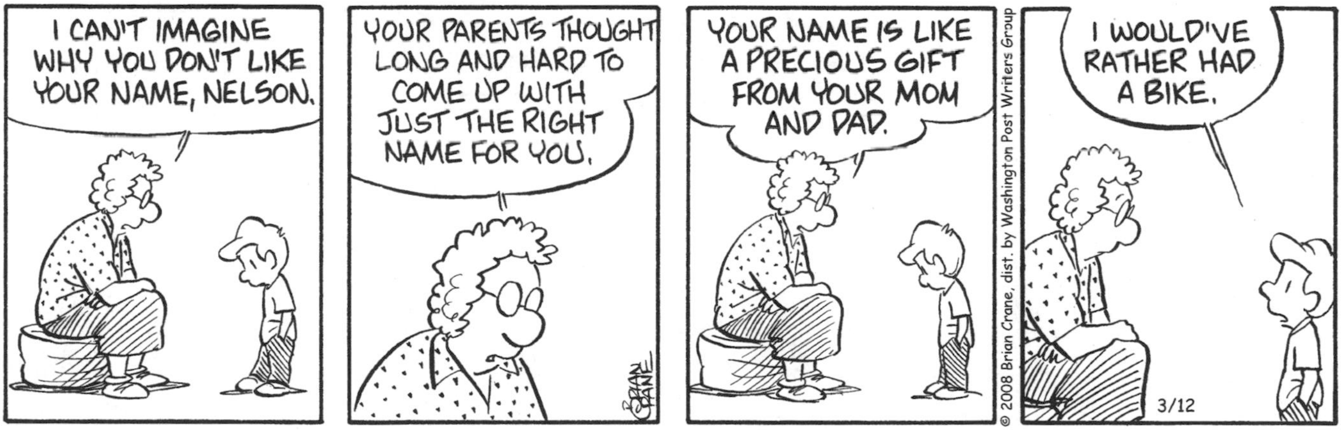
I CAN'T IMAGINE WHY YOU DON'T LIKE YOUR NAME, NELSON.
YOUR PARENTS THOUGHT LONG AND HARD TO COME UP WITH JUST THE RIGHT NAME FOR YOU.
YOUR NAME IS LIKE A PRECIOUS GIFT FROM YOUR MOM AND DAD.
I WOULD'VE RATHER HAD A BIKE.
3/12
© 2008 Brian Crane, dist. by Washington Post Writers Group

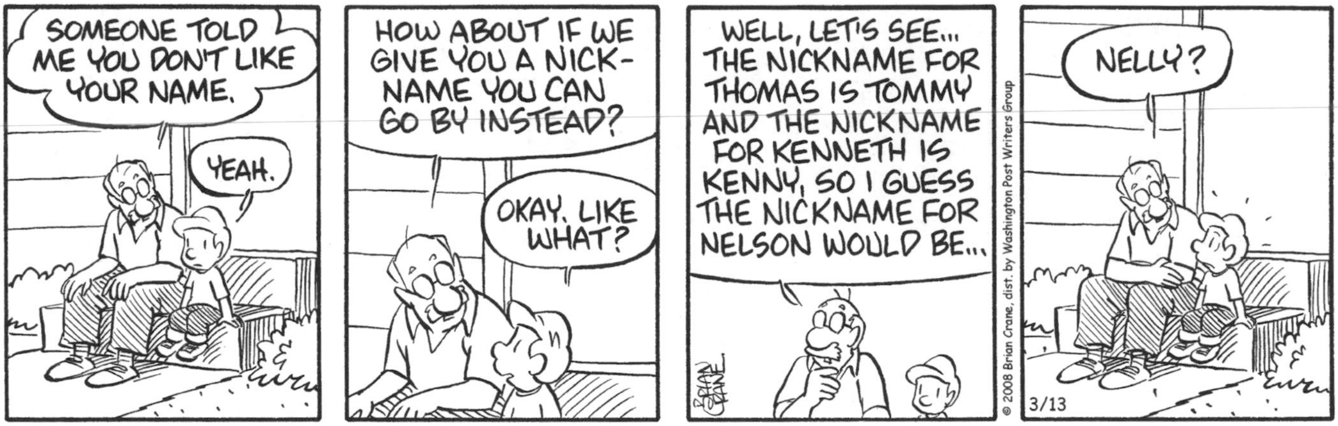
SOMEONE TOLD ME YOU DON'T LIKE YOUR NAME.
YEAH.
HOW ABOUT IF WE GIVE YOU A NICK-NAME YOU CAN GO BY INSTEAD?
OKAY. LIKE WHAT?
WELL, LET'S SEE... THE NICKNAME FOR THOMAS IS TOMMY AND THE NICKNAME FOR KENNETH IS KENNY, SO I GUESS THE NICKNAME FOR NELSON WOULD BE...
BRIAN CRANE
© 2008 Brian Crane, dist. by Washington Post Writers Group
NELLY?
3/13

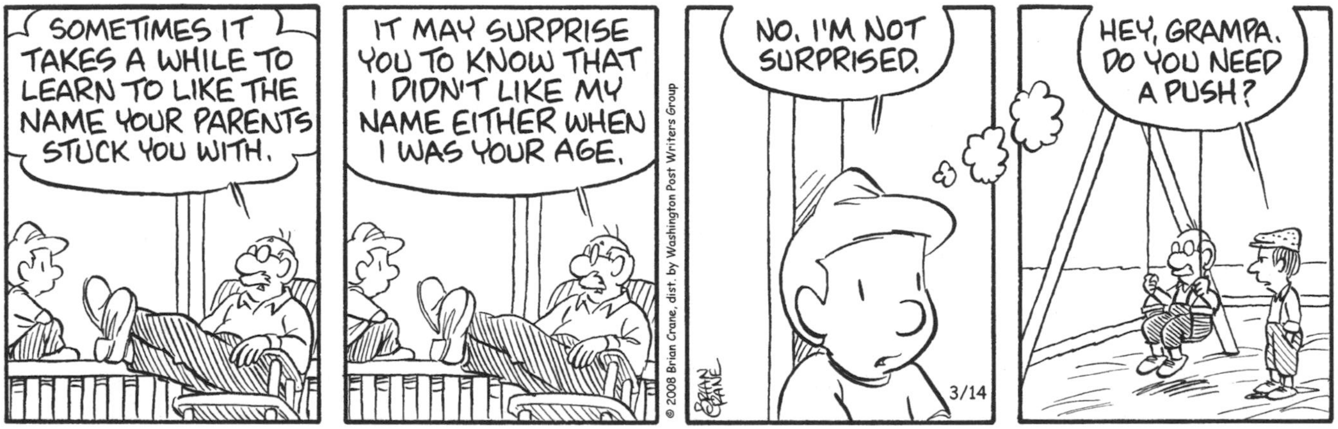
SOMETIMES IT TAKES A WHILE TO LEARN TO LIKE THE NAME YOUR PARENTS STUCK YOU WITH.
IT MAY SURPRISE YOU TO KNOW THAT I DIDN'T LIKE MY NAME EITHER WHEN I WAS YOUR AGE.
© 2008 Brian Crane, dist. by Washington Post Writers Group
BRIAN CRANE
NO. I'M NOT SURPRISED.
3/14
HEY, GRAMPA. DO YOU NEED A PUSH?

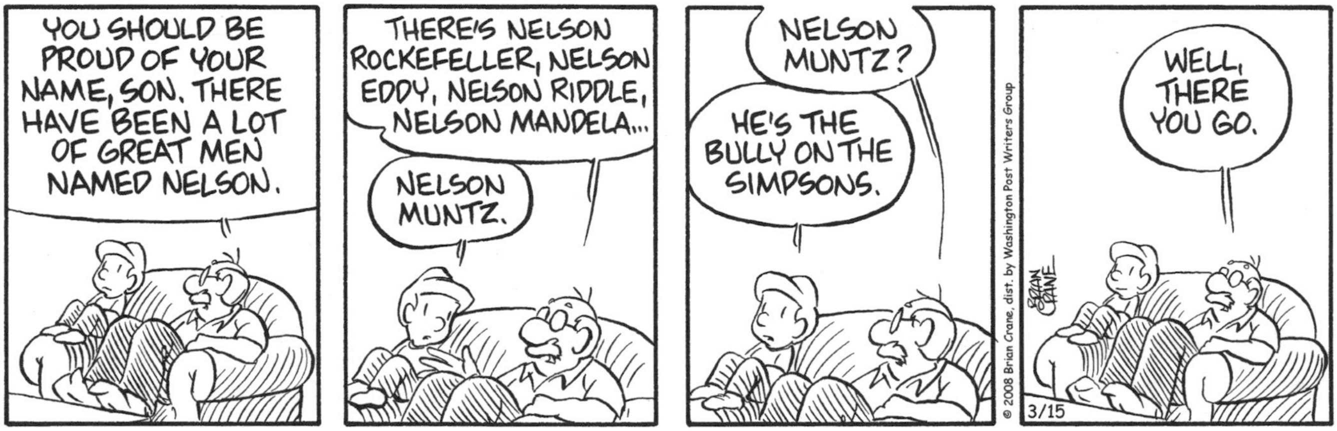
YOU SHOULD BE PROUD OF YOUR NAME, SON. THERE HAVE BEEN A LOT OF GREAT MEN NAMED NELSON.
THERE'S NELSON ROCKEFELLER, NELSON EDDY, NELSON RIDDLE, NELSON MANDELA...
NELSON MUNTZ.
NELSON MUNTZ?
HE'S THE BULLY ON THE SIMPSONS.
© 2008 Brian Crane, dist. by Washington Post Writers Group
BRIAN CRANE
WELL, THERE YOU GO.
3/15

SundayPickles

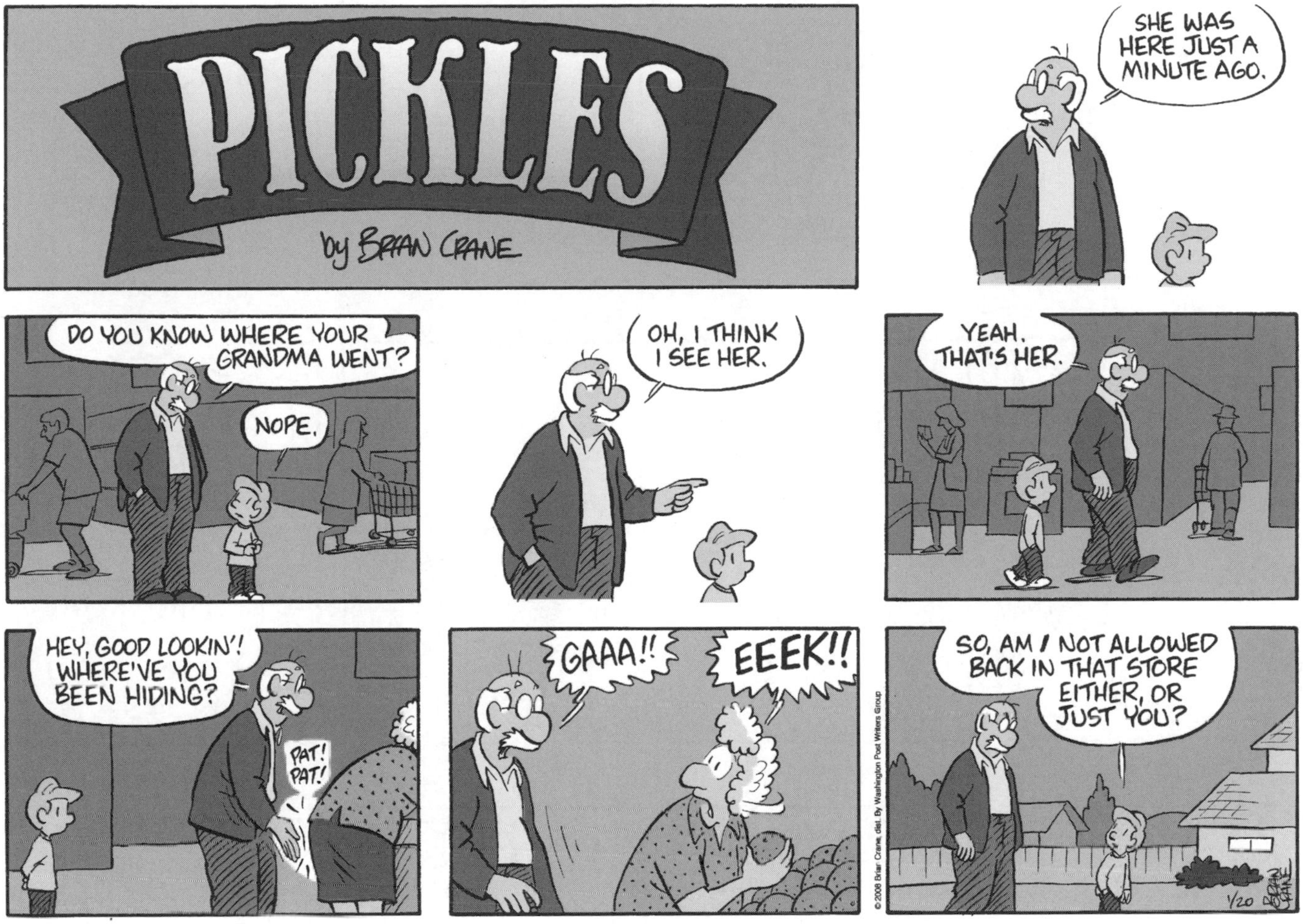
PICKLES
by BRIAN CRANE
SHE WAS HERE JUST A MINUTE AGO.
DO YOU KNOW WHERE YOUR GRANDMA WENT?
NOPE.
OH, I THINK I SEE HER.
YEAH. THAT'S HER.
HEY, GOOD LOOKIN'! WHERE'VE YOU BEEN HIDING?
PAT! PAT!
GAAA!!
EEEK!!
© 2008 Brian Crane, dist. By Washington Post Writers Group
SO, AM I NOT ALLOWED BACK IN THAT STORE EITHER, OR JUST YOU?
1/20

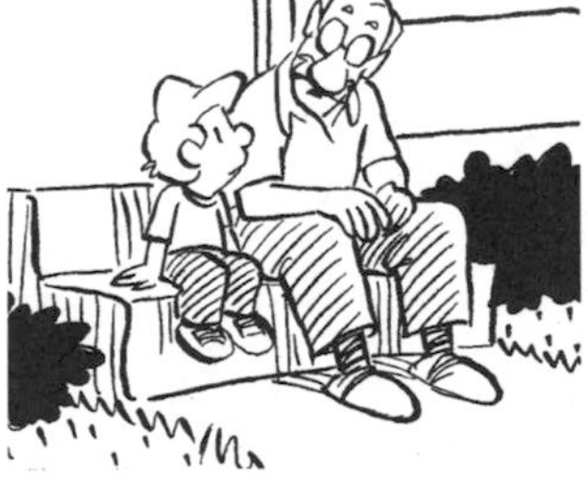

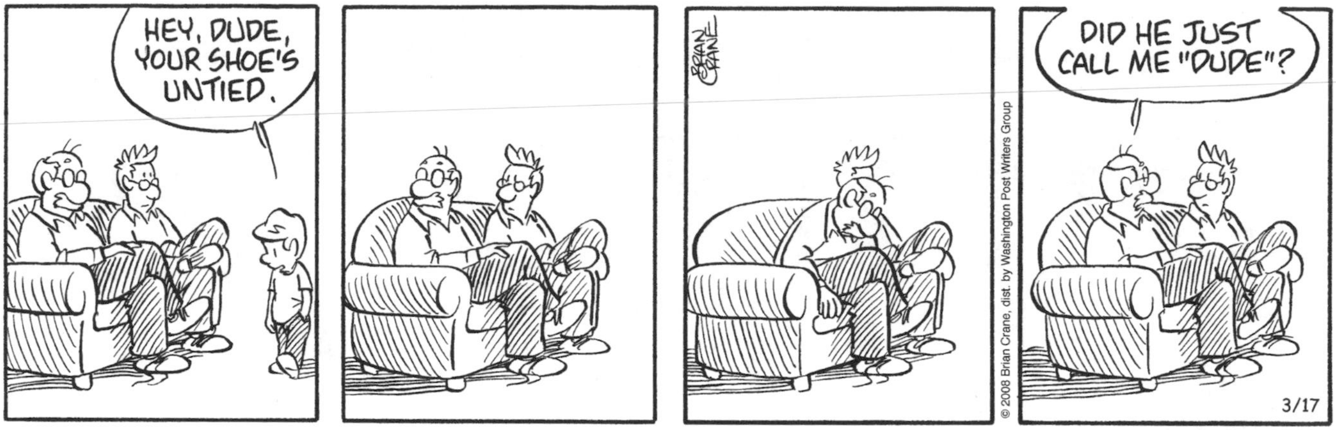
HEY, DUDE, YOUR SHOE'S UNTIED.
BRIAN CRANE
DID HE JUST CALL ME "DUDE"?
© 2008 Brian Crane, dist. by Washington Post Writers Group
3/17

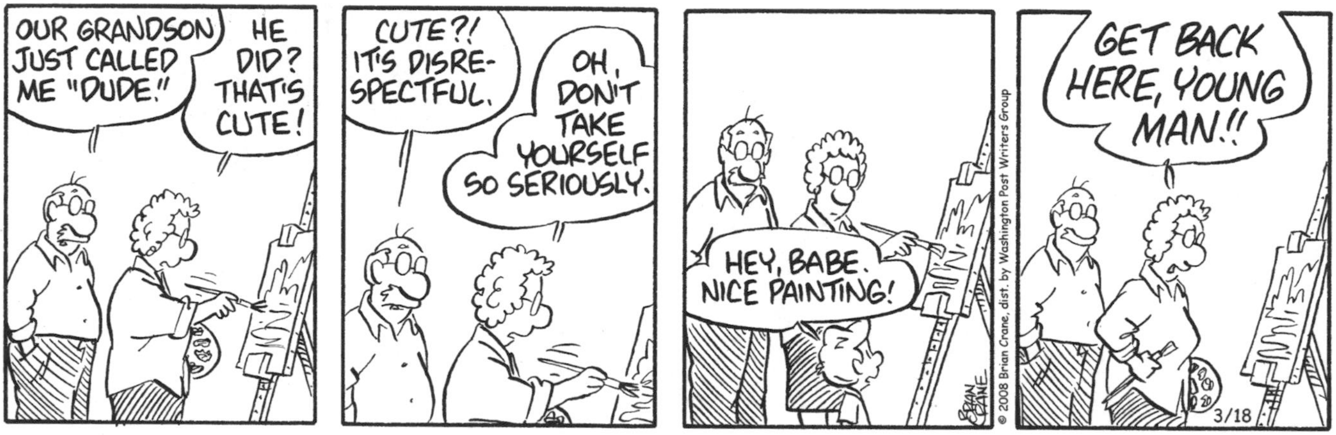
OUR GRANDSON JUST CALLED ME "DUDE."
HE DID? THAT'S CUTE!
CUTE?! IT'S DISRESPECTFUL.
OH, DON'T TAKE YOURSELF SO SERIOUSLY.
HEY, BABE. NICE PAINTING!
BRIAN CRANE
© 2008 Brian Crane, dist. by Washington Post Writers Group
GET BACK HERE, YOUNG MAN!!
3/18

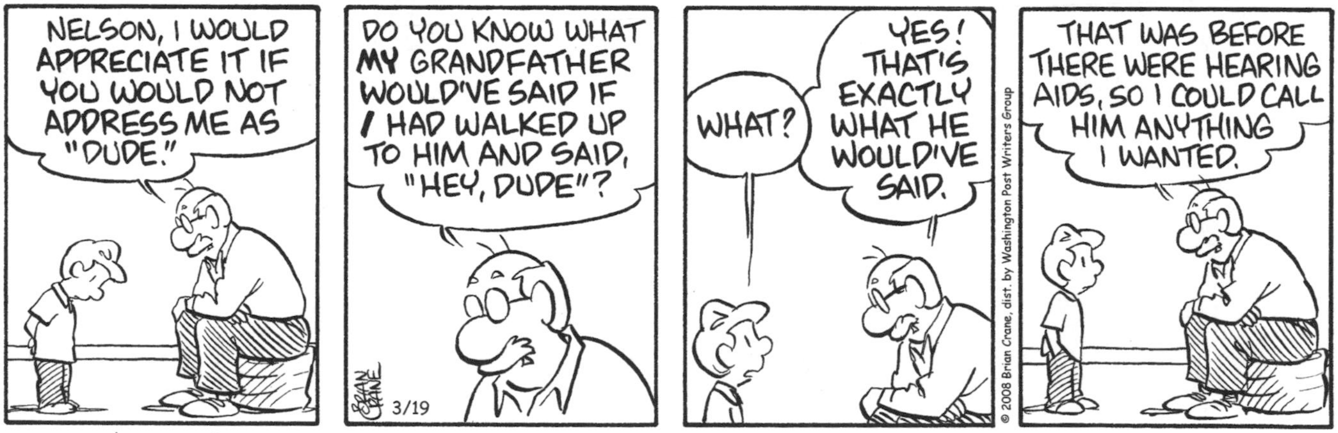
NELSON, I WOULD APPRECIATE IT IF YOU WOULD NOT ADDRESS ME AS "DUDE."
DO YOU KNOW WHAT MY GRANDFATHER WOULD'VE SAID IF I HAD WALKED UP TO HIM AND SAID, "HEY, DUDE"?
BRIAN CRANE
3/19
WHAT?
YES! THAT'S EXACTLY WHAT HE WOULD'VE SAID.
© 2008 Brian Crane, dist. by Washington Post Writers Group
THAT WAS BEFORE THERE WERE HEARING AIDS, SO I COULD CALL HIM ANYTHING I WANTED.

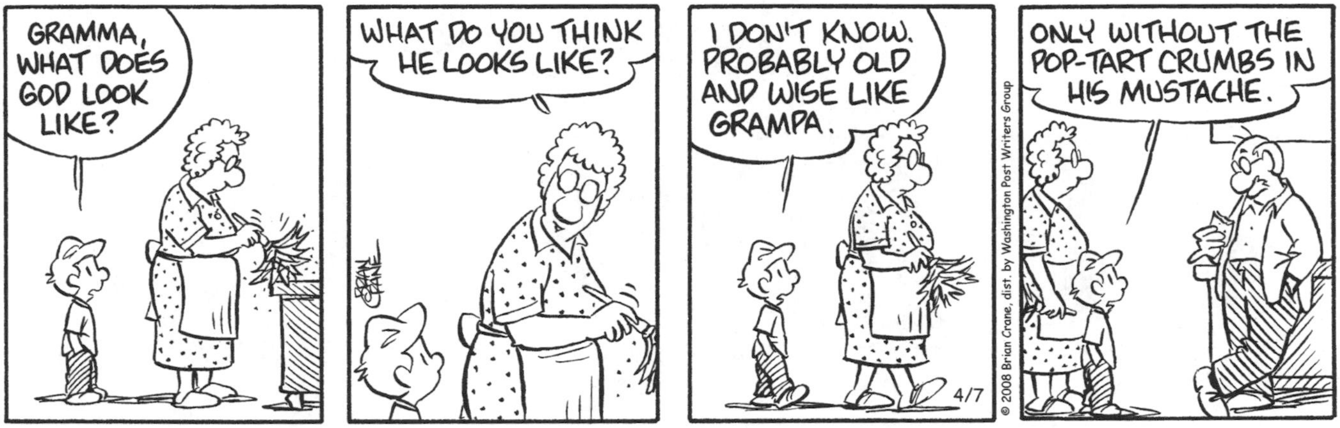
GRAMMA, WHAT DOES GOD LOOK LIKE?
WHAT DO YOU THINK HE LOOKS LIKE?
I DON'T KNOW. PROBABLY OLD AND WISE LIKE GRAMPA.
ONLY WITHOUT THE POP-TART CRUMBS IN HIS MUSTACHE.
4/7

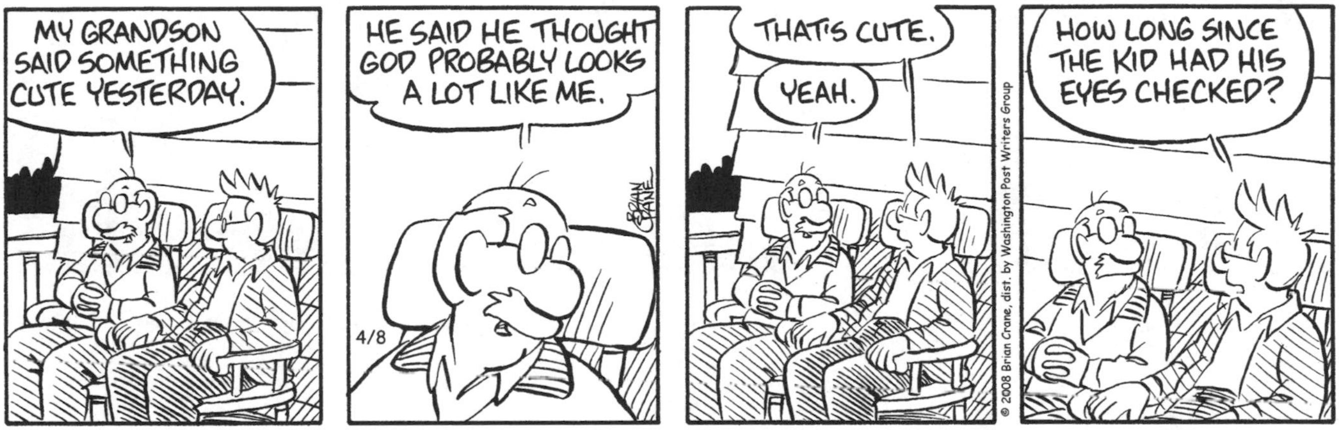
MY GRANDSON SAID SOMETHING CUTE YESTERDAY.
HE SAID HE THOUGHT GOD PROBABLY LOOKS A LOT LIKE ME.
4/8
THAT'S CUTE.
YEAH.
HOW LONG SINCE THE KID HAD HIS EYES CHECKED?

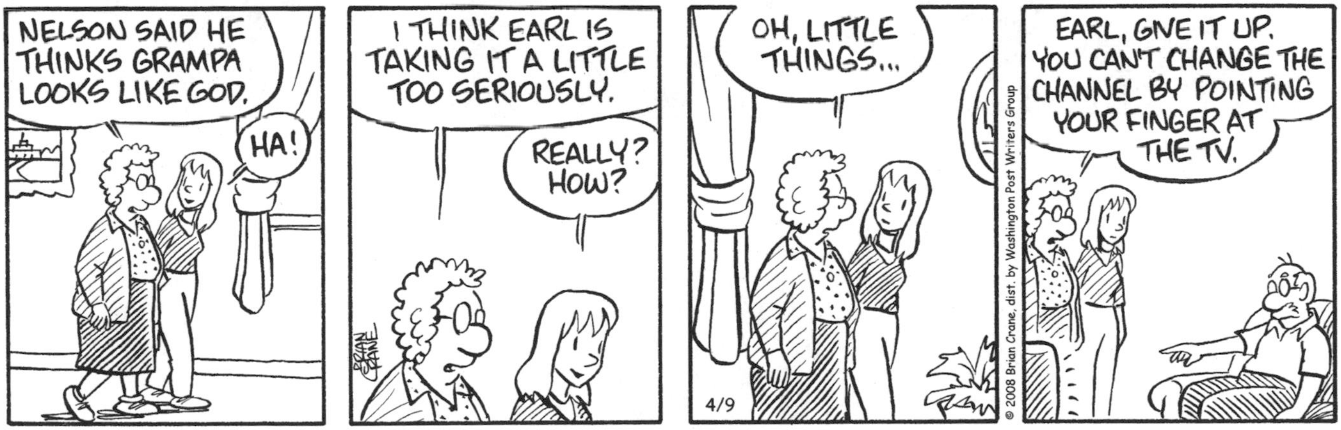
NELSON SAID HE THINKS GRAMPA LOOKS LIKE GOD.
HA!
I THINK EARL IS TAKING IT A LITTLE TOO SERIOUSLY.
REALLY? HOW?
OH, LITTLE THINGS...
4/9
EARL, GIVE IT UP. YOU CAN'T CHANGE THE CHANNEL BY POINTING YOUR FINGER AT THE TV.

SundayPickles

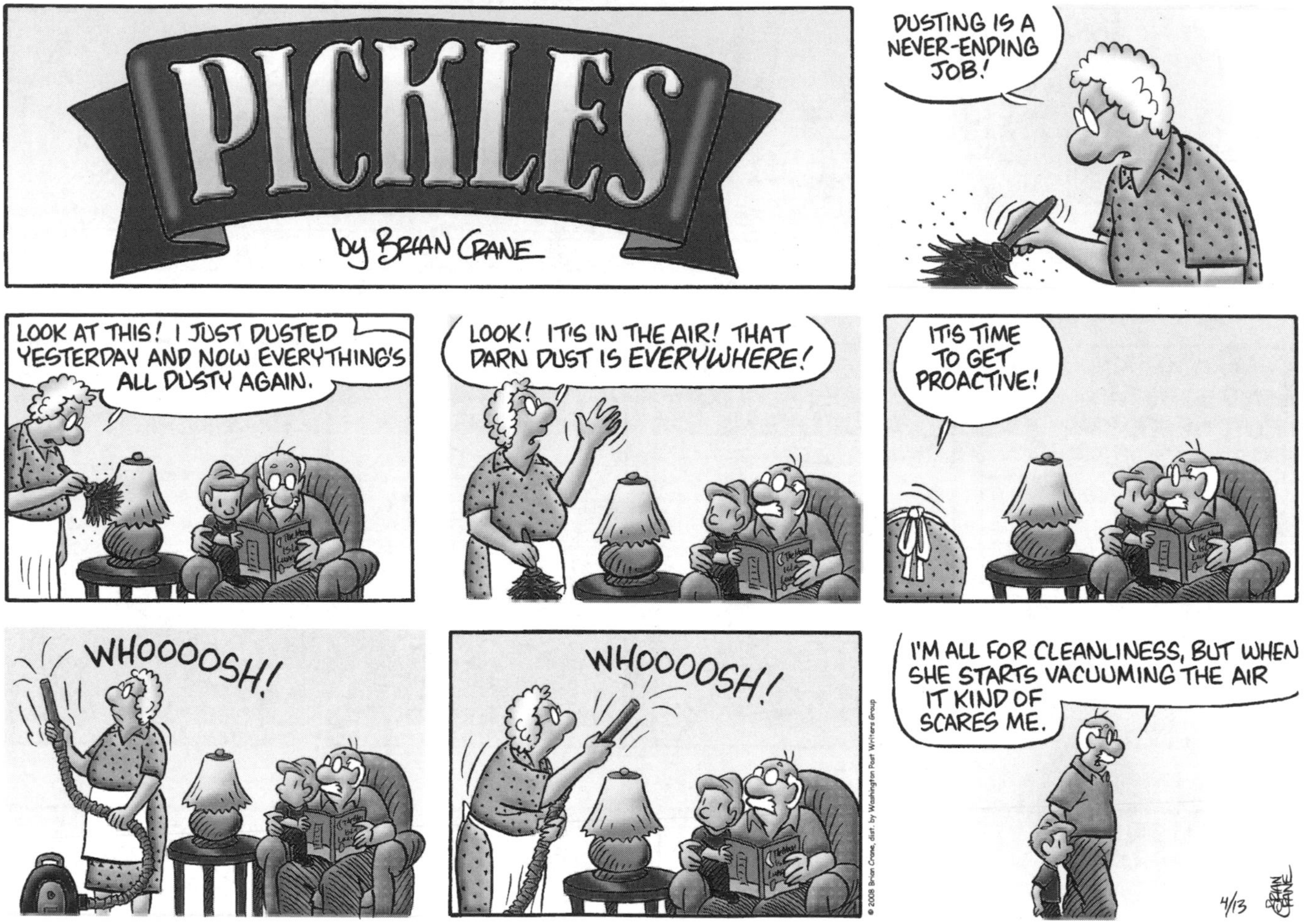
PICKLES
by BRIAN CRANE
DUSTING IS A NEVER-ENDING JOB!
LOOK AT THIS! I JUST DUSTED YESTERDAY AND NOW EVERYTHING'S ALL DUSTY AGAIN.
LOOK! IT'S IN THE AIR! THAT DARN DUST IS EVERYWHERE!
IT'S TIME TO GET PROACTIVE!
WHOOOOSH!
WHOOOOSH!
I'M ALL FOR CLEANLINESS, BUT WHEN SHE STARTS VACUUMING THE AIR IT KIND OF SCARES ME.
© 2008 Brian Crane, dist. by Washington Post Writers Group
4/13

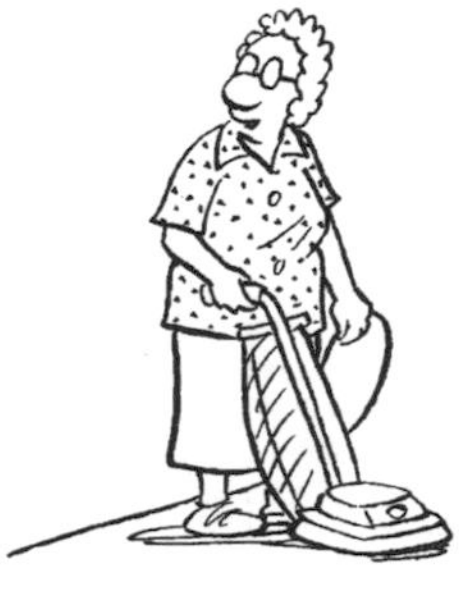

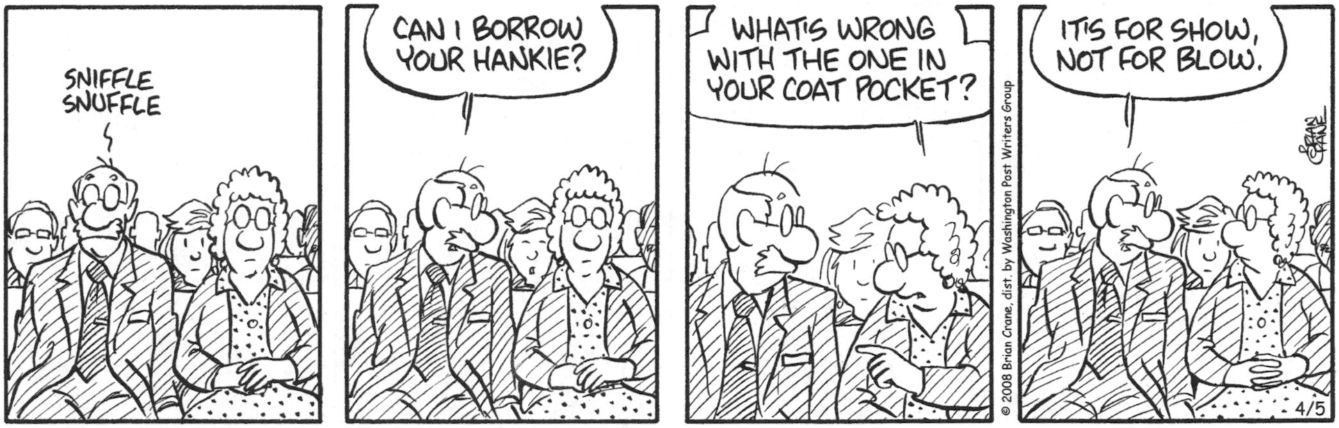
SNIFFLE SNUFFLE
CAN I BORROW YOUR HANKIE?
WHAT'S WRONG WITH THE ONE IN YOUR COAT POCKET?
IT'S FOR SHOW, NOT FOR BLOW.
© 2008 Brian Crane, dist. by Washington Post Writers Group
4/5

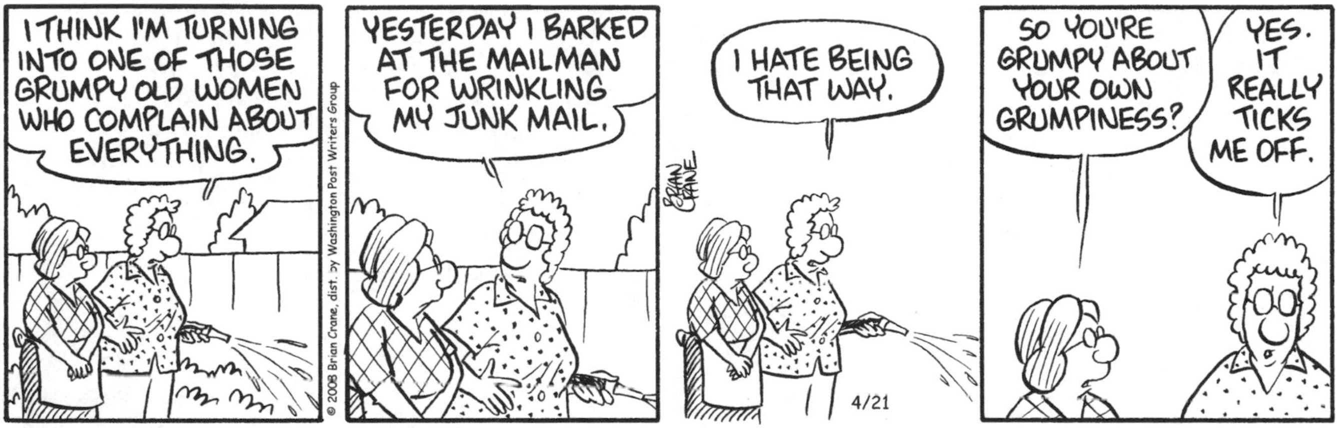
I THINK I'M TURNING INTO ONE OF THOSE GRUMPY OLD WOMEN WHO COMPLAIN ABOUT EVERYTHING.
© 2008 Brian Crane, dist. by Washington Post Writers Group
YESTERDAY I BARKED AT THE MAILMAN FOR WRINKLING MY JUNK MAIL.
I HATE BEING THAT WAY.
4/21
SO YOU'RE GRUMPY ABOUT YOUR OWN GRUMPINESS?
YES. IT REALLY TICKS ME OFF.

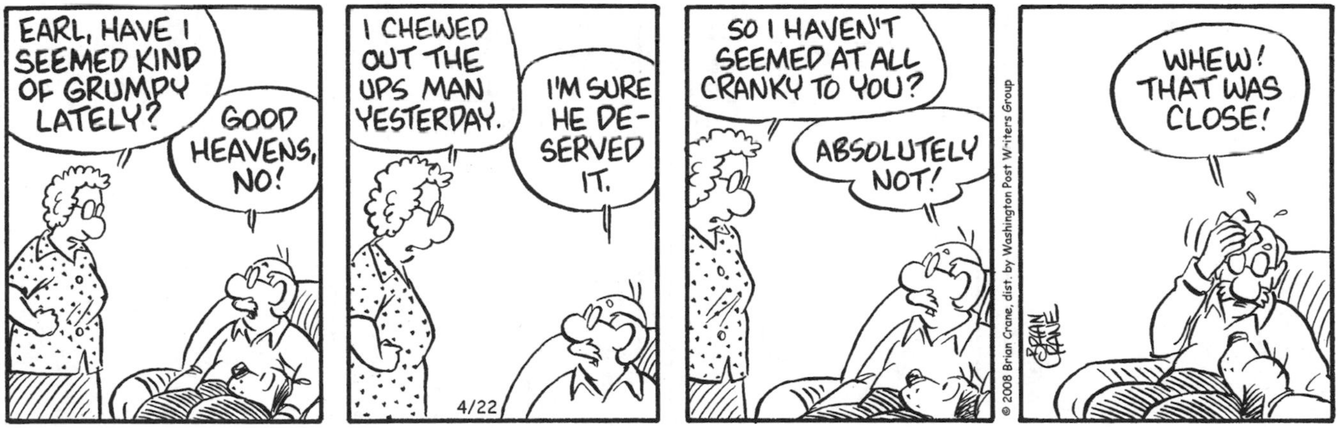
EARL, HAVE I SEEMED KIND OF GRUMPY LATELY?
GOOD HEAVENS, NO!
I CHEWED OUT THE UPS MAN YESTERDAY.
I'M SURE HE DESERVED IT.
4/22
SO I HAVEN'T SEEMED AT ALL CRANKY TO YOU?
ABSOLUTELY NOT!
© 2008 Brian Crane, dist. by Washington Post Writers Group
WHEW! THAT WAS CLOSE!

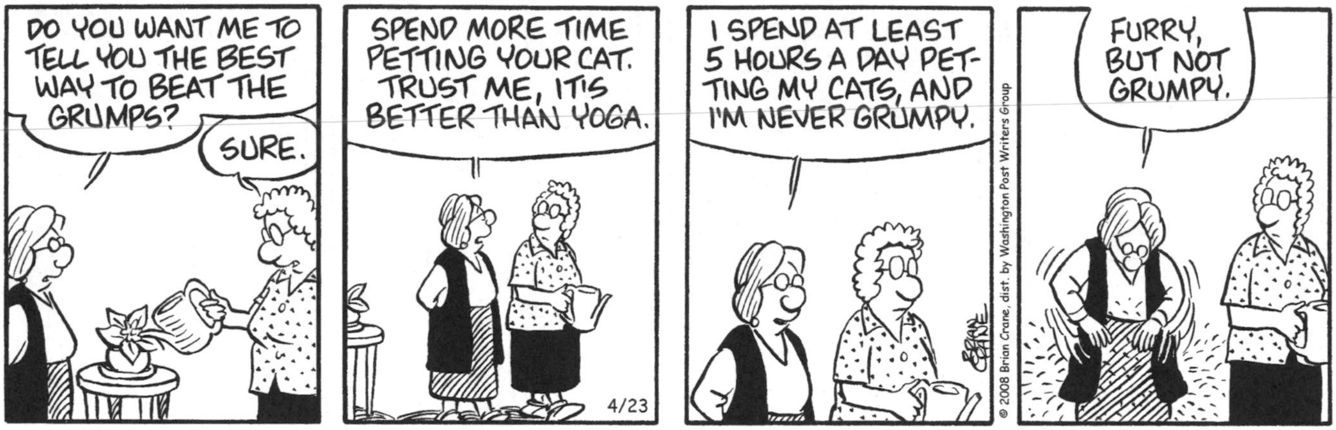
DO YOU WANT ME TO TELL YOU THE BEST WAY TO BEAT THE GRUMPS?
SURE.
SPEND MORE TIME PETTING YOUR CAT. TRUST ME, IT'S BETTER THAN YOGA.
4/23
I SPEND AT LEAST 5 HOURS A DAY PETTING MY CATS, AND I'M NEVER GRUMPY.
FURRY, BUT NOT GRUMPY.
© 2008 Brian Crane, dist. by Washington Post Writers Group

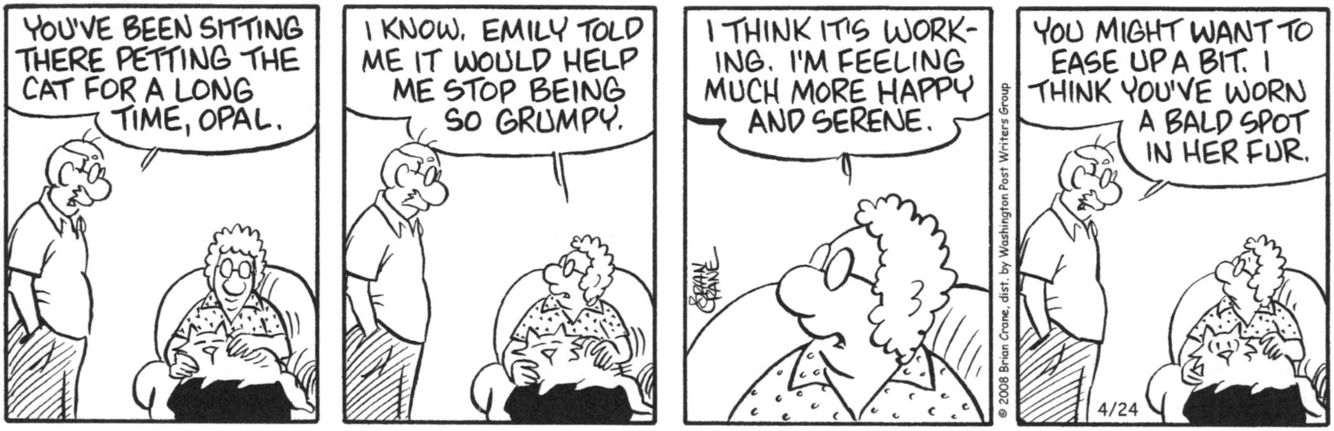
YOU'VE BEEN SITTING THERE PETTING THE CAT FOR A LONG TIME, OPAL.
I KNOW. EMILY TOLD ME IT WOULD HELP ME STOP BEING SO GRUMPY.
I THINK IT'S WORKING. I'M FEELING MUCH MORE HAPPY AND SERENE.
YOU MIGHT WANT TO EASE UP A BIT. I THINK YOU'VE WORN A BALD SPOT IN HER FUR.
4/24
© 2008 Brian Crane, dist. by Washington Post Writers Group

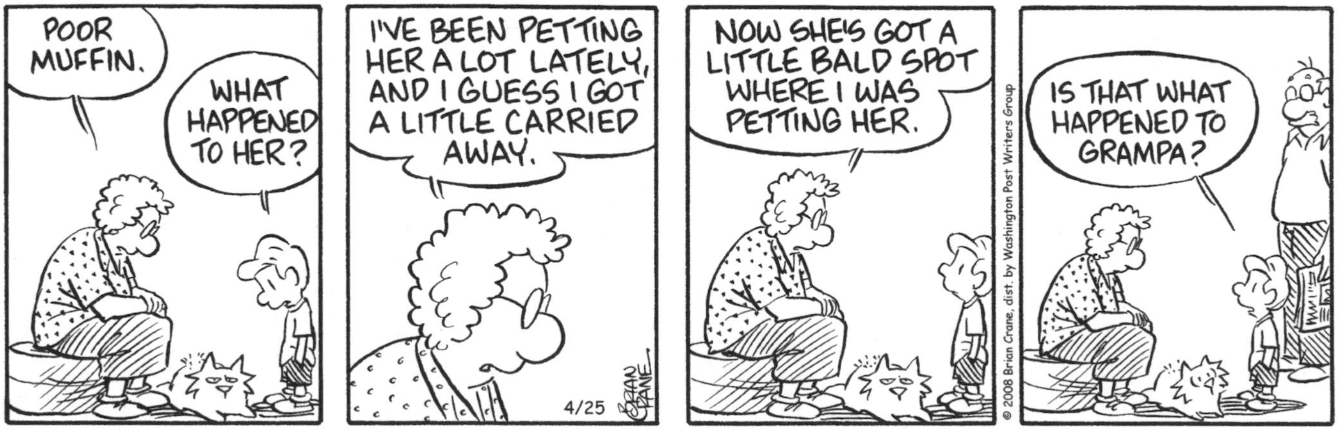
POOR MUFFIN.
WHAT HAPPENED TO HER?
I'VE BEEN PETTING HER A LOT LATELY, AND I GUESS I GOT A LITTLE CARRIED AWAY.
4/25
NOW SHE'S GOT A LITTLE BALD SPOT WHERE I WAS PETTING HER.
IS THAT WHAT HAPPENED TO GRAMPA?
© 2008 Brian Crane, dist. by Washington Post Writers Group

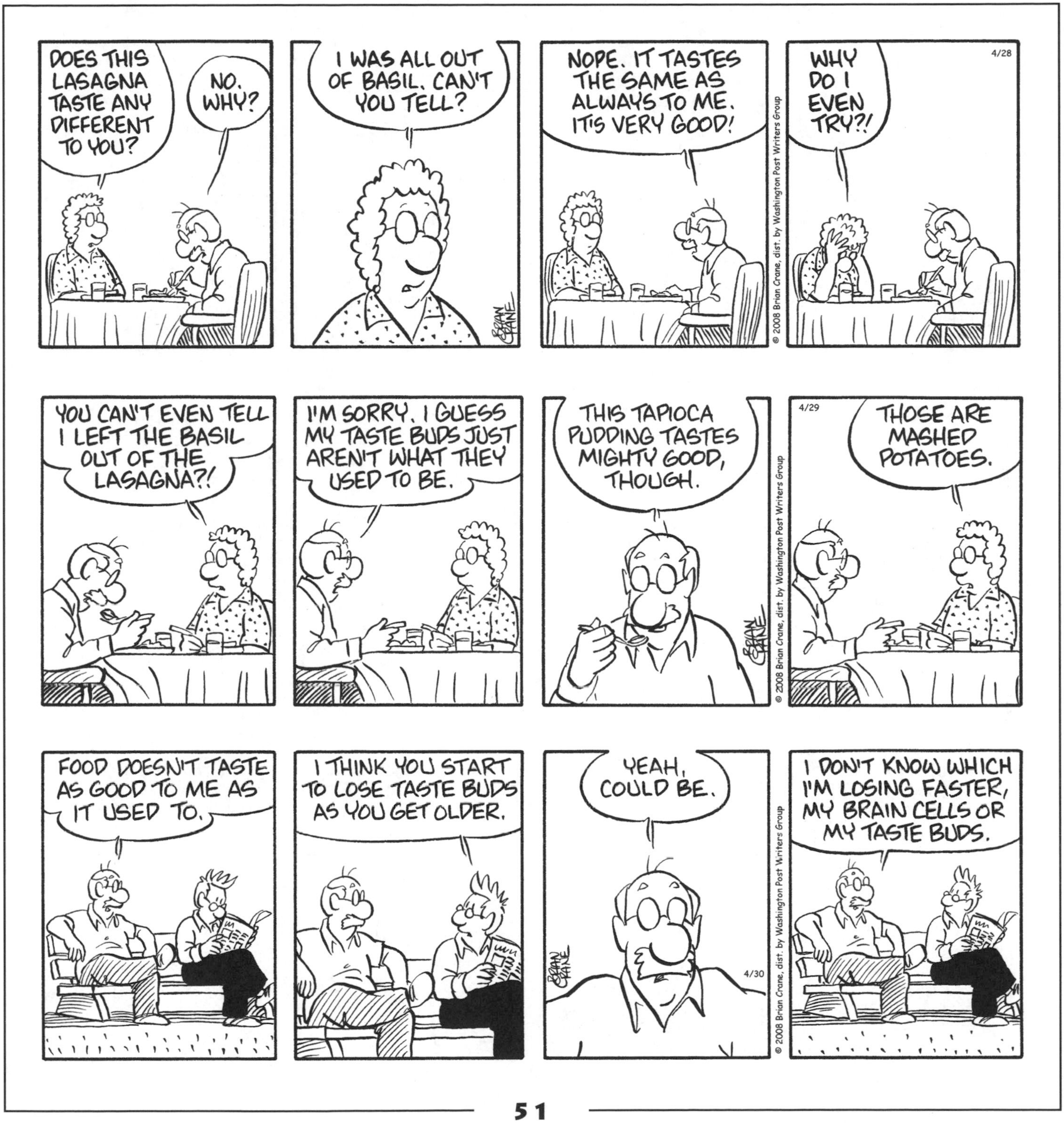
DOES THIS LASAGNA TASTE ANY DIFFERENT TO YOU?
NO. WHY?
I WAS ALL OUT OF BASIL. CAN'T YOU TELL?
BRIAN CRANE
NOPE. IT TASTES THE SAME AS ALWAYS TO ME. IT'S VERY GOOD!
© 2008 Brian Crane, dist. by Washington Post Writers Group
WHY DO I EVEN TRY?!
4/28
YOU CAN'T EVEN TELL I LEFT THE BASIL OUT OF THE LASAGNA?!
I'M SORRY. I GUESS MY TASTE BUDS JUST AREN'T WHAT THEY USED TO BE.
THIS TAPIOCA PUDDING TASTES MIGHTY GOOD, THOUGH.
BRIAN CRANE
© 2008 Brian Crane, dist. by Washington Post Writers Group
4/29
THOSE ARE MASHED POTATOES.
FOOD DOESN'T TASTE AS GOOD TO ME AS IT USED TO.
I THINK YOU START TO LOSE TASTE BUDS AS YOU GET OLDER.
YEAH, COULD BE.
BRIAN CRANE
4/30
© 2008 Brian Crane, dist. by Washington Post Writers Group
I DON'T KNOW WHICH I'M LOSING FASTER, MY BRAIN CELLS OR MY TASTE BUDS.

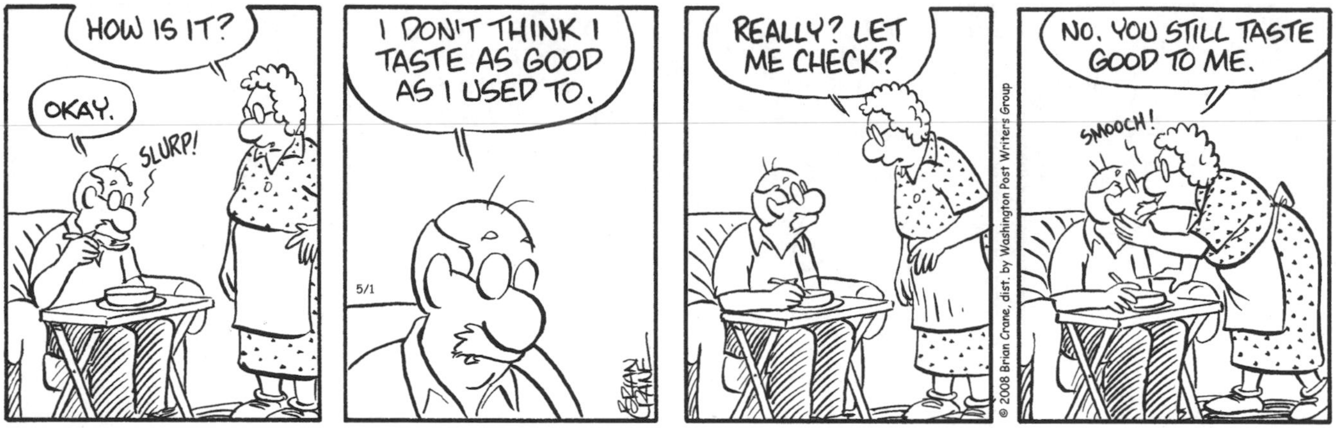
HOW IS IT?
OKAY.
SLURP!
I DON'T THINK I TASTE AS GOOD AS I USED TO.
5/1
BRIAN CRANE
REALLY? LET ME CHECK?
SMOOCH!
NO. YOU STILL TASTE GOOD TO ME.

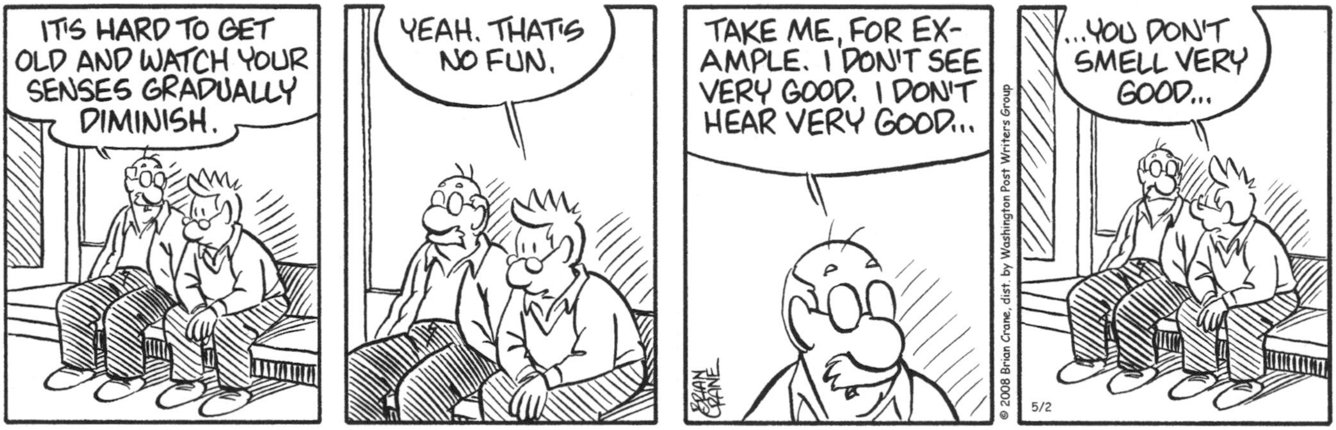
IT'S HARD TO GET OLD AND WATCH YOUR SENSES GRADUALLY DIMINISH.
YEAH. THAT'S NO FUN.
TAKE ME, FOR EXAMPLE. I DON'T SEE VERY GOOD. I DON'T HEAR VERY GOOD...
BRIAN CRANE
...YOU DON'T SMELL VERY GOOD...
5/2

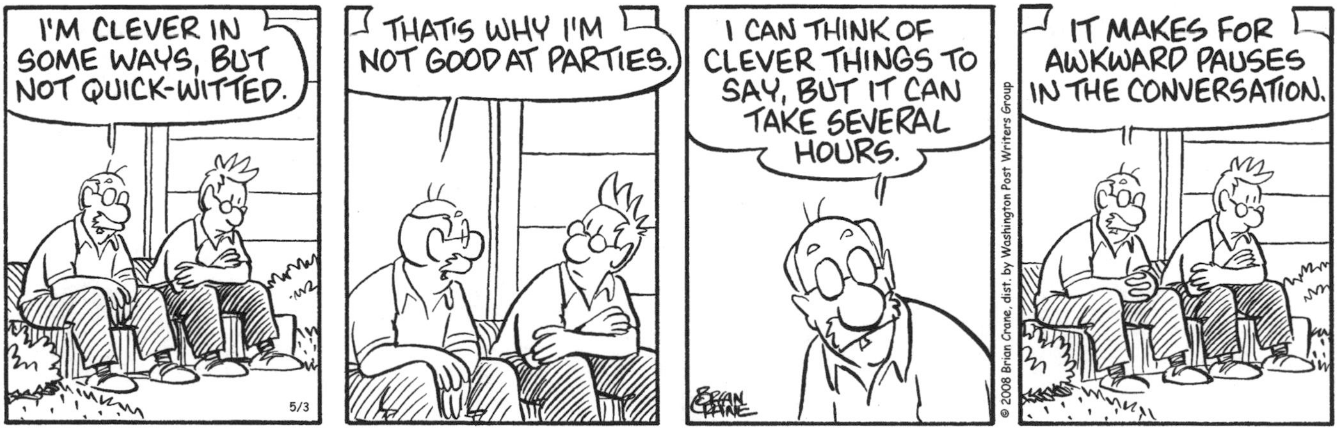
I'M CLEVER IN SOME WAYS, BUT NOT QUICK-WITTED.
5/3
THAT'S WHY I'M NOT GOOD AT PARTIES.
I CAN THINK OF CLEVER THINGS TO SAY, BUT IT CAN TAKE SEVERAL HOURS.
BRIAN CRANE
IT MAKES FOR AWKWARD PAUSES IN THE CONVERSATION.

Sunday Pickles

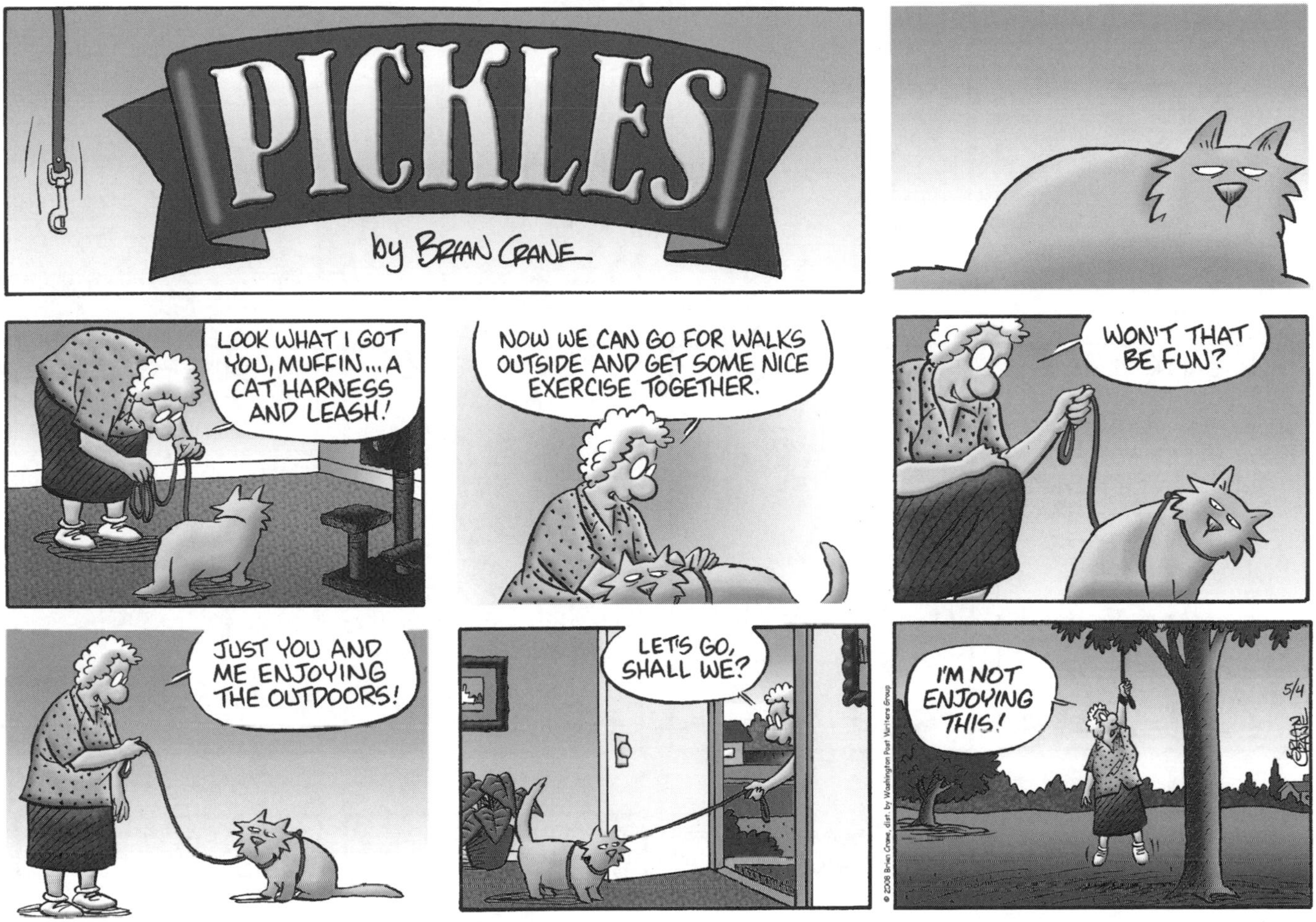
PICKLES
by BRIAN CRANE
LOOK WHAT I GOT YOU, MUFFIN... A CAT HARNESS AND LEASH!
NOW WE CAN GO FOR WALKS OUTSIDE AND GET SOME NICE EXERCISE TOGETHER.
WON'T THAT BE FUN?
JUST YOU AND ME ENJOYING THE OUTDOORS!
LET'S GO, SHALL WE?
© 2008 Brian Crane, dist. by Washington Post Writers Group
I'M NOT ENJOYING THIS!
5/4

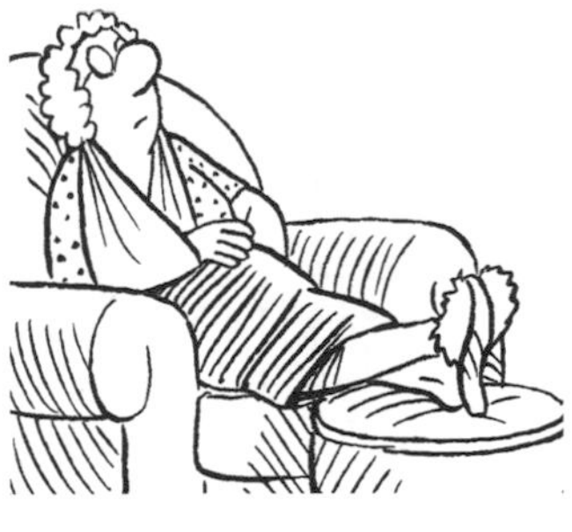

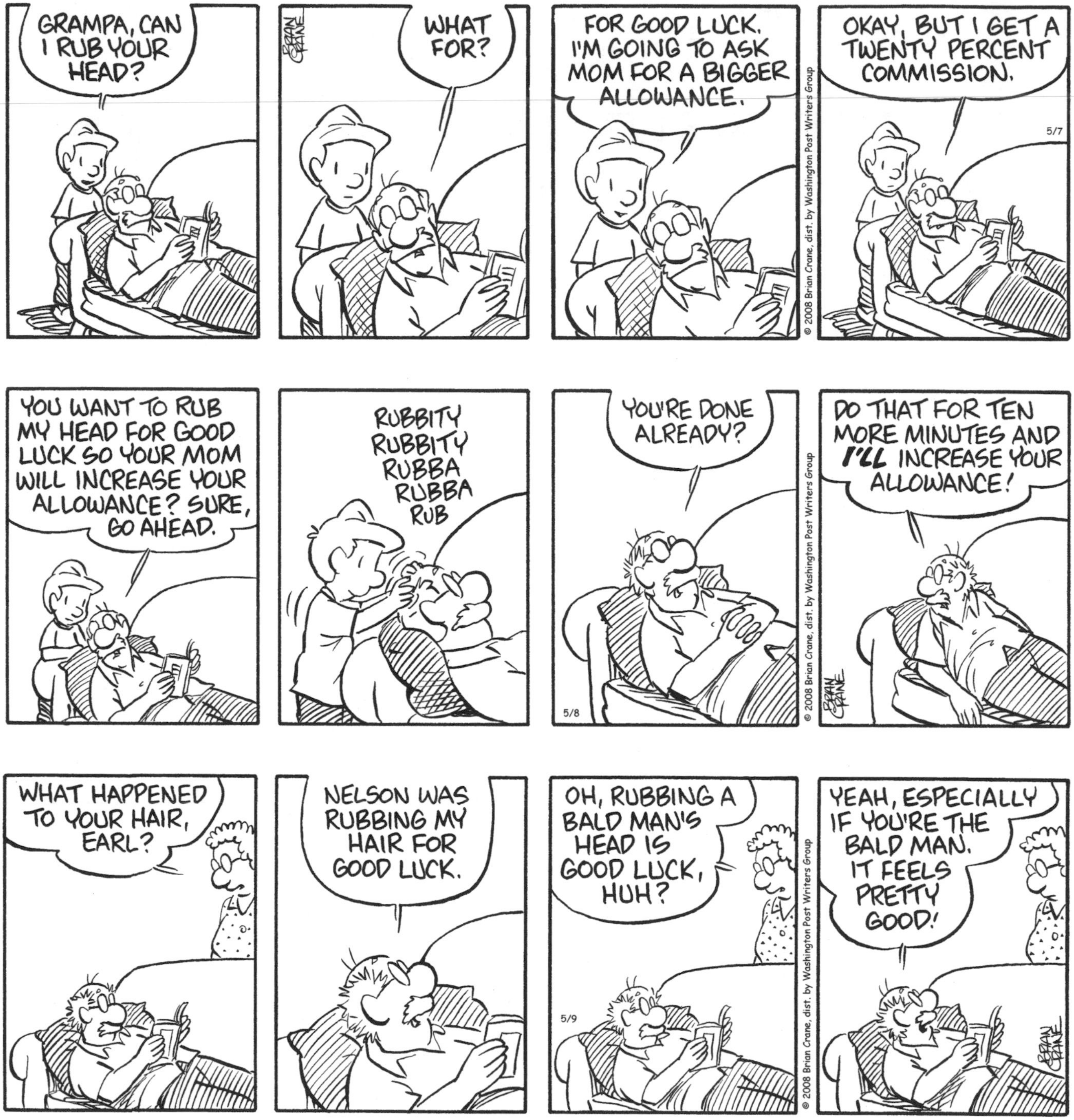

GRAMPA, CAN I RUB YOUR HEAD?
BRIAN CRANE
WHAT FOR?
FOR GOOD LUCK. I'M GOING TO ASK MOM FOR A BIGGER ALLOWANCE.
© 2008 Brian Crane, dist. by Washington Post Writers Group
OKAY, BUT I GET A TWENTY PERCENT COMMISSION.
5/7
YOU WANT TO RUB MY HEAD FOR GOOD LUCK SO YOUR MOM WILL INCREASE YOUR ALLOWANCE? SURE, GO AHEAD.
RUBBITY RUBBITY RUBBA RUBBA RUB
YOU'RE DONE ALREADY?
5/8
© 2008 Brian Crane, dist. by Washington Post Writers Group
BRIAN CRANE
DO THAT FOR TEN MORE MINUTES AND ***I'LL*** INCREASE YOUR ALLOWANCE!
WHAT HAPPENED TO YOUR HAIR, EARL?
NELSON WAS RUBBING MY HAIR FOR GOOD LUCK.
OH, RUBBING A BALD MAN'S HEAD IS GOOD LUCK, HUH?
5/9
© 2008 Brian Crane, dist. by Washington Post Writers Group
YEAH, ESPECIALLY IF YOU'RE THE BALD MAN. IT FEELS PRETTY GOOD!
BRIAN CRANE

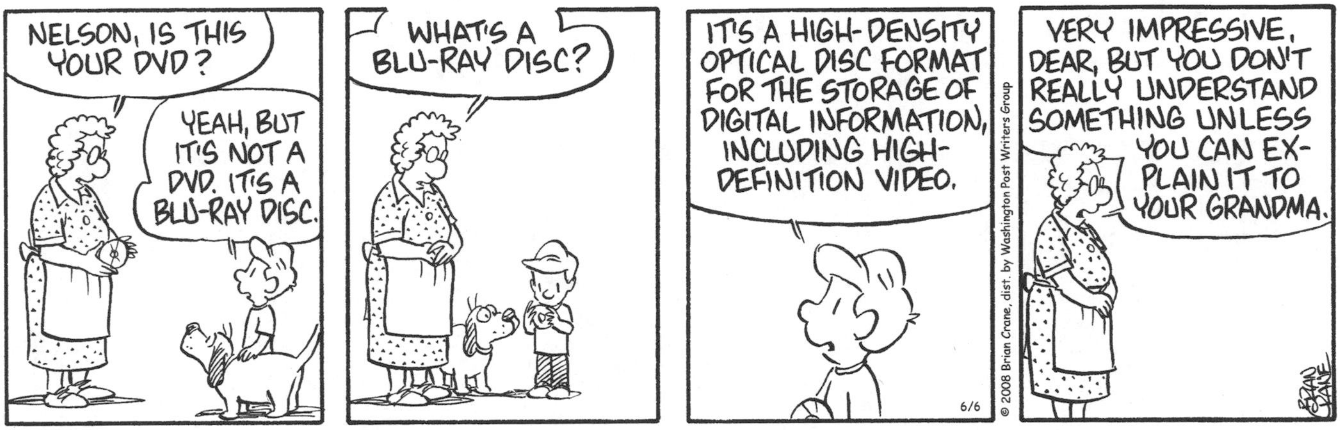
NELSON, IS THIS YOUR DVD?
YEAH, BUT IT'S NOT A DVD. IT'S A BLU-RAY DISC.
WHAT'S A BLU-RAY DISC?
IT'S A HIGH-DENSITY OPTICAL DISC FORMAT FOR THE STORAGE OF DIGITAL INFORMATION, INCLUDING HIGH-DEFINITION VIDEO.
6/6
© 2008 Brian Crane, dist. by Washington Post Writers Group
VERY IMPRESSIVE, DEAR, BUT YOU DON'T REALLY UNDERSTAND SOMETHING UNLESS YOU CAN EX-PLAIN IT TO YOUR GRANDMA.
BRIAN CRANE

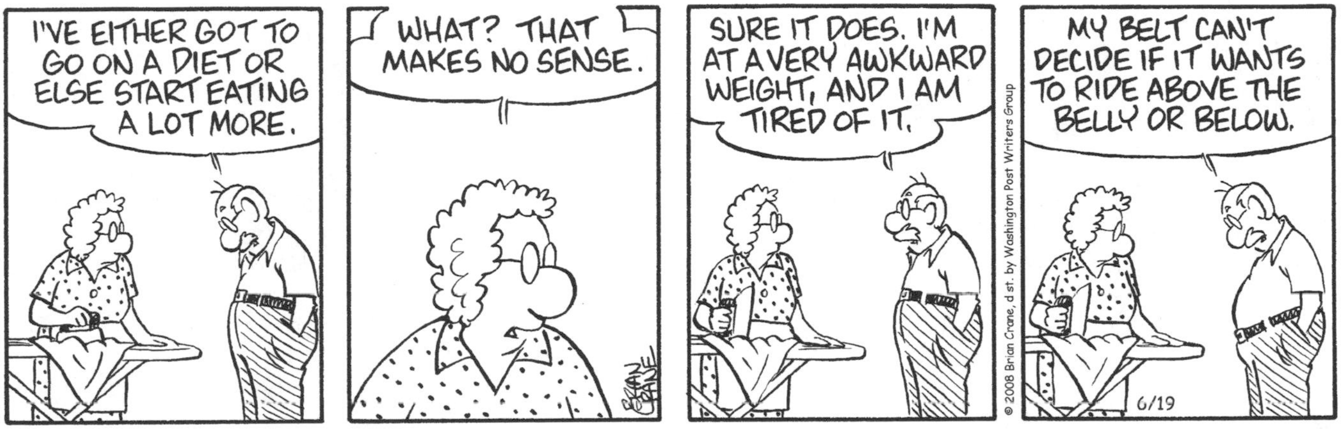
I'VE EITHER GOT TO GO ON A DIET OR ELSE START EATING A LOT MORE.
WHAT? THAT MAKES NO SENSE.
BRIAN CRANE
SURE IT DOES. I'M AT A VERY AWKWARD WEIGHT, AND I AM TIRED OF IT.
© 2008 Brian Crane, dist. by Washington Post Writers Group
MY BELT CAN'T DECIDE IF IT WANTS TO RIDE ABOVE THE BELLY OR BELOW.
6/19

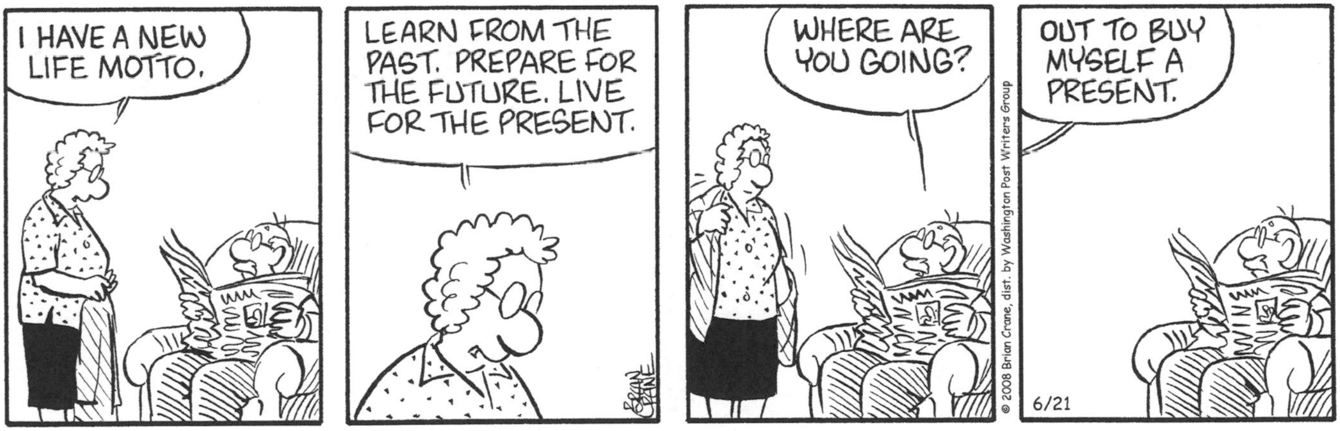
I HAVE A NEW LIFE MOTTO.
LEARN FROM THE PAST. PREPARE FOR THE FUTURE. LIVE FOR THE PRESENT.
BRIAN CRANE
WHERE ARE YOU GOING?
© 2008 Brian Crane, dist. by Washington Post Writers Group
OUT TO BUY MYSELF A PRESENT.
6/21

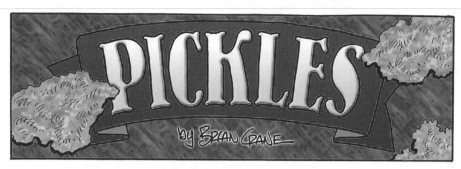

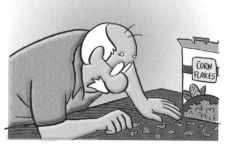

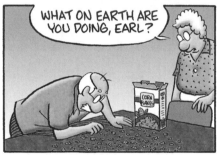

SundayPickles

PICKLES
by BRIAN CRANE
CORN FLAKES
WHAT ON EARTH ARE YOU DOING, EARL?
I READ ABOUT SOME LADY WHO FOUND A CORN FLAKE SHAPED LIKE ILLINOIS. SHE SOLD IT ON EBAY FOR $1350!
I DON'T SEE WHY I COULDN'T DO THE SAME.
ALL I HAVE TO DO IS FIND A FLAKE SHAPED LIKE A STATE.
AND FIGURE OUT WHAT AN EBAY IS.
BRIAN CRANE
5/18
© 2008 Brian Crane, dist. by Washington Post Writers Group
I SEE A FLAKE SHAPED LIKE MY HUSBAND.

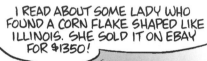

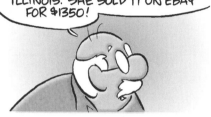

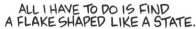

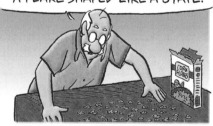

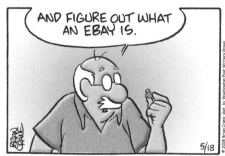

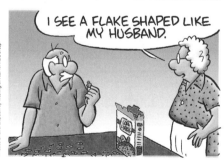

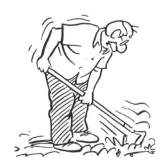

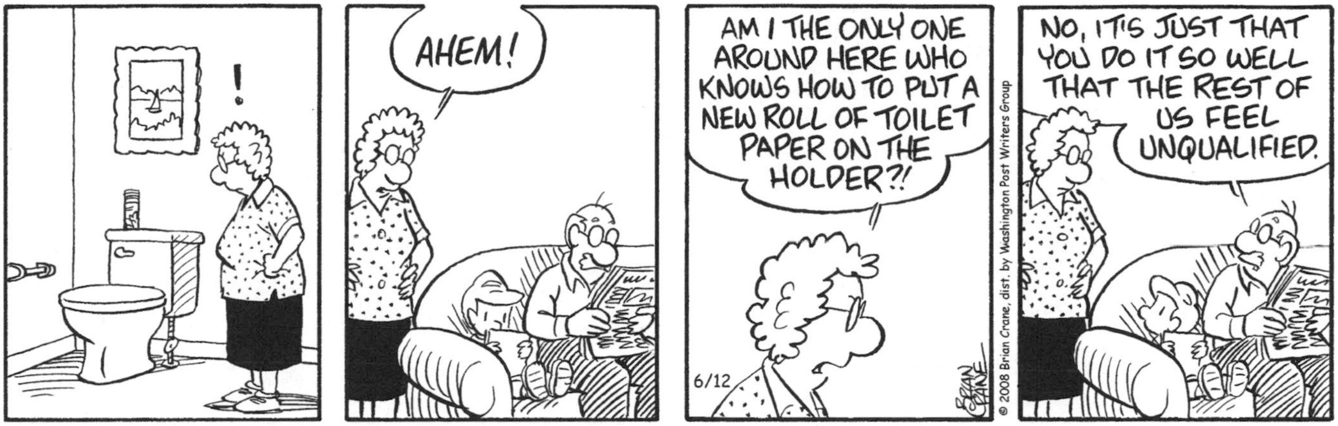
!
AHEM!
AM I THE ONLY ONE AROUND HERE WHO KNOWS HOW TO PUT A NEW ROLL OF TOILET PAPER ON THE HOLDER?!
6/12
© 2008 Brian Crane, dist. by Washington Post Writers Group
NO, IT'S JUST THAT YOU DO IT SO WELL THAT THE REST OF US FEEL UNQUALIFIED.

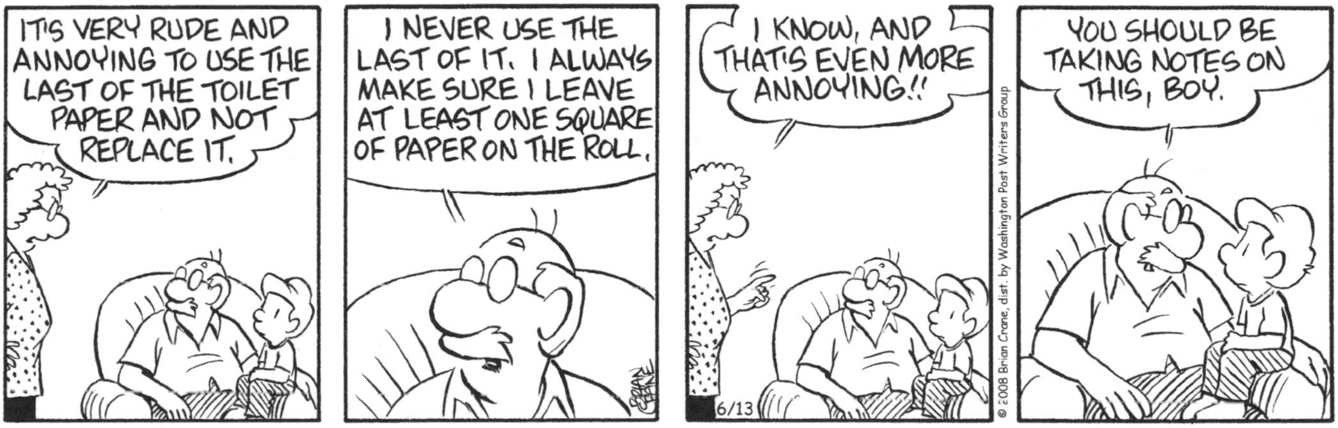
IT'S VERY RUDE AND ANNOYING TO USE THE LAST OF THE TOILET PAPER AND NOT REPLACE IT.
I NEVER USE THE LAST OF IT. I ALWAYS MAKE SURE I LEAVE AT LEAST ONE SQUARE OF PAPER ON THE ROLL.
I KNOW, AND THAT'S EVEN MORE ANNOYING!!
6/13
© 2008 Brian Crane, dist. by Washington Post Writers Group
YOU SHOULD BE TAKING NOTES ON THIS, BOY.

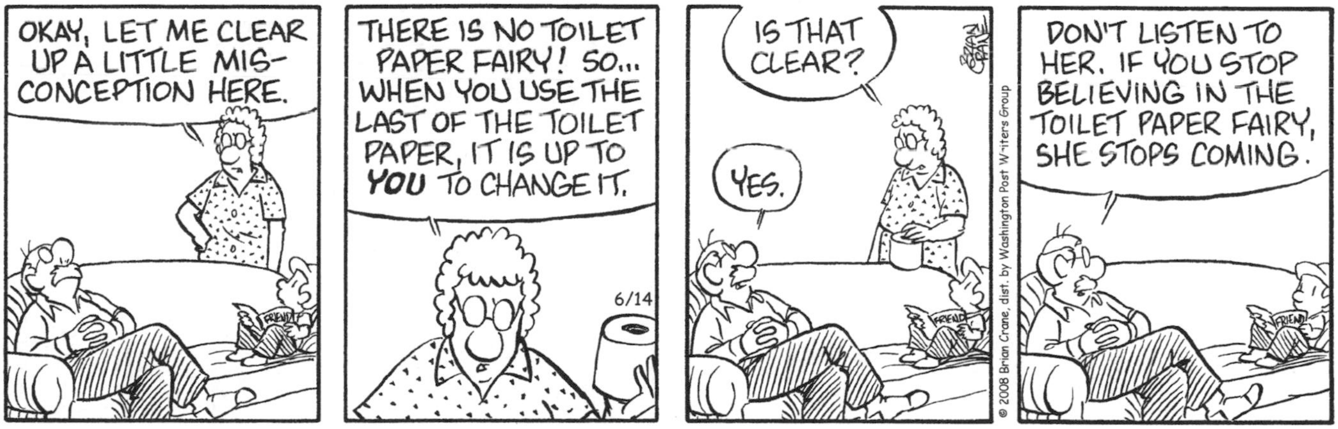
OKAY, LET ME CLEAR UP A LITTLE MIS-CONCEPTION HERE.
THERE IS NO TOILET PAPER FAIRY! SO... WHEN YOU USE THE LAST OF THE TOILET PAPER, IT IS UP TO YOU TO CHANGE IT.
6/14
IS THAT CLEAR?
YES.
© 2008 Brian Crane, dist. by Washington Post Writers Group
DON'T LISTEN TO HER. IF YOU STOP BELIEVING IN THE TOILET PAPER FAIRY, SHE STOPS COMING.

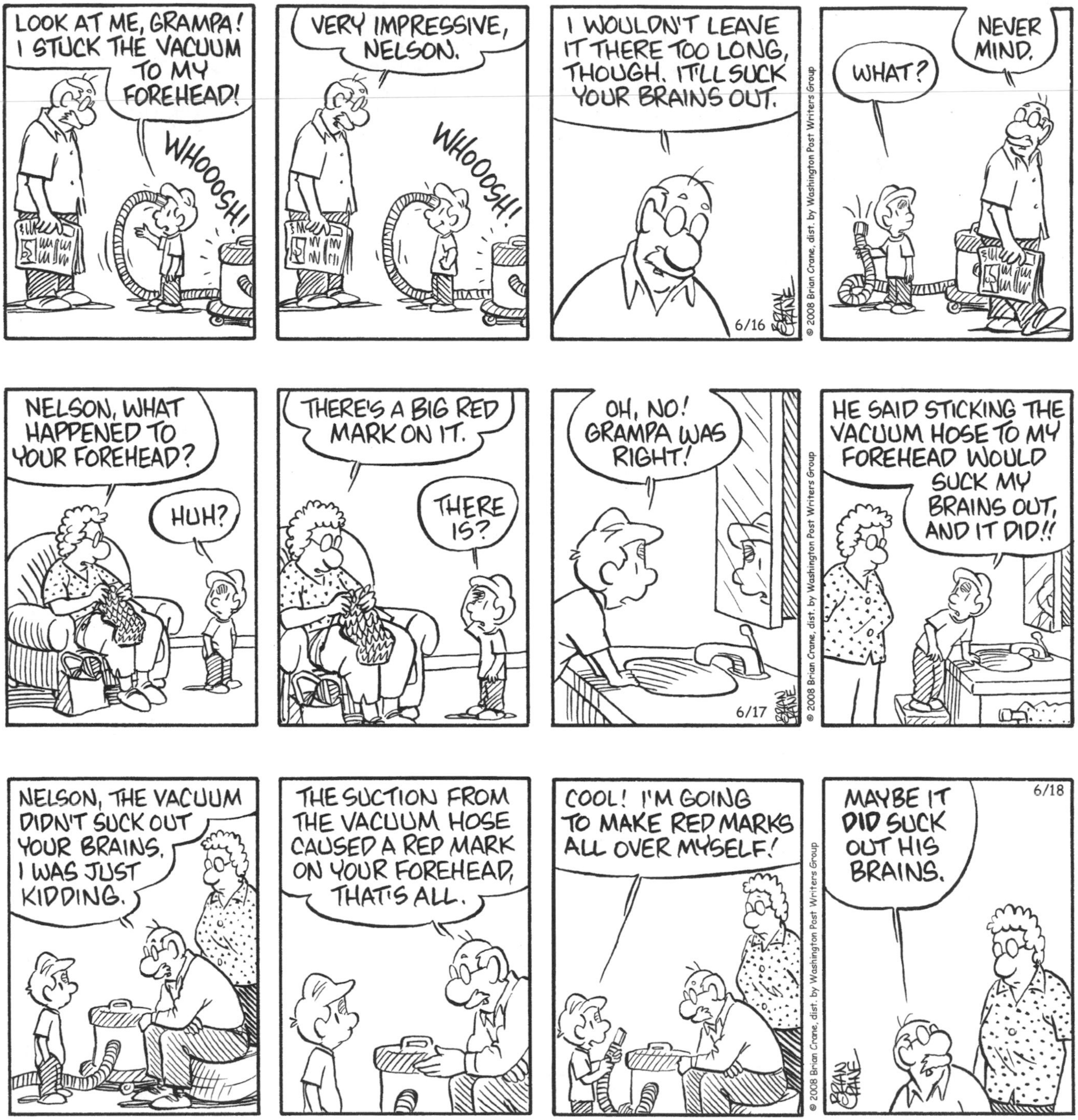
LOOK AT ME, GRAMPA! I STUCK THE VACUUM TO MY FOREHEAD!
WHOOOSH!
VERY IMPRESSIVE, NELSON.
WHOOOSH!
I WOULDN'T LEAVE IT THERE TOO LONG, THOUGH. IT'LL SUCK YOUR BRAINS OUT.
6/16
BRIAN CRANE
© 2008 Brian Crane, dist. by Washington Post Writers Group
WHAT?
NEVER MIND.
NELSON, WHAT HAPPENED TO YOUR FOREHEAD?
HUH?
THERE'S A BIG RED MARK ON IT.
THERE IS?
OH, NO! GRAMPA WAS RIGHT!
6/17
BRIAN CRANE
© 2008 Brian Crane, dist. by Washington Post Writers Group
HE SAID STICKING THE VACUUM HOSE TO MY FOREHEAD WOULD SUCK MY BRAINS OUT, AND IT DID!!
NELSON, THE VACUUM DIDN'T SUCK OUT YOUR BRAINS, I WAS JUST KIDDING.
THE SUCTION FROM THE VACUUM HOSE CAUSED A RED MARK ON YOUR FOREHEAD, THAT'S ALL.
COOL! I'M GOING TO MAKE RED MARKS ALL OVER MYSELF!
© 2008 Brian Crane, dist. by Washington Post Writers Group
6/18
MAYBE IT **DID** SUCK OUT HIS BRAINS.
BRIAN CRANE

SundayPickles

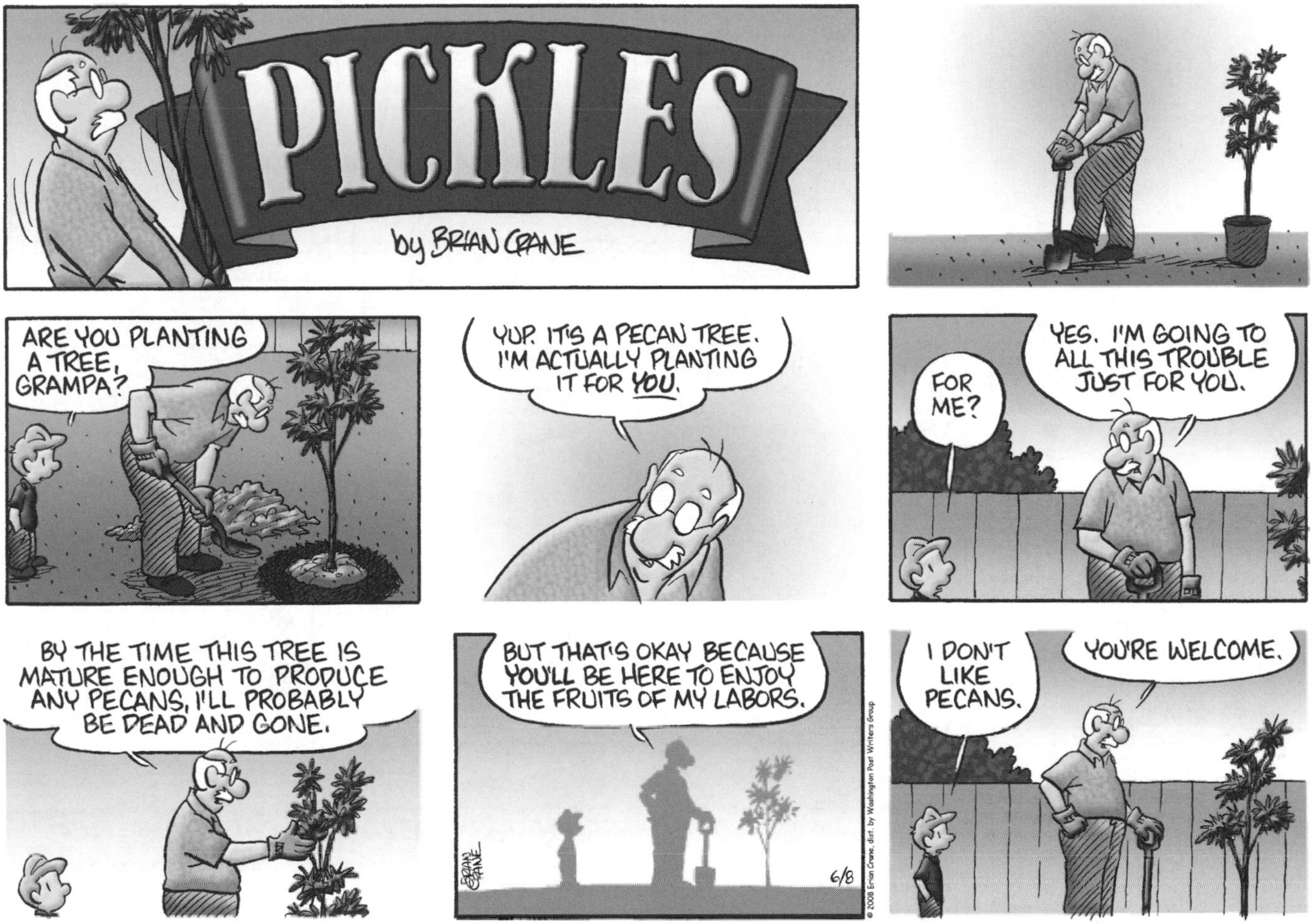
PICKLES
by BRIAN CRANE
ARE YOU PLANTING A TREE, GRAMPA?
YUP. IT'S A PECAN TREE. I'M ACTUALLY PLANTING IT FOR YOU.
FOR ME?
YES. I'M GOING TO ALL THIS TROUBLE JUST FOR YOU.
BY THE TIME THIS TREE IS MATURE ENOUGH TO PRODUCE ANY PECANS, I'LL PROBABLY BE DEAD AND GONE.
BUT THAT'S OKAY BECAUSE YOU'LL BE HERE TO ENJOY THE FRUITS OF MY LABORS.
6/8
© 2008 Brian Crane, dist. by Washington Post Writers Group
I DON'T LIKE PECANS.
YOU'RE WELCOME.

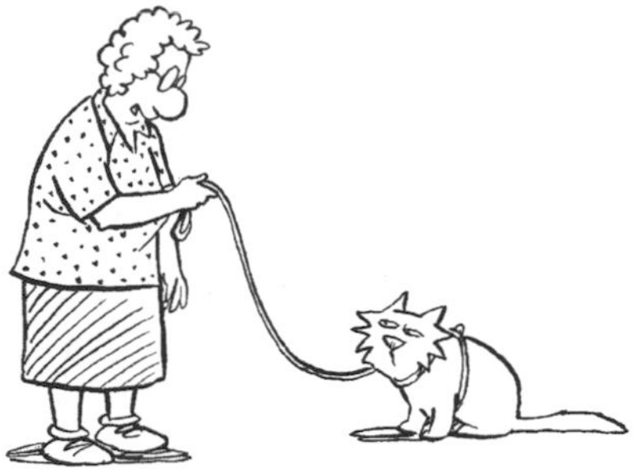

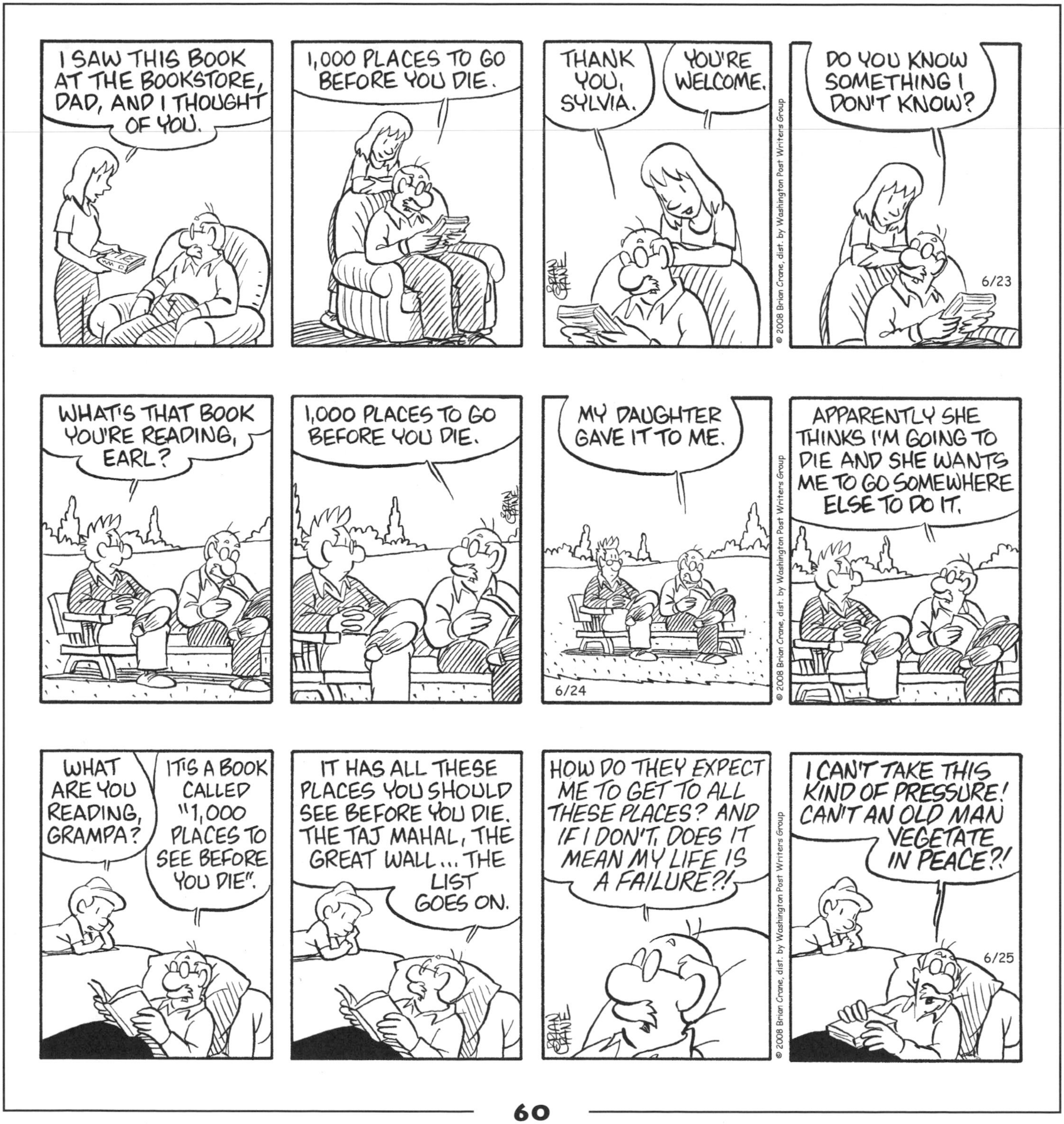
I SAW THIS BOOK AT THE BOOKSTORE, DAD, AND I THOUGHT OF YOU.
1,000 PLACES TO GO BEFORE YOU DIE.
THANK YOU, SYLVIA.
YOU'RE WELCOME.
DO YOU KNOW SOMETHING I DON'T KNOW?
6/23
© 2008 Brian Crane, dist. by Washington Post Writers Group
WHAT'S THAT BOOK YOU'RE READING, EARL?
1,000 PLACES TO GO BEFORE YOU DIE.
MY DAUGHTER GAVE IT TO ME.
APPARENTLY SHE THINKS I'M GOING TO DIE AND SHE WANTS ME TO GO SOMEWHERE ELSE TO DO IT.
6/24
© 2008 Brian Crane, dist. by Washington Post Writers Group
WHAT ARE YOU READING, GRAMPA?
IT'S A BOOK CALLED "1,000 PLACES TO SEE BEFORE YOU DIE".
IT HAS ALL THESE PLACES YOU SHOULD SEE BEFORE YOU DIE. THE TAJ MAHAL, THE GREAT WALL... THE LIST GOES ON.
HOW DO THEY EXPECT ME TO GET TO ALL THESE PLACES? AND IF I DON'T, DOES IT MEAN MY LIFE IS A FAILURE?!
I CAN'T TAKE THIS KIND OF PRESSURE! CAN'T AN OLD MAN VEGETATE IN PEACE?!
6/25
© 2008 Brian Crane, dist. by Washington Post Writers Group

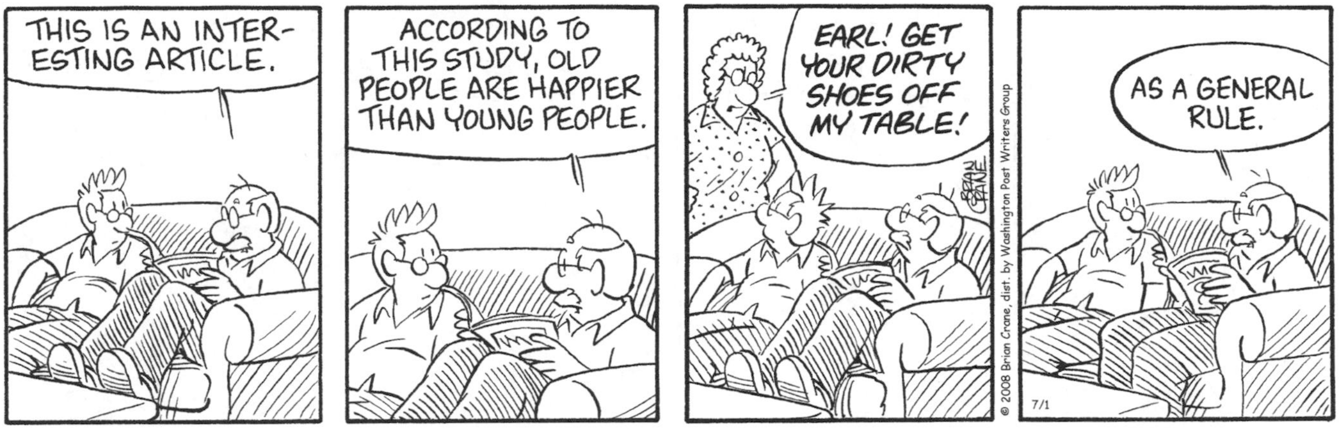
THIS IS AN INTERESTING ARTICLE.
ACCORDING TO THIS STUDY, OLD PEOPLE ARE HAPPIER THAN YOUNG PEOPLE.
EARL! GET YOUR DIRTY SHOES OFF MY TABLE!
© 2008 Brian Crane, dist. by Washington Post Writers Group
AS A GENERAL RULE.
7/1

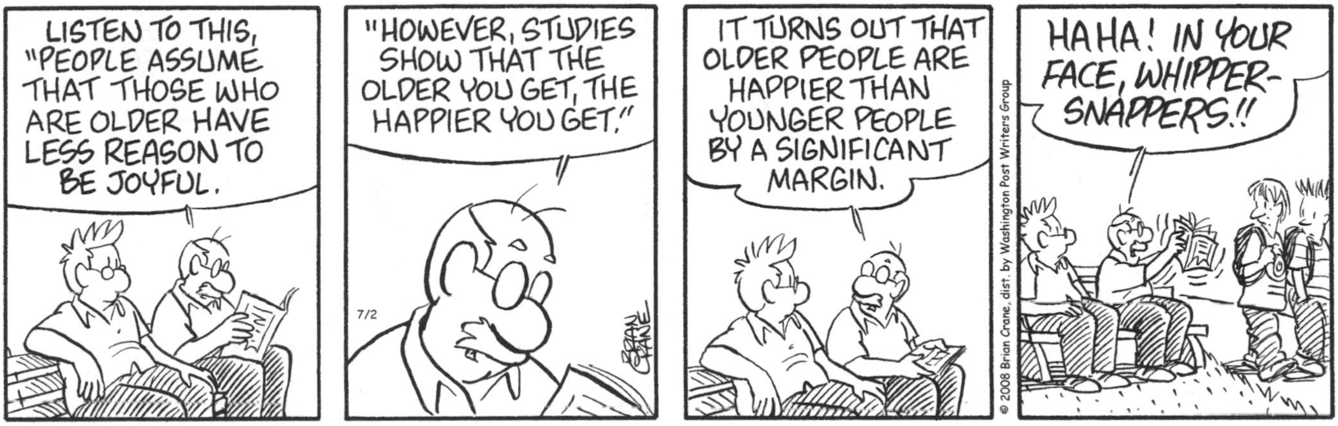
LISTEN TO THIS, "PEOPLE ASSUME THAT THOSE WHO ARE OLDER HAVE LESS REASON TO BE JOYFUL.
"HOWEVER, STUDIES SHOW THAT THE OLDER YOU GET, THE HAPPIER YOU GET."
7/2
IT TURNS OUT THAT OLDER PEOPLE ARE HAPPIER THAN YOUNGER PEOPLE BY A SIGNIFICANT MARGIN.
© 2008 Brian Crane, dist. by Washington Post Writers Group
HA HA! IN YOUR FACE, WHIPPER-SNAPPERS!!

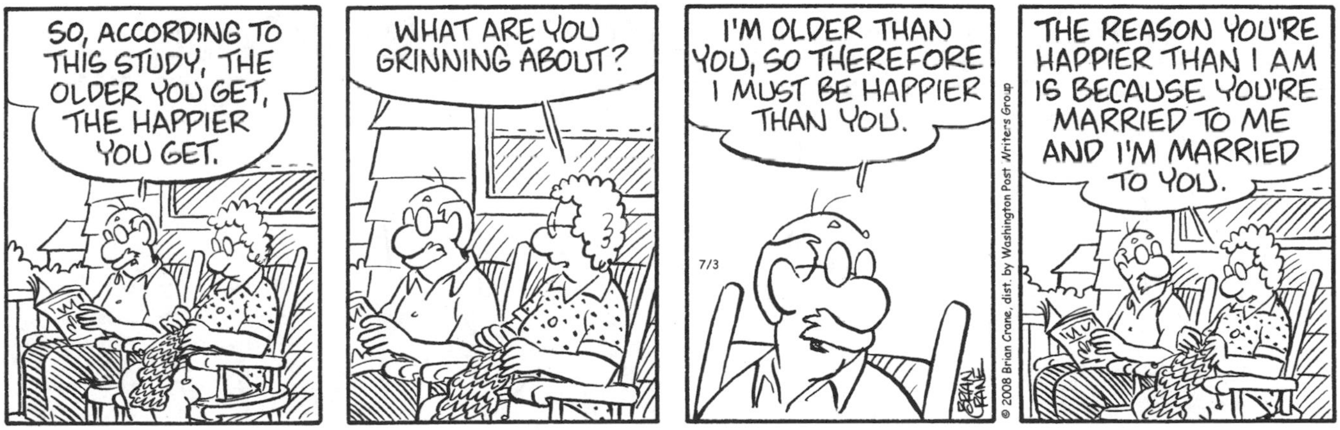
SO, ACCORDING TO THIS STUDY, THE OLDER YOU GET, THE HAPPIER YOU GET.
WHAT ARE YOU GRINNING ABOUT?
I'M OLDER THAN YOU, SO THEREFORE I MUST BE HAPPIER THAN YOU.
7/3
© 2008 Brian Crane, dist. by Washington Post Writers Group
THE REASON YOU'RE HAPPIER THAN I AM IS BECAUSE YOU'RE MARRIED TO ME AND I'M MARRIED TO YOU.

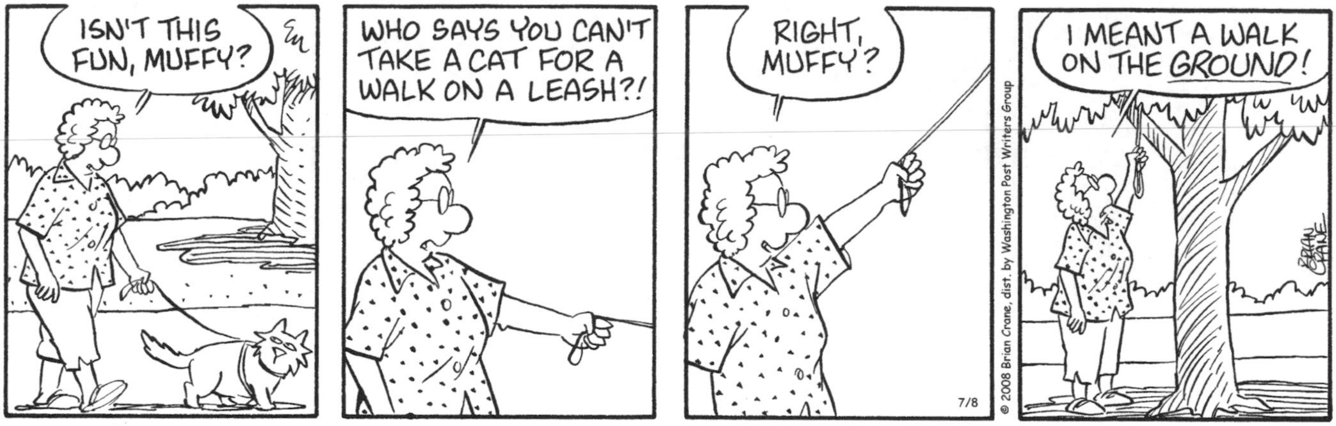
ISN'T THIS FUN, MUFFY?
WHO SAYS YOU CAN'T TAKE A CAT FOR A WALK ON A LEASH?!
RIGHT, MUFFY?
7/8
© 2008 Brian Crane, dist. by Washington Post Writers Group
I MEANT A WALK ON THE GROUND!
BRIAN CRANE

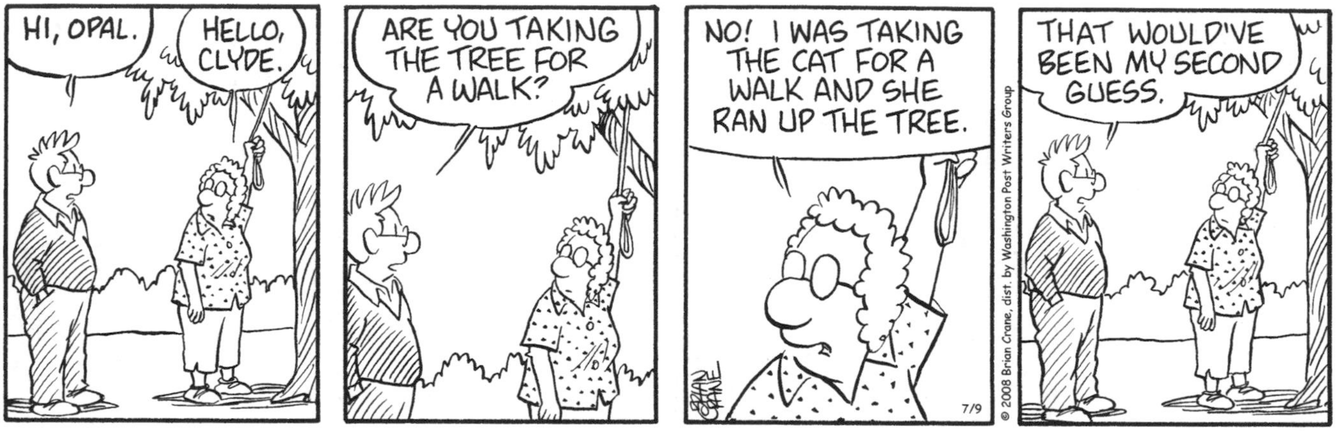
HI, OPAL.
HELLO, CLYDE.
ARE YOU TAKING THE TREE FOR A WALK?
NO! I WAS TAKING THE CAT FOR A WALK AND SHE RAN UP THE TREE.
BRIAN CRANE
7/9
© 2008 Brian Crane, dist. by Washington Post Writers Group
THAT WOULD'VE BEEN MY SECOND GUESS.

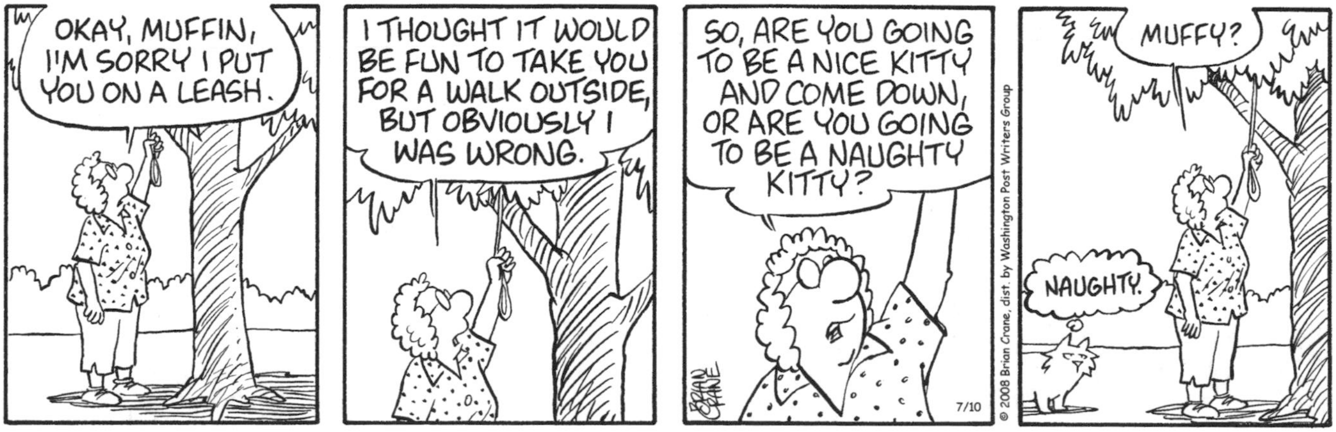
OKAY, MUFFIN, I'M SORRY I PUT YOU ON A LEASH.
I THOUGHT IT WOULD BE FUN TO TAKE YOU FOR A WALK OUTSIDE, BUT OBVIOUSLY I WAS WRONG.
SO, ARE YOU GOING TO BE A NICE KITTY AND COME DOWN, OR ARE YOU GOING TO BE A NAUGHTY KITTY?
BRIAN CRANE
7/10
© 2008 Brian Crane, dist. by Washington Post Writers Group
MUFFY?
NAUGHTY.

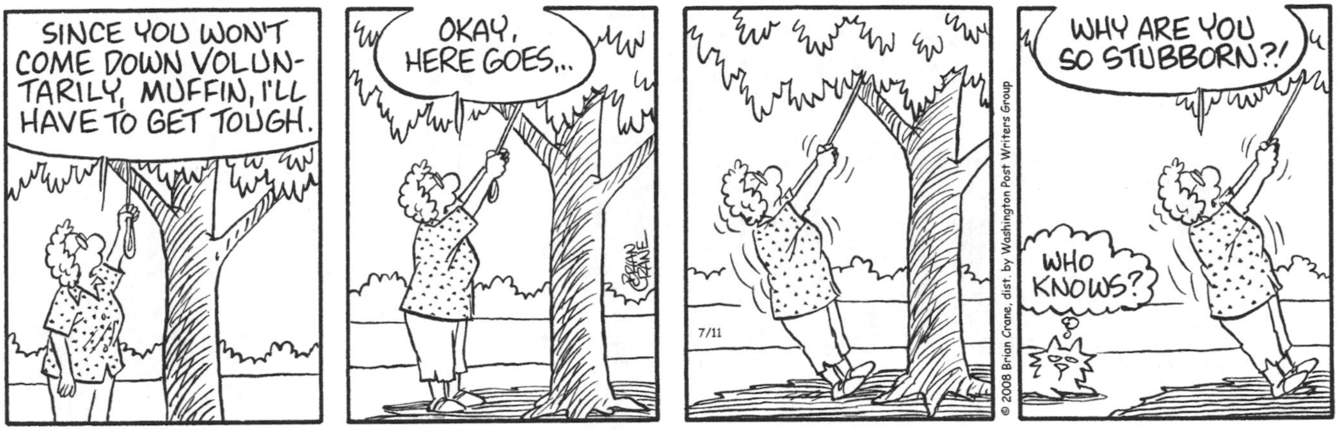
SINCE YOU WON'T COME DOWN VOLUNTARILY, MUFFIN, I'LL HAVE TO GET TOUGH.
OKAY, HERE GOES...
7/11
WHY ARE YOU SO STUBBORN?!
WHO KNOWS?
© 2008 Brian Crane, dist. by Washington Post Writers Group

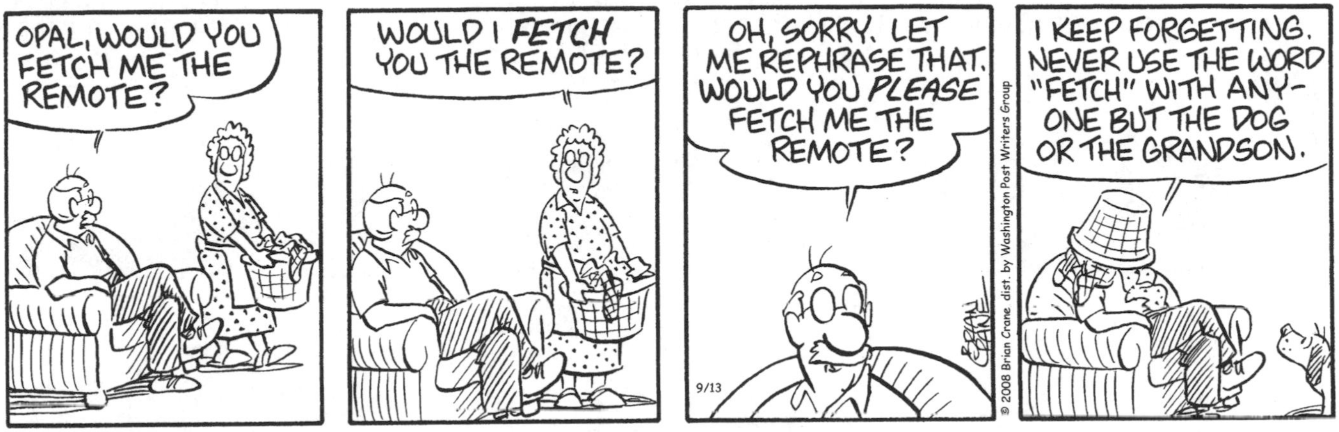
OPAL, WOULD YOU FETCH ME THE REMOTE?
WOULD I **FETCH** YOU THE REMOTE?
OH, SORRY. LET ME REPHRASE THAT. WOULD YOU *PLEASE* FETCH ME THE REMOTE?
9/13
I KEEP FORGETTING. NEVER USE THE WORD "FETCH" WITH ANYONE BUT THE DOG OR THE GRANDSON.
© 2008 Brian Crane, dist. by Washington Post Writers Group

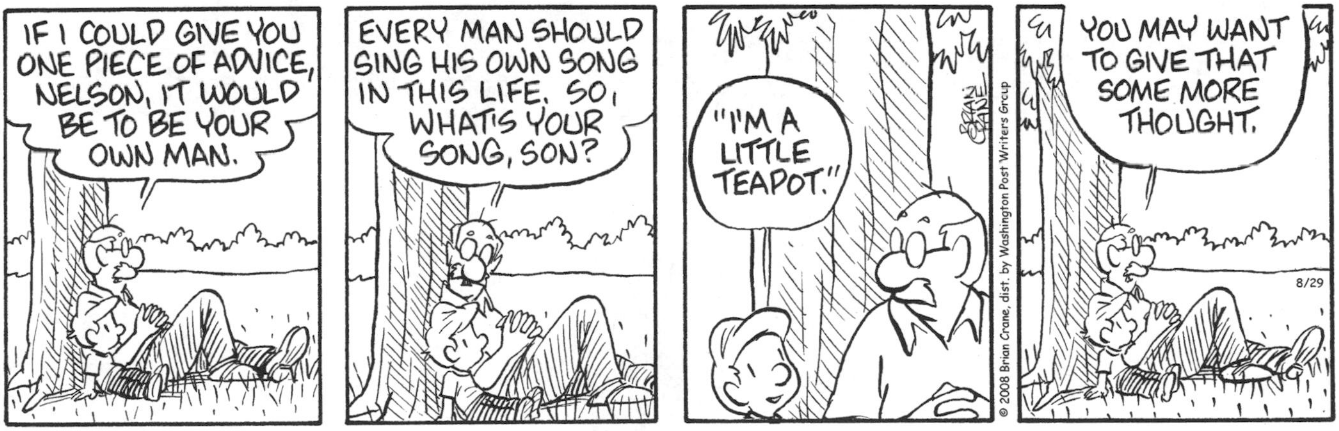
IF I COULD GIVE YOU ONE PIECE OF ADVICE, NELSON, IT WOULD BE TO BE YOUR OWN MAN.
EVERY MAN SHOULD SING HIS OWN SONG IN THIS LIFE. SO, WHAT'S YOUR SONG, SON?
"I'M A LITTLE TEAPOT."
YOU MAY WANT TO GIVE THAT SOME MORE THOUGHT.
8/29
© 2008 Brian Crane, dist. by Washington Post Writers Group

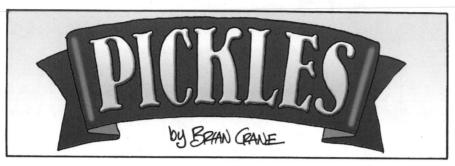

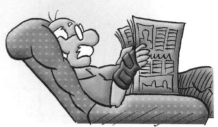

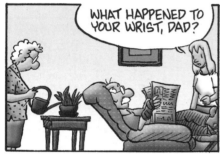

SundayPickles

PICKLES
by BRIAN CRANE
WHAT HAPPENED TO YOUR WRIST, DAD?
I INJURED IT WORKING WITH A POWER TOOL. I GUESS I GOT A LITTLE CARRIED AWAY.
OH, NO! YOU SHOULD BE MORE CAREFUL WITH THAT KIND OF EQUIPMENT.
YEAH, I KNOW.
HERE, LET ME KISS IT AND MAKE IT BETTER.
SMACK!
WHAT ARE YOU GRINNING ABOUT?!
OH, NOTHING.
A TV REMOTE IS A POWER TOOL!
8/3
BRIAN CRANE
© 2008 Brian Crane, dist. by Washington Post Writers Group

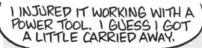

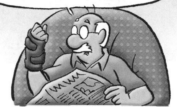

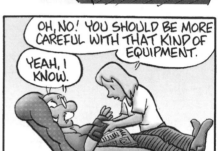

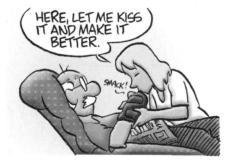

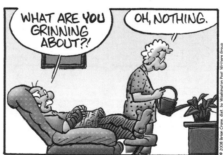

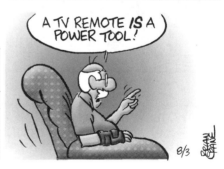

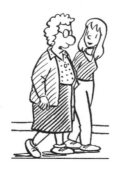

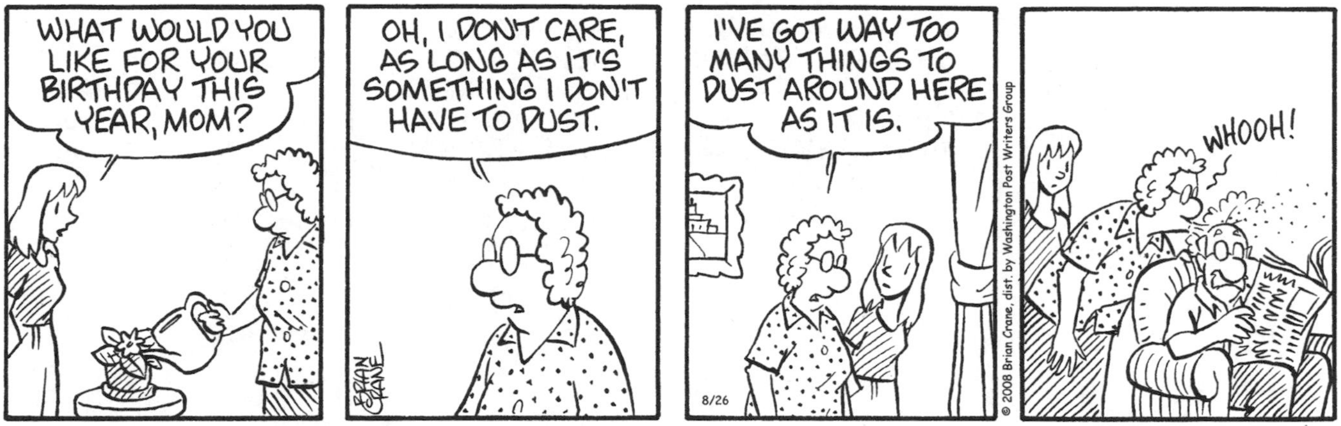
WHAT WOULD YOU LIKE FOR YOUR BIRTHDAY THIS YEAR, MOM?
OH, I DON'T CARE, AS LONG AS IT'S SOMETHING I DON'T HAVE TO DUST.
I'VE GOT WAY TOO MANY THINGS TO DUST AROUND HERE AS IT IS.
WHOOH!
8/26

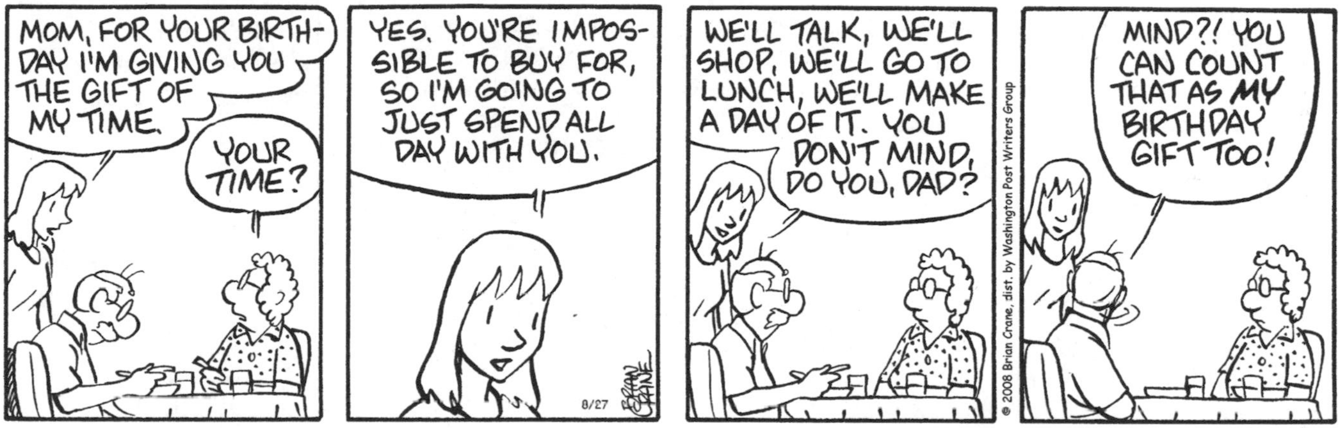
MOM, FOR YOUR BIRTHDAY I'M GIVING YOU THE GIFT OF MY TIME.
YOUR TIME?
YES. YOU'RE IMPOSSIBLE TO BUY FOR, SO I'M GOING TO JUST SPEND ALL DAY WITH YOU.
WE'LL TALK, WE'LL SHOP, WE'LL GO TO LUNCH, WE'LL MAKE A DAY OF IT. YOU DON'T MIND, DO YOU, DAD?
MIND?! YOU CAN COUNT THAT AS MY BIRTHDAY GIFT TOO!
8/27

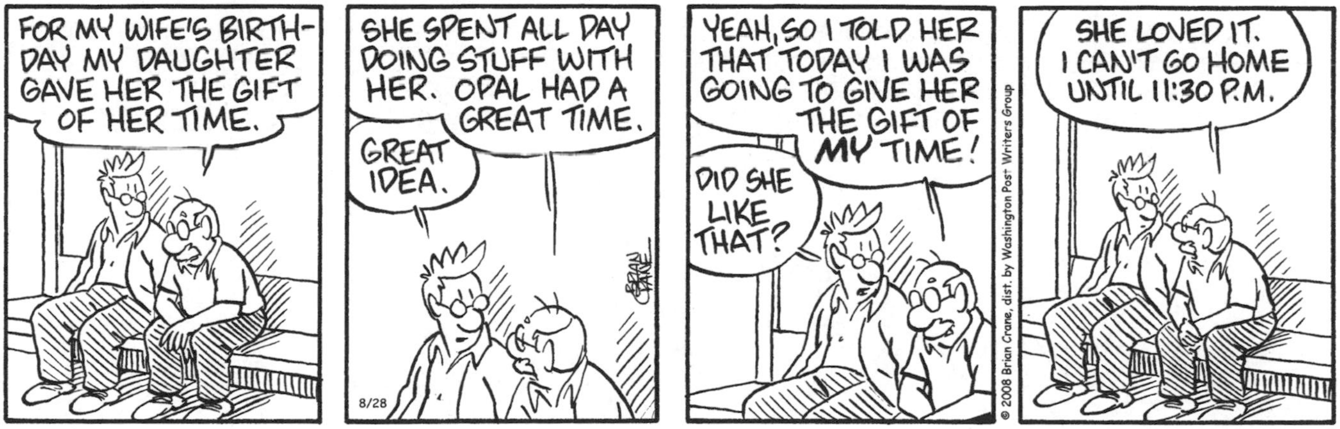
FOR MY WIFE'S BIRTHDAY MY DAUGHTER GAVE HER THE GIFT OF HER TIME.
SHE SPENT ALL DAY DOING STUFF WITH HER. OPAL HAD A GREAT TIME.
GREAT IDEA.
YEAH, SO I TOLD HER THAT TODAY I WAS GOING TO GIVE HER THE GIFT OF MY TIME!
DID SHE LIKE THAT?
SHE LOVED IT. I CAN'T GO HOME UNTIL 11:30 P.M.
8/28

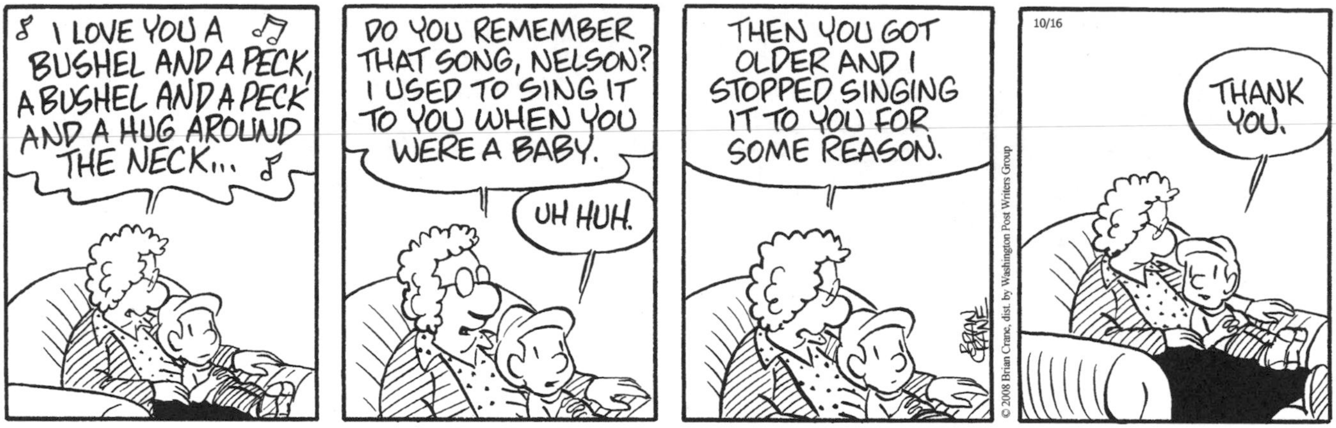
I LOVE YOU A BUSHEL AND A PECK, A BUSHEL AND A PECK AND A HUG AROUND THE NECK...
DO YOU REMEMBER THAT SONG, NELSON? I USED TO SING IT TO YOU WHEN YOU WERE A BABY.
UH HUH.
THEN YOU GOT OLDER AND I STOPPED SINGING IT TO YOU FOR SOME REASON.
BRIAN CRANE
10/16
THANK YOU.

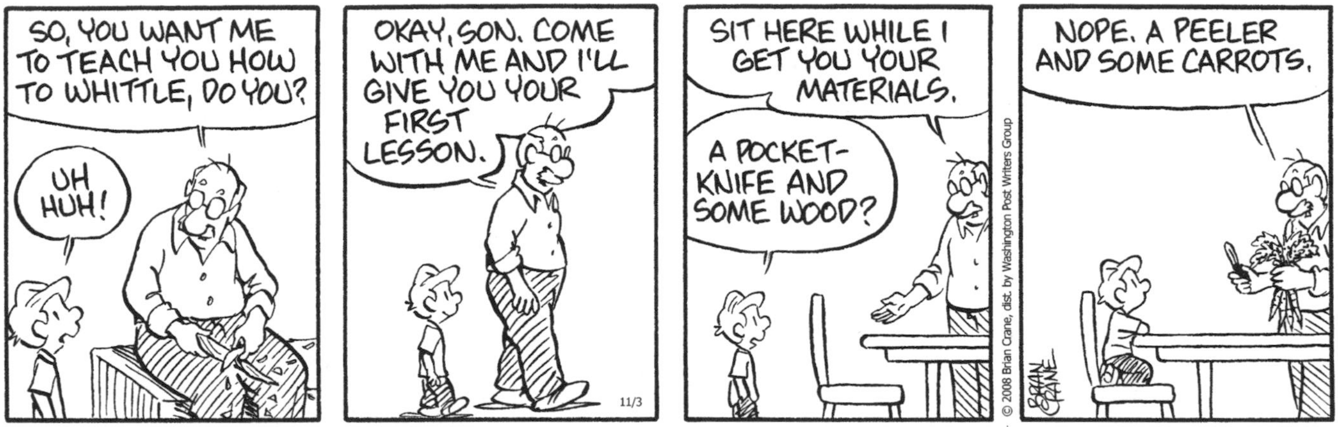
SO, YOU WANT ME TO TEACH YOU HOW TO WHITTLE, DO YOU?
UH HUH!
OKAY, SON. COME WITH ME AND I'LL GIVE YOU YOUR FIRST LESSON.
11/3
SIT HERE WHILE I GET YOU YOUR MATERIALS.
A POCKET-KNIFE AND SOME WOOD?
NOPE. A PEELER AND SOME CARROTS.
BRIAN CRANE

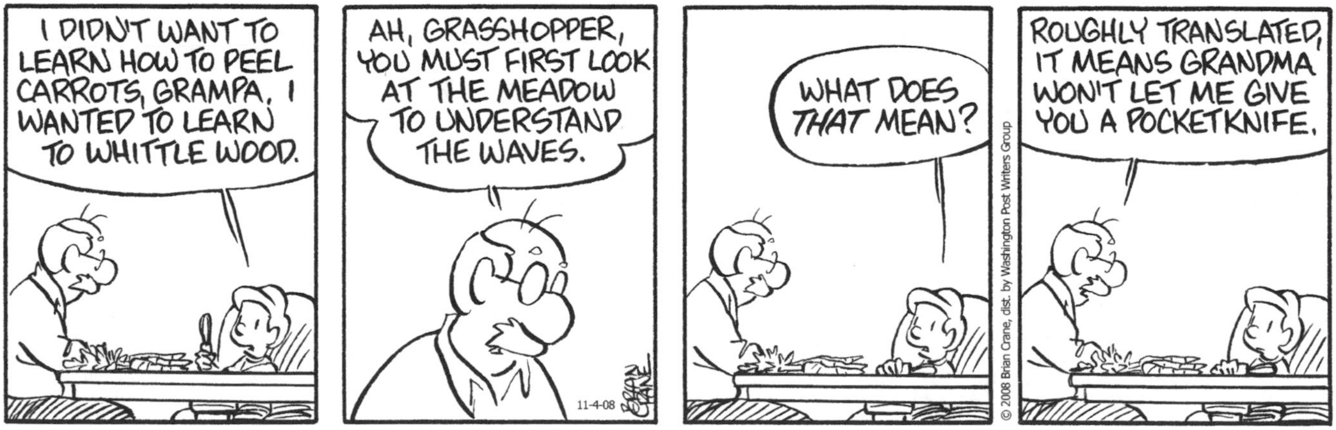
I DIDN'T WANT TO LEARN HOW TO PEEL CARROTS, GRAMPA. I WANTED TO LEARN TO WHITTLE WOOD.
AH, GRASSHOPPER, YOU MUST FIRST LOOK AT THE MEADOW TO UNDERSTAND THE WAVES.
11-4-08
BRIAN CRANE
WHAT DOES *THAT* MEAN?
ROUGHLY TRANSLATED, IT MEANS GRANDMA WON'T LET ME GIVE YOU A POCKETKNIFE.

SundayPickles

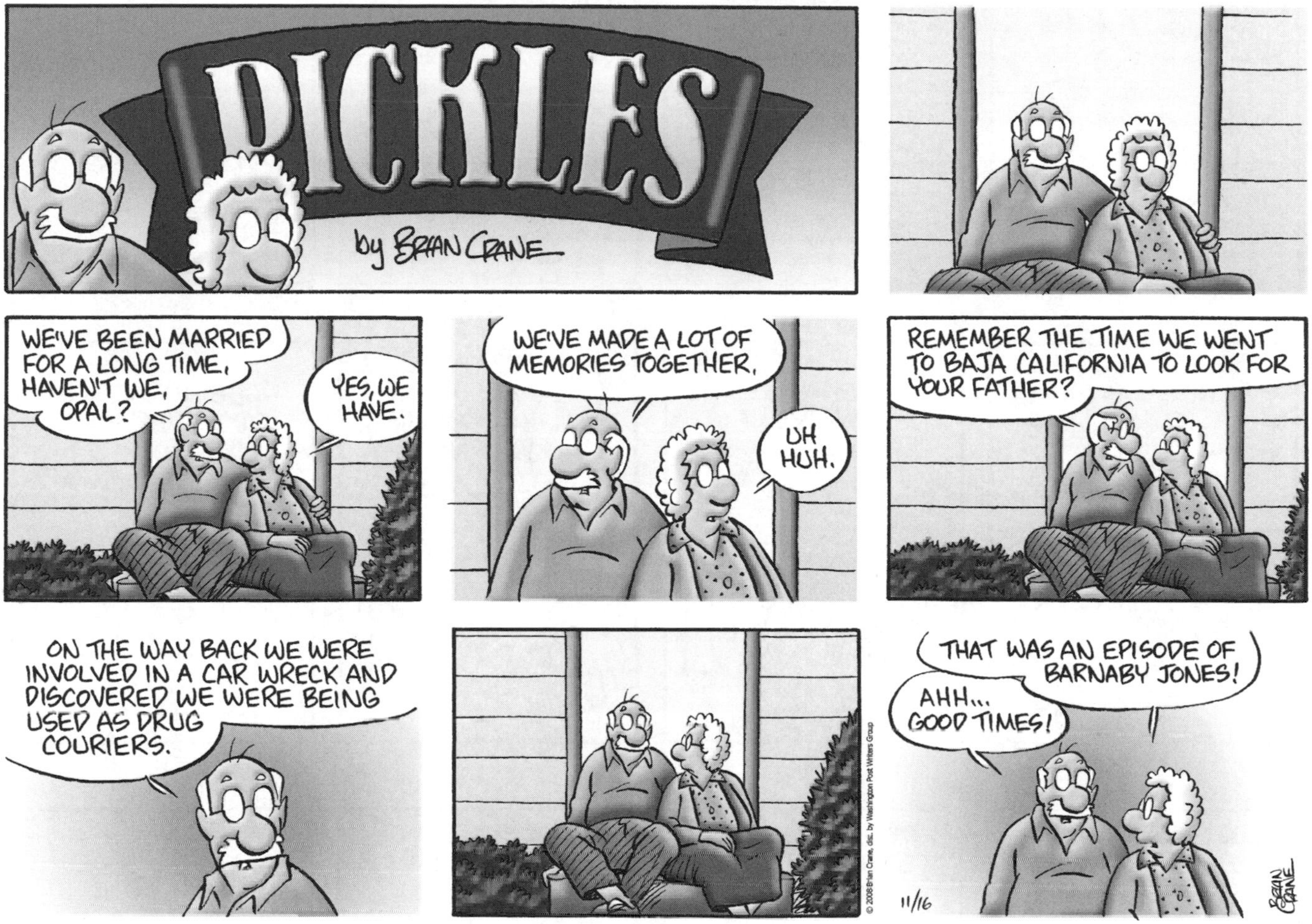
PICKLES
by BRIAN CRANE
WE'VE BEEN MARRIED FOR A LONG TIME, HAVEN'T WE, OPAL?
YES, WE HAVE.
WE'VE MADE A LOT OF MEMORIES TOGETHER.
UH HUH.
REMEMBER THE TIME WE WENT TO BAJA CALIFORNIA TO LOOK FOR YOUR FATHER?
ON THE WAY BACK WE WERE INVOLVED IN A CAR WRECK AND DISCOVERED WE WERE BEING USED AS DRUG COURIERS.
THAT WAS AN EPISODE OF BARNABY JONES!
AHH... GOOD TIMES!
11/16
BRIAN CRANE

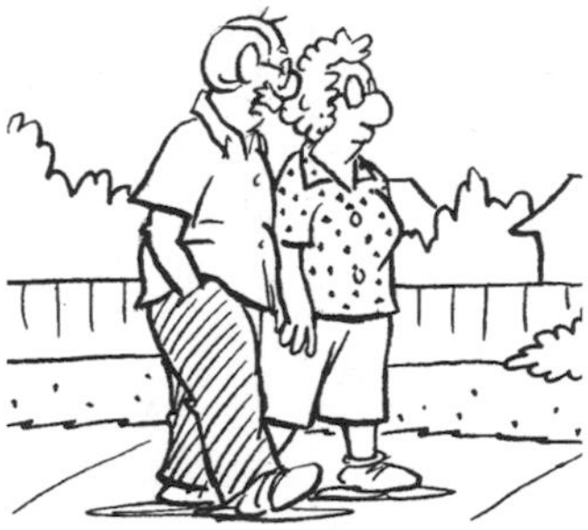

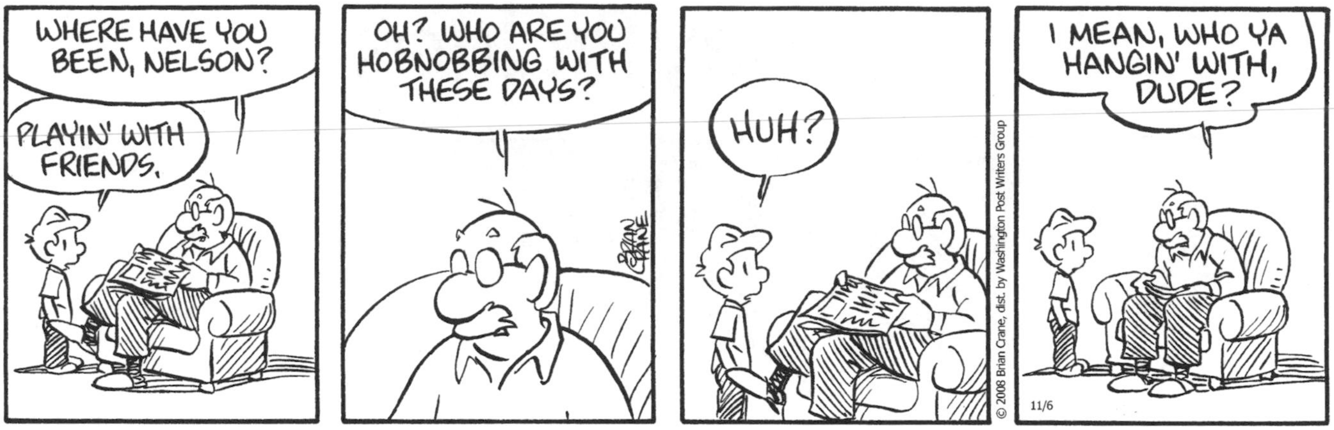
WHERE HAVE YOU BEEN, NELSON?
PLAYIN' WITH FRIENDS.
OH? WHO ARE YOU HOBNOBBING WITH THESE DAYS?
HUH?
I MEAN, WHO YA HANGIN' WITH, DUDE?
© 2008 Brian Crane, dist. by Washington Post Writers Group
11/6

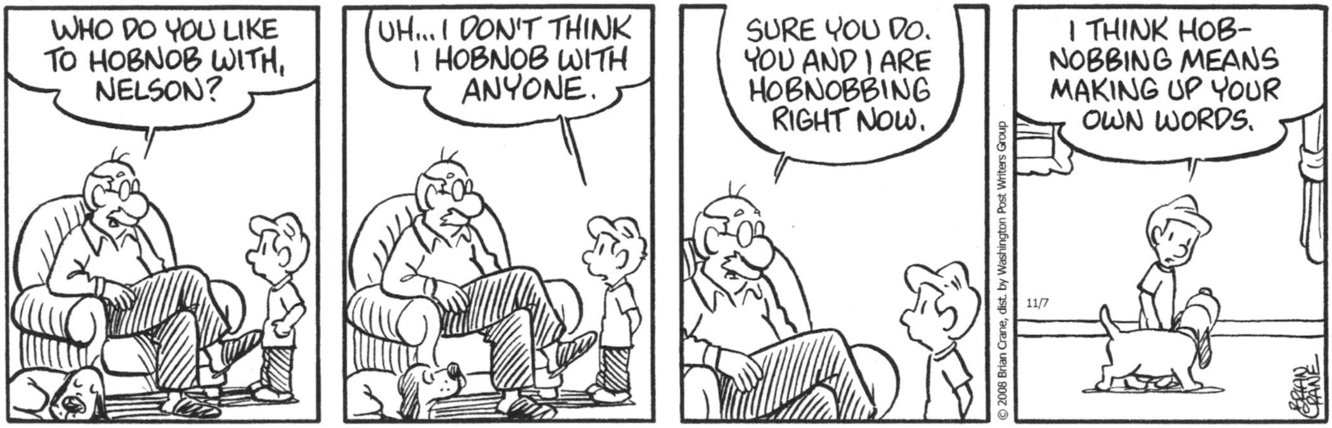
WHO DO YOU LIKE TO HOBNOB WITH, NELSON?
UH... I DON'T THINK I HOBNOB WITH ANYONE.
SURE YOU DO. YOU AND I ARE HOBNOBBING RIGHT NOW.
I THINK HOB-NOBBING MEANS MAKING UP YOUR OWN WORDS.
© 2008 Brian Crane, dist. by Washington Post Writers Group
11/7

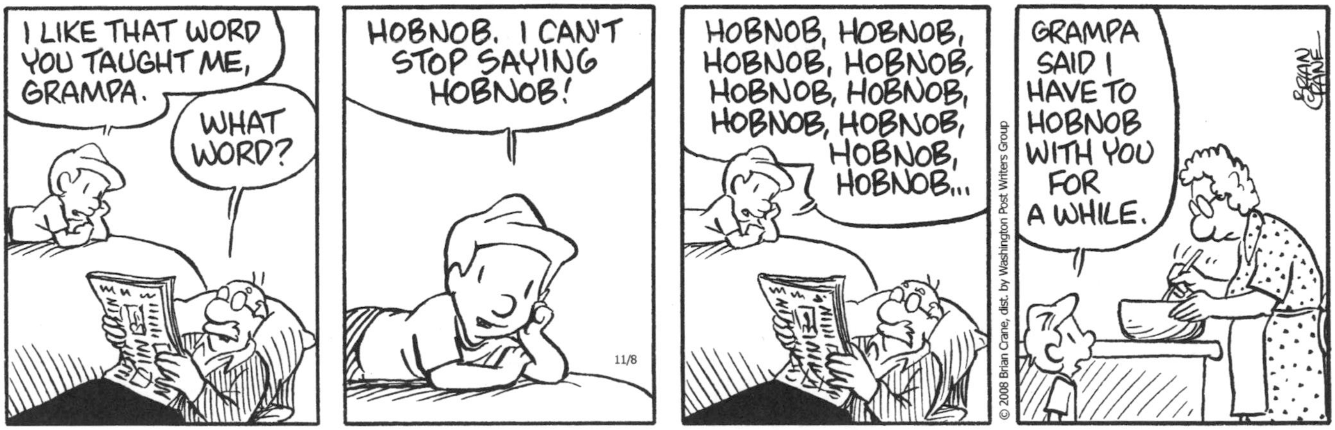
I LIKE THAT WORD YOU TAUGHT ME, GRAMPA.
WHAT WORD?
HOBNOB. I CAN'T STOP SAYING HOBNOB!
11/8
HOBNOB, HOBNOB, HOBNOB, HOBNOB, HOBNOB, HOBNOB, HOBNOB, HOBNOB, HOBNOB, HOBNOB...
© 2008 Brian Crane, dist. by Washington Post Writers Group
GRAMPA SAID I HAVE TO HOBNOB WITH YOU FOR A WHILE.

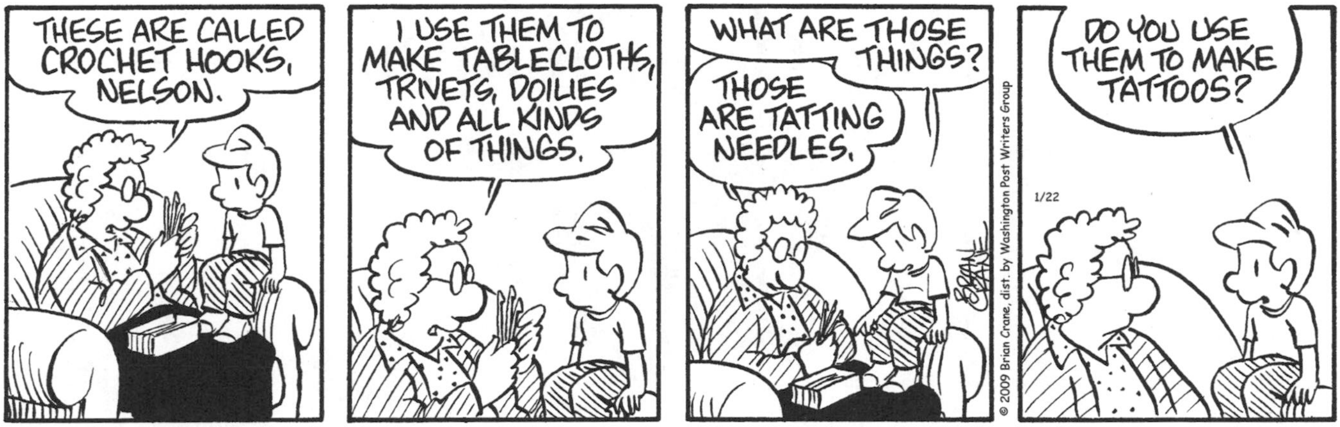
THESE ARE CALLED CROCHET HOOKS, NELSON.
I USE THEM TO MAKE TABLECLOTHS, TRIVETS, DOILIES AND ALL KINDS OF THINGS.
WHAT ARE THOSE THINGS?
THOSE ARE TATTING NEEDLES.
© 2009 Brian Crane, dist. by Washington Post Writers Group
1/22
DO YOU USE THEM TO MAKE TATTOOS?

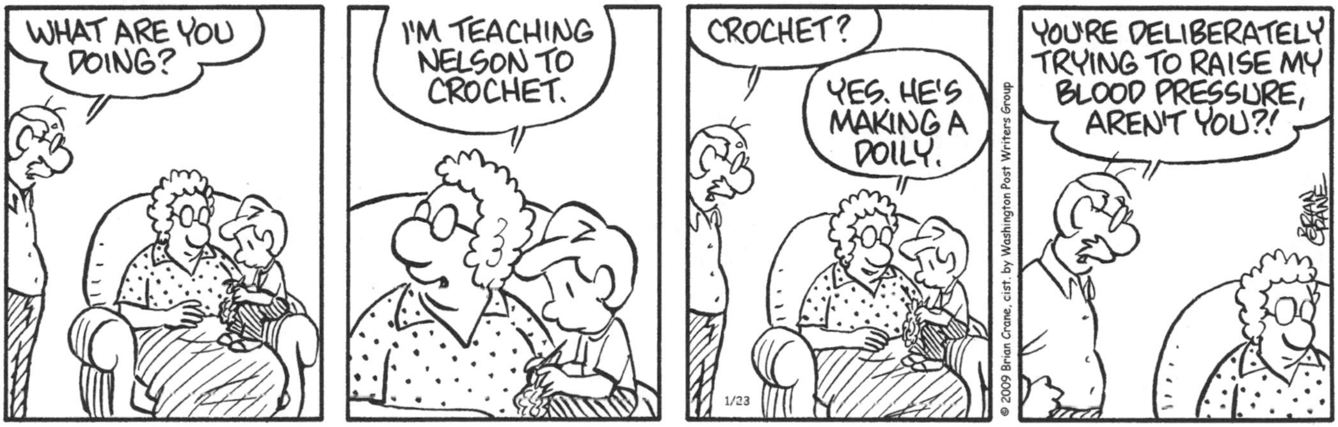
WHAT ARE YOU DOING?
I'M TEACHING NELSON TO CROCHET.
CROCHET?
YES. HE'S MAKING A DOILY.
1/23
© 2009 Brian Crane, cist. by Washington Post Writers Group
YOU'RE DELIBERATELY TRYING TO RAISE MY BLOOD PRESSURE, AREN'T YOU?!

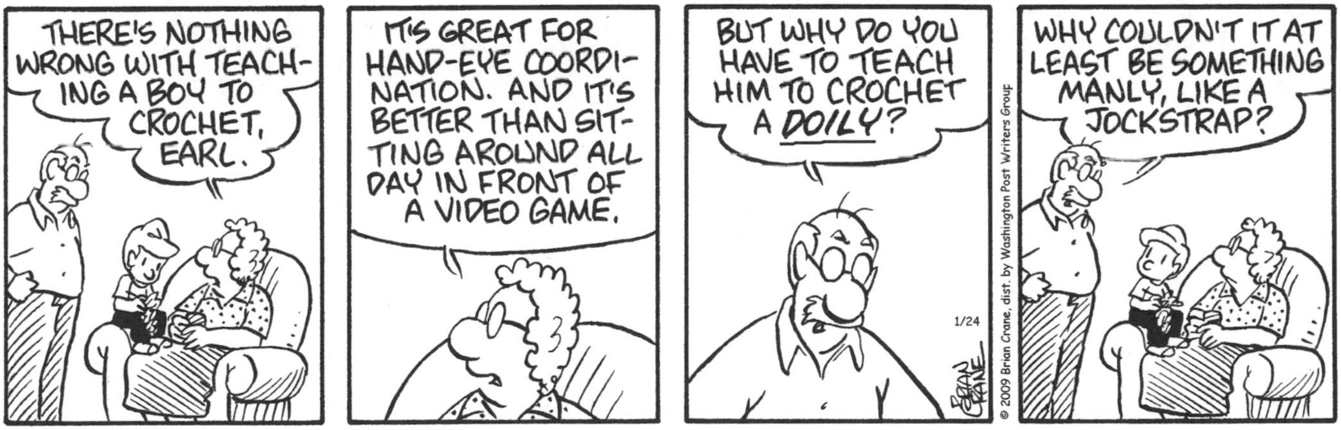
THERE'S NOTHING WRONG WITH TEACHING A BOY TO CROCHET, EARL.
IT'S GREAT FOR HAND-EYE COORDINATION. AND IT'S BETTER THAN SITTING AROUND ALL DAY IN FRONT OF A VIDEO GAME.
BUT WHY DO YOU HAVE TO TEACH HIM TO CROCHET A DOILY?
1/24
© 2009 Brian Crane, dist. by Washington Post Writers Group
WHY COULDN'T IT AT LEAST BE SOMETHING MANLY, LIKE A JOCKSTRAP?

SundayPickles

PICKLES
RING!
BY BRIAN CRANE
HELLO?
HELLO, I'M CALLING WITH A VERY IMPORTANT MESSAGE FOR YOU ABOUT AN EXTREMELY EXCITING OPPORTUNITY.
OH, I AM VERY INTERESTED! PLEASE TELL ME ALL ABOUT IT.
WHAT IF I TOLD YOU THAT FOR A SMALL MONTHLY FEE WE COULD REDUCE YOUR ENERGY BILLS, HELP SAVE THE PLANET AND IMPROVE YOUR LOVE LIFE?
I KNOW WHAT YOU'RE THINKING... HOW IS THIS POSSIBLE? ALLOW ME TO EXPLAIN...
11/30
MMPHFLURL BLARGHMFFT
© 2008 Brian Crane, dist. by Washington Post Writers Group
ISN'T THAT UNCOMFORTABLE?
A LITTLE, BUT IT'S WORTH IT.
MRPLFF
BRIAN CRANE

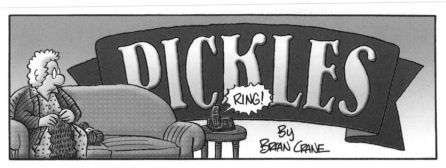

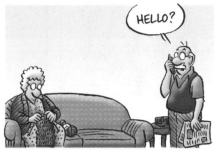

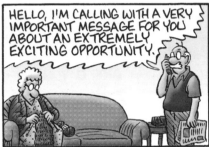

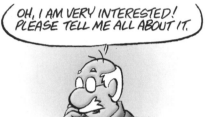

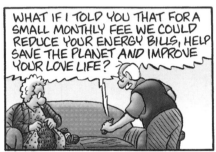

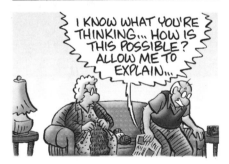

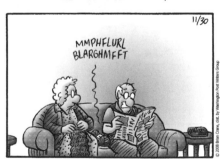

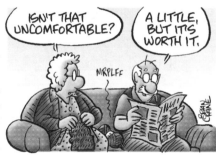

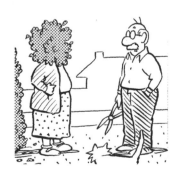

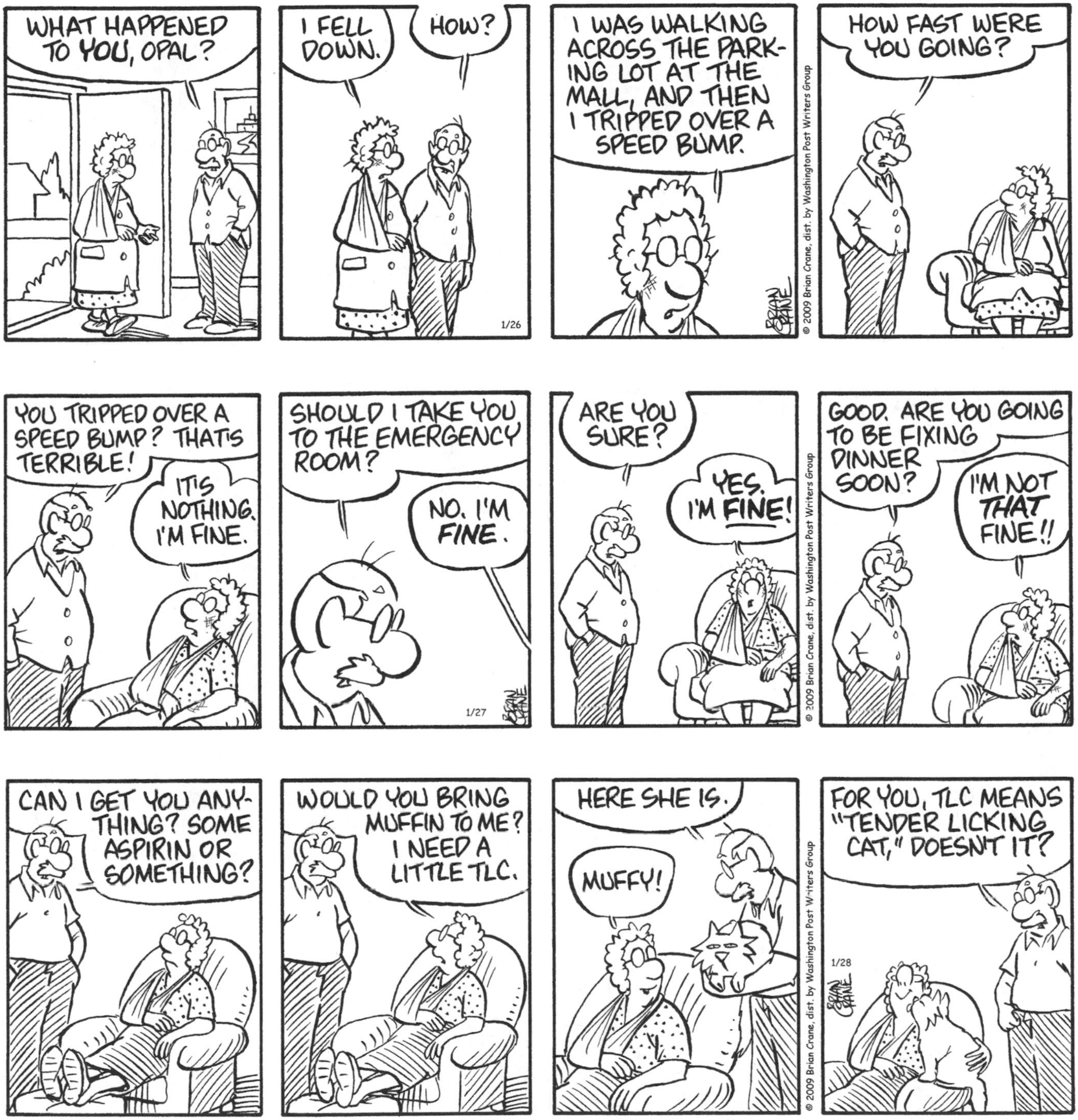
WHAT HAPPENED TO YOU, OPAL?
I FELL DOWN.
HOW?
I WAS WALKING ACROSS THE PARKING LOT AT THE MALL, AND THEN I TRIPPED OVER A SPEED BUMP.
HOW FAST WERE YOU GOING?
1/26
BRIAN CRANE
© 2009 Brian Crane, dist. by Washington Post Writers Group
YOU TRIPPED OVER A SPEED BUMP? THAT'S TERRIBLE!
IT'S NOTHING. I'M FINE.
SHOULD I TAKE YOU TO THE EMERGENCY ROOM?
NO. I'M FINE.
ARE YOU SURE?
YES. I'M FINE!
GOOD. ARE YOU GOING TO BE FIXING DINNER SOON?
I'M NOT THAT FINE!!
1/27
BRIAN CRANE
© 2009 Brian Crane, dist. by Washington Post Writers Group
CAN I GET YOU ANYTHING? SOME ASPIRIN OR SOMETHING?
WOULD YOU BRING MUFFIN TO ME? I NEED A LITTLE TLC.
HERE SHE IS.
MUFFY!
FOR YOU, TLC MEANS "TENDER LICKING CAT," DOESN'T IT?
1/28
BRIAN CRANE
© 2009 Brian Crane, dist. by Washington Post Writers Group

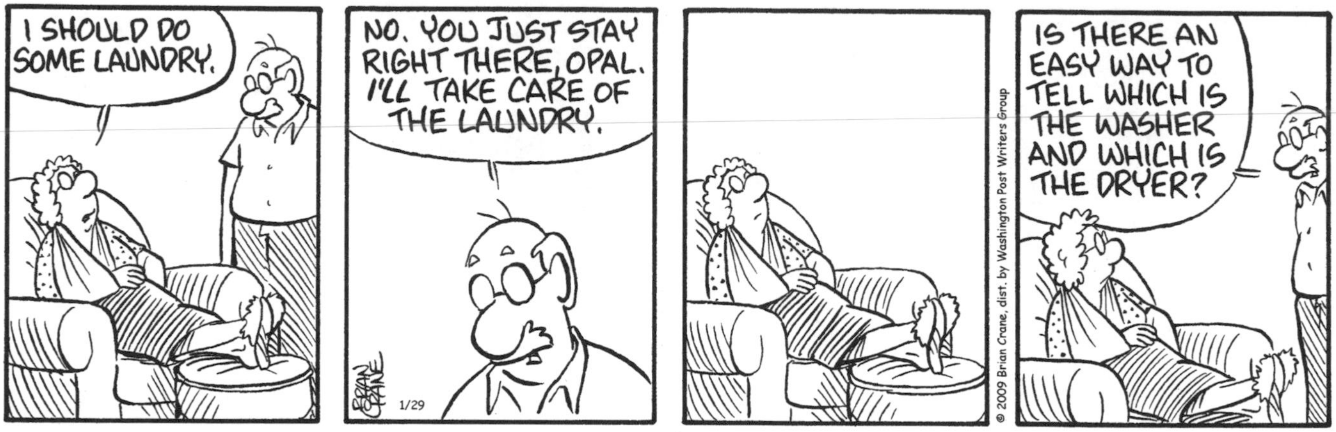
I SHOULD DO SOME LAUNDRY.
NO. YOU JUST STAY RIGHT THERE, OPAL. I'LL TAKE CARE OF THE LAUNDRY.
BRIAN CRANE
1/29
© 2009 Brian Crane, dist. by Washington Post Writers Group
IS THERE AN EASY WAY TO TELL WHICH IS THE WASHER AND WHICH IS THE DRYER?

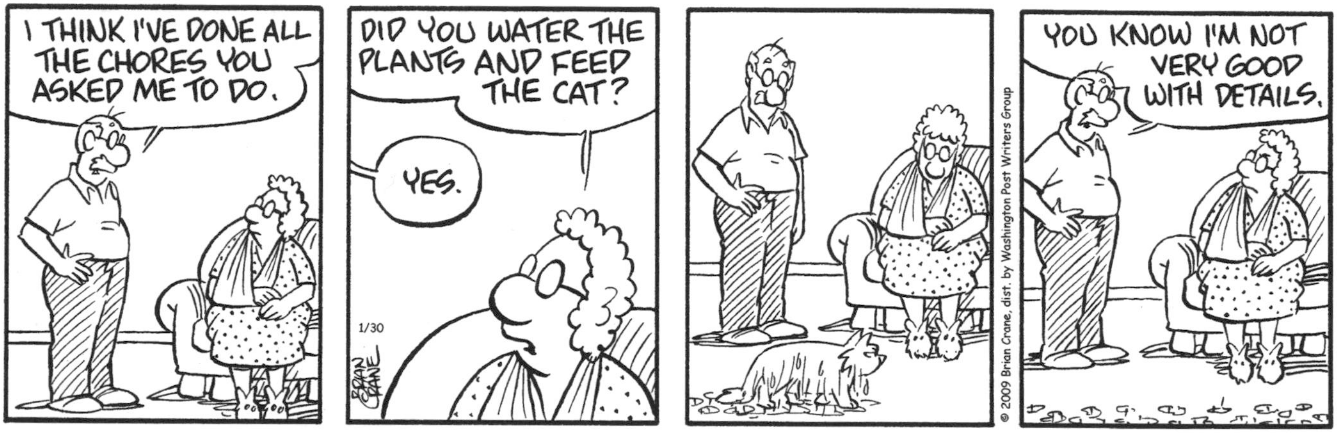
I THINK I'VE DONE ALL THE CHORES YOU ASKED ME TO DO.
DID YOU WATER THE PLANTS AND FEED THE CAT?
YES.
1/30
BRIAN CRANE
© 2009 Brian Crane, dist. by Washington Post Writers Group
YOU KNOW I'M NOT VERY GOOD WITH DETAILS.

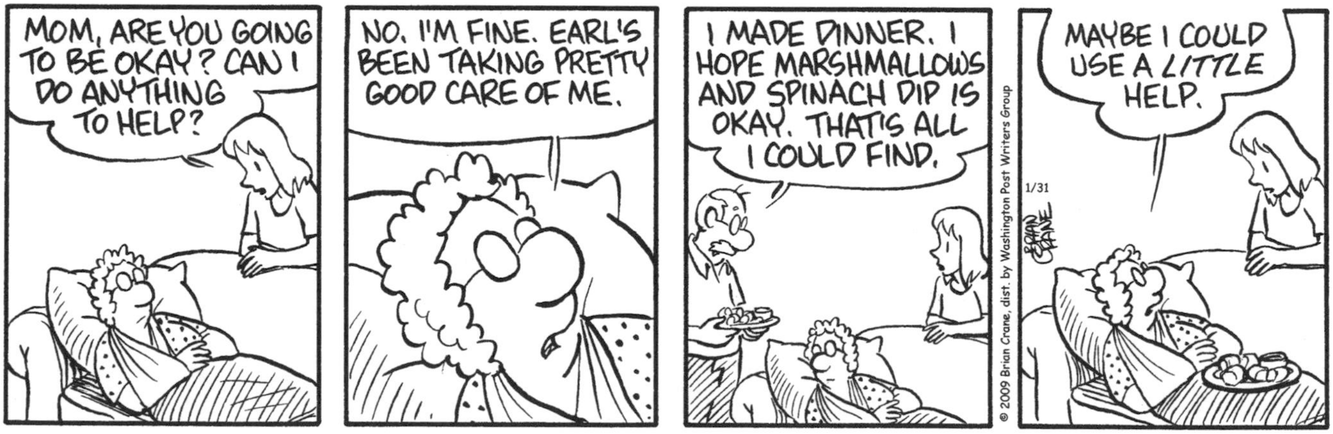
MOM, ARE YOU GOING TO BE OKAY? CAN I DO ANYTHING TO HELP?
NO. I'M FINE. EARL'S BEEN TAKING PRETTY GOOD CARE OF ME.
I MADE DINNER. I HOPE MARSHMALLOWS AND SPINACH DIP IS OKAY. THAT'S ALL I COULD FIND.
© 2009 Brian Crane, dist. by Washington Post Writers Group
1/31
BRIAN CRANE
MAYBE I COULD USE A *LITTLE* HELP.

Sunday Pickles

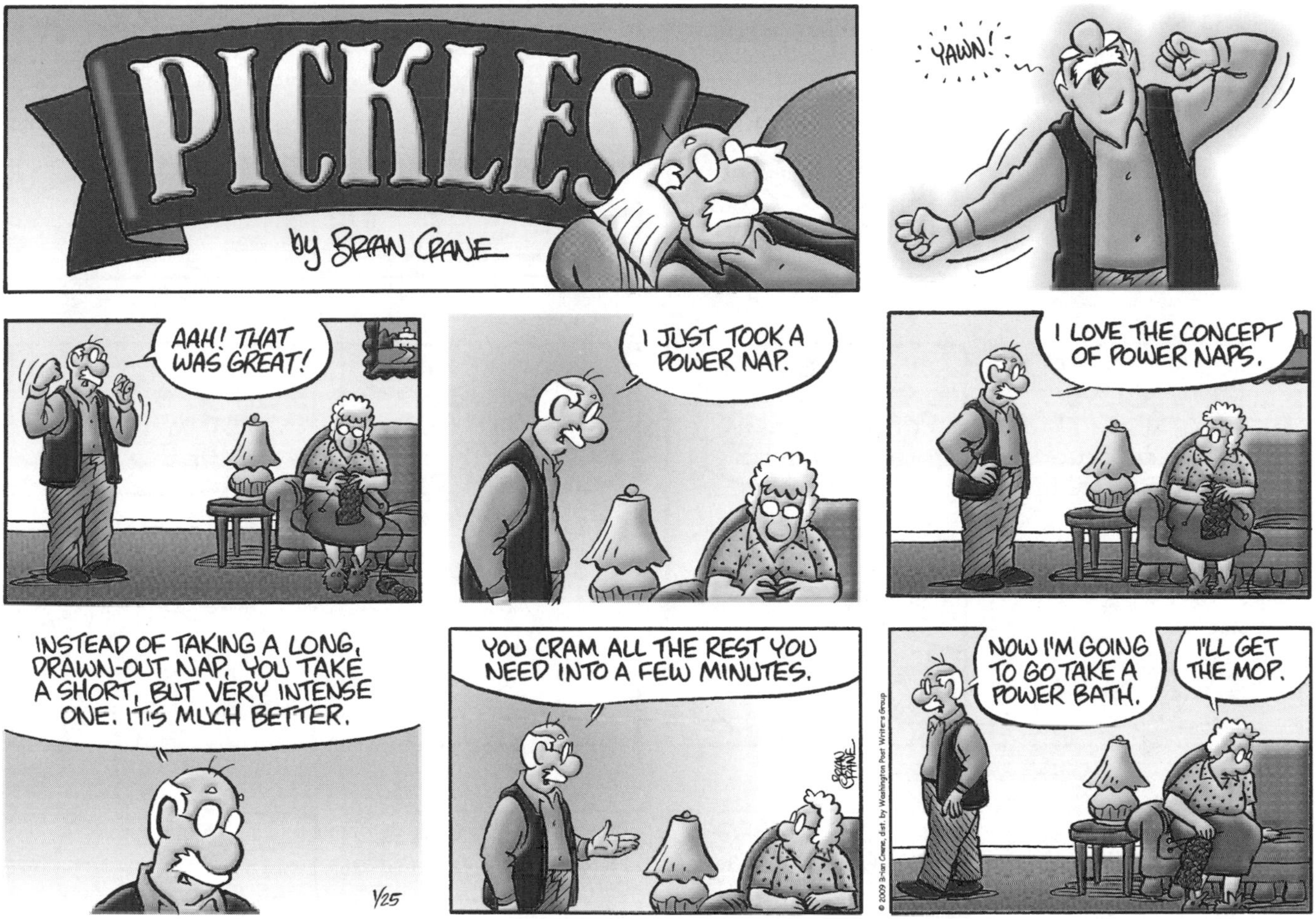
PICKLES
by BRIAN CRANE
YAWN!
AAH! THAT WAS GREAT!
I JUST TOOK A POWER NAP.
I LOVE THE CONCEPT OF POWER NAPS.
INSTEAD OF TAKING A LONG, DRAWN-OUT NAP, YOU TAKE A SHORT, BUT VERY INTENSE ONE. IT'S MUCH BETTER.
1/25
YOU CRAM ALL THE REST YOU NEED INTO A FEW MINUTES.
BRIAN CRANE
© 2009 Brian Crane, dist. by Washington Post Writers Group
NOW I'M GOING TO GO TAKE A POWER BATH.
I'LL GET THE MOP.

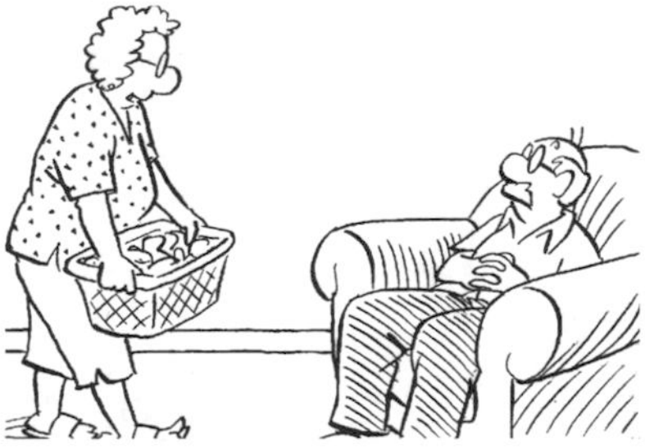

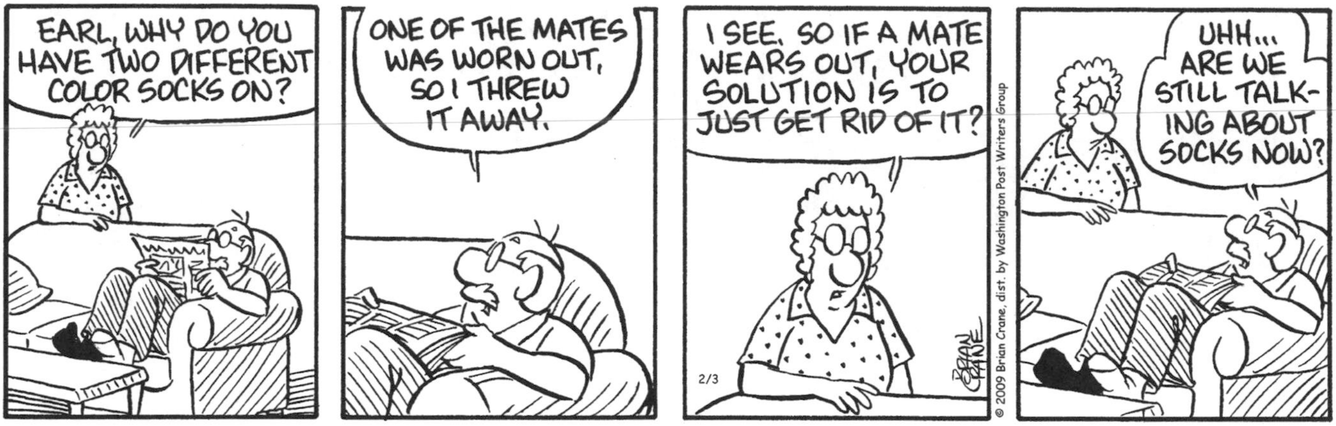
EARL, WHY DO YOU HAVE TWO DIFFERENT COLOR SOCKS ON?
ONE OF THE MATES WAS WORN OUT, SO I THREW IT AWAY.
I SEE. SO IF A MATE WEARS OUT, YOUR SOLUTION IS TO JUST GET RID OF IT?
2/3
UHH... ARE WE STILL TALKING ABOUT SOCKS NOW?
© 2009 Brian Crane, dist. by Washington Post Writers Group

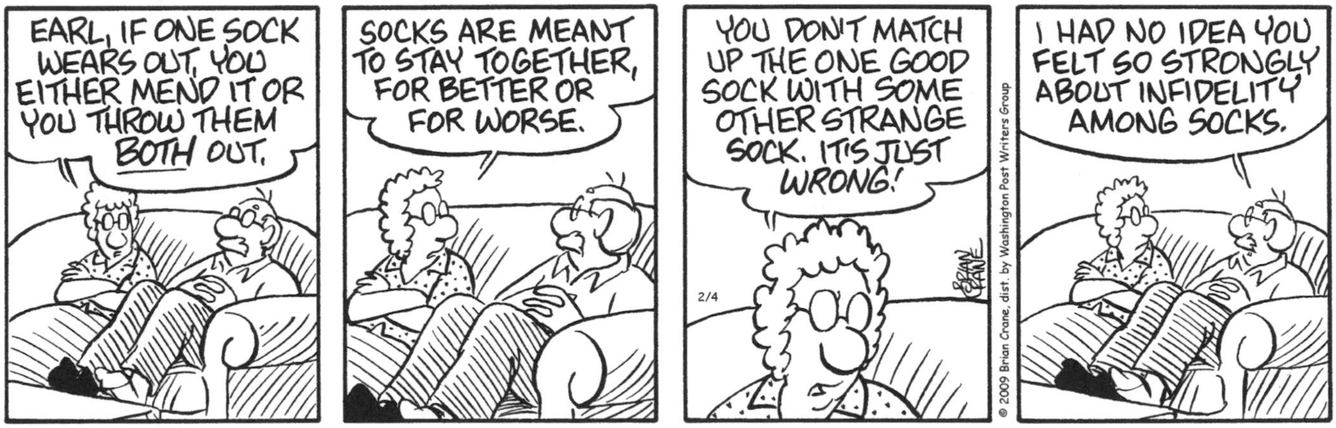
EARL, IF ONE SOCK WEARS OUT, YOU EITHER MEND IT OR YOU THROW THEM BOTH OUT.
SOCKS ARE MEANT TO STAY TOGETHER, FOR BETTER OR FOR WORSE.
YOU DON'T MATCH UP THE ONE GOOD SOCK WITH SOME OTHER STRANGE SOCK. IT'S JUST WRONG!
2/4
I HAD NO IDEA YOU FELT SO STRONGLY ABOUT INFIDELITY AMONG SOCKS.
© 2009 Brian Crane, dist. by Washington Post Writers Group

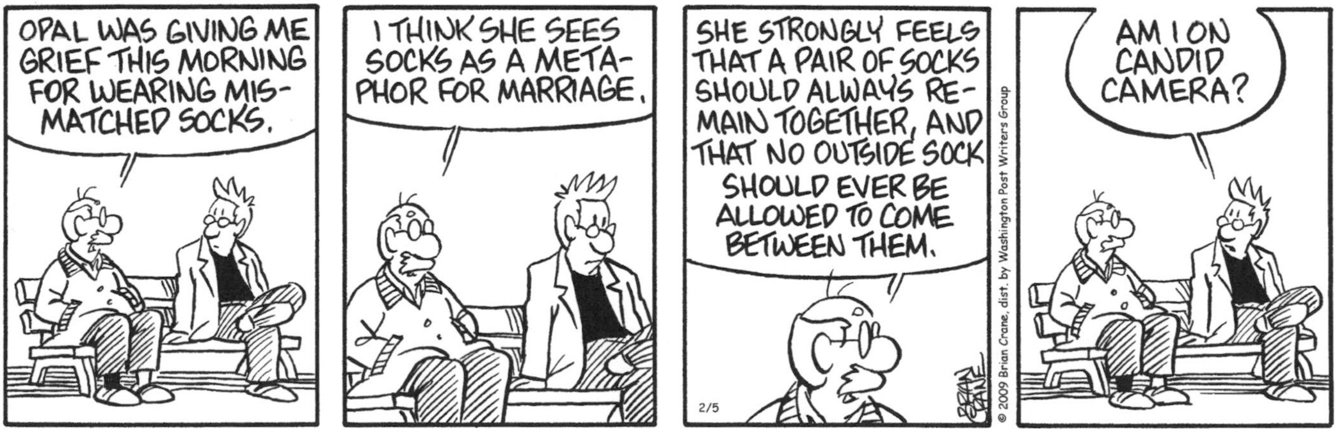
OPAL WAS GIVING ME GRIEF THIS MORNING FOR WEARING MIS-MATCHED SOCKS.
I THINK SHE SEES SOCKS AS A METAPHOR FOR MARRIAGE.
SHE STRONGLY FEELS THAT A PAIR OF SOCKS SHOULD ALWAYS REMAIN TOGETHER, AND THAT NO OUTSIDE SOCK SHOULD EVER BE ALLOWED TO COME BETWEEN THEM.
2/5
AM I ON CANDID CAMERA?
© 2009 Brian Crane, dist. by Washington Post Writers Group

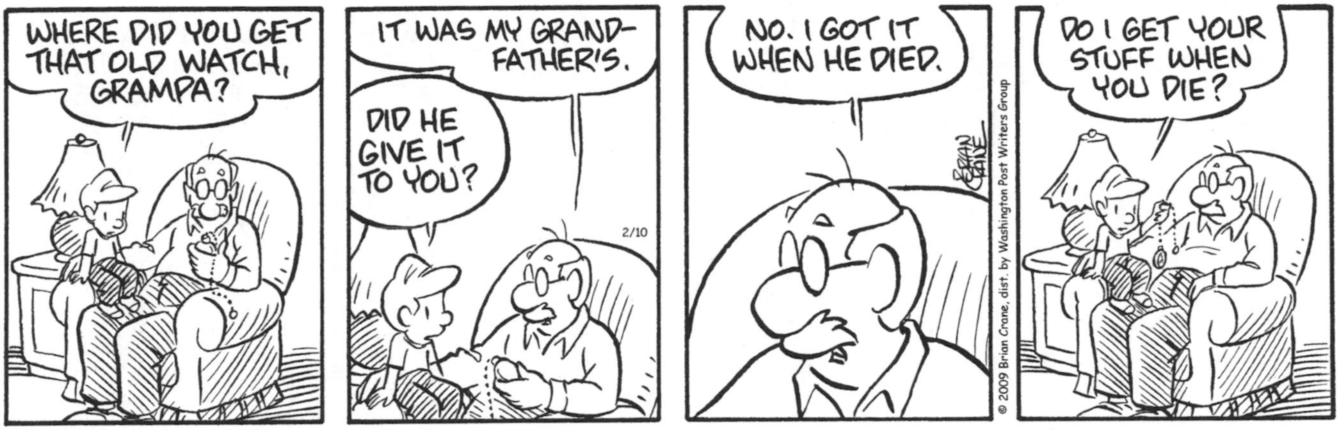
WHERE DID YOU GET THAT OLD WATCH, GRAMPA?
IT WAS MY GRANDFATHER'S.
DID HE GIVE IT TO YOU?
2/10
NO. I GOT IT WHEN HE DIED.
BRIAN CRANE
DO I GET YOUR STUFF WHEN YOU DIE?
© 2009 Brian Crane, dist. by Washington Post Writers Group

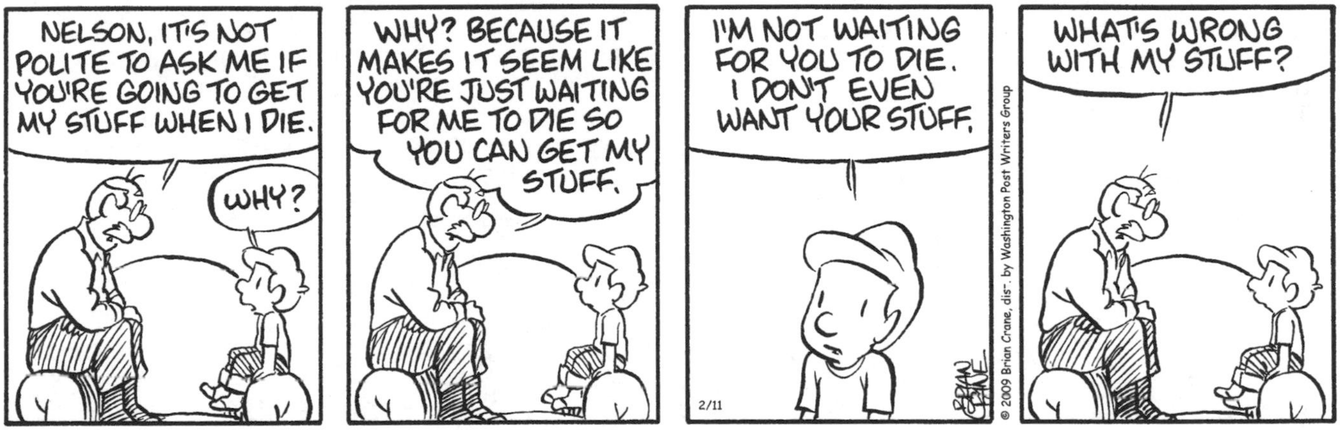
NELSON, IT'S NOT POLITE TO ASK ME IF YOU'RE GOING TO GET MY STUFF WHEN I DIE.
WHY?
WHY? BECAUSE IT MAKES IT SEEM LIKE YOU'RE JUST WAITING FOR ME TO DIE SO YOU CAN GET MY STUFF.
I'M NOT WAITING FOR YOU TO DIE. I DON'T EVEN WANT YOUR STUFF.
2/11
BRIAN CRANE
WHAT'S WRONG WITH MY STUFF?
© 2009 Brian Crane, dist. by Washington Post Writers Group

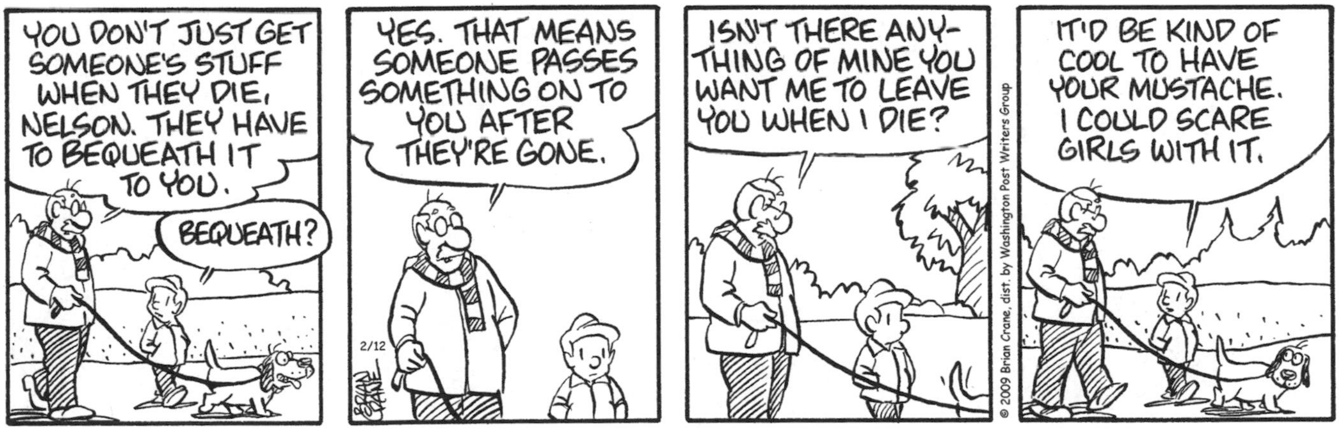
YOU DON'T JUST GET SOMEONE'S STUFF WHEN THEY DIE, NELSON. THEY HAVE TO BEQUEATH IT TO YOU.
BEQUEATH?
YES. THAT MEANS SOMEONE PASSES SOMETHING ON TO YOU AFTER THEY'RE GONE.
2/12
BRIAN CRANE
ISN'T THERE ANYTHING OF MINE YOU WANT ME TO LEAVE YOU WHEN I DIE?
IT'D BE KIND OF COOL TO HAVE YOUR MUSTACHE. I COULD SCARE GIRLS WITH IT.
© 2009 Brian Crane, dist. by Washington Post Writers Group

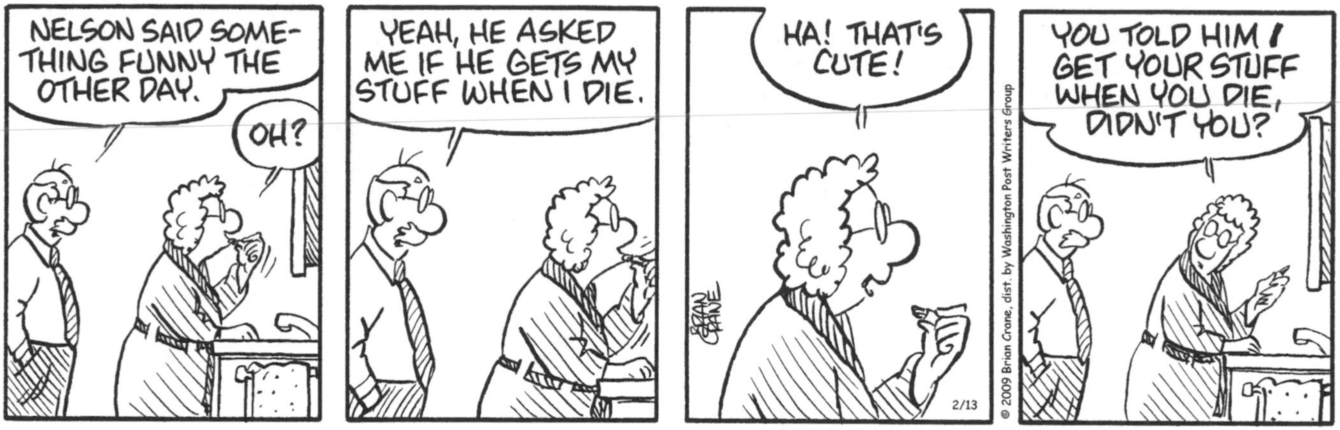
NELSON SAID SOMETHING FUNNY THE OTHER DAY.
OH?
YEAH, HE ASKED ME IF HE GETS MY STUFF WHEN I DIE.
HA! THAT'S CUTE!
BRIAN CRANE
2/13
© 2009 Brian Crane, dist. by Washington Post Writers Group
YOU TOLD HIM I GET YOUR STUFF WHEN YOU DIE, DIDN'T YOU?

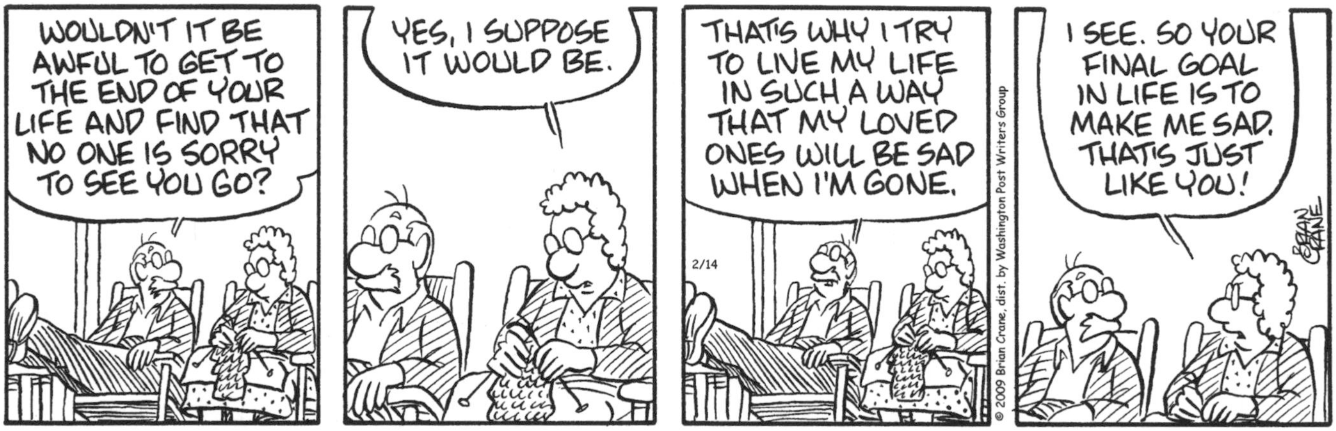
WOULDN'T IT BE AWFUL TO GET TO THE END OF YOUR LIFE AND FIND THAT NO ONE IS SORRY TO SEE YOU GO?
YES, I SUPPOSE IT WOULD BE.
THAT'S WHY I TRY TO LIVE MY LIFE IN SUCH A WAY THAT MY LOVED ONES WILL BE SAD WHEN I'M GONE.
2/14
© 2009 Brian Crane, dist. by Washington Post Writers Group
I SEE. SO YOUR FINAL GOAL IN LIFE IS TO MAKE ME SAD. THAT'S JUST LIKE YOU!
BRIAN CRANE

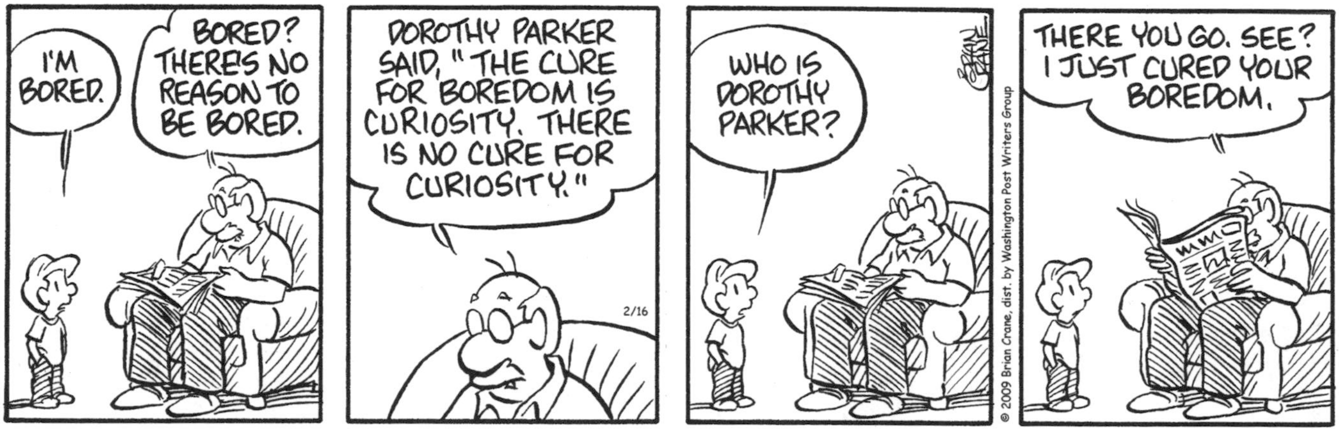
I'M BORED.
BORED? THERE'S NO REASON TO BE BORED.
2/16
DOROTHY PARKER SAID, "THE CURE FOR BOREDOM IS CURIOSITY. THERE IS NO CURE FOR CURIOSITY."
WHO IS DOROTHY PARKER?
BRIAN CRANE
© 2009 Brian Crane, dist. by Washington Post Writers Group
THERE YOU GO. SEE? I JUST CURED YOUR BOREDOM.

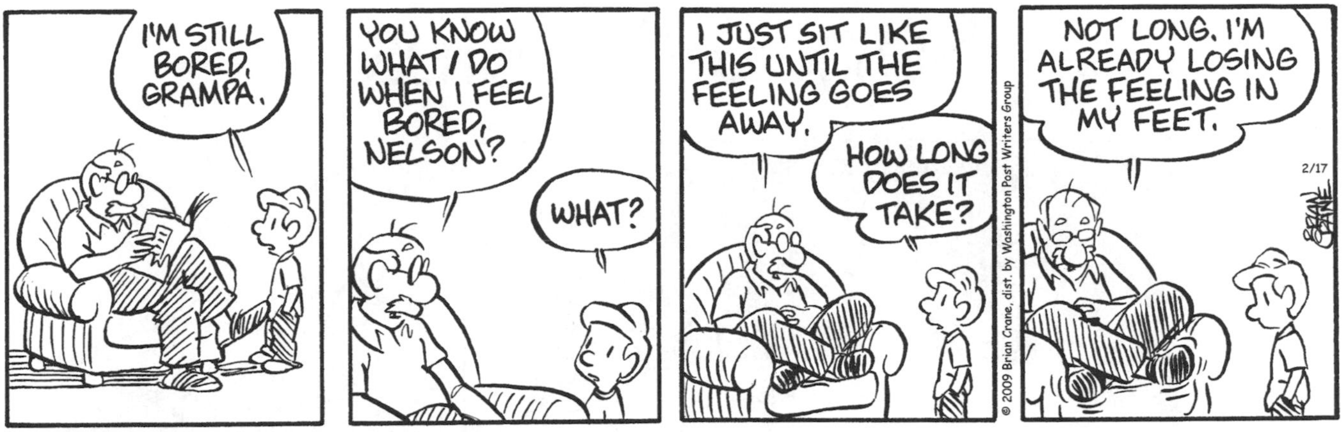
I'M STILL BORED, GRAMPA.
YOU KNOW WHAT I DO WHEN I FEEL BORED, NELSON?
WHAT?
I JUST SIT LIKE THIS UNTIL THE FEELING GOES AWAY.
HOW LONG DOES IT TAKE?
NOT LONG. I'M ALREADY LOSING THE FEELING IN MY FEET.
2/17
© 2009 Brian Crane, dist. by Washington Post Writers Group

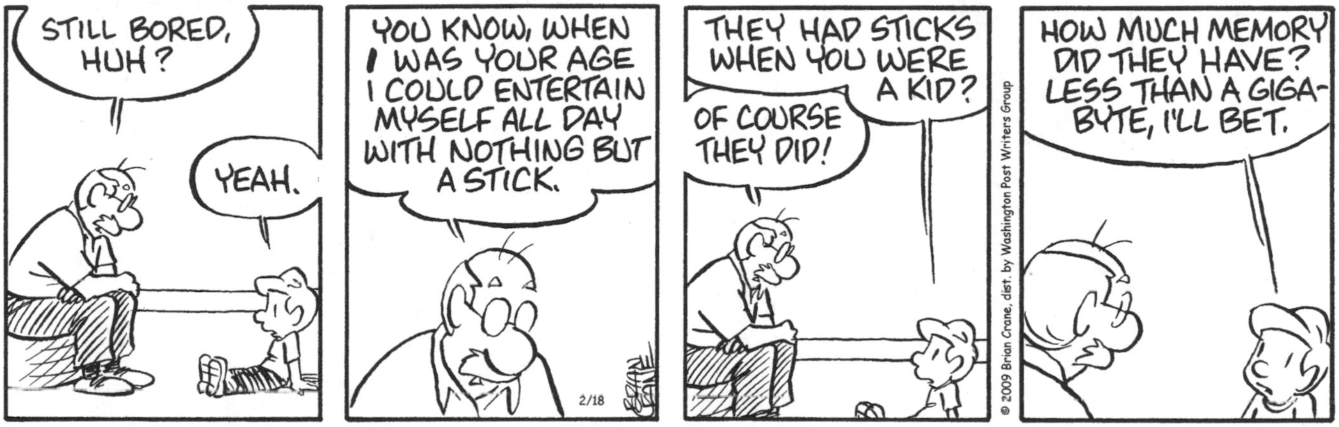
STILL BORED, HUH?
YEAH.
YOU KNOW, WHEN I WAS YOUR AGE I COULD ENTERTAIN MYSELF ALL DAY WITH NOTHING BUT A STICK.
2/18
THEY HAD STICKS WHEN YOU WERE A KID?
OF COURSE THEY DID!
HOW MUCH MEMORY DID THEY HAVE? LESS THAN A GIGA-BYTE, I'LL BET.
© 2009 Brian Crane, dist. by Washington Post Writers Group

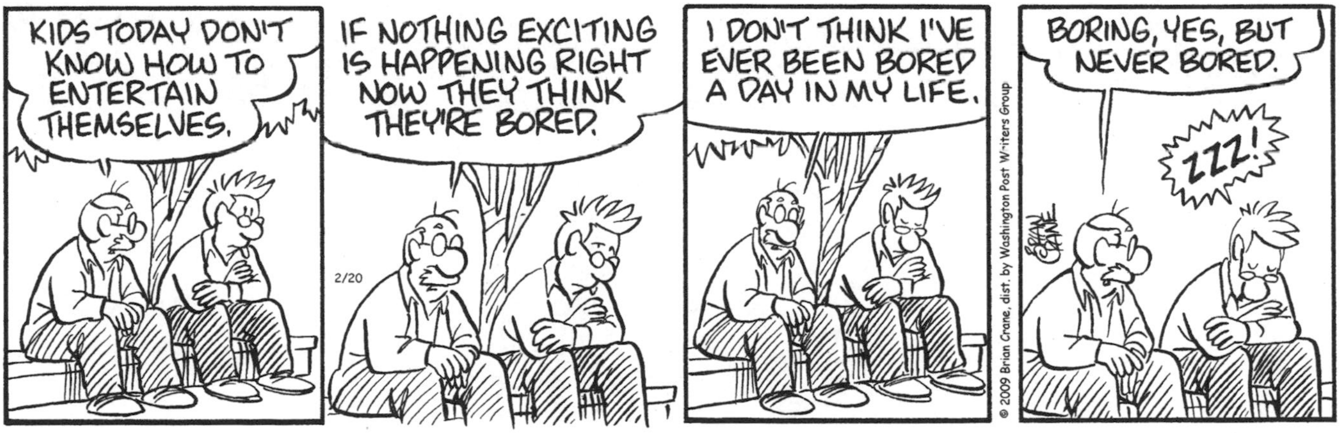
KIDS TODAY DON'T KNOW HOW TO ENTERTAIN THEMSELVES.
IF NOTHING EXCITING IS HAPPENING RIGHT NOW THEY THINK THEY'RE BORED.
2/20
I DON'T THINK I'VE EVER BEEN BORED A DAY IN MY LIFE.
BORING, YES, BUT NEVER BORED.
ZZZ!
© 2009 Brian Crane, dist. by Washington Post Writers Group

Sunday Pickles

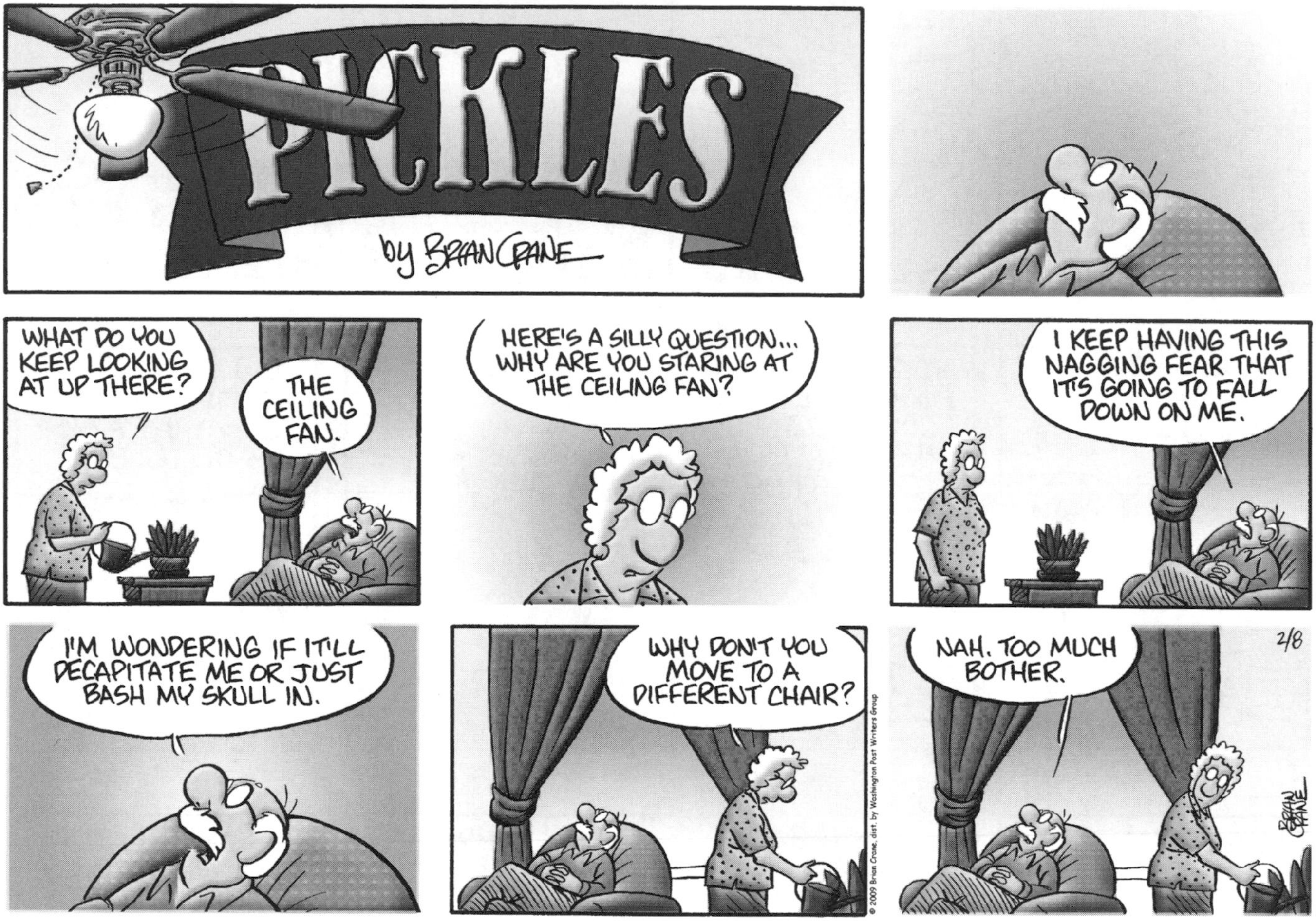
PICKLES
by BRIAN CRANE
WHAT DO YOU KEEP LOOKING AT UP THERE?
THE CEILING FAN.
HERE'S A SILLY QUESTION... WHY ARE YOU STARING AT THE CEILING FAN?
I KEEP HAVING THIS NAGGING FEAR THAT IT'S GOING TO FALL DOWN ON ME.
I'M WONDERING IF IT'LL DECAPITATE ME OR JUST BASH MY SKULL IN.
WHY DON'T YOU MOVE TO A DIFFERENT CHAIR?
NAH. TOO MUCH BOTHER.
2/8
BRIAN CRANE
© 2009 Brian Crane, dist. by Washington Post Writers Group

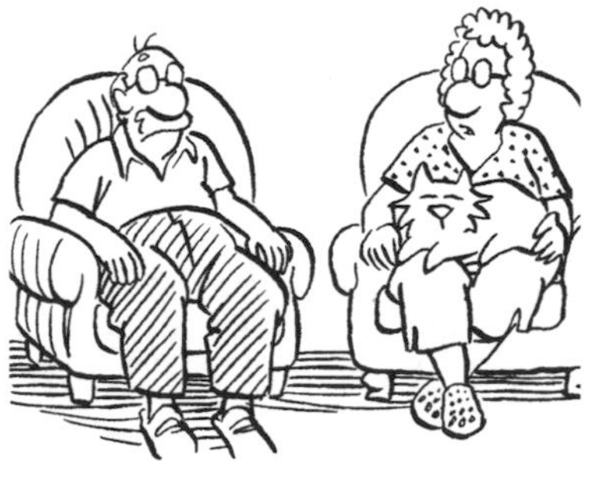

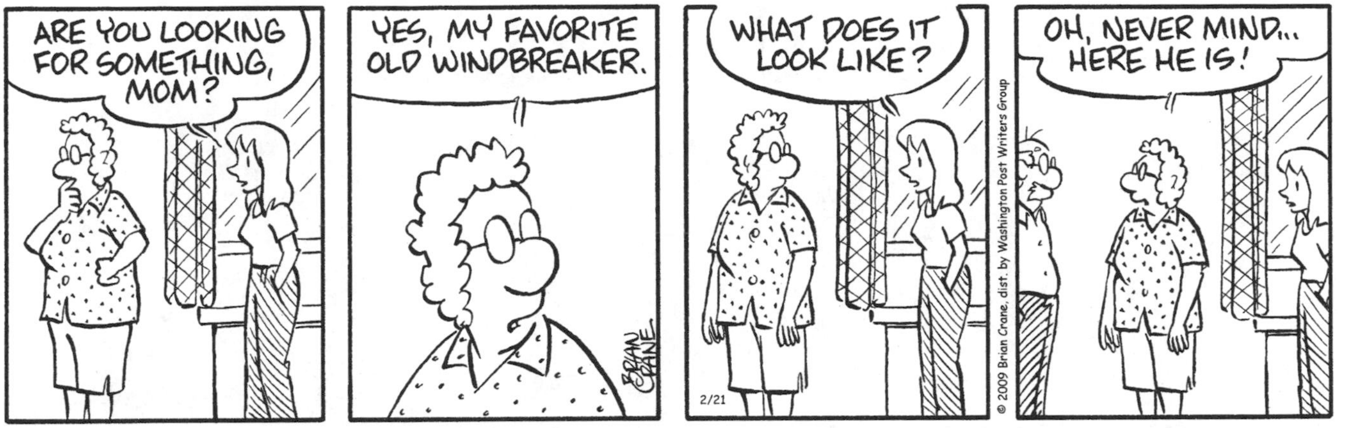

ARE YOU LOOKING FOR SOMETHING, MOM?
YES, MY FAVORITE OLD WINDBREAKER.
BRIAN CRANE
2/21
WHAT DOES IT LOOK LIKE?
© 2009 Brian Crane, dist. by Washington Post Writers Group
OH, NEVER MIND... HERE HE IS!

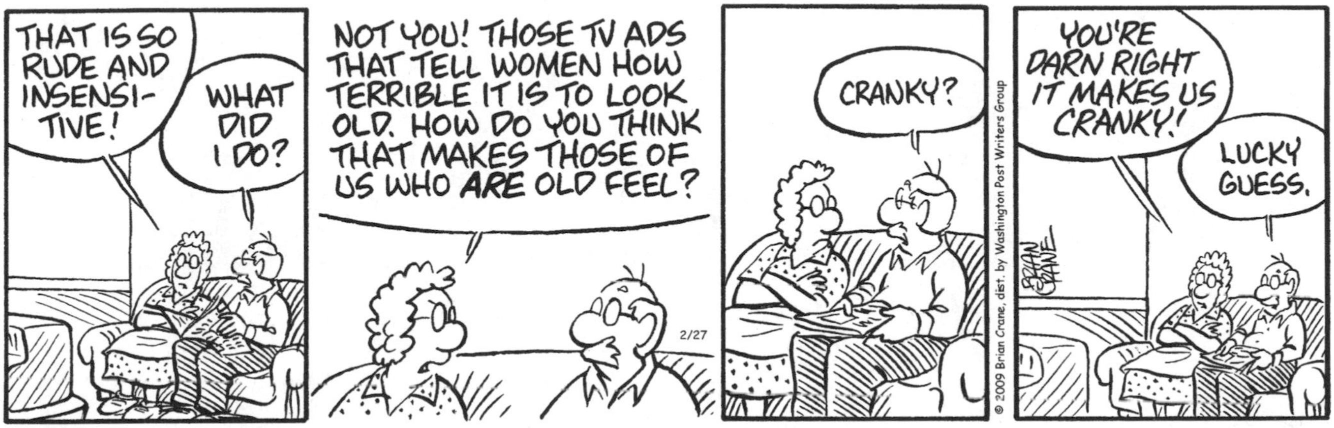

THAT IS SO RUDE AND INSENSI-TIVE!
WHAT DID I DO?
NOT YOU! THOSE TV ADS THAT TELL WOMEN HOW TERRIBLE IT IS TO LOOK OLD. HOW DO YOU THINK THAT MAKES THOSE OF US WHO ARE OLD FEEL?
2/27
CRANKY?
© 2009 Brian Crane, dist. by Washington Post Writers Group
YOU'RE DARN RIGHT IT MAKES US CRANKY!
LUCKY GUESS.
BRIAN CRANE

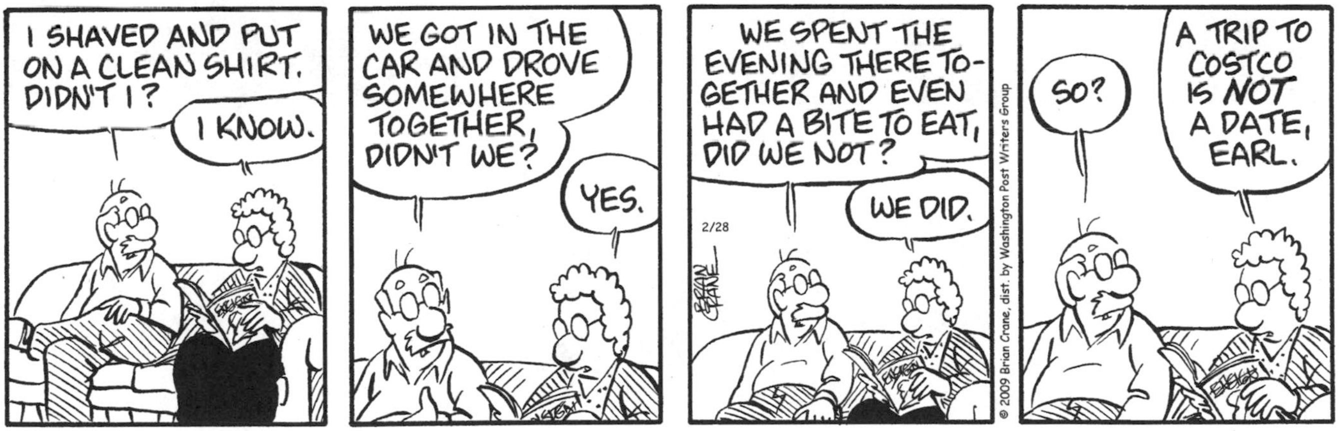

I SHAVED AND PUT ON A CLEAN SHIRT. DIDN'T I?
I KNOW.
WE GOT IN THE CAR AND DROVE SOMEWHERE TOGETHER, DIDN'T WE?
YES.
WE SPENT THE EVENING THERE TO-GETHER AND EVEN HAD A BITE TO EAT, DID WE NOT?
WE DID.
2/28
BRIAN CRANE
© 2009 Brian Crane, dist. by Washington Post Writers Group
SO?
A TRIP TO COSTCO IS NOT A DATE, EARL.

Sunday Pickles

GORGLE!
PICKLES
by BRIAN CRANE
GLURPLE!
EARL! ARE YOU GOING TO UNPLUG THE SINK OR NOT?!
GLORP!
I'VE ASKED YOU THREE TIMES ALREADY!
OKAY. JUST A SEC.
THAT'S WHAT YOU SAID LAST TIME! I'M TIRED OF WAITING FOR SECS!
I SPEND HALF MY TIME WAITING FOR SECS! I DON'T WANT TO HEAR ANY MORE ABOUT SECS!
© 2009 Brian Crane, dist. by Washington Post Writers Group
BRIAN CRANE 3/15
WHAT ON EARTH ARE YOU LAUGHING ABOUT?

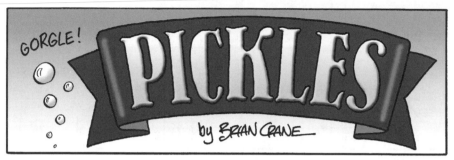

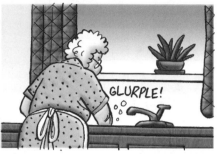

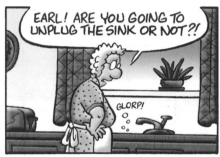

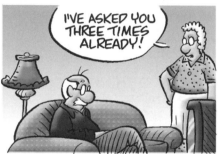

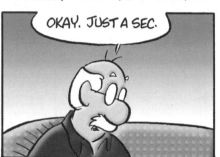

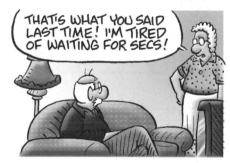

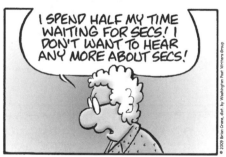

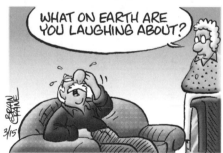

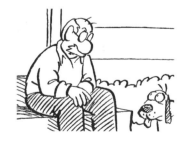

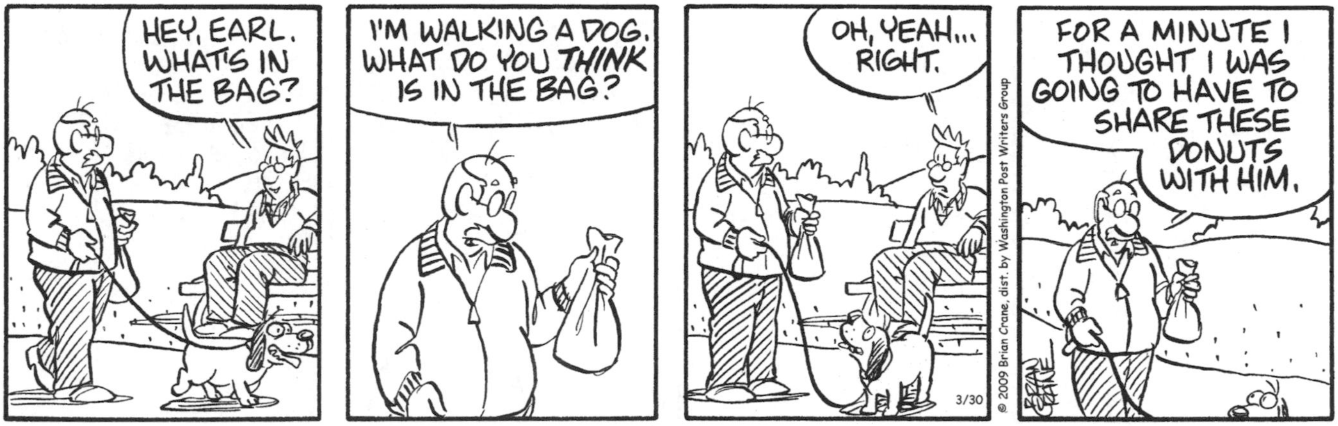
HEY, EARL. WHAT'S IN THE BAG?
I'M WALKING A DOG. WHAT DO YOU *THINK* IS IN THE BAG?
OH, YEAH... RIGHT.
FOR A MINUTE I THOUGHT I WAS GOING TO HAVE TO SHARE THESE DONUTS WITH HIM.
3/30
© 2009 Brian Crane, dist. by Washington Post Writers Group

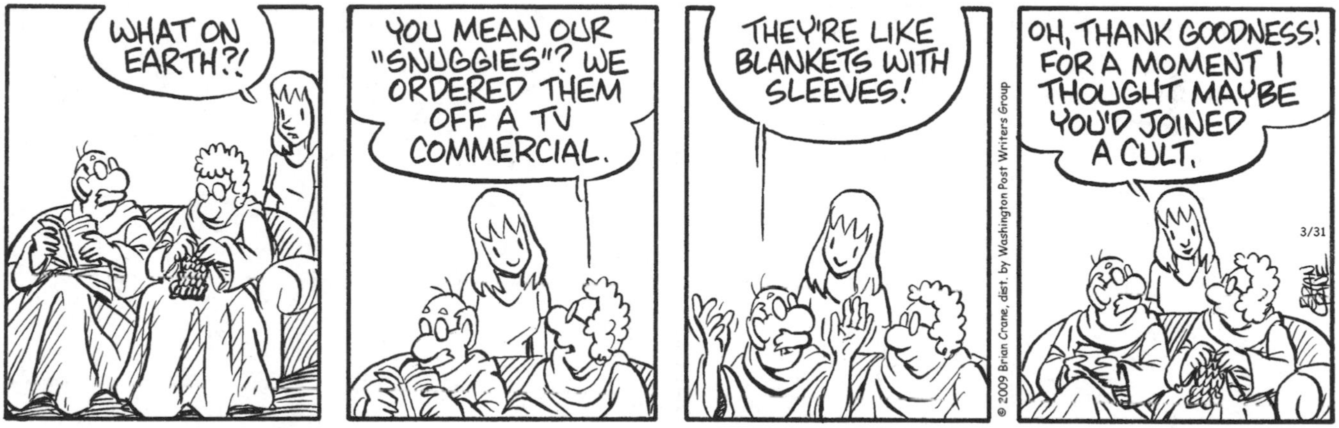
WHAT ON EARTH?!
YOU MEAN OUR "SNUGGIES"? WE ORDERED THEM OFF A TV COMMERCIAL.
THEY'RE LIKE BLANKETS WITH SLEEVES!
OH, THANK GOODNESS! FOR A MOMENT I THOUGHT MAYBE YOU'D JOINED A CULT.
3/31
© 2009 Brian Crane, dist. by Washington Post Writers Group

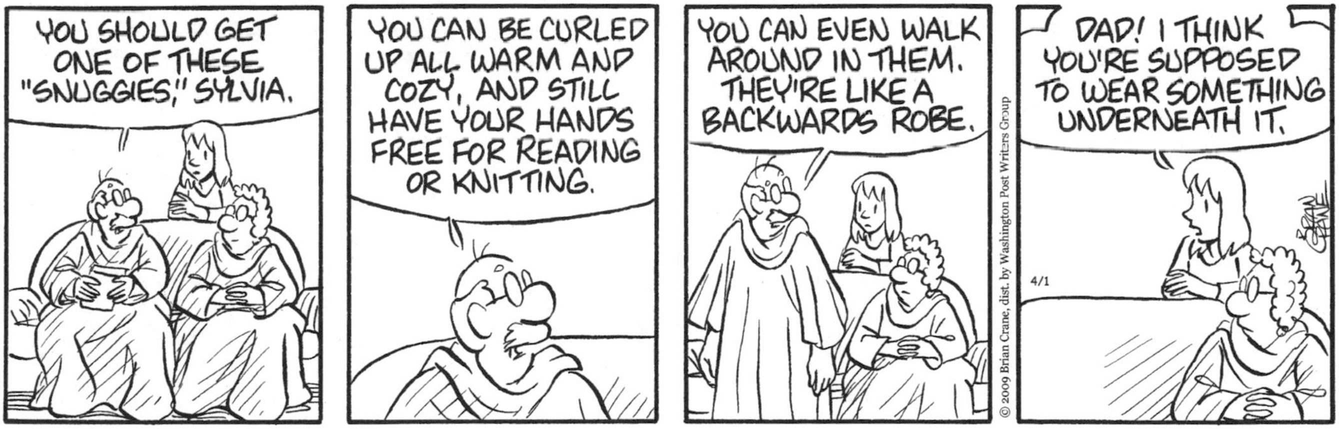
YOU SHOULD GET ONE OF THESE "SNUGGIES," SYLVIA.
YOU CAN BE CURLED UP ALL WARM AND COZY, AND STILL HAVE YOUR HANDS FREE FOR READING OR KNITTING.
YOU CAN EVEN WALK AROUND IN THEM. THEY'RE LIKE A BACKWARDS ROBE.
DAD! I THINK YOU'RE SUPPOSED TO WEAR SOMETHING UNDERNEATH IT.
4/1
© 2009 Brian Crane, dist. by Washington Post Writers Group

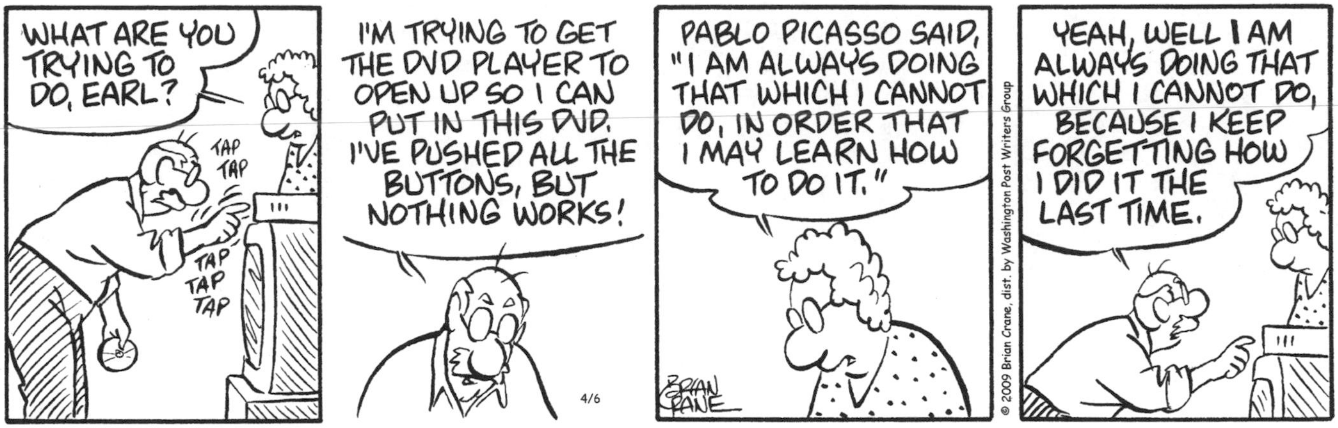
WHAT ARE YOU TRYING TO DO, EARL?
TAP TAP
TAP TAP TAP
I'M TRYING TO GET THE DVD PLAYER TO OPEN UP SO I CAN PUT IN THIS DVD. I'VE PUSHED ALL THE BUTTONS, BUT NOTHING WORKS!
4/6
PABLO PICASSO SAID, "I AM ALWAYS DOING THAT WHICH I CANNOT DO, IN ORDER THAT I MAY LEARN HOW TO DO IT."
BRIAN CRANE
YEAH, WELL I AM ALWAYS DOING THAT WHICH I CANNOT DO, BECAUSE I KEEP FORGETTING HOW I DID IT THE LAST TIME.
© 2009 Brian Crane, dist. by Washington Post Writers Group

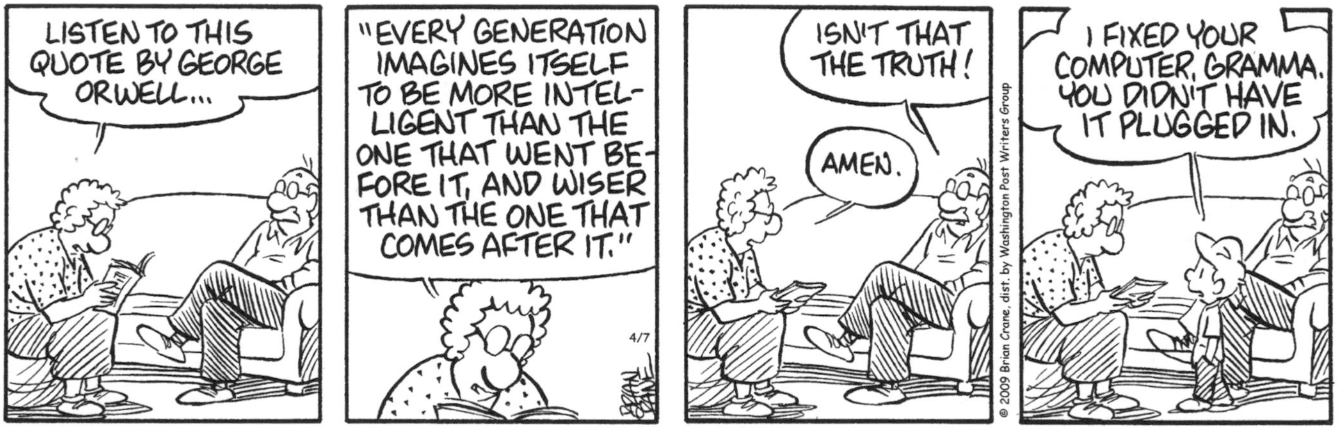
LISTEN TO THIS QUOTE BY GEORGE ORWELL...
"EVERY GENERATION IMAGINES ITSELF TO BE MORE INTEL-LIGENT THAN THE ONE THAT WENT BE-FORE IT, AND WISER THAN THE ONE THAT COMES AFTER IT."
4/7
ISN'T THAT THE TRUTH!
AMEN.
© 2009 Brian Crane, dist. by Washington Post Writers Group
I FIXED YOUR COMPUTER, GRAMMA. YOU DIDN'T HAVE IT PLUGGED IN.

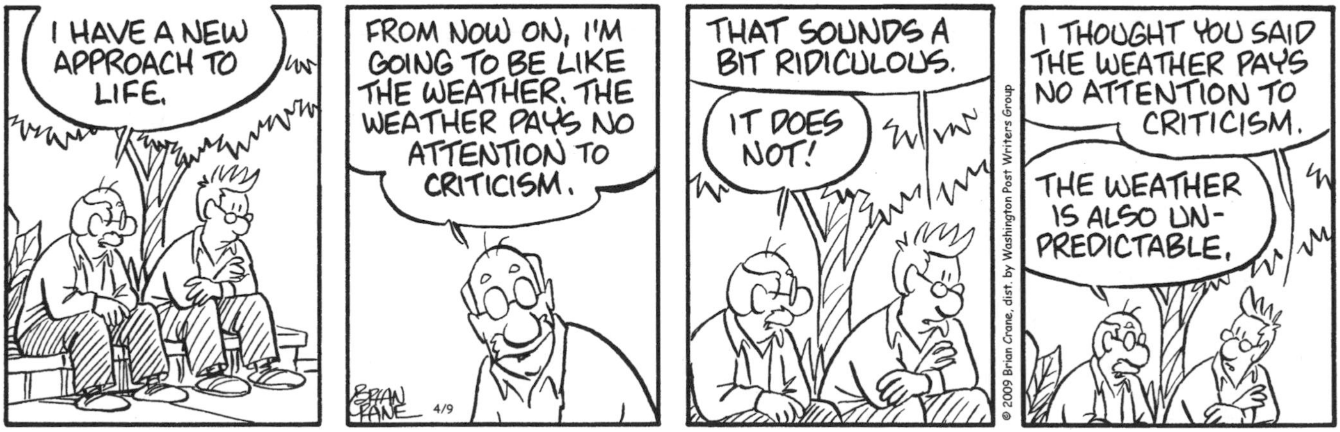
I HAVE A NEW APPROACH TO LIFE.
FROM NOW ON, I'M GOING TO BE LIKE THE WEATHER. THE WEATHER PAYS NO ATTENTION TO CRITICISM.
BRIAN CRANE
4/9
THAT SOUNDS A BIT RIDICULOUS.
IT DOES NOT!
© 2009 Brian Crane, dist. by Washington Post Writers Group
I THOUGHT YOU SAID THE WEATHER PAYS NO ATTENTION TO CRITICISM.
THE WEATHER IS ALSO UN-PREDICTABLE.

SundayPickles

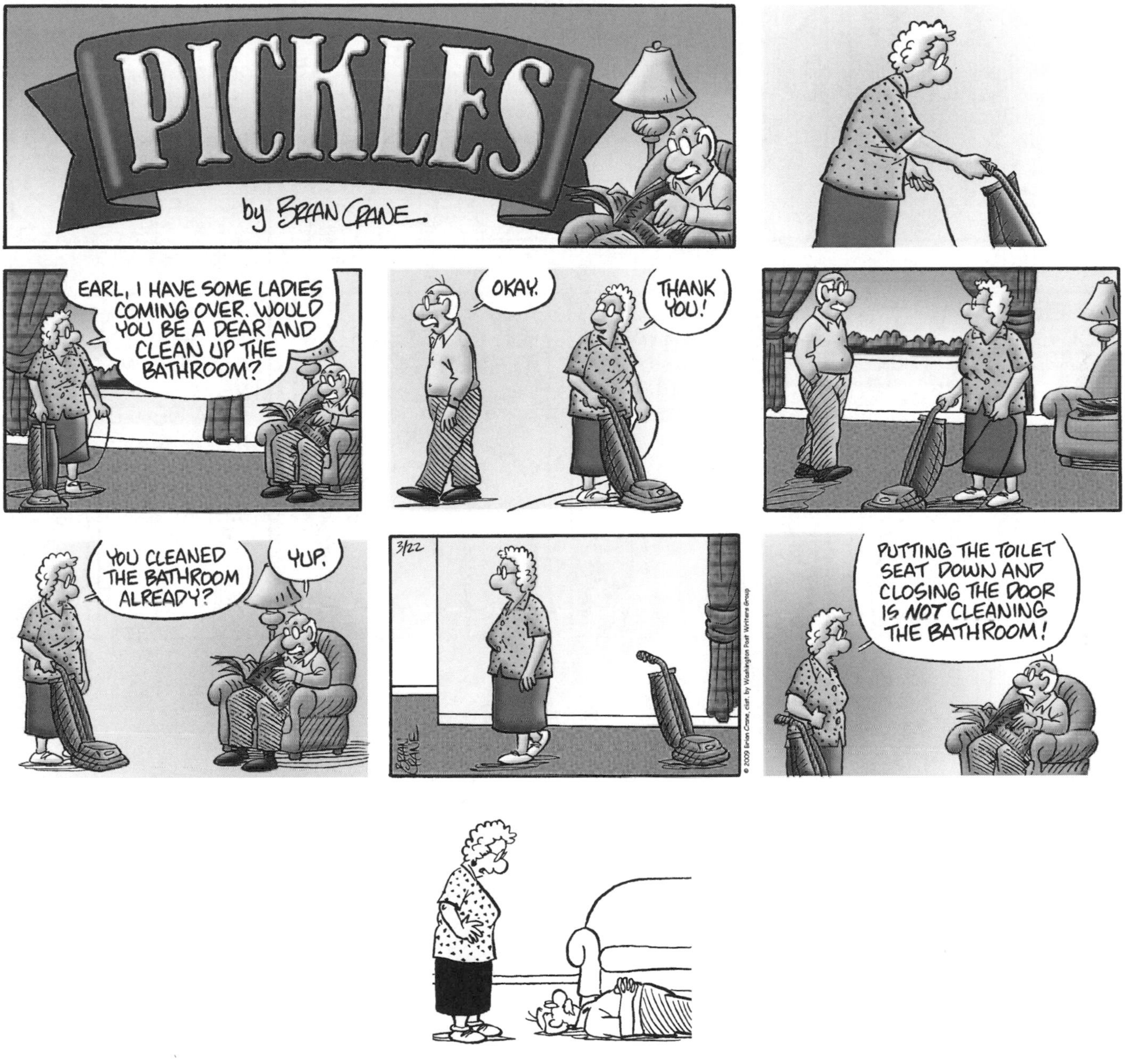
PICKLES
by BRIAN CRANE
EARL, I HAVE SOME LADIES COMING OVER. WOULD YOU BE A DEAR AND CLEAN UP THE BATHROOM?
OKAY.
THANK YOU!
YOU CLEANED THE BATHROOM ALREADY?
YUP.
3/22
© 2009 Brian Crane, dist. by Washington Post Writers Group
PUTTING THE TOILET SEAT DOWN AND CLOSING THE DOOR IS NOT CLEANING THE BATHROOM!

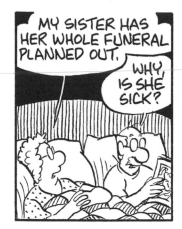

MY SISTER HAS HER WHOLE FUNERAL PLANNED OUT.
WHY, IS SHE SICK?
NO, SHE'S JUST NOT A SPONTANEOUS PERSON. SHE LIKES TO PLAN THINGS IN ADVANCE.
4/10
BRIAN CRANE
HAVE YOU EVER THOUGHT WHAT KIND OF FUNERAL YOU WANT WHEN THE TIME COMES?
© 2009 Brian Crane, dist. by Washington Post Writers Group
I DON'T WANT A LONG ONE. IF IT GOES OVER AN HOUR I'M GOING TO GET UP AND WALK OUT.

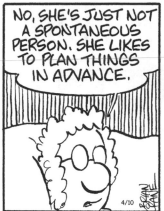

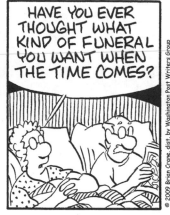

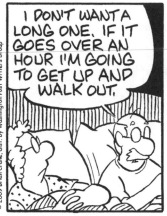

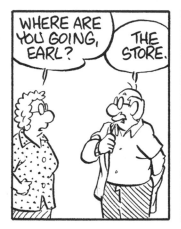

WHERE ARE YOU GOING, EARL?
THE STORE.
WHAT FOR?
I'M LOOKING FOR A PAIR OF SUNGLASSES I LOST.
ZIP!
AND YOU THINK YOU LOST THEM AT THE STORE?
NO.
4/13
© 2009 Brian Crane, dist. by Washington Post Writers Group
BUT I'VE FOUND THAT THE BEST WAY TO LOCATE SOMETHING I'VE LOST IS TO BUY A NEW ONE.
BRIAN CRANE

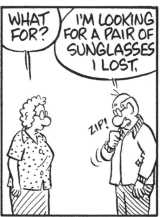

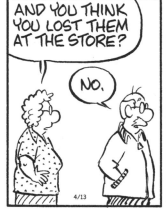

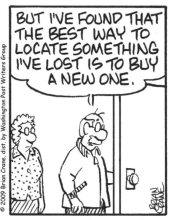

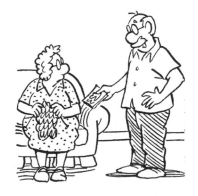

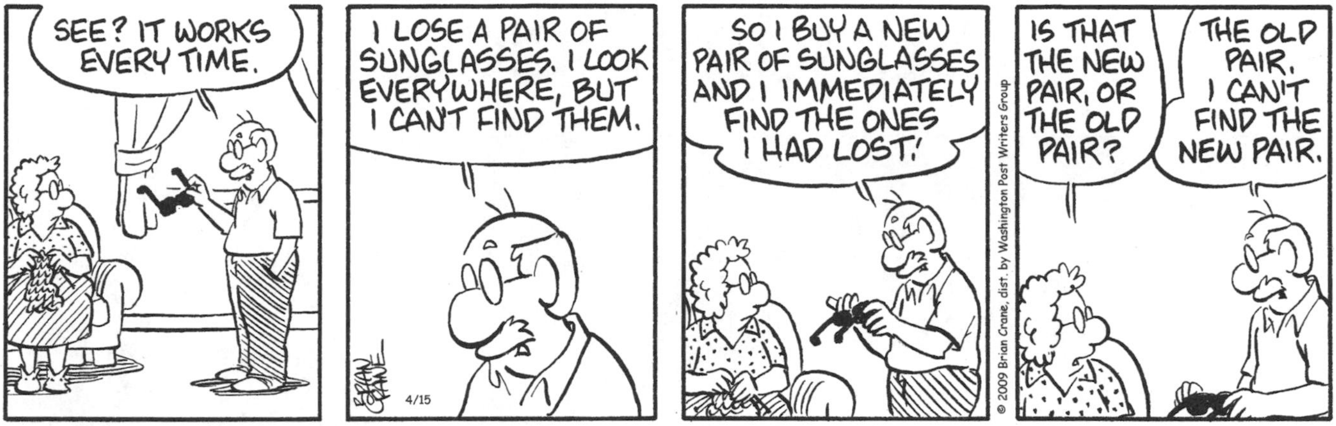
SEE? IT WORKS EVERY TIME.
I LOSE A PAIR OF SUNGLASSES. I LOOK EVERYWHERE, BUT I CAN'T FIND THEM.
4/15
SO I BUY A NEW PAIR OF SUNGLASSES AND I IMMEDIATELY FIND THE ONES I HAD LOST!
IS THAT THE NEW PAIR, OR THE OLD PAIR?
THE OLD PAIR. I CAN'T FIND THE NEW PAIR.
© 2009 Brian Crane, dist. by Washington Post Writers Group

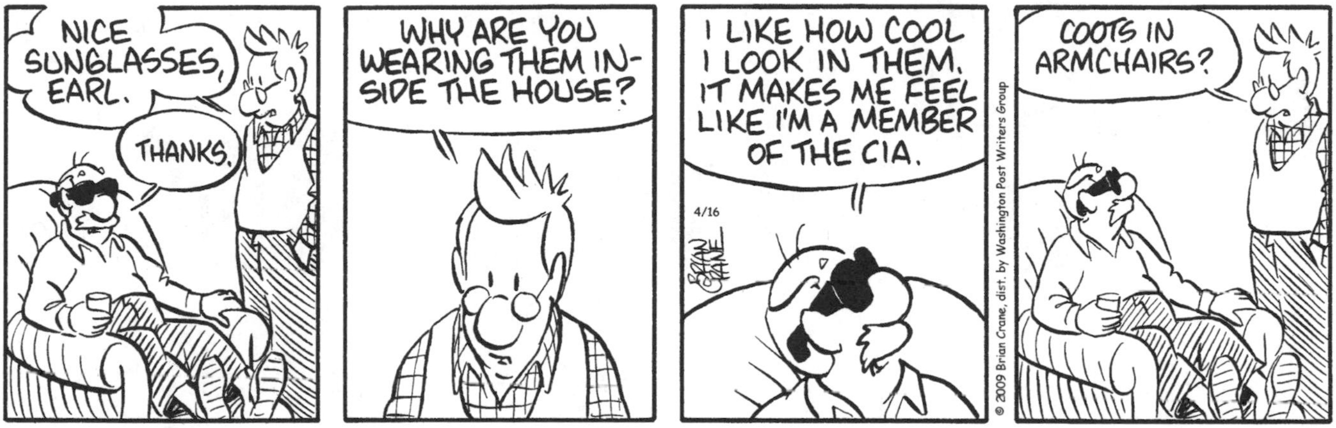
NICE SUNGLASSES, EARL.
THANKS.
WHY ARE YOU WEARING THEM INSIDE THE HOUSE?
I LIKE HOW COOL I LOOK IN THEM. IT MAKES ME FEEL LIKE I'M A MEMBER OF THE CIA.
4/16
COOTS IN ARMCHAIRS?
© 2009 Brian Crane, dist. by Washington Post Writers Group

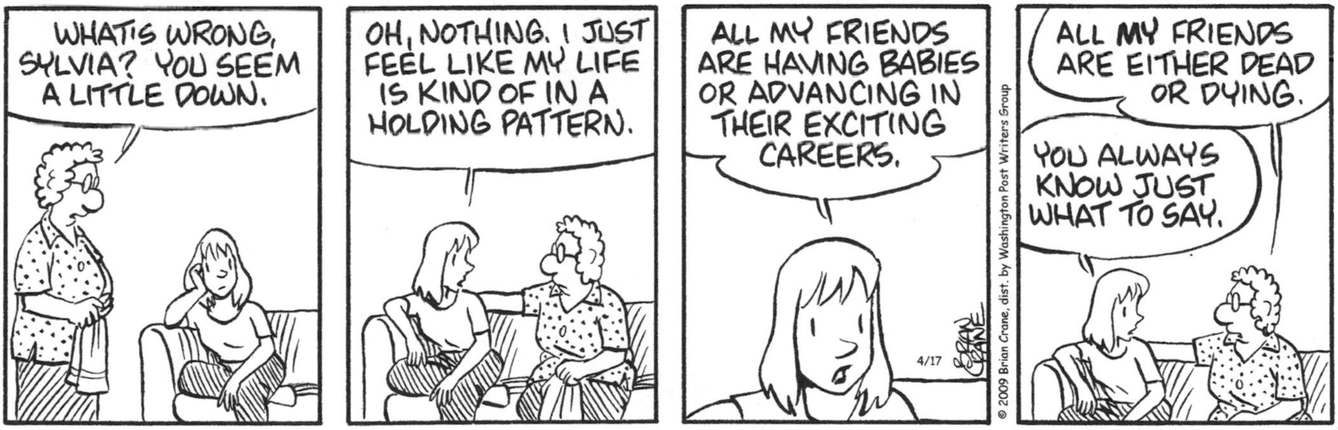
WHAT'S WRONG, SYLVIA? YOU SEEM A LITTLE DOWN.
OH, NOTHING. I JUST FEEL LIKE MY LIFE IS KIND OF IN A HOLDING PATTERN.
ALL MY FRIENDS ARE HAVING BABIES OR ADVANCING IN THEIR EXCITING CAREERS.
4/17
ALL MY FRIENDS ARE EITHER DEAD OR DYING.
YOU ALWAYS KNOW JUST WHAT TO SAY.
© 2009 Brian Crane, dist. by Washington Post Writers Group

SundayPickles

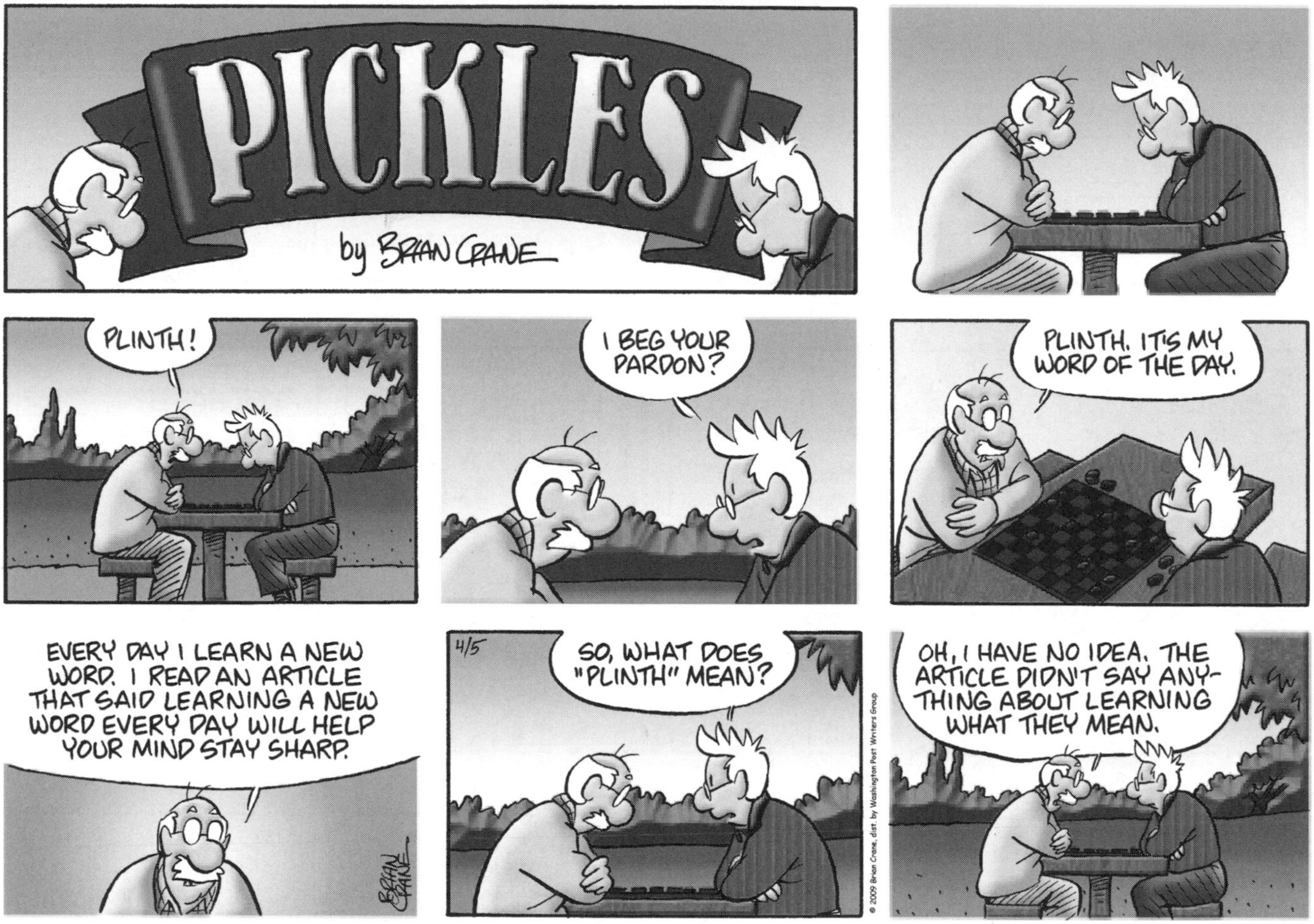
PICKLES
by BRIAN CRANE
PLINTH!
I BEG YOUR PARDON?
PLINTH. IT'S MY WORD OF THE DAY.
EVERY DAY I LEARN A NEW WORD. I READ AN ARTICLE THAT SAID LEARNING A NEW WORD EVERY DAY WILL HELP YOUR MIND STAY SHARP.
4/5
SO, WHAT DOES "PLINTH" MEAN?
© 2009 Brian Crane, dist. by Washington Post Writers Group
OH, I HAVE NO IDEA. THE ARTICLE DIDN'T SAY ANY-THING ABOUT LEARNING WHAT THEY MEAN.

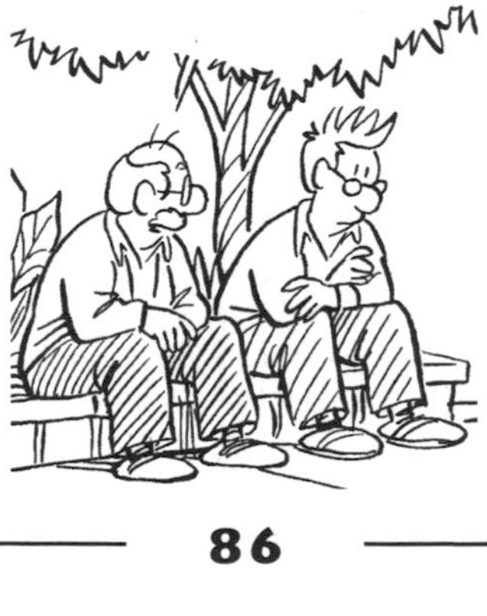

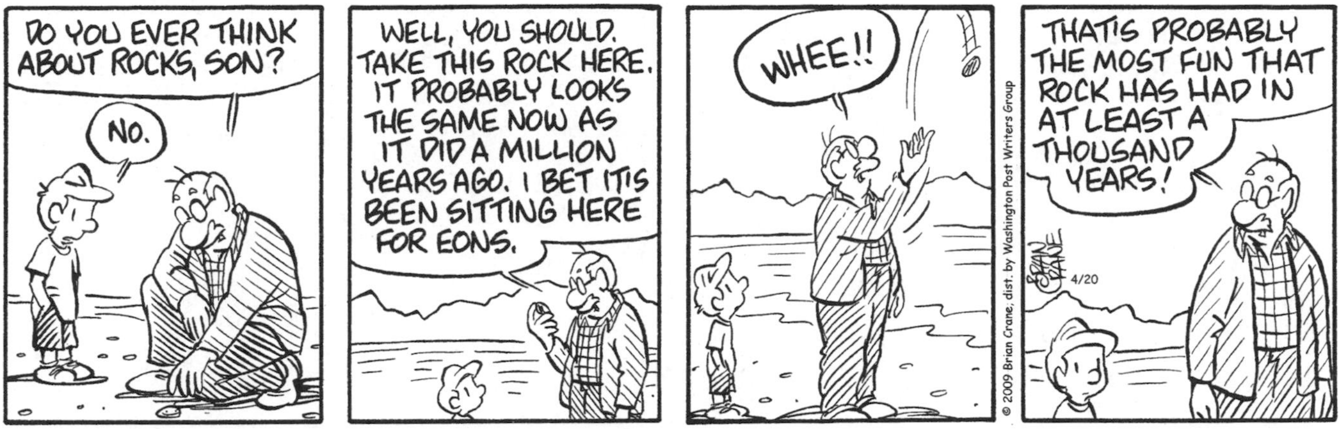
DO YOU EVER THINK ABOUT ROCKS, SON?
NO.
WELL, YOU SHOULD. TAKE THIS ROCK HERE. IT PROBABLY LOOKS THE SAME NOW AS IT DID A MILLION YEARS AGO. I BET IT'S BEEN SITTING HERE FOR EONS.
WHEE!!
THAT'S PROBABLY THE MOST FUN THAT ROCK HAS HAD IN AT LEAST A THOUSAND YEARS!
BRIAN CRANE
4/20
© 2009 Brian Crane, dist. by Washington Post Writers Group

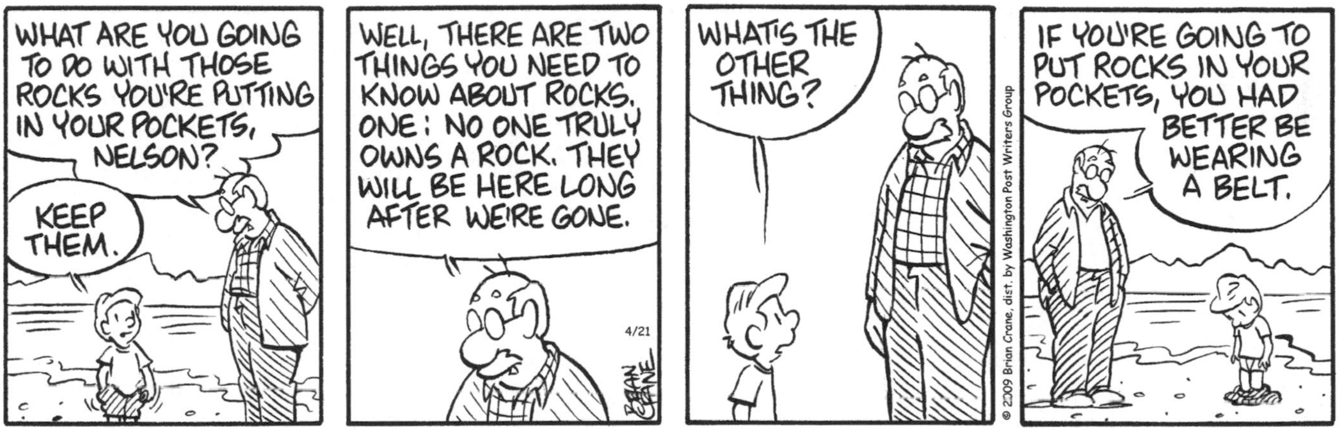
WHAT ARE YOU GOING TO DO WITH THOSE ROCKS YOU'RE PUTTING IN YOUR POCKETS, NELSON?
KEEP THEM.
WELL, THERE ARE TWO THINGS YOU NEED TO KNOW ABOUT ROCKS. ONE: NO ONE TRULY OWNS A ROCK. THEY WILL BE HERE LONG AFTER WE'RE GONE.
4/21
BRIAN CRANE
WHAT'S THE OTHER THING?
IF YOU'RE GOING TO PUT ROCKS IN YOUR POCKETS, YOU HAD BETTER BE WEARING A BELT.
© 2009 Brian Crane, dist. by Washington Post Writers Group

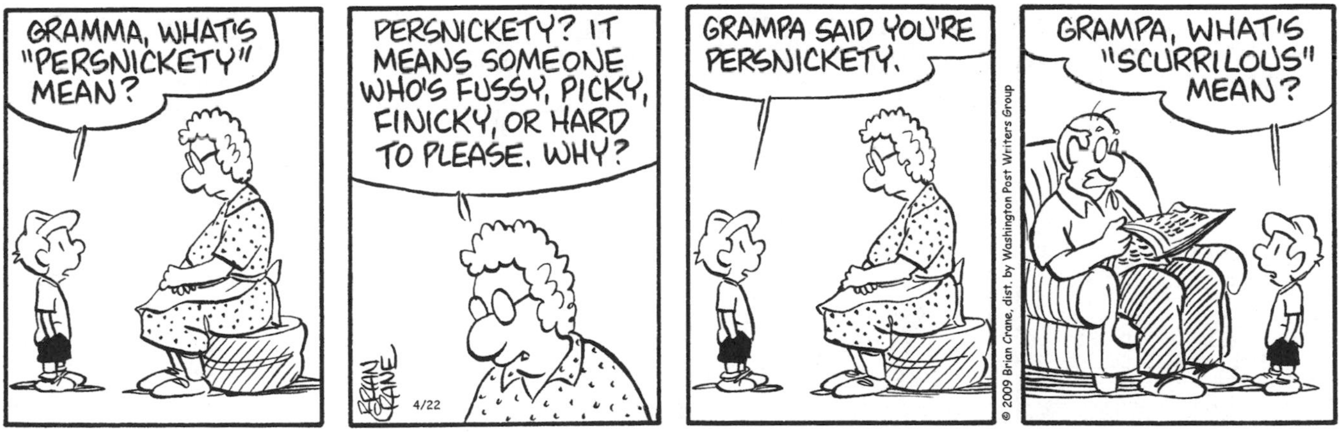
GRAMMA, WHAT'S "PERSNICKETY" MEAN?
PERSNICKETY? IT MEANS SOMEONE WHO'S FUSSY, PICKY, FINICKY, OR HARD TO PLEASE. WHY?
BRIAN CRANE
4/22
GRAMPA SAID YOU'RE PERSNICKETY.
GRAMPA, WHAT'S "SCURRILOUS" MEAN?
© 2009 Brian Crane, dist. by Washington Post Writers Group

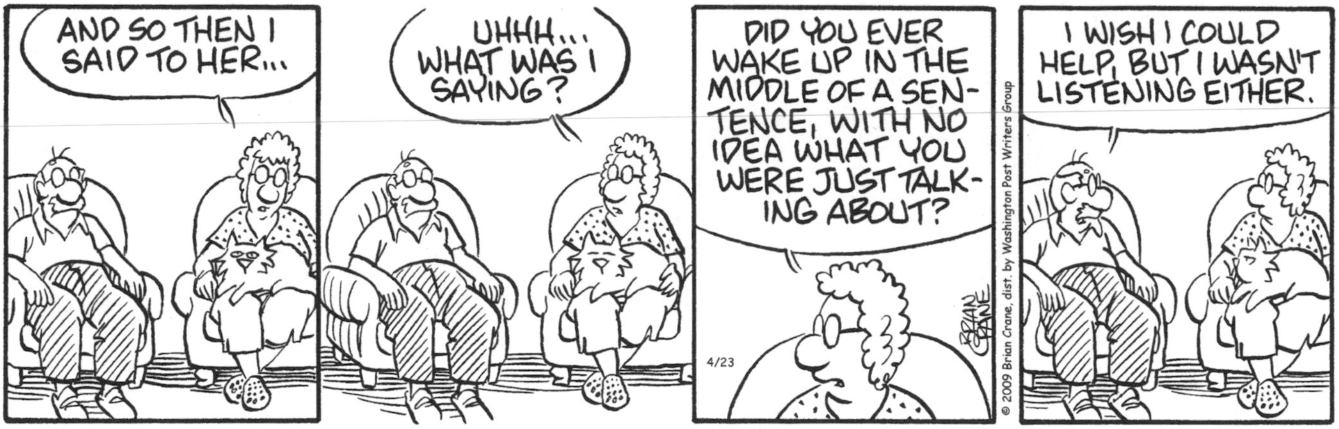
AND SO THEN I SAID TO HER...
UHHH... WHAT WAS I SAYING?
DID YOU EVER WAKE UP IN THE MIDDLE OF A SENTENCE, WITH NO IDEA WHAT YOU WERE JUST TALKING ABOUT?
4/23
© 2009 Brian Crane, dist. by Washington Post Writers Group
I WISH I COULD HELP, BUT I WASN'T LISTENING EITHER.

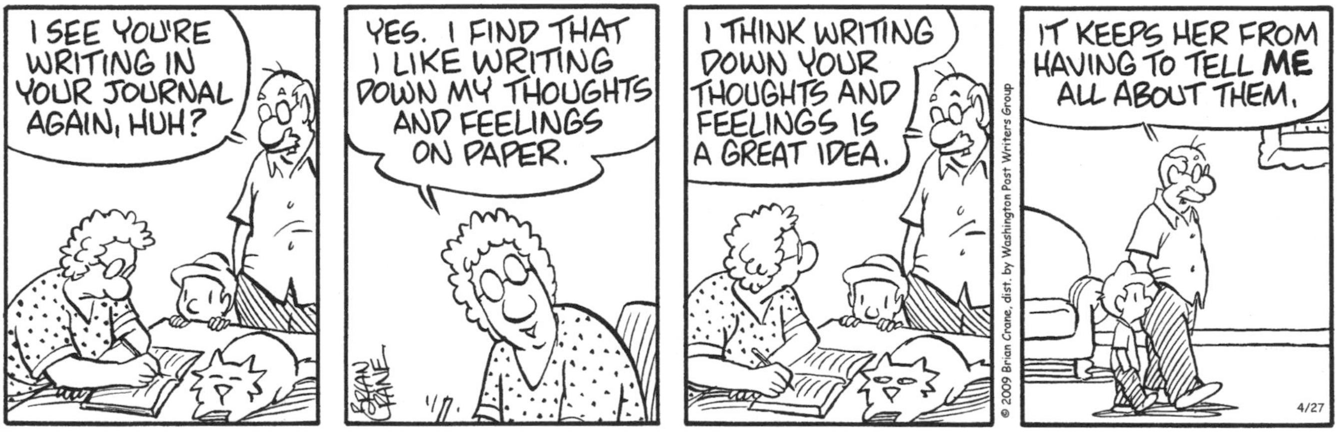
I SEE YOU'RE WRITING IN YOUR JOURNAL AGAIN, HUH?
YES. I FIND THAT I LIKE WRITING DOWN MY THOUGHTS AND FEELINGS ON PAPER.
I THINK WRITING DOWN YOUR THOUGHTS AND FEELINGS IS A GREAT IDEA.
© 2009 Brian Crane, dist. by Washington Post Writers Group
IT KEEPS HER FROM HAVING TO TELL **ME** ALL ABOUT THEM.
4/27

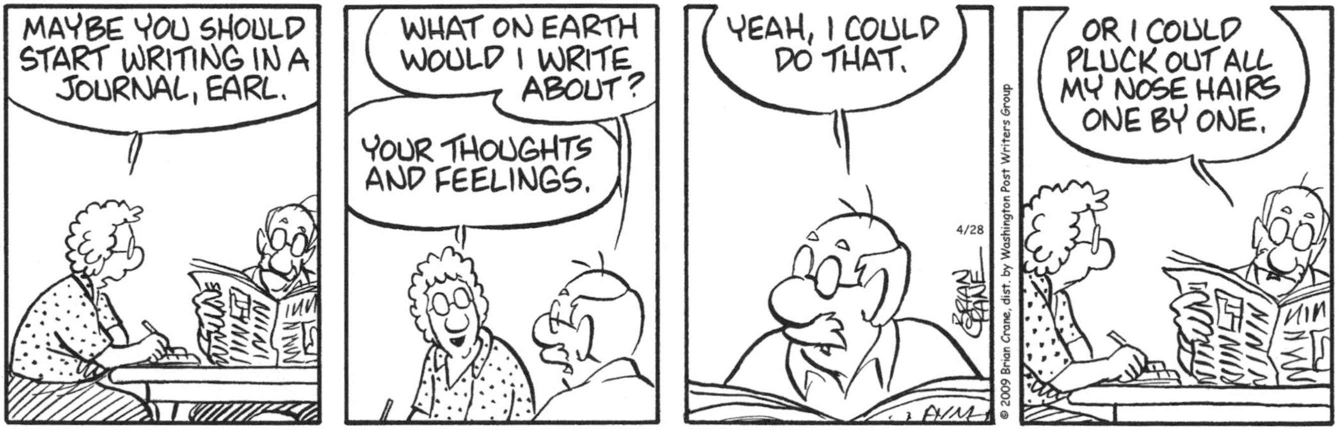
MAYBE YOU SHOULD START WRITING IN A JOURNAL, EARL.
WHAT ON EARTH WOULD I WRITE ABOUT?
YOUR THOUGHTS AND FEELINGS.
YEAH, I COULD DO THAT.
4/28
© 2009 Brian Crane, dist. by Washington Post Writers Group
OR I COULD PLUCK OUT ALL MY NOSE HAIRS ONE BY ONE.

Sunday Pickles

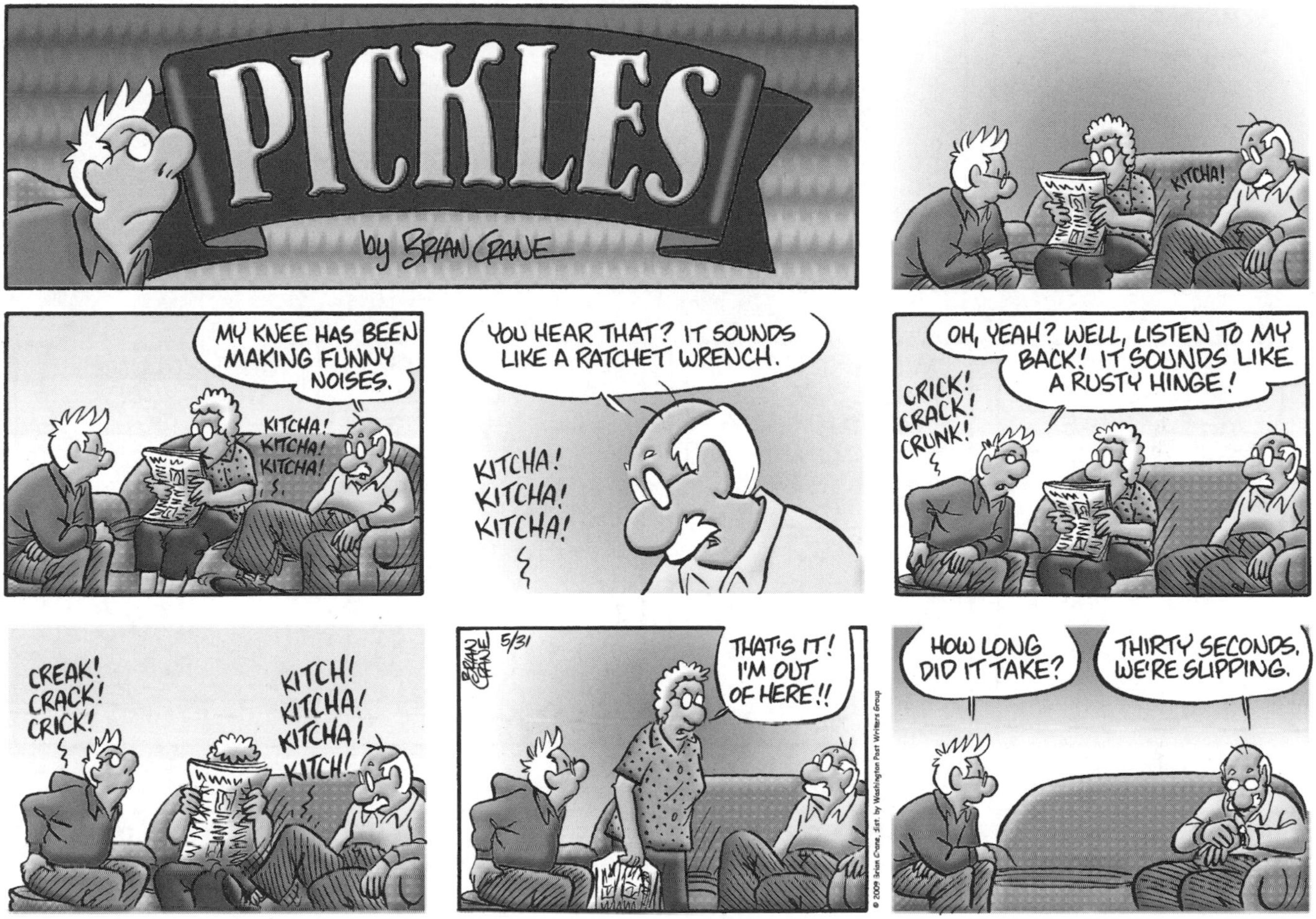
PICKLES
by BRIAN CRANE
KITCHA!
MY KNEE HAS BEEN MAKING FUNNY NOISES.
KITCHA! KITCHA! KITCHA!
YOU HEAR THAT? IT SOUNDS LIKE A RATCHET WRENCH.
KITCHA! KITCHA! KITCHA!
CRICK! CRACK! CRUNK!
OH, YEAH? WELL, LISTEN TO MY BACK! IT SOUNDS LIKE A RUSTY HINGE!
CREAK! CRACK! CRICK!
KITCH! KITCHA! KITCHA! KITCH!
BRIAN CRANE 5/31
THAT'S IT! I'M OUT OF HERE!!
© 2009 Brian Crane, dist. by Washington Post Writers Group
HOW LONG DID IT TAKE?
THIRTY SECONDS. WE'RE SLIPPING.

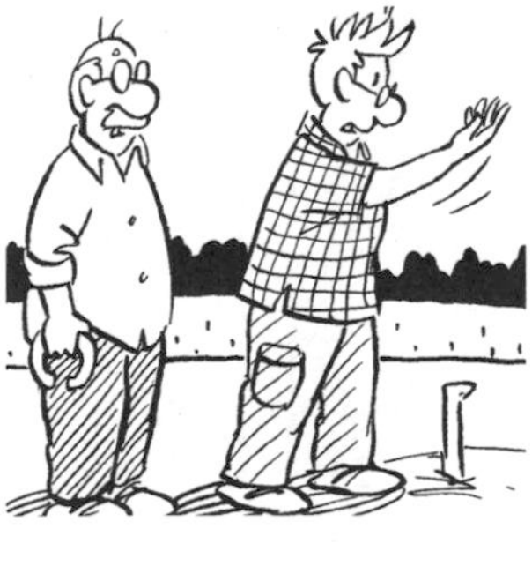

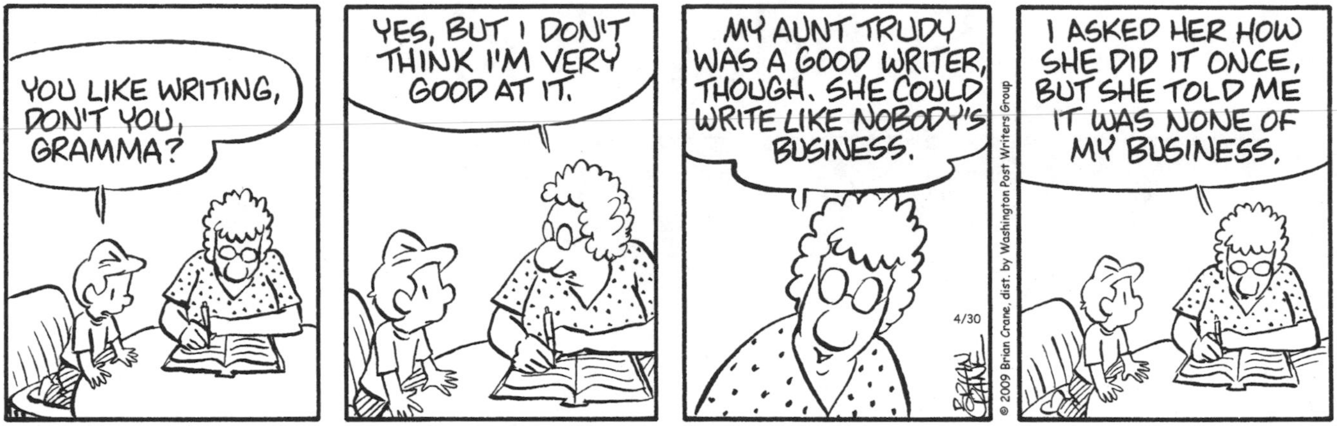
YOU LIKE WRITING, DON'T YOU, GRAMMA?
YES, BUT I DON'T THINK I'M VERY GOOD AT IT.
MY AUNT TRUDY WAS A GOOD WRITER, THOUGH. SHE COULD WRITE LIKE NOBODY'S BUSINESS.
I ASKED HER HOW SHE DID IT ONCE, BUT SHE TOLD ME IT WAS NONE OF MY BUSINESS.
4/30
BRIAN CRANE
© 2009 Brian Crane, dist. by Washington Post Writers Group

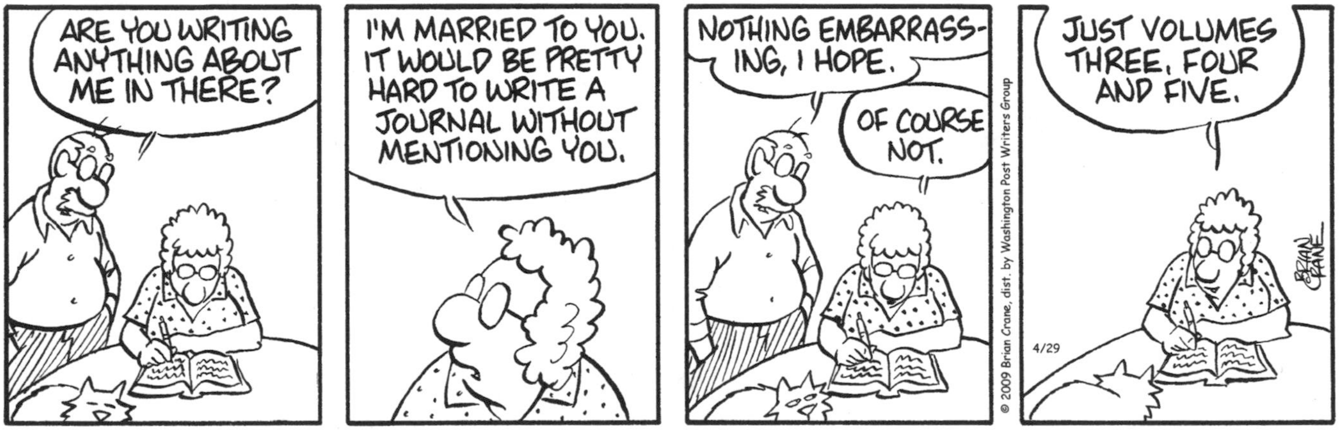
ARE YOU WRITING ANYTHING ABOUT ME IN THERE?
I'M MARRIED TO YOU. IT WOULD BE PRETTY HARD TO WRITE A JOURNAL WITHOUT MENTIONING YOU.
NOTHING EMBARRASS-ING, I HOPE.
OF COURSE NOT.
JUST VOLUMES THREE, FOUR AND FIVE.
BRIAN CRANE
4/29
© 2009 Brian Crane, dist. by Washington Post Writers Group

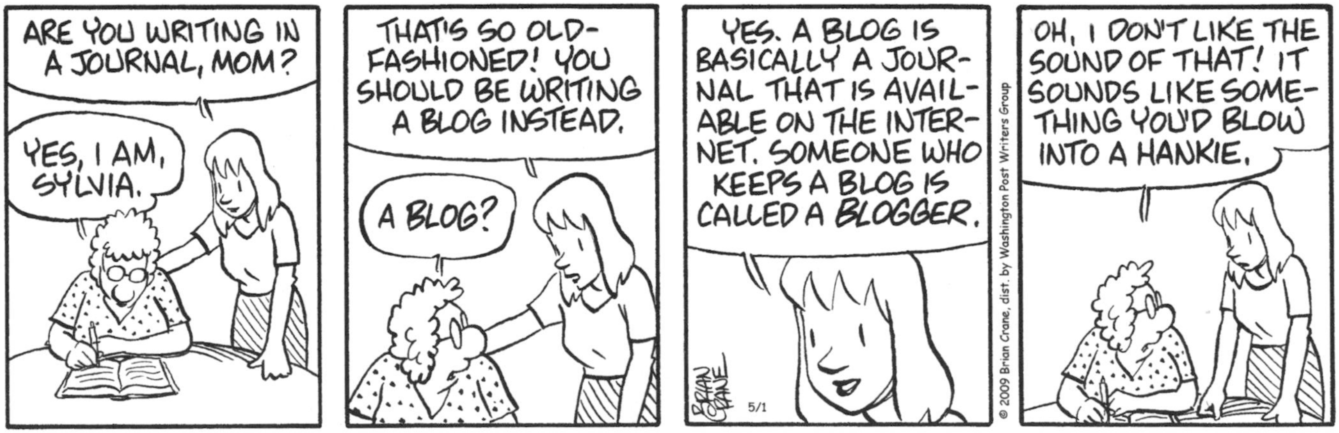
ARE YOU WRITING IN A JOURNAL, MOM?
YES, I AM, SYLVIA.
THAT'S SO OLD-FASHIONED! YOU SHOULD BE WRITING A BLOG INSTEAD.
A BLOG?
YES. A BLOG IS BASICALLY A JOUR-NAL THAT IS AVAIL-ABLE ON THE INTER-NET. SOMEONE WHO KEEPS A BLOG IS CALLED A *BLOGGER*.
BRIAN CRANE
5/1
© 2009 Brian Crane, dist. by Washington Post Writers Group
OH, I DON'T LIKE THE SOUND OF THAT! IT SOUNDS LIKE SOME-THING YOU'D BLOW INTO A HANKIE.

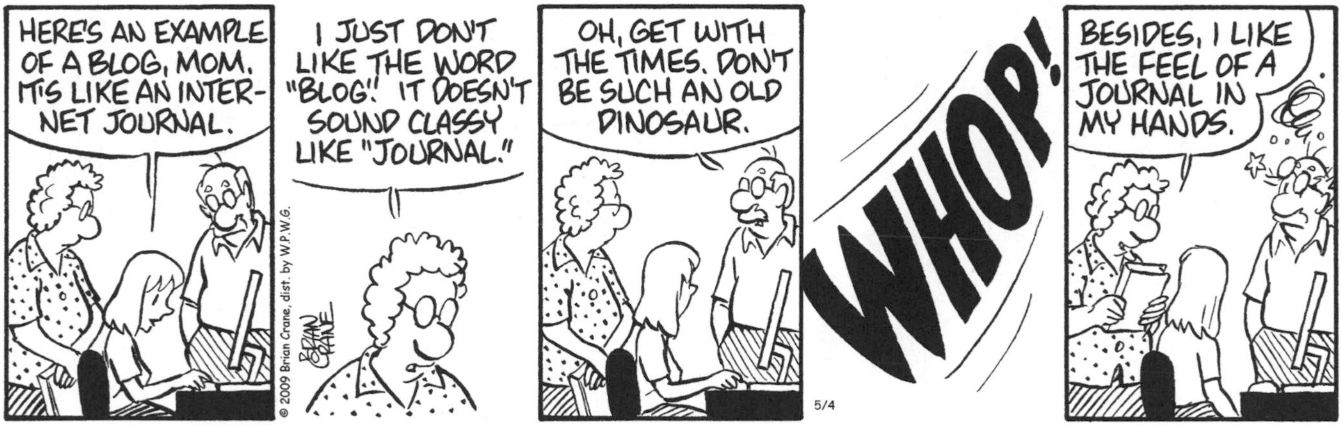
HERE'S AN EXAMPLE OF A BLOG, MOM. IT'S LIKE AN INTER-NET JOURNAL.
I JUST DON'T LIKE THE WORD "BLOG." IT DOESN'T SOUND CLASSY LIKE "JOURNAL."
OH, GET WITH THE TIMES. DON'T BE SUCH AN OLD DINOSAUR.
WHOP!
BESIDES, I LIKE THE FEEL OF A JOURNAL IN MY HANDS.
© 2009 Brian Crane, dist. by W.P.W.G.
BRIAN CRANE
5/4

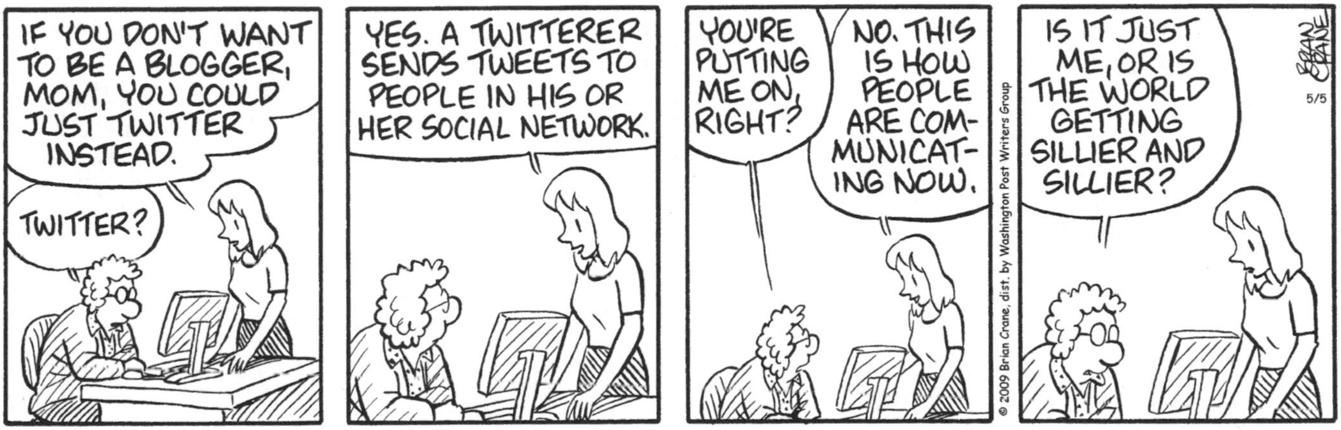
IF YOU DON'T WANT TO BE A BLOGGER, MOM, YOU COULD JUST TWITTER INSTEAD.
TWITTER?
YES. A TWITTERER SENDS TWEETS TO PEOPLE IN HIS OR HER SOCIAL NETWORK.
YOU'RE PUTTING ME ON, RIGHT?
NO. THIS IS HOW PEOPLE ARE COM-MUNICAT-ING NOW.
IS IT JUST ME, OR IS THE WORLD GETTING SILLIER AND SILLIER?
BRIAN CRANE
5/5
© 2009 Brian Crane, dist. by Washington Post Writers Group

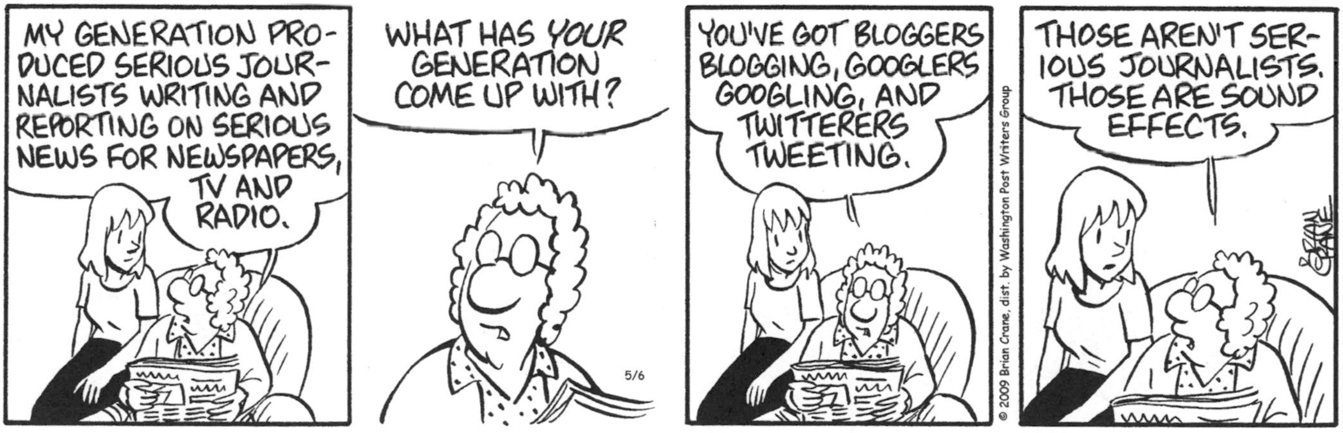
MY GENERATION PRO-DUCED SERIOUS JOUR-NALISTS WRITING AND REPORTING ON SERIOUS NEWS FOR NEWSPAPERS, TV AND RADIO.
WHAT HAS YOUR GENERATION COME UP WITH?
5/6
YOU'VE GOT BLOGGERS BLOGGING, GOOGLERS GOOGLING, AND TWITTERERS TWEETING.
THOSE AREN'T SER-IOUS JOURNALISTS. THOSE ARE SOUND EFFECTS.
BRIAN CRANE
© 2009 Brian Crane, dist. by Washington Post Writers Group

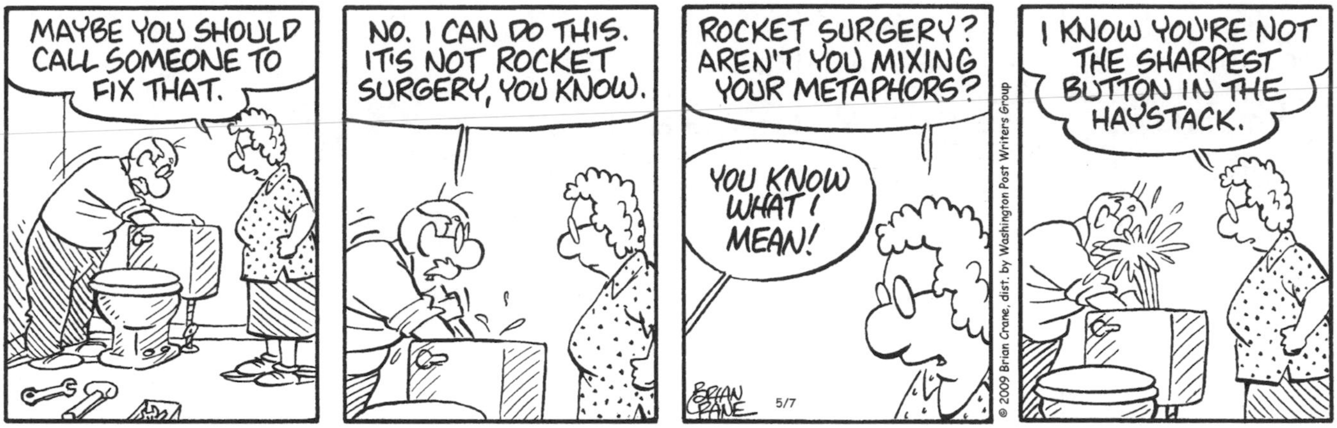
MAYBE YOU SHOULD CALL SOMEONE TO FIX THAT.
NO. I CAN DO THIS. IT'S NOT ROCKET SURGERY, YOU KNOW.
ROCKET SURGERY? AREN'T YOU MIXING YOUR METAPHORS?
YOU KNOW WHAT I MEAN!
BRIAN CRANE 5/7
© 2009 Brian Crane, dist. by Washington Post Writers Group
I KNOW YOU'RE NOT THE SHARPEST BUTTON IN THE HAYSTACK.

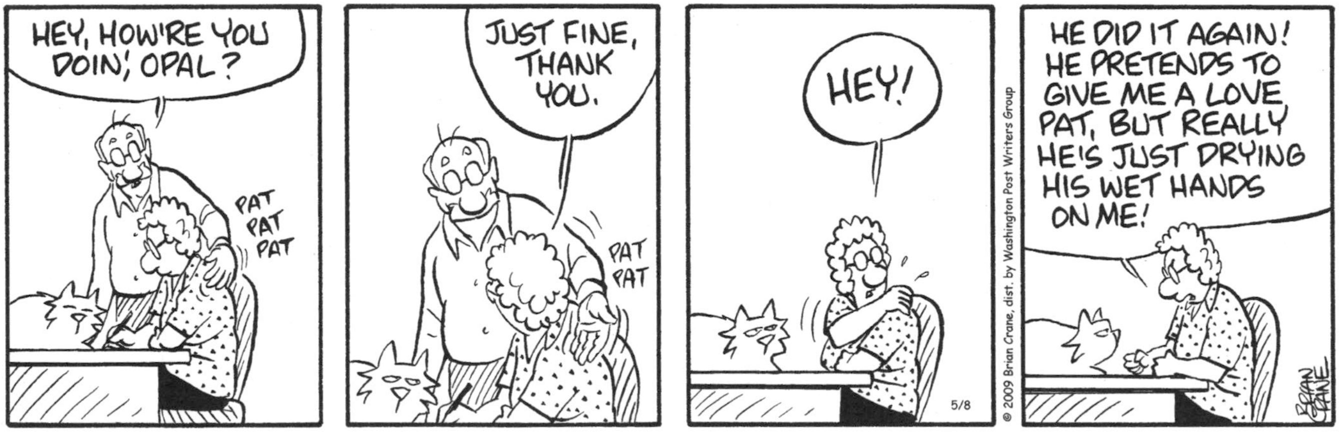
HEY, HOW'RE YOU DOIN', OPAL?
PAT PAT PAT
JUST FINE, THANK YOU.
PAT PAT
HEY!
5/8
© 2009 Brian Crane, dist. by Washington Post Writers Group
HE DID IT AGAIN! HE PRETENDS TO GIVE ME A LOVE PAT, BUT REALLY HE'S JUST DRYING HIS WET HANDS ON ME!
BRIAN CRANE

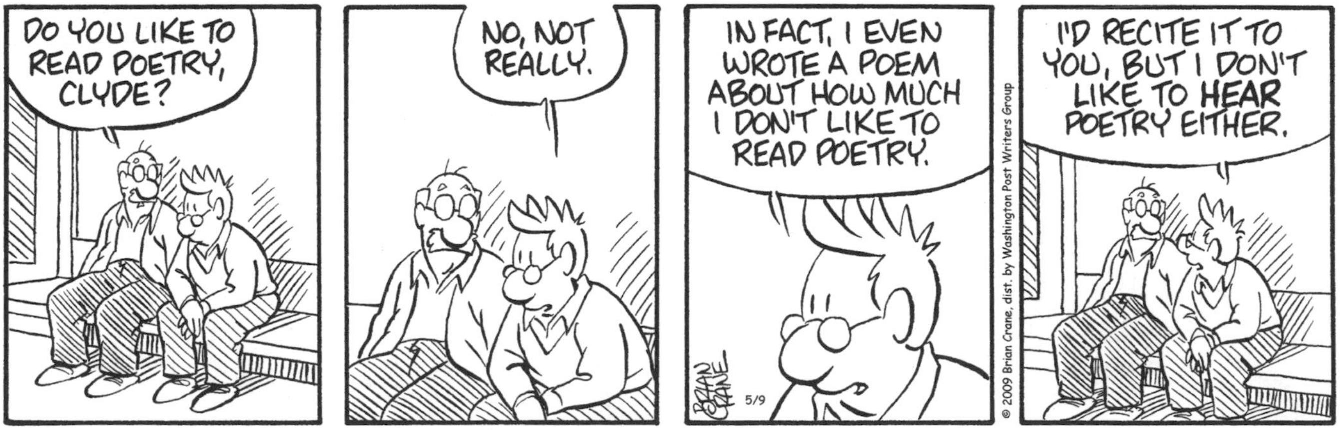
DO YOU LIKE TO READ POETRY, CLYDE?
NO, NOT REALLY.
IN FACT, I EVEN WROTE A POEM ABOUT HOW MUCH I DON'T LIKE TO READ POETRY.
BRIAN CRANE 5/9
© 2009 Brian Crane, dist. by Washington Post Writers Group
I'D RECITE IT TO YOU, BUT I DON'T LIKE TO HEAR POETRY EITHER.

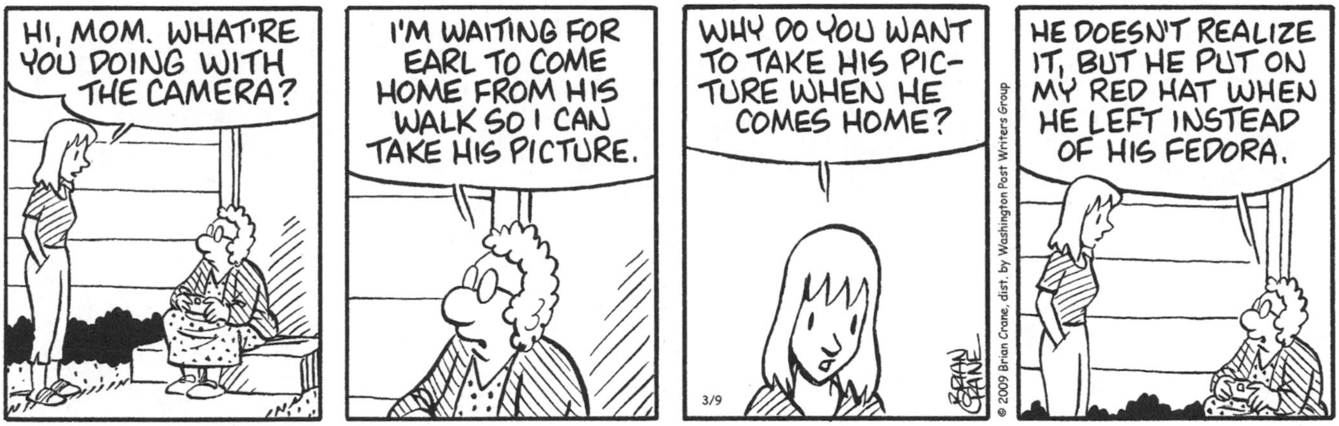
HI, MOM. WHAT'RE YOU DOING WITH THE CAMERA?
I'M WAITING FOR EARL TO COME HOME FROM HIS WALK SO I CAN TAKE HIS PICTURE.
WHY DO YOU WANT TO TAKE HIS PIC-TURE WHEN HE COMES HOME?
HE DOESN'T REALIZE IT, BUT HE PUT ON MY RED HAT WHEN HE LEFT INSTEAD OF HIS FEDORA.
3/9

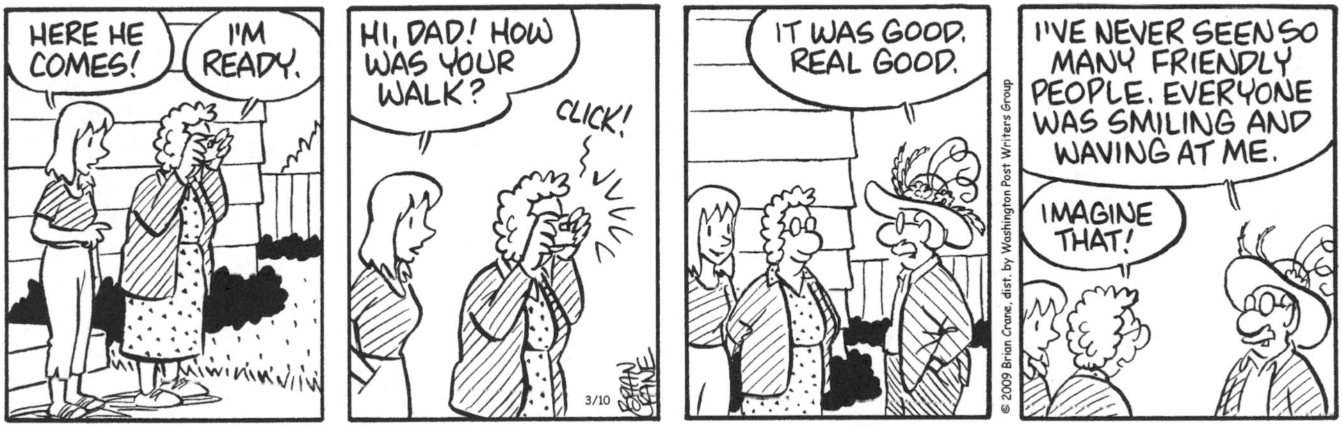
HERE HE COMES!
I'M READY.
HI, DAD! HOW WAS YOUR WALK?
CLICK!
3/10
IT WAS GOOD. REAL GOOD.
I'VE NEVER SEEN SO MANY FRIENDLY PEOPLE. EVERYONE WAS SMILING AND WAVING AT ME.
IMAGINE THAT!

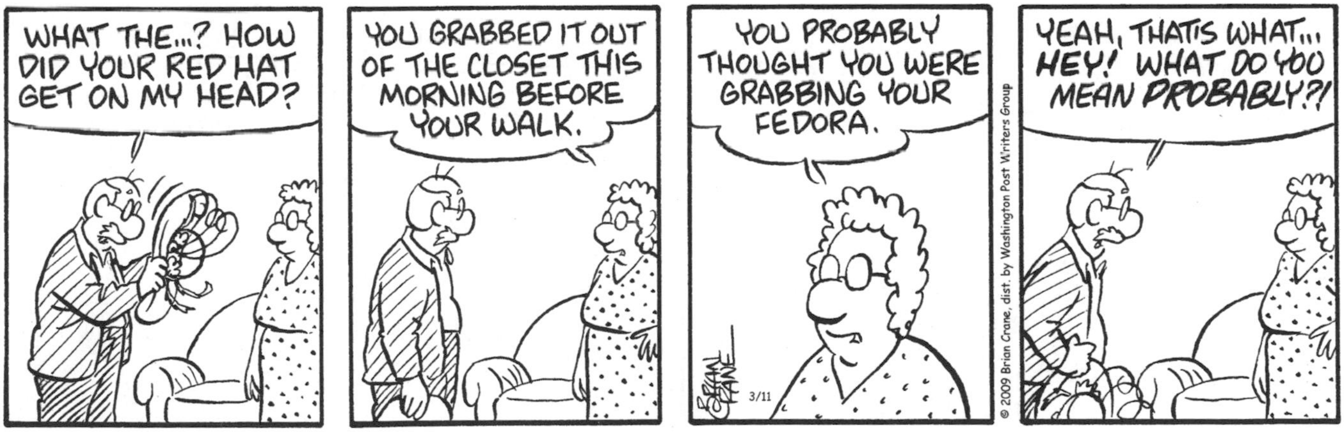
WHAT THE...? HOW DID YOUR RED HAT GET ON MY HEAD?
YOU GRABBED IT OUT OF THE CLOSET THIS MORNING BEFORE YOUR WALK.
YOU PROBABLY THOUGHT YOU WERE GRABBING YOUR FEDORA.
3/11
YEAH, THAT IS WHAT... HEY! WHAT DO YOU MEAN PROBABLY?!

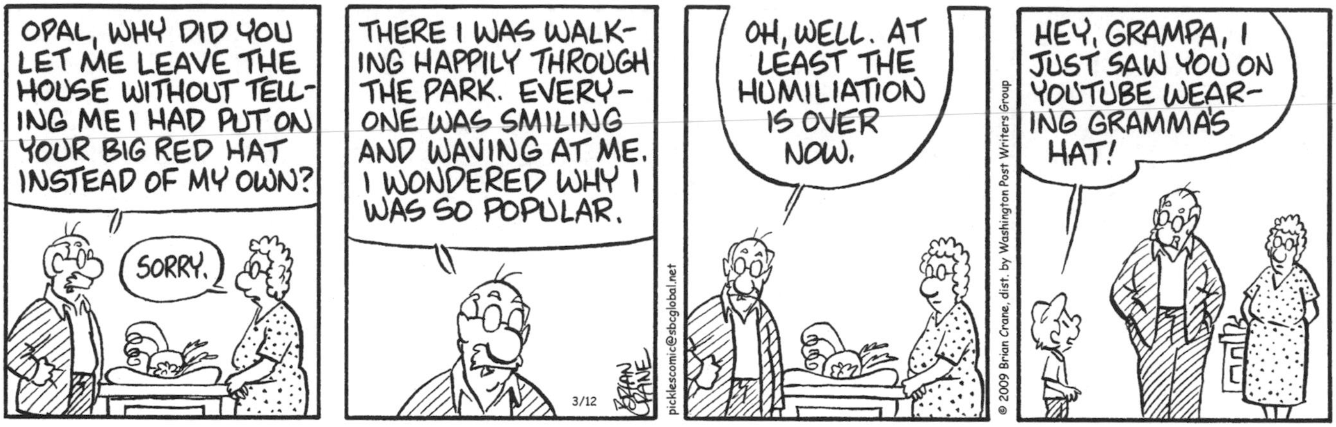
OPAL, WHY DID YOU LET ME LEAVE THE HOUSE WITHOUT TELLING ME I HAD PUT ON YOUR BIG RED HAT INSTEAD OF MY OWN?
SORRY.
THERE I WAS WALKING HAPPILY THROUGH THE PARK. EVERYONE WAS SMILING AND WAVING AT ME. I WONDERED WHY I WAS SO POPULAR.
3/12
BRIAN CRANE
picklescomic@sbcglobal.net
OH, WELL. AT LEAST THE HUMILIATION IS OVER NOW.
© 2009 Brian Crane, dist. by Washington Post Writers Group
HEY, GRAMPA, I JUST SAW YOU ON YOUTUBE WEARING GRAMMA'S HAT!

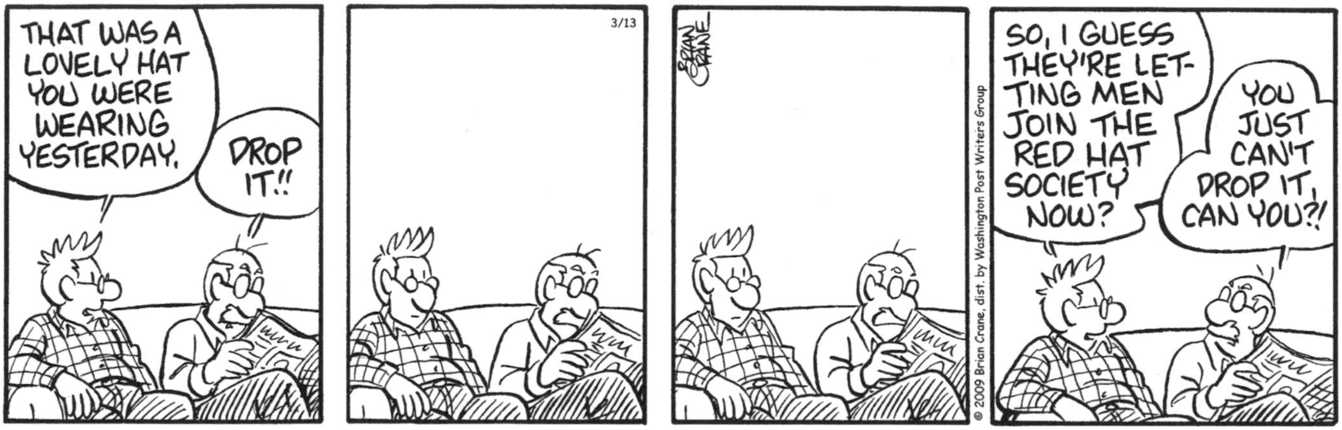
THAT WAS A LOVELY HAT YOU WERE WEARING YESTERDAY.
DROP IT!!
3/13
BRIAN CRANE
© 2009 Brian Crane, dist. by Washington Post Writers Group
SO, I GUESS THEY'RE LETTING MEN JOIN THE RED HAT SOCIETY NOW?
YOU JUST CAN'T DROP IT, CAN YOU?!

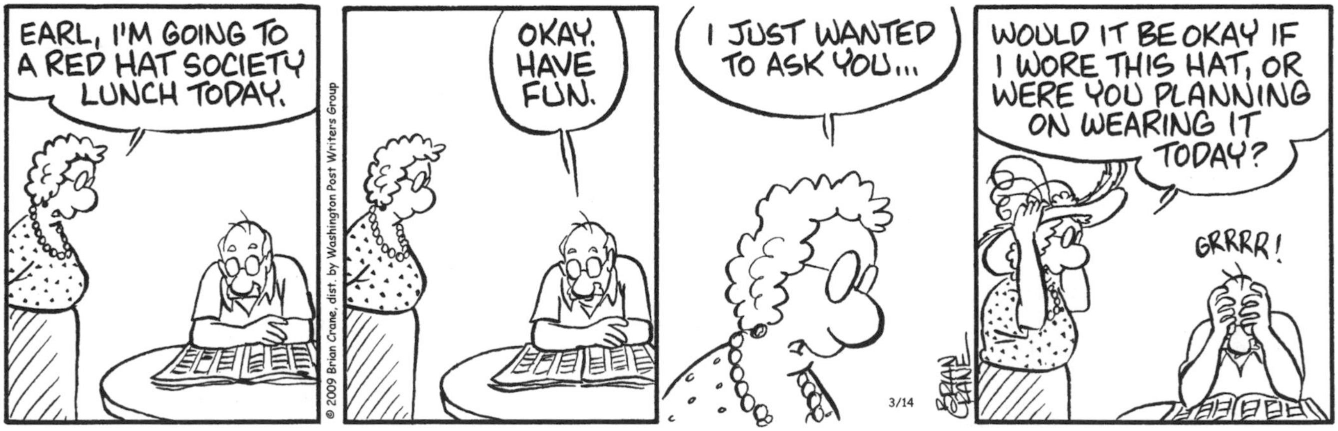
EARL, I'M GOING TO A RED HAT SOCIETY LUNCH TODAY.
© 2009 Brian Crane, dist. by Washington Post Writers Group
OKAY. HAVE FUN.
I JUST WANTED TO ASK YOU...
3/14
BRIAN CRANE
WOULD IT BE OKAY IF I WORE THIS HAT, OR WERE YOU PLANNING ON WEARING IT TODAY?
GRRRR!

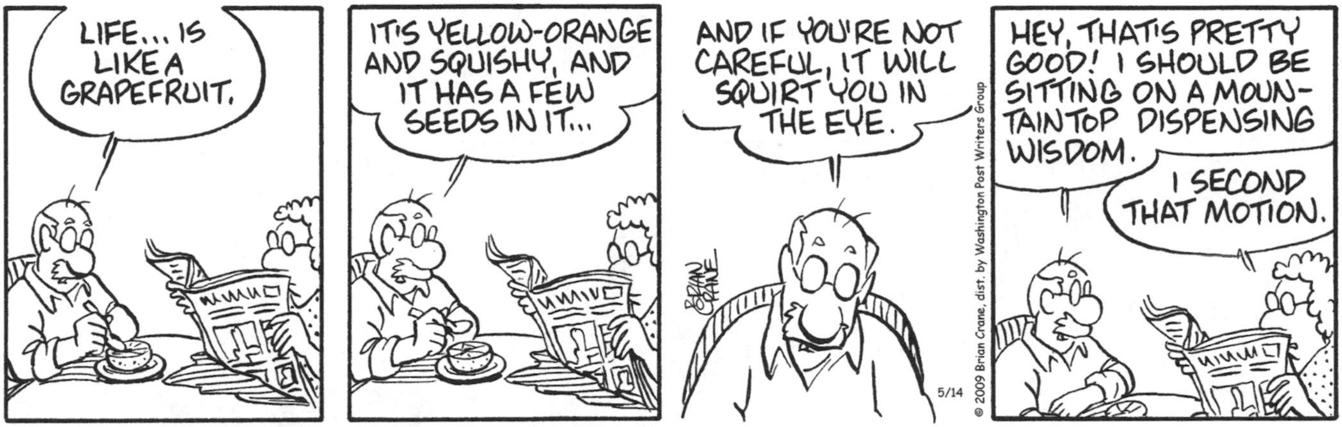
LIFE... IS LIKE A GRAPEFRUIT.
IT'S YELLOW-ORANGE AND SQUISHY, AND IT HAS A FEW SEEDS IN IT...
AND IF YOU'RE NOT CAREFUL, IT WILL SQUIRT YOU IN THE EYE.
BRIAN CRANE
5/14
© 2009 Brian Crane, dist. by Washington Post Writers Group
HEY, THAT'S PRETTY GOOD! I SHOULD BE SITTING ON A MOUNTAINTOP DISPENSING WISDOM.
I SECOND THAT MOTION.

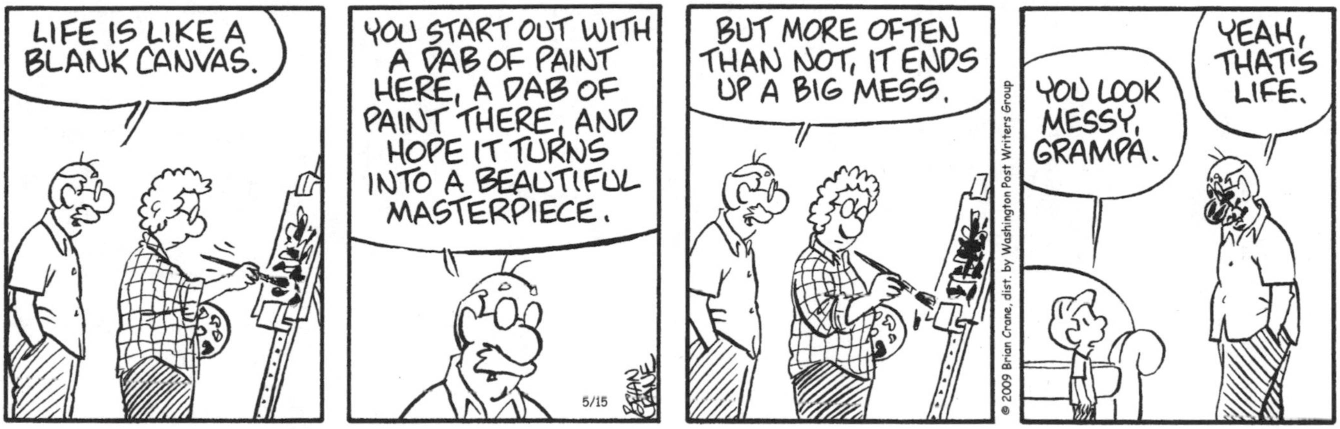
LIFE IS LIKE A BLANK CANVAS.
YOU START OUT WITH A DAB OF PAINT HERE, A DAB OF PAINT THERE, AND HOPE IT TURNS INTO A BEAUTIFUL MASTERPIECE.
5/15
BRIAN CRANE
BUT MORE OFTEN THAN NOT, IT ENDS UP A BIG MESS.
© 2009 Brian Crane, dist. by Washington Post Writers Group
YOU LOOK MESSY, GRAMPA.
YEAH, THAT'S LIFE.

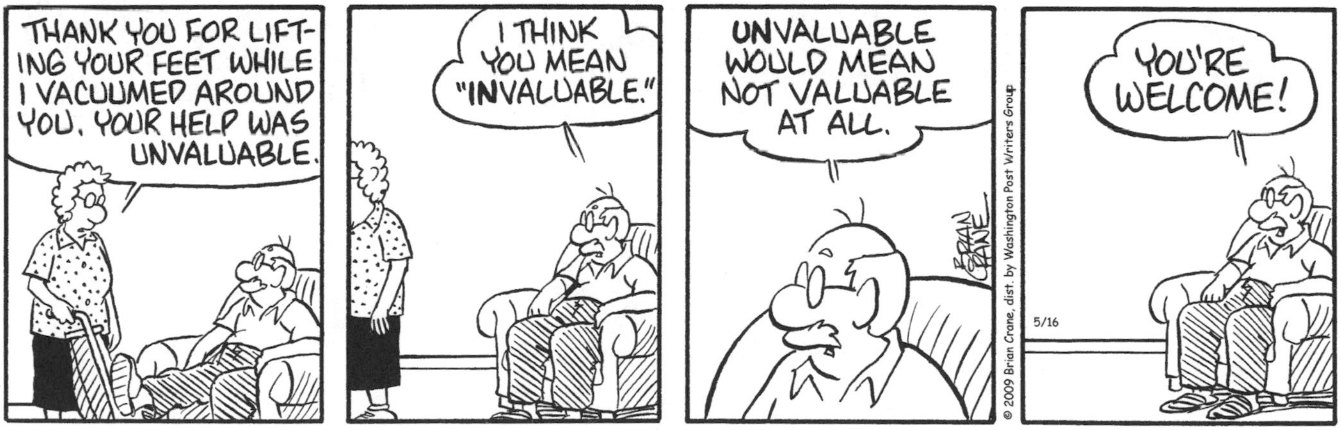
THANK YOU FOR LIFTING YOUR FEET WHILE I VACUUMED AROUND YOU. YOUR HELP WAS UNVALUABLE.
I THINK YOU MEAN "INVALUABLE."
UNVALUABLE WOULD MEAN NOT VALUABLE AT ALL.
BRIAN CRANE
© 2009 Brian Crane, dist. by Washington Post Writers Group
5/16
YOU'RE WELCOME!

Sunday Pickles

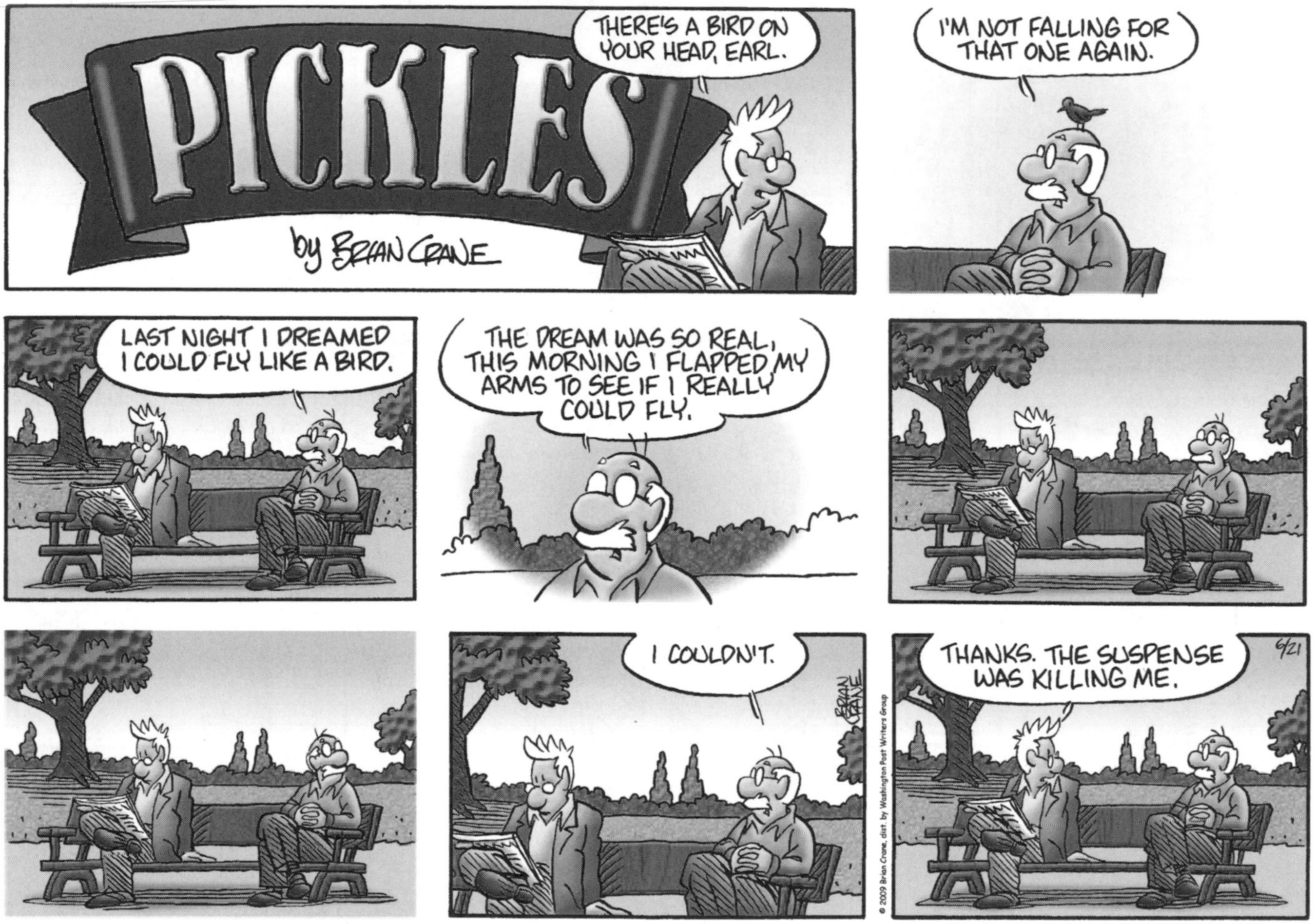
PICKLES
by BRIAN CRANE
THERE'S A BIRD ON YOUR HEAD, EARL.
I'M NOT FALLING FOR THAT ONE AGAIN.
LAST NIGHT I DREAMED I COULD FLY LIKE A BIRD.
THE DREAM WAS SO REAL, THIS MORNING I FLAPPED MY ARMS TO SEE IF I REALLY COULD FLY.
I COULDN'T.
BRIAN CRANE
© 2009 Brian Crane, dist. by Washington Post Writers Group
THANKS. THE SUSPENSE WAS KILLING ME.
6/21

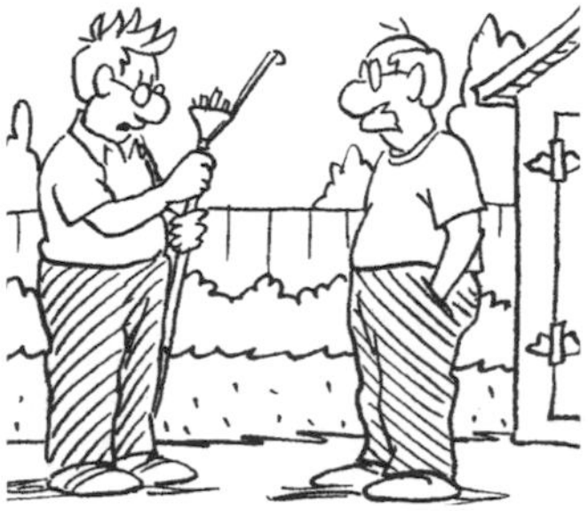

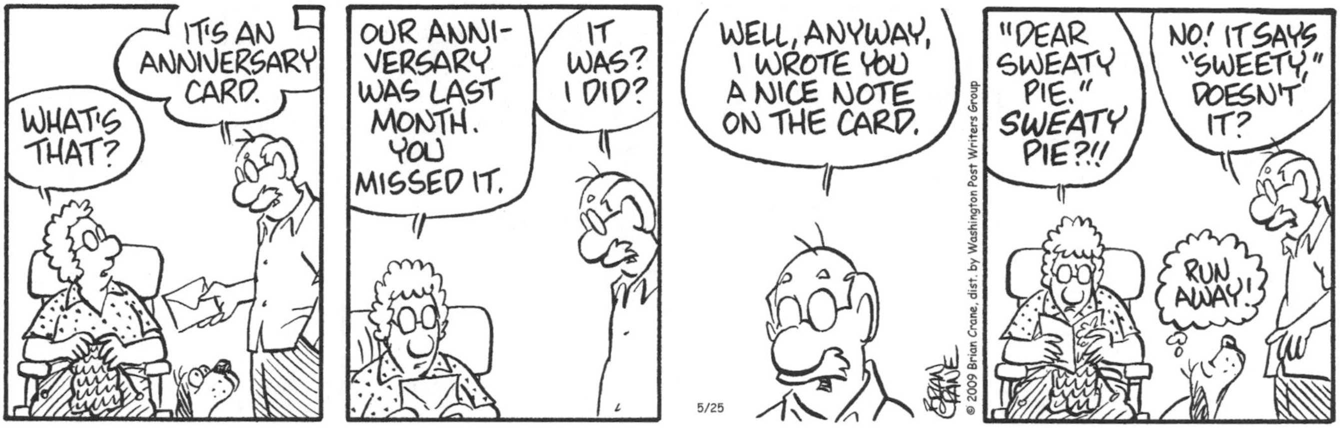
WHAT'S THAT?
IT'S AN ANNIVERSARY CARD.
OUR ANNIVERSARY WAS LAST MONTH. YOU MISSED IT.
IT WAS? I DID?
WELL, ANYWAY, I WROTE YOU A NICE NOTE ON THE CARD.
5/25
"DEAR SWEATY PIE." SWEATY PIE?!!
NO! IT SAYS "SWEETY," DOESN'T IT?
RUN AWAY!
© 2009 Brian Crane, dist. by Washington Post Writers Group

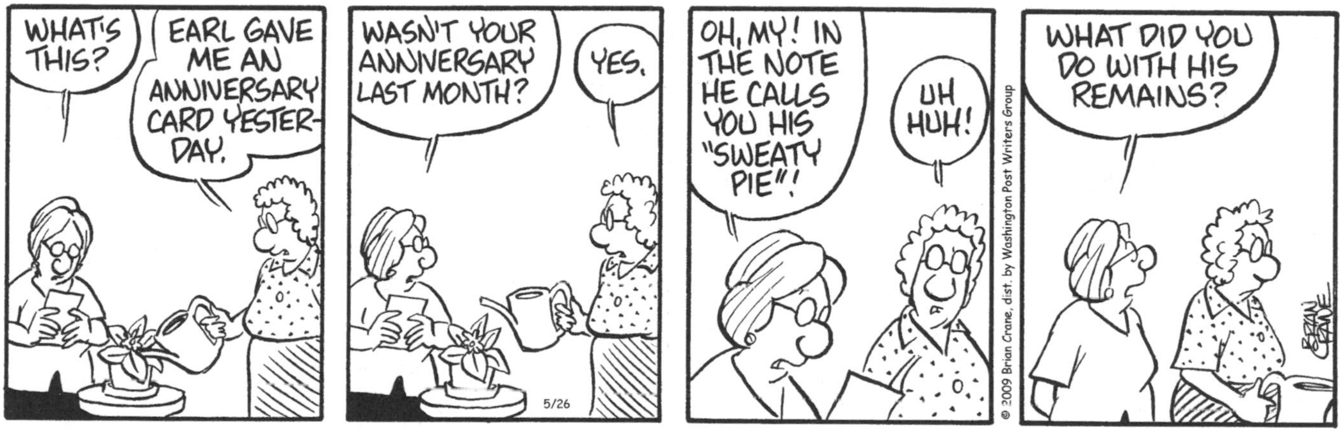
WHAT'S THIS?
EARL GAVE ME AN ANNIVERSARY CARD YESTERDAY.
WASN'T YOUR ANNIVERSARY LAST MONTH?
YES.
5/26
OH, MY! IN THE NOTE HE CALLS YOU HIS "SWEATY PIE"!
UH HUH!
WHAT DID YOU DO WITH HIS REMAINS?
© 2009 Brian Crane, dist. by Washington Post Writers Group

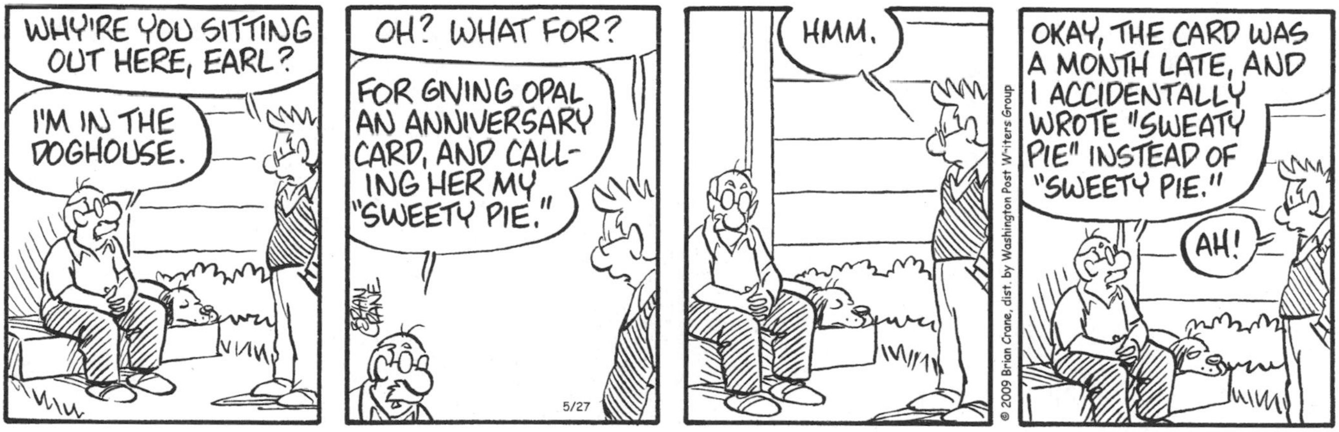
WHY'RE YOU SITTING OUT HERE, EARL?
I'M IN THE DOGHOUSE.
OH? WHAT FOR?
FOR GIVING OPAL AN ANNIVERSARY CARD, AND CALLING HER MY "SWEETY PIE."
5/27
HMM.
OKAY, THE CARD WAS A MONTH LATE, AND I ACCIDENTALLY WROTE "SWEATY PIE" INSTEAD OF "SWEETY PIE."
AH!
© 2009 Brian Crane, dist. by Washington Post Writers Group

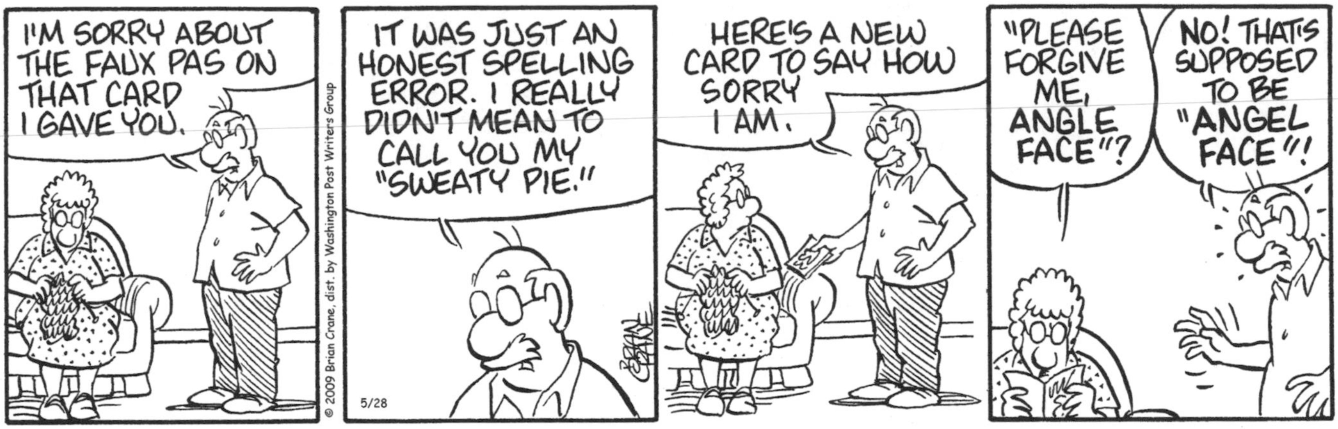
I'M SORRY ABOUT THE FAUX PAS ON THAT CARD I GAVE YOU.
IT WAS JUST AN HONEST SPELLING ERROR. I REALLY DIDN'T MEAN TO CALL YOU MY "SWEATY PIE."
HERE'S A NEW CARD TO SAY HOW SORRY I AM.
"PLEASE FORGIVE ME, ANGLE FACE"?
NO! THAT'S SUPPOSED TO BE "ANGEL FACE"!
© 2009 Brian Crane, dist. by Washington Post Writers Group
5/28

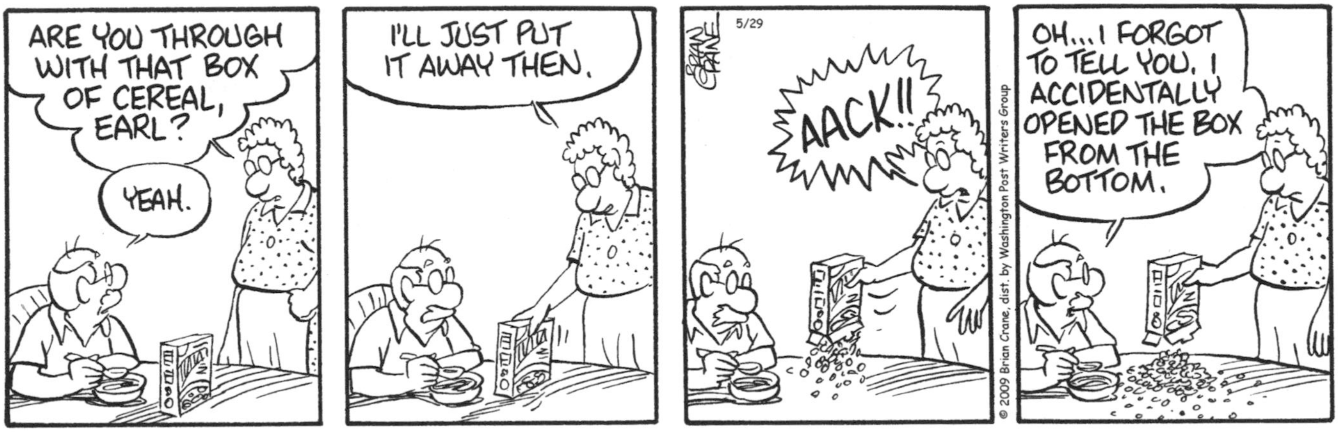
ARE YOU THROUGH WITH THAT BOX OF CEREAL, EARL?
YEAH.
I'LL JUST PUT IT AWAY THEN.
5/29
AACK!!
OH... I FORGOT TO TELL YOU. I ACCIDENTALLY OPENED THE BOX FROM THE BOTTOM.
© 2009 Brian Crane, dist. by Washington Post Writers Group

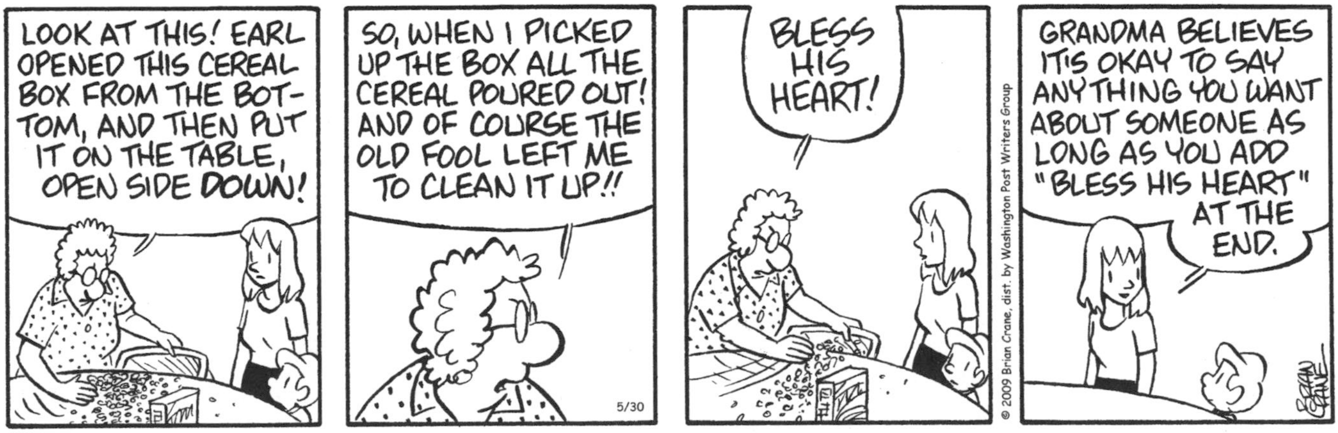
LOOK AT THIS! EARL OPENED THIS CEREAL BOX FROM THE BOTTOM, AND THEN PUT IT ON THE TABLE, OPEN SIDE DOWN!
SO, WHEN I PICKED UP THE BOX ALL THE CEREAL POURED OUT! AND OF COURSE THE OLD FOOL LEFT ME TO CLEAN IT UP!!
5/30
BLESS HIS HEART!
GRANDMA BELIEVES IT'S OKAY TO SAY ANYTHING YOU WANT ABOUT SOMEONE AS LONG AS YOU ADD "BLESS HIS HEART" AT THE END.
© 2009 Brian Crane, dist. by Washington Post Writers Group

SundayPickles

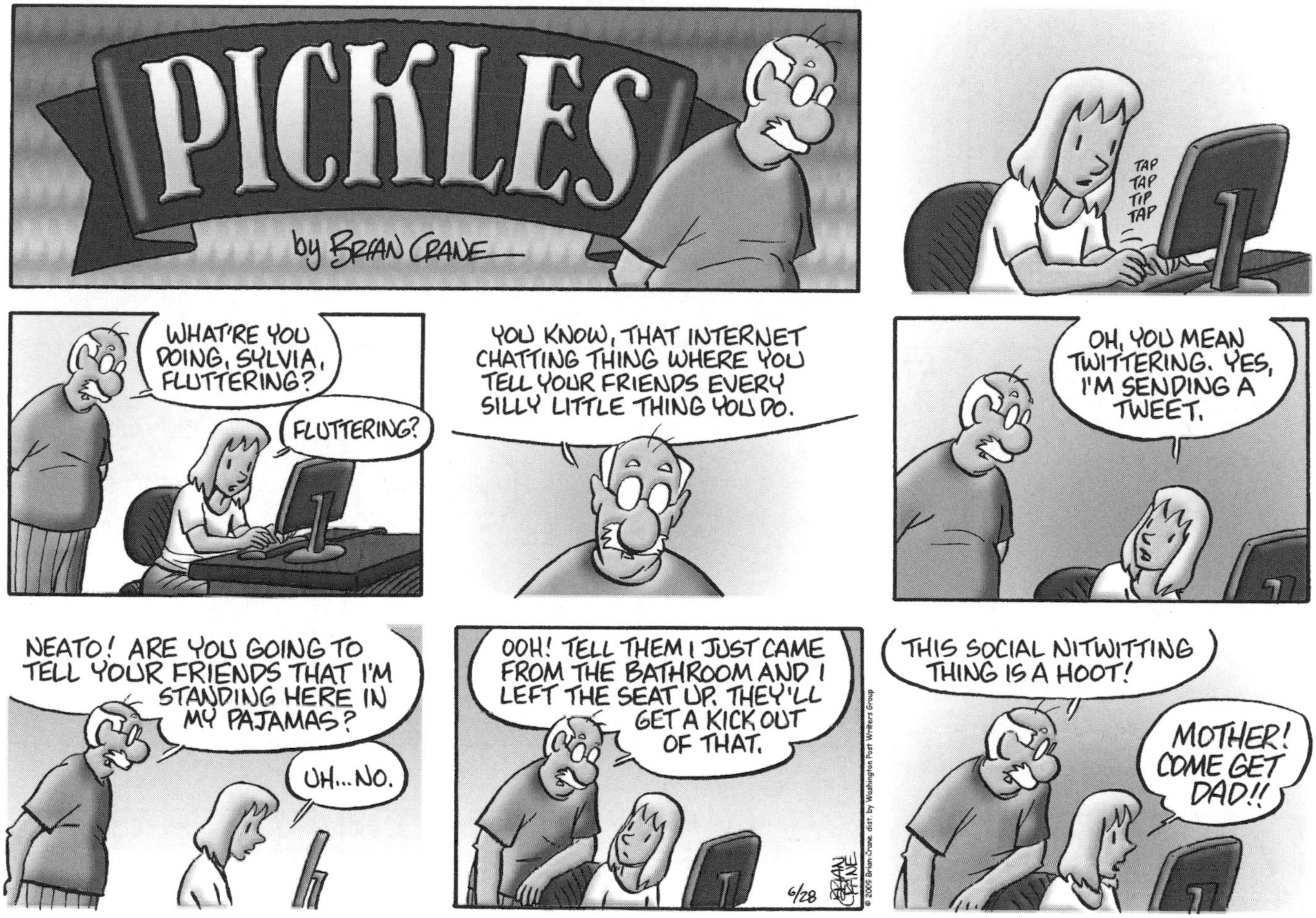
PICKLES
by BRIAN CRANE
TAP TAP TIP TAP
WHAT'RE YOU DOING, SYLVIA, FLUTTERING?
FLUTTERING?
YOU KNOW, THAT INTERNET CHATTING THING WHERE YOU TELL YOUR FRIENDS EVERY SILLY LITTLE THING YOU DO.
OH, YOU MEAN TWITTERING. YES, I'M SENDING A TWEET.
NEATO! ARE YOU GOING TO TELL YOUR FRIENDS THAT I'M STANDING HERE IN MY PAJAMAS?
UH...NO.
OOH! TELL THEM I JUST CAME FROM THE BATHROOM AND I LEFT THE SEAT UP. THEY'LL GET A KICK OUT OF THAT.
6/28
BRIAN CRANE
© 2009 Brian Crane. dist. by Washington Post Writers Group
THIS SOCIAL NITWITTING THING IS A HOOT!
MOTHER! COME GET DAD!!

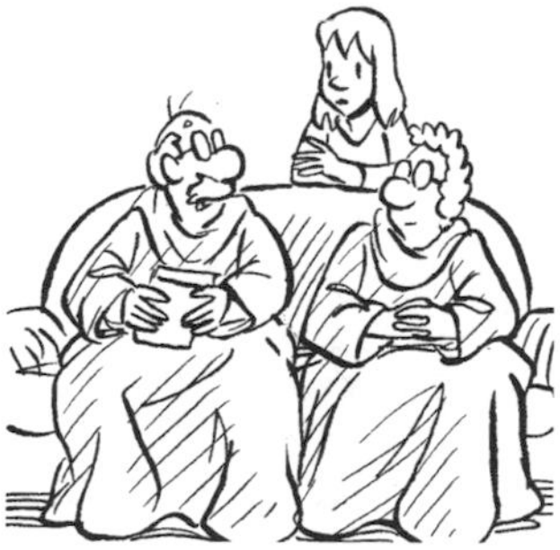

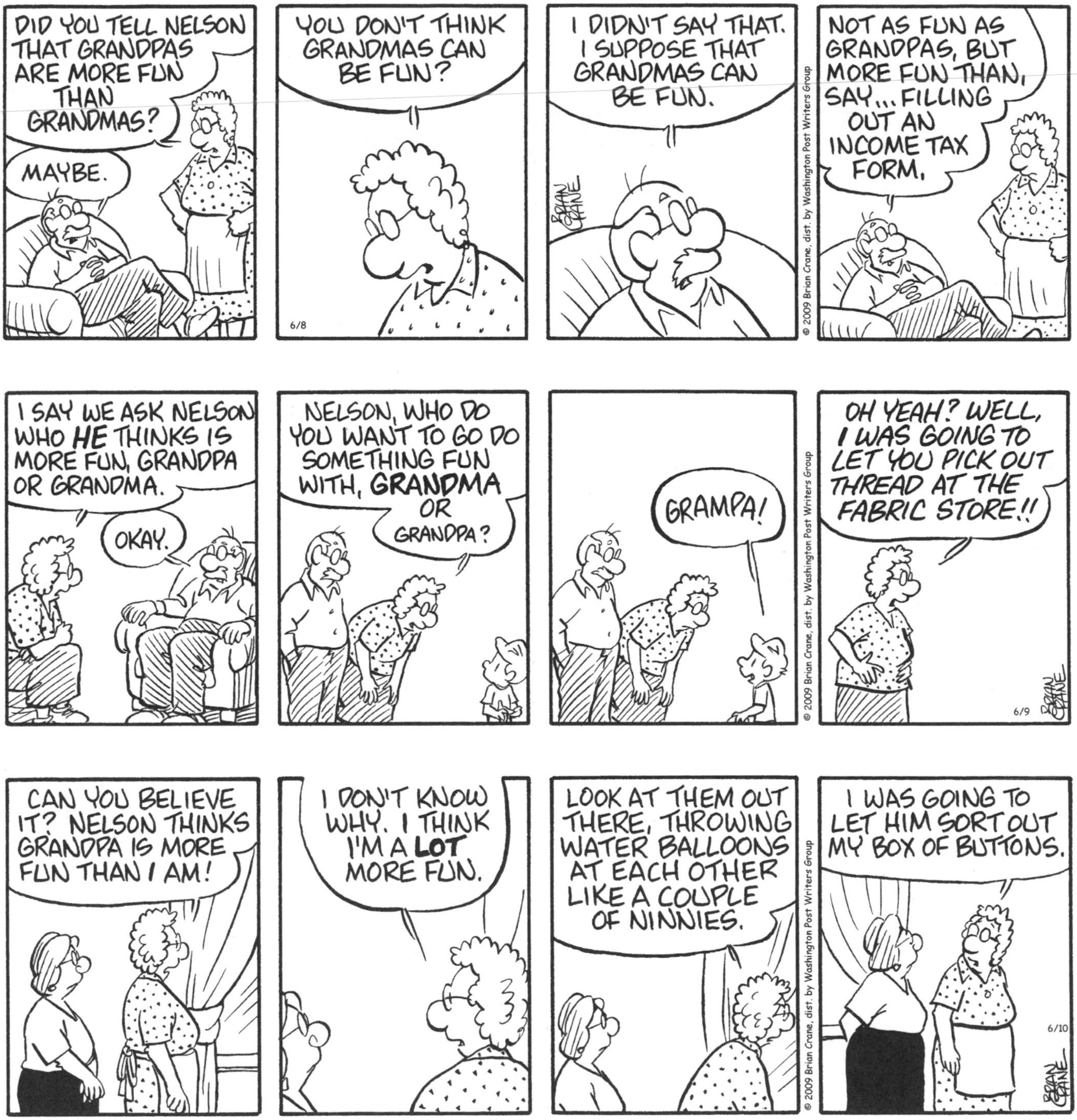
DID YOU TELL NELSON THAT GRANDPAS ARE MORE FUN THAN GRANDMAS?
MAYBE.
YOU DON'T THINK GRANDMAS CAN BE FUN?
I DIDN'T SAY THAT. I SUPPOSE THAT GRANDMAS CAN BE FUN.
BRIAN CRANE
NOT AS FUN AS GRANDPAS, BUT MORE FUN THAN, SAY... FILLING OUT AN INCOME TAX FORM.
6/8
© 2009 Brian Crane, dist. by Washington Post Writers Group
I SAY WE ASK NELSON WHO **HE** THINKS IS MORE FUN, GRANDPA OR GRANDMA.
OKAY.
NELSON, WHO DO YOU WANT TO GO DO SOMETHING FUN WITH, **GRANDMA** OR GRANDPA?
GRAMPA!
OH YEAH? WELL, ***I*** WAS GOING TO LET YOU PICK OUT THREAD AT THE FABRIC STORE!!
6/9
BRIAN CRANE
© 2009 Brian Crane, dist. by Washington Post Writers Group
CAN YOU BELIEVE IT? NELSON THINKS GRANDPA IS MORE FUN THAN ***I*** AM!
I DON'T KNOW WHY. I THINK I'M A **LOT** MORE FUN.
LOOK AT THEM OUT THERE, THROWING WATER BALLOONS AT EACH OTHER LIKE A COUPLE OF NINNIES.
I WAS GOING TO LET HIM SORT OUT MY BOX OF BUTTONS.
6/10
BRIAN CRANE
© 2009 Brian Crane, dist. by Washington Post Writers Group

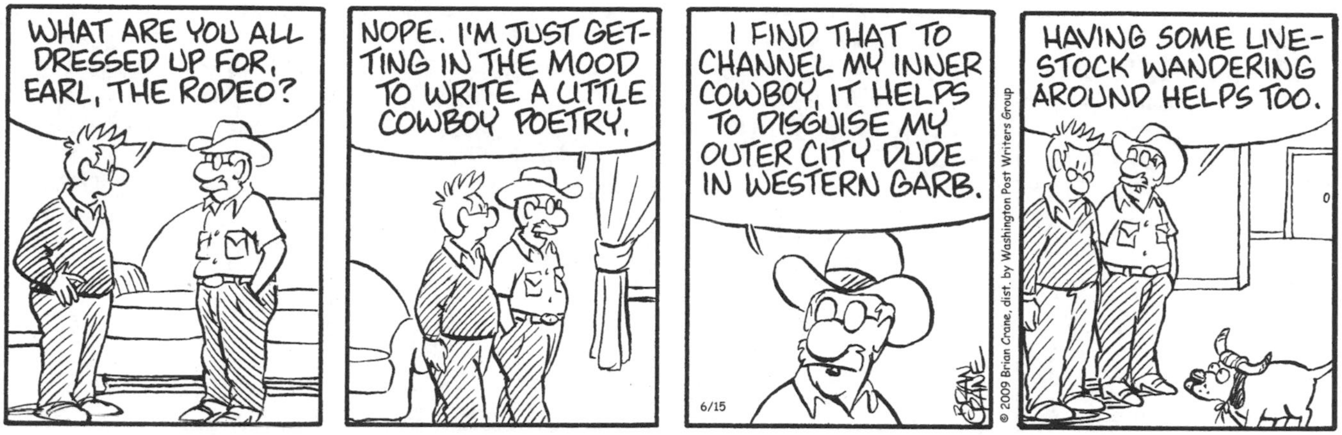
WHAT ARE YOU ALL DRESSED UP FOR, EARL, THE RODEO?
NOPE. I'M JUST GETTING IN THE MOOD TO WRITE A LITTLE COWBOY POETRY.
I FIND THAT TO CHANNEL MY INNER COWBOY, IT HELPS TO DISGUISE MY OUTER CITY DUDE IN WESTERN GARB.
HAVING SOME LIVESTOCK WANDERING AROUND HELPS TOO.

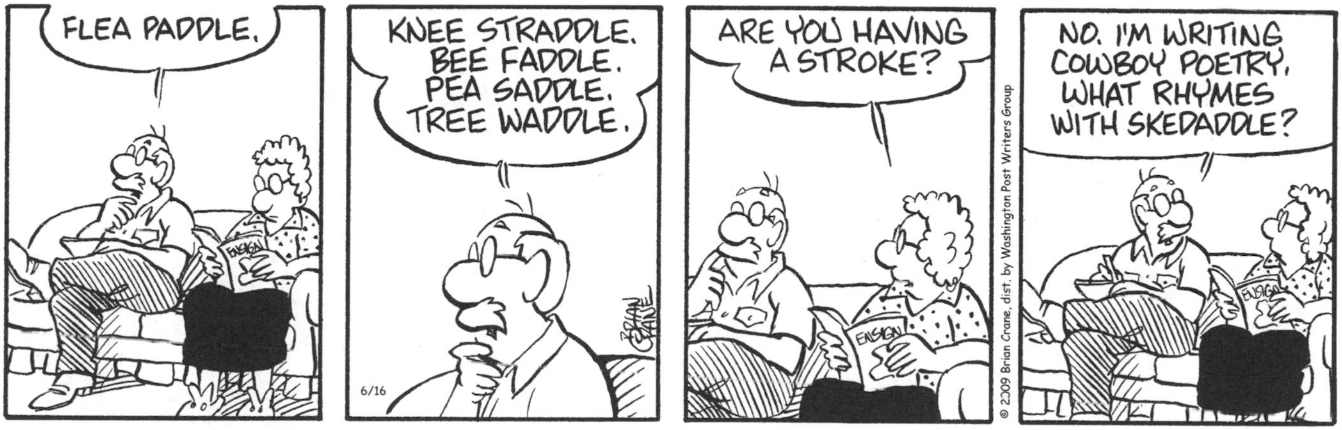
FLEA PADDLE.
KNEE STRADDLE. BEE FADDLE. PEA SADDLE. TREE WADDLE.
ARE YOU HAVING A STROKE?
NO. I'M WRITING COWBOY POETRY. WHAT RHYMES WITH SKEDADDLE?

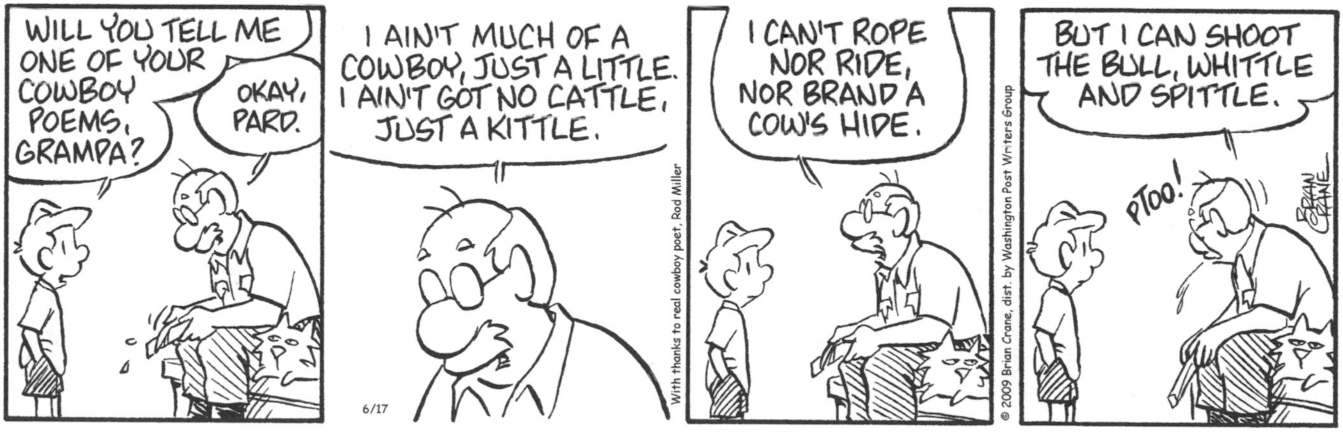
WILL YOU TELL ME ONE OF YOUR COWBOY POEMS, GRAMPA?
OKAY, PARD.
I AIN'T MUCH OF A COWBOY, JUST A LITTLE. I AIN'T GOT NO CATTLE, JUST A KITTLE.
With thanks to real cowboy poet, Rod Miller
I CAN'T ROPE NOR RIDE, NOR BRAND A COW'S HIDE.
BUT I CAN SHOOT THE BULL, WHITTLE AND SPITTLE.
PTOO!

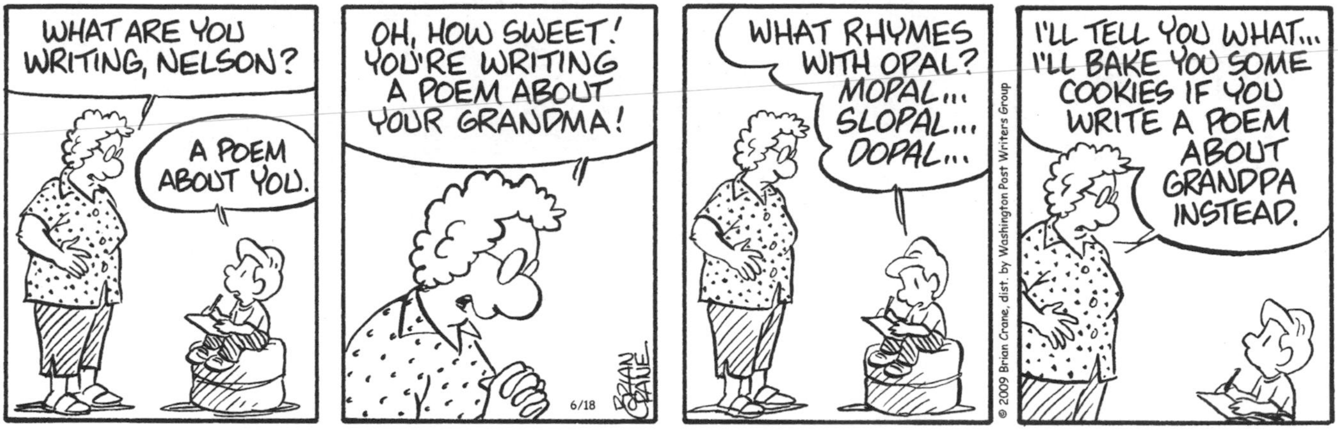
WHAT ARE YOU WRITING, NELSON?
A POEM ABOUT YOU.
OH, HOW SWEET! YOU'RE WRITING A POEM ABOUT YOUR GRANDMA!
6/18
BRIAN CRANE
WHAT RHYMES WITH OPAL? MOPAL... SLOPAL... DOPAL...
© 2009 Brian Crane, dist. by Washington Post Writers Group
I'LL TELL YOU WHAT... I'LL BAKE YOU SOME COOKIES IF YOU WRITE A POEM ABOUT GRANDPA INSTEAD.

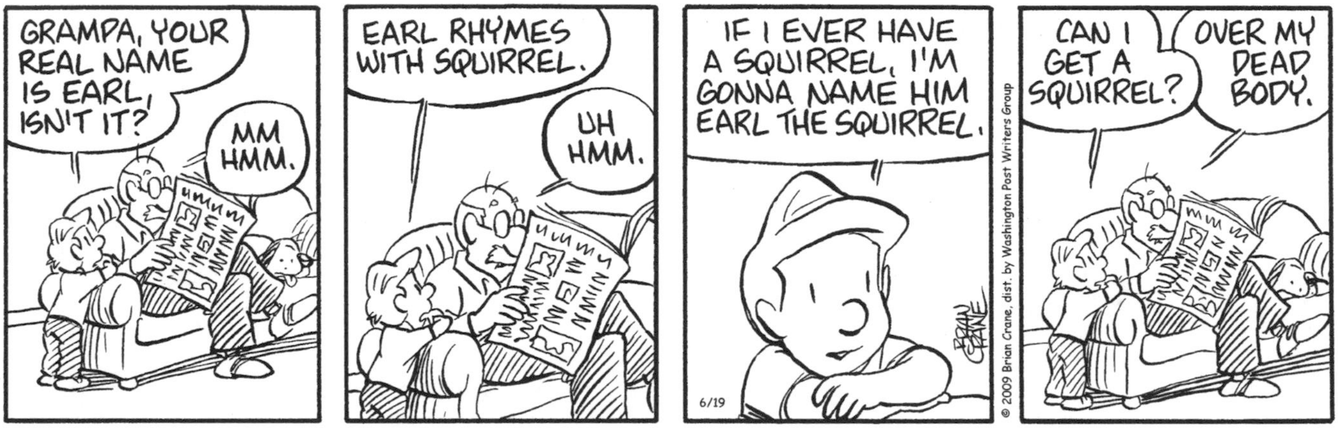
GRAMPA, YOUR REAL NAME IS EARL, ISN'T IT?
MM HMM.
EARL RHYMES WITH SQUIRREL.
UH HMM.
IF I EVER HAVE A SQUIRREL, I'M GONNA NAME HIM EARL THE SQUIRREL.
BRIAN CRANE
6/19
© 2009 Brian Crane, dist. by Washington Post Writers Group
CAN I GET A SQUIRREL?
OVER MY DEAD BODY.

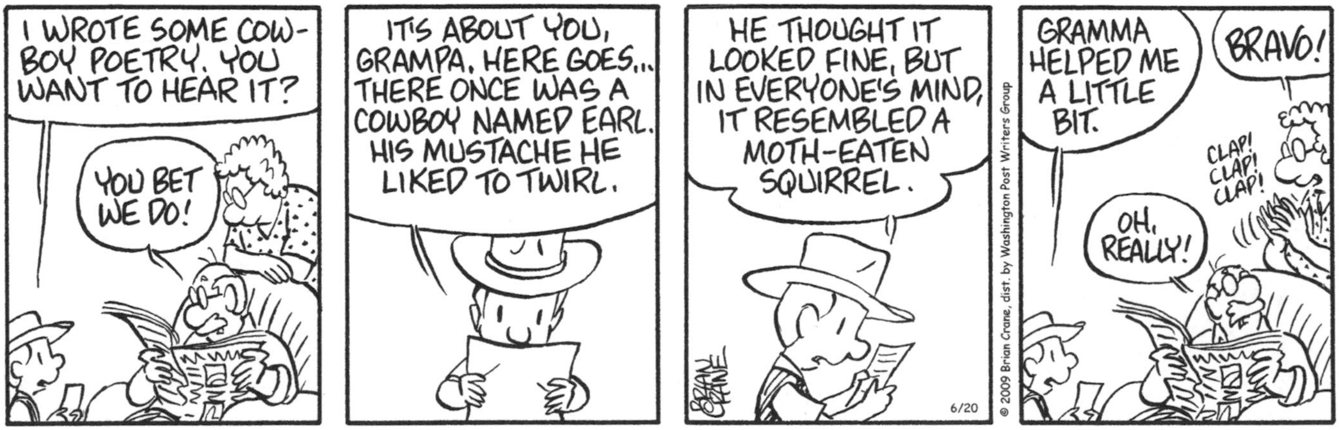
I WROTE SOME COW-BOY POETRY. YOU WANT TO HEAR IT?
YOU BET WE DO!
IT'S ABOUT YOU, GRAMPA. HERE GOES... THERE ONCE WAS A COWBOY NAMED EARL. HIS MUSTACHE HE LIKED TO TWIRL.
HE THOUGHT IT LOOKED FINE, BUT IN EVERYONE'S MIND, IT RESEMBLED A MOTH-EATEN SQUIRREL.
BRIAN CRANE
6/20
© 2009 Brian Crane, dist. by Washington Post Writers Group
GRAMMA HELPED ME A LITTLE BIT.
BRAVO!
CLAP! CLAP! CLAP!
OH, REALLY!

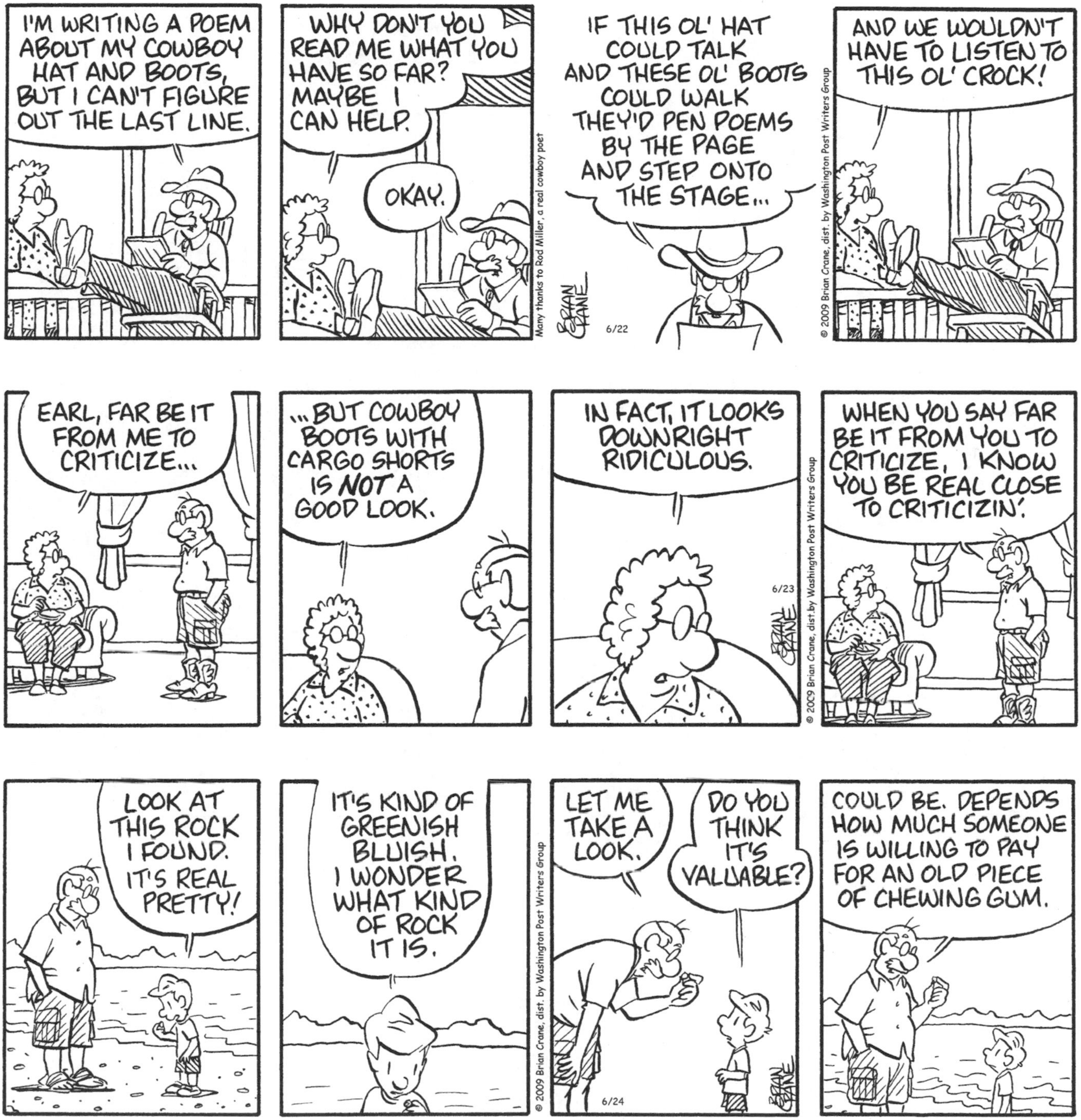

I'M WRITING A POEM ABOUT MY COWBOY HAT AND BOOTS, BUT I CAN'T FIGURE OUT THE LAST LINE.
WHY DON'T YOU READ ME WHAT YOU HAVE SO FAR? MAYBE I CAN HELP.
OKAY.
IF THIS OL' HAT COULD TALK AND THESE OL' BOOTS COULD WALK THEY'D PEN POEMS BY THE PAGE AND STEP ONTO THE STAGE...
Many thanks to Rod Miller, a real cowboy poet
BRIAN CRANE
6/22
AND WE WOULDN'T HAVE TO LISTEN TO THIS OL' CROCK!
© 2009 Brian Crane, dist. by Washington Post Writers Group
EARL, FAR BE IT FROM ME TO CRITICIZE...
...BUT COWBOY BOOTS WITH CARGO SHORTS IS NOT A GOOD LOOK.
IN FACT, IT LOOKS DOWNRIGHT RIDICULOUS.
6/23
BRIAN CRANE
© 2009 Brian Crane, dist. by Washington Post Writers Group
WHEN YOU SAY FAR BE IT FROM YOU TO CRITICIZE, I KNOW YOU BE REAL CLOSE TO CRITICIZIN'.
LOOK AT THIS ROCK I FOUND. IT'S REAL PRETTY!
IT'S KIND OF GREENISH BLUISH. I WONDER WHAT KIND OF ROCK IT IS.
© 2009 Brian Crane, dist. by Washington Post Writers Group
LET ME TAKE A LOOK.
DO YOU THINK IT'S VALUABLE?
6/24
BRIAN CRANE
COULD BE. DEPENDS HOW MUCH SOMEONE IS WILLING TO PAY FOR AN OLD PIECE OF CHEWING GUM.

SundayPickles

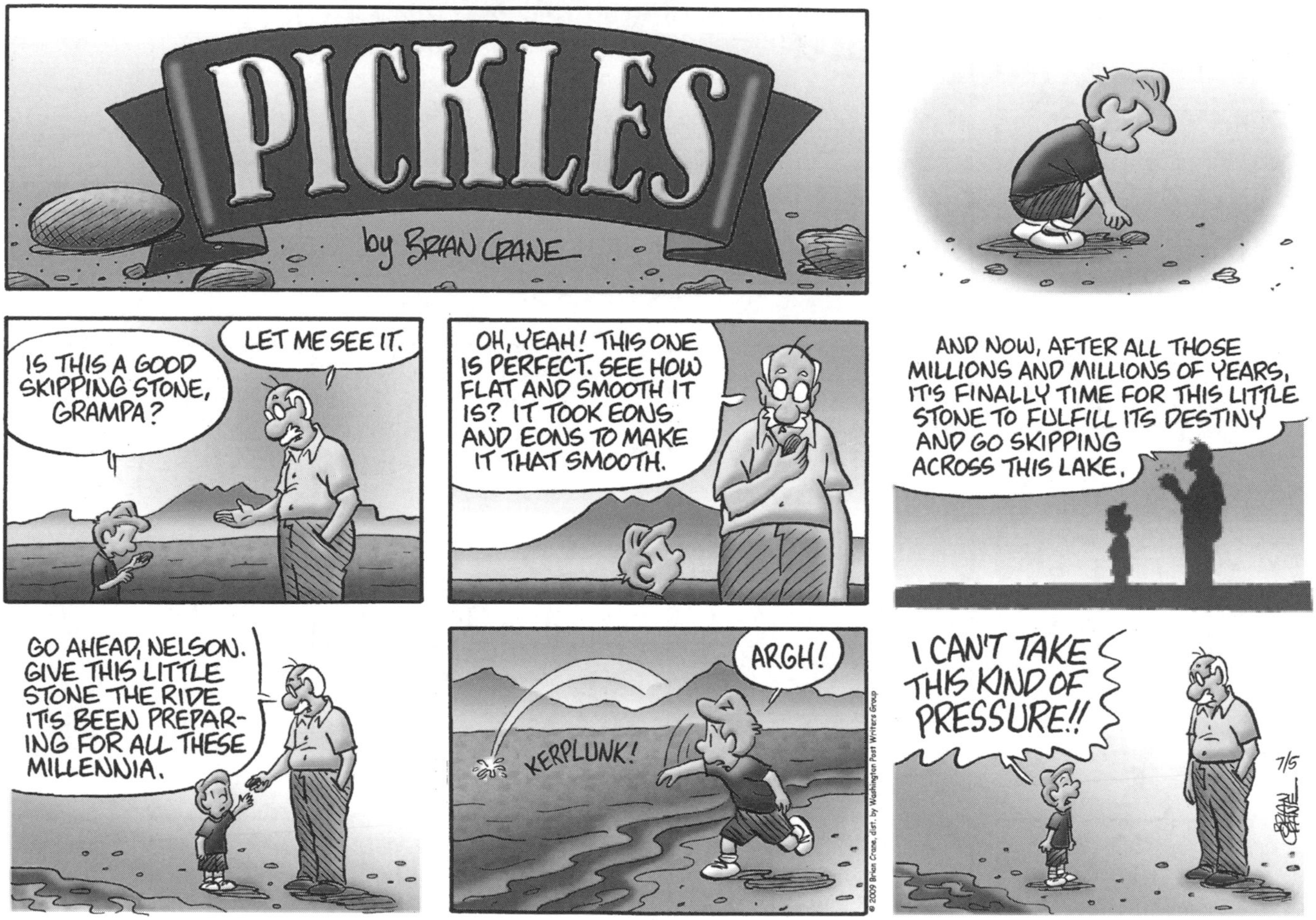
PICKLES
by BRIAN CRANE
IS THIS A GOOD SKIPPING STONE, GRAMPA?
LET ME SEE IT.
OH, YEAH! THIS ONE IS PERFECT. SEE HOW FLAT AND SMOOTH IT IS? IT TOOK EONS AND EONS TO MAKE IT THAT SMOOTH.
AND NOW, AFTER ALL THOSE MILLIONS AND MILLIONS OF YEARS, IT'S FINALLY TIME FOR THIS LITTLE STONE TO FULFILL ITS DESTINY AND GO SKIPPING ACROSS THIS LAKE.
GO AHEAD, NELSON. GIVE THIS LITTLE STONE THE RIDE IT'S BEEN PREPARING FOR ALL THESE MILLENNIA.
ARGH!
KERPLUNK!
I CAN'T TAKE THIS KIND OF PRESSURE!!
7/5
© 2009 Brian Crane, dist. by Washington Post Writers Group

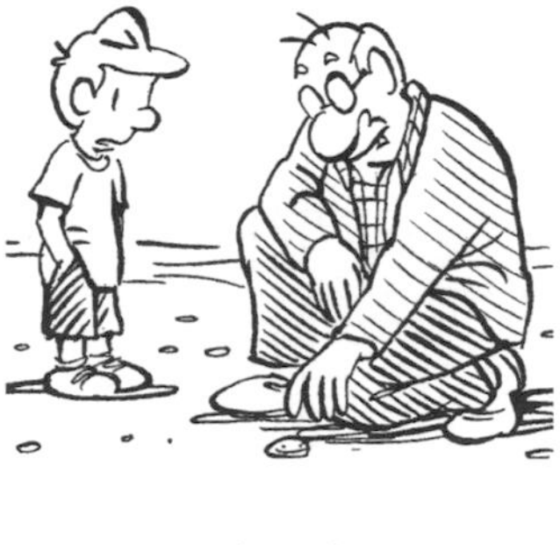

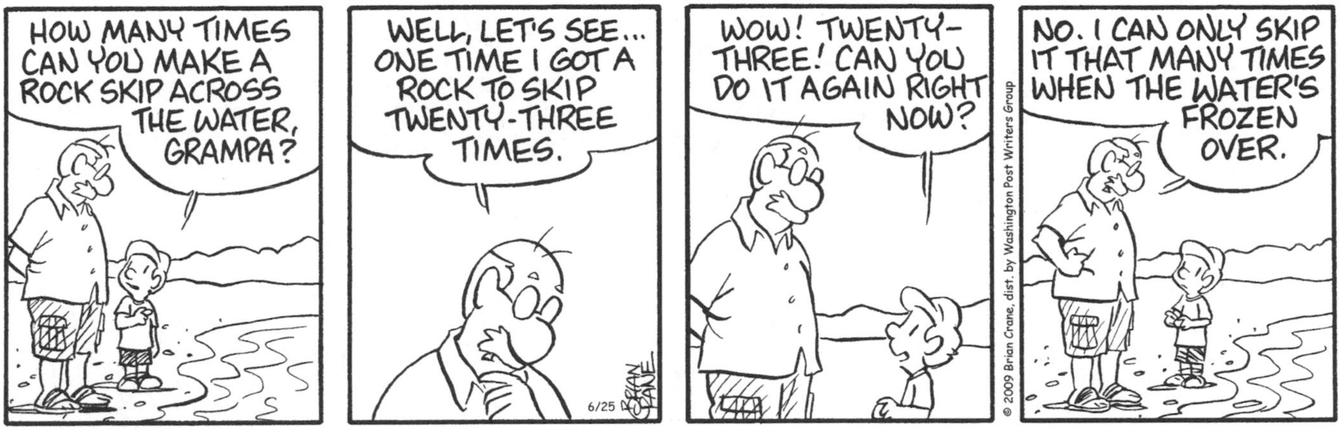
HOW MANY TIMES CAN YOU MAKE A ROCK SKIP ACROSS THE WATER, GRAMPA?
WELL, LET'S SEE... ONE TIME I GOT A ROCK TO SKIP TWENTY-THREE TIMES.
6/25
BRIAN CRANE
WOW! TWENTY-THREE! CAN YOU DO IT AGAIN RIGHT NOW?
© 2009 Brian Crane, dist. by Washington Post Writers Group
NO. I CAN ONLY SKIP IT THAT MANY TIMES WHEN THE WATER'S FROZEN OVER.

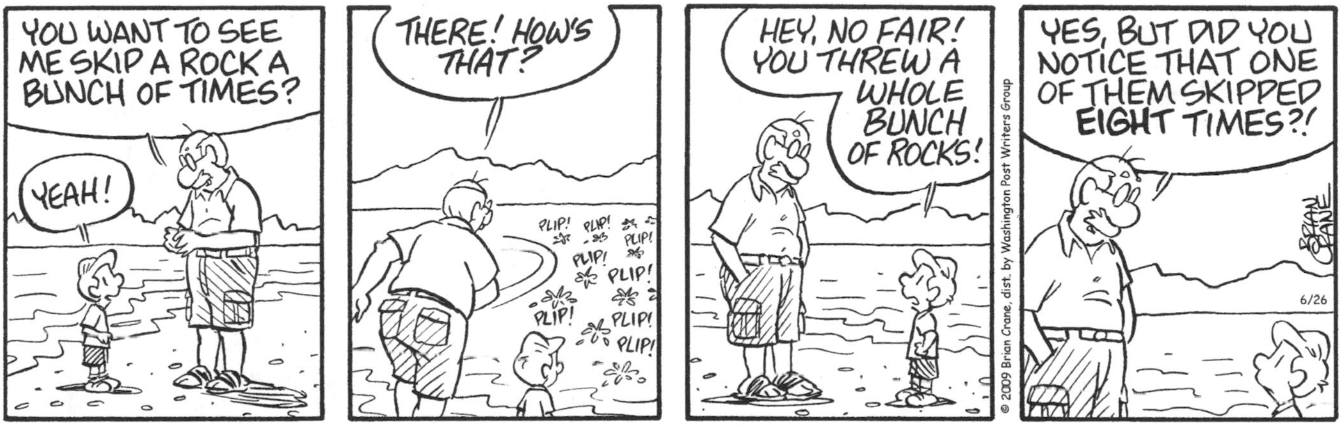
YOU WANT TO SEE ME SKIP A ROCK A BUNCH OF TIMES?
YEAH!
THERE! HOW'S THAT?
PLIP! PLIP! PLIP! PLIP! PLIP! PLIP! PLIP! PLIP! PLIP!
HEY, NO FAIR! YOU THREW A WHOLE BUNCH OF ROCKS!
© 2009 Brian Crane, dist. by Washington Post Writers Group
YES, BUT DID YOU NOTICE THAT ONE OF THEM SKIPPED **EIGHT** TIMES?!
BRIAN CRANE
6/26

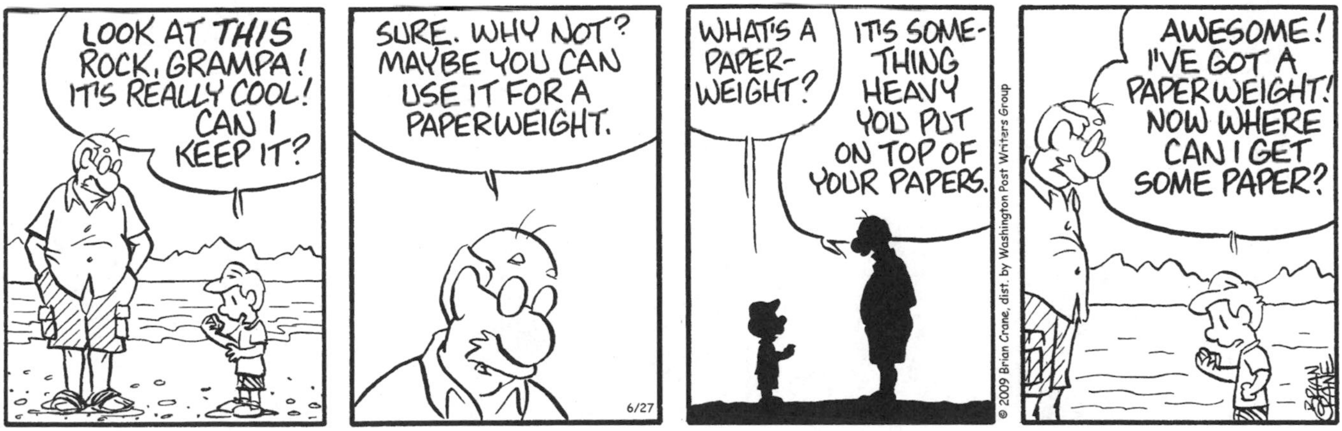
LOOK AT *THIS* ROCK, GRAMPA! IT'S REALLY COOL! CAN I KEEP IT?
SURE. WHY NOT? MAYBE YOU CAN USE IT FOR A PAPERWEIGHT.
6/27
WHAT'S A PAPER-WEIGHT?
IT'S SOME-THING HEAVY YOU PUT ON TOP OF YOUR PAPERS.
© 2009 Brian Crane, dist. by Washington Post Writers Group
AWESOME! I'VE GOT A PAPERWEIGHT! NOW WHERE CAN I GET SOME PAPER?
BRIAN CRANE

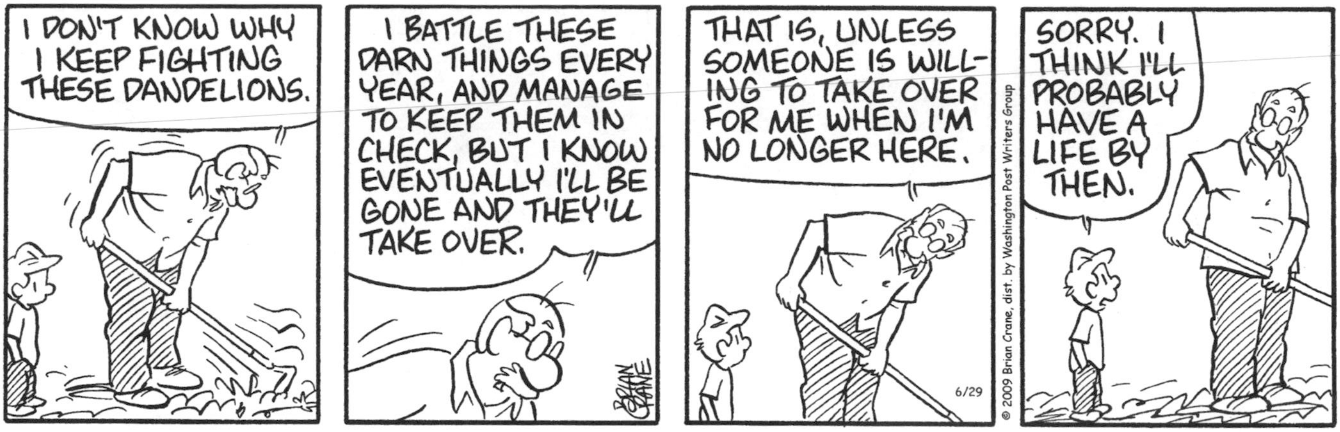
I DON'T KNOW WHY I KEEP FIGHTING THESE DANDELIONS.
I BATTLE THESE DARN THINGS EVERY YEAR, AND MANAGE TO KEEP THEM IN CHECK, BUT I KNOW EVENTUALLY I'LL BE GONE AND THEY'LL TAKE OVER.
BRIAN CRANE
THAT IS, UNLESS SOMEONE IS WILLING TO TAKE OVER FOR ME WHEN I'M NO LONGER HERE.
6/29
SORRY. I THINK I'LL PROBABLY HAVE A LIFE BY THEN.

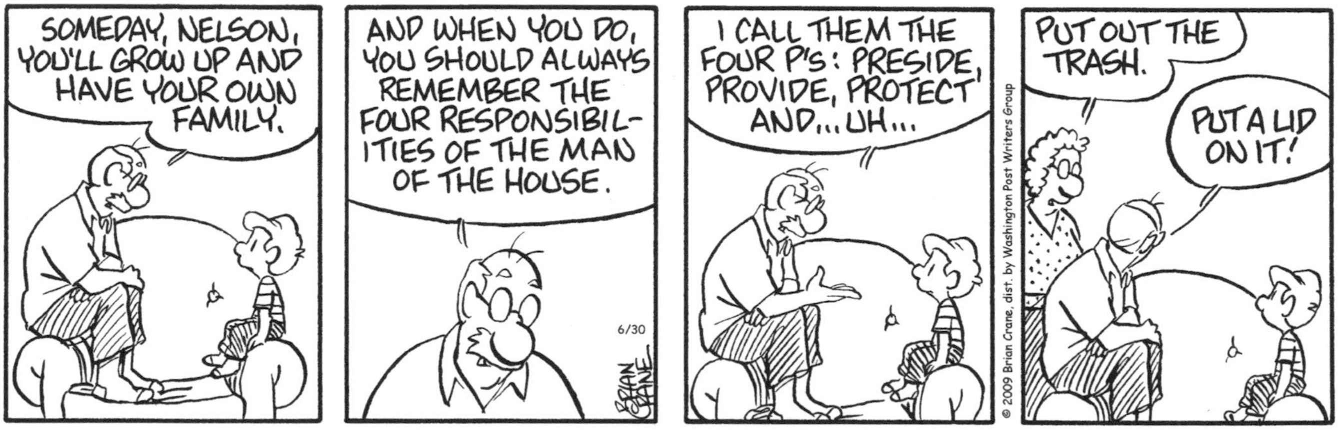
SOMEDAY, NELSON, YOU'LL GROW UP AND HAVE YOUR OWN FAMILY.
AND WHEN YOU DO, YOU SHOULD ALWAYS REMEMBER THE FOUR RESPONSIBILITIES OF THE MAN OF THE HOUSE.
6/30
BRIAN CRANE
I CALL THEM THE FOUR P'S: PRESIDE, PROVIDE, PROTECT AND... UH...
PUT OUT THE TRASH.
PUT A LID ON IT!

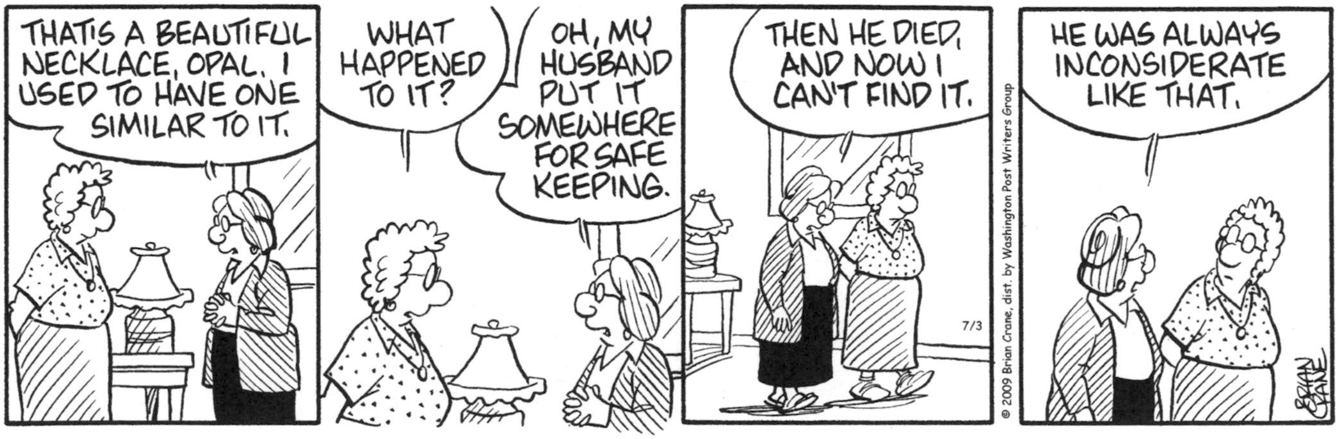
THAT'S A BEAUTIFUL NECKLACE, OPAL. I USED TO HAVE ONE SIMILAR TO IT.
WHAT HAPPENED TO IT?
OH, MY HUSBAND PUT IT SOMEWHERE FOR SAFE KEEPING.
THEN HE DIED, AND NOW I CAN'T FIND IT.
7/3
HE WAS ALWAYS INCONSIDERATE LIKE THAT.
BRIAN CRANE

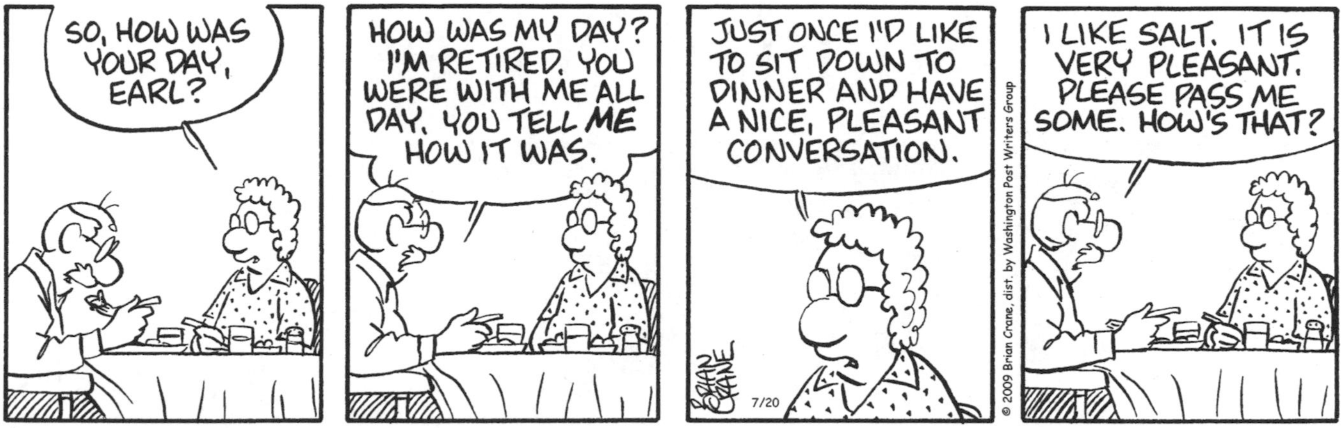
SO, HOW WAS YOUR DAY, EARL?
HOW WAS MY DAY? I'M RETIRED. YOU WERE WITH ME ALL DAY. YOU TELL ME HOW IT WAS.
JUST ONCE I'D LIKE TO SIT DOWN TO DINNER AND HAVE A NICE, PLEASANT CONVERSATION.
BRIAN CRANE
7/20
I LIKE SALT. IT IS VERY PLEASANT. PLEASE PASS ME SOME. HOW'S THAT?

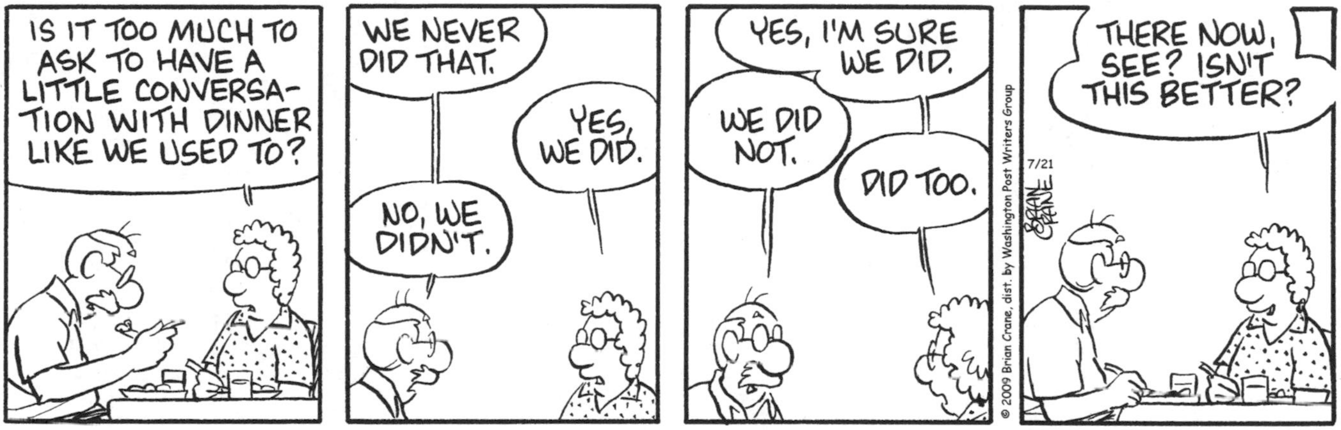
IS IT TOO MUCH TO ASK TO HAVE A LITTLE CONVERSATION WITH DINNER LIKE WE USED TO?
WE NEVER DID THAT.
YES, WE DID.
NO, WE DIDN'T.
YES, I'M SURE WE DID.
WE DID NOT.
DID TOO.
7/21
BRIAN CRANE
THERE NOW, SEE? ISN'T THIS BETTER?

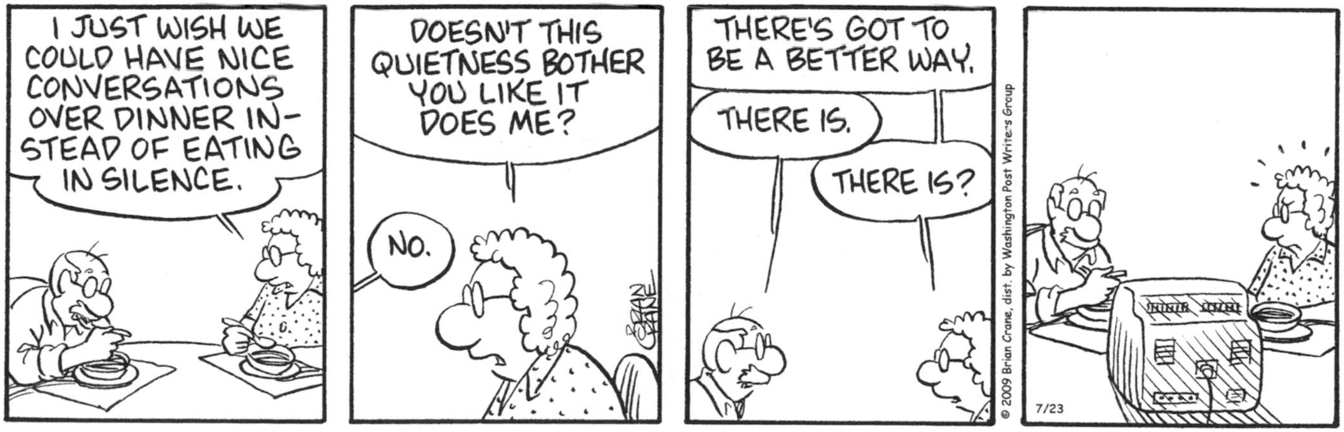
I JUST WISH WE COULD HAVE NICE CONVERSATIONS OVER DINNER INSTEAD OF EATING IN SILENCE.
DOESN'T THIS QUIETNESS BOTHER YOU LIKE IT DOES ME?
NO.
BRIAN CRANE
THERE'S GOT TO BE A BETTER WAY.
THERE IS.
THERE IS?
7/23

SundayPickles

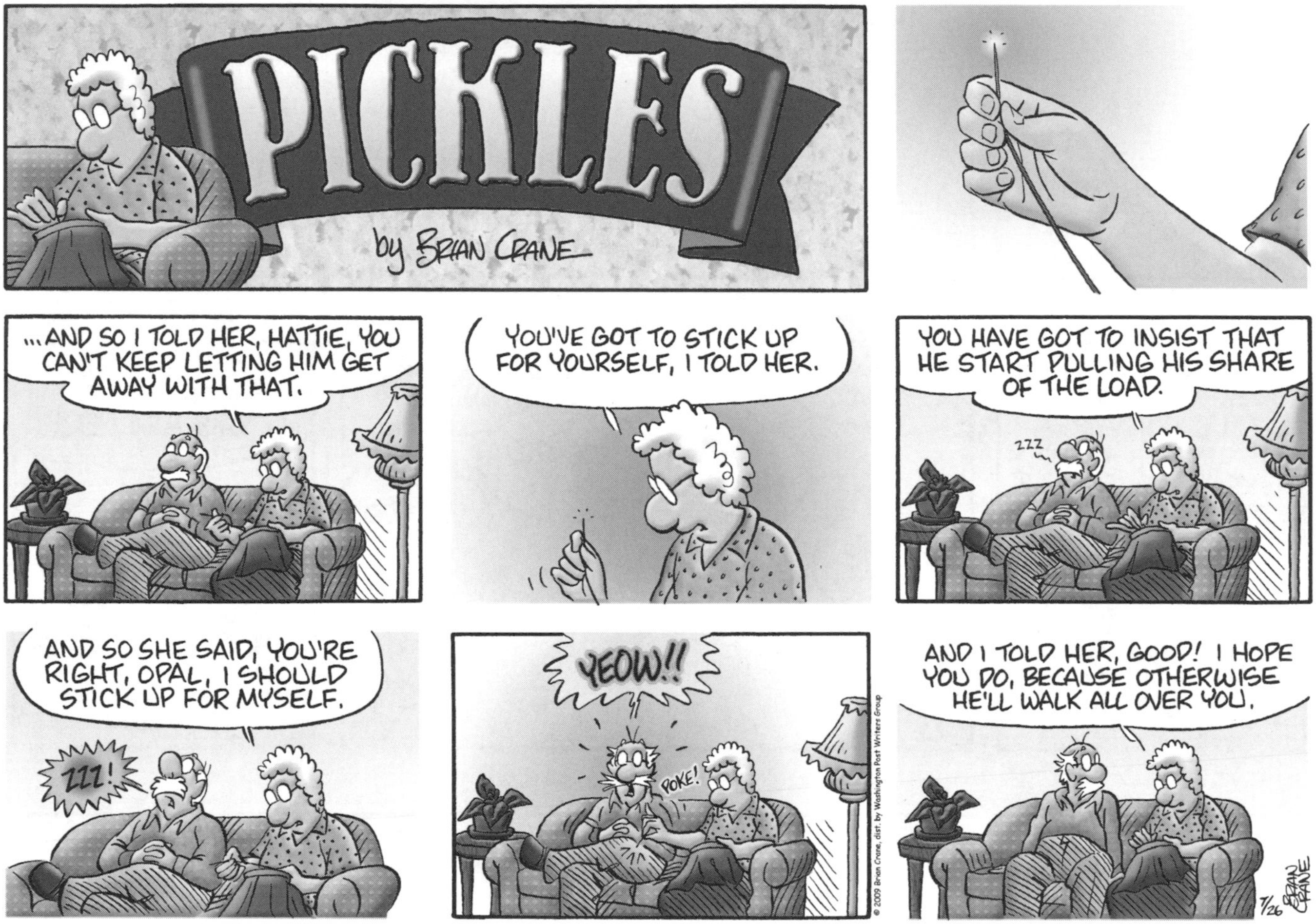
PICKLES
by BRIAN CRANE
...AND SO I TOLD HER, HATTIE, YOU CAN'T KEEP LETTING HIM GET AWAY WITH THAT.
YOU'VE GOT TO STICK UP FOR YOURSELF, I TOLD HER.
YOU HAVE GOT TO INSIST THAT HE START PULLING HIS SHARE OF THE LOAD.
ZZZ
AND SO SHE SAID, YOU'RE RIGHT, OPAL, I SHOULD STICK UP FOR MYSELF.
ZZZ!
YEOW!!
POKE!
© 2009 Brian Crane, dist. by Washington Post Writers Group
AND I TOLD HER, GOOD! I HOPE YOU DO, BECAUSE OTHERWISE HE'LL WALK ALL OVER YOU.
7/26
BRIAN CRANE

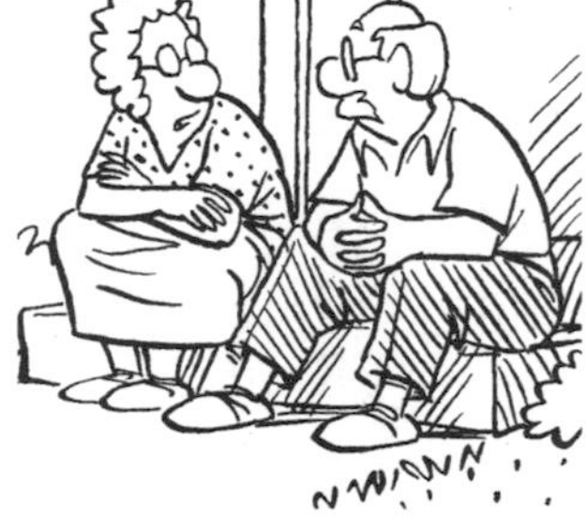

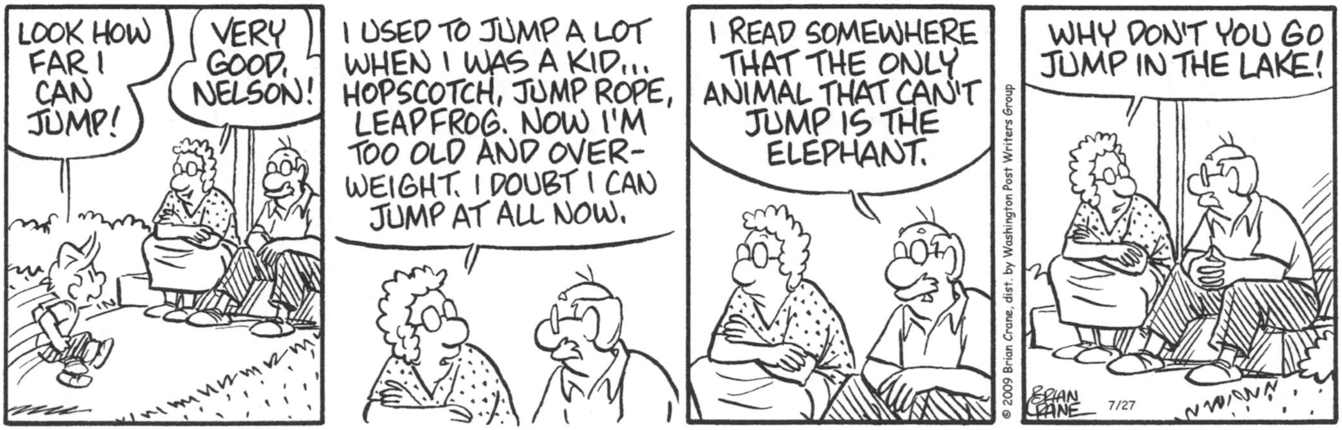
LOOK HOW FAR I CAN JUMP!
VERY GOOD, NELSON!
I USED TO JUMP A LOT WHEN I WAS A KID... HOPSCOTCH, JUMP ROPE, LEAPFROG. NOW I'M TOO OLD AND OVER-WEIGHT. I DOUBT I CAN JUMP AT ALL NOW.
I READ SOMEWHERE THAT THE ONLY ANIMAL THAT CAN'T JUMP IS THE ELEPHANT.
WHY DON'T YOU GO JUMP IN THE LAKE!
© 2009 Brian Crane, dist. by Washington Post Writers Group
BRIAN CRANE 7/27

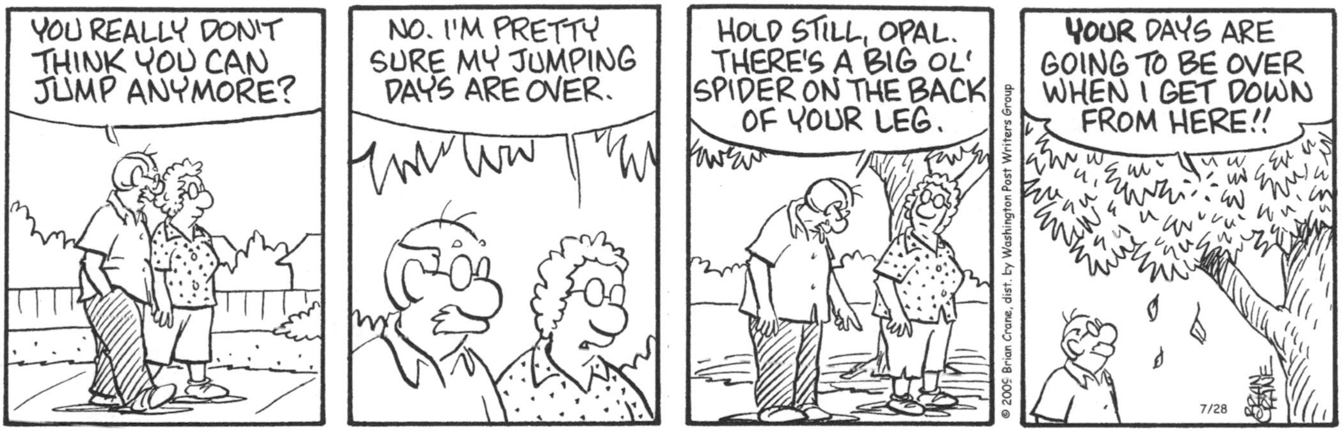
YOU REALLY DON'T THINK YOU CAN JUMP ANYMORE?
NO. I'M PRETTY SURE MY JUMPING DAYS ARE OVER.
HOLD STILL, OPAL. THERE'S A BIG OL' SPIDER ON THE BACK OF YOUR LEG.
YOUR DAYS ARE GOING TO BE OVER WHEN I GET DOWN FROM HERE!!
© 2005 Brian Crane, dist. by Washington Post Writers Group
7/28

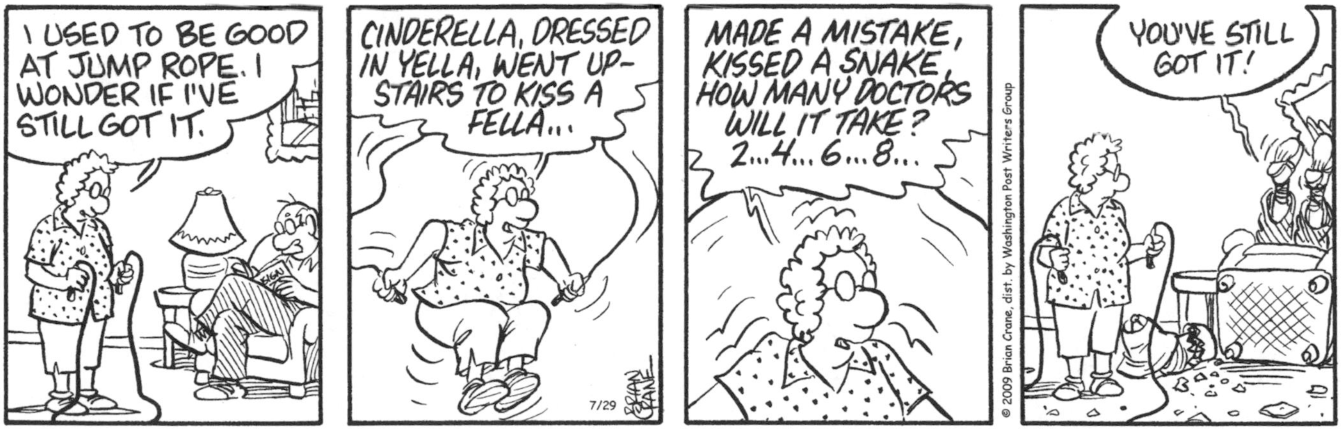
I USED TO BE GOOD AT JUMP ROPE. I WONDER IF I'VE STILL GOT IT.
CINDERELLA, DRESSED IN YELLA, WENT UP-STAIRS TO KISS A FELLA...
7/29 BRIAN CRANE
MADE A MISTAKE, KISSED A SNAKE, HOW MANY DOCTORS WILL IT TAKE? 2...4...6...8...
YOU'VE STILL GOT IT!
© 2009 Brian Crane, dist. by Washington Post Writers Group

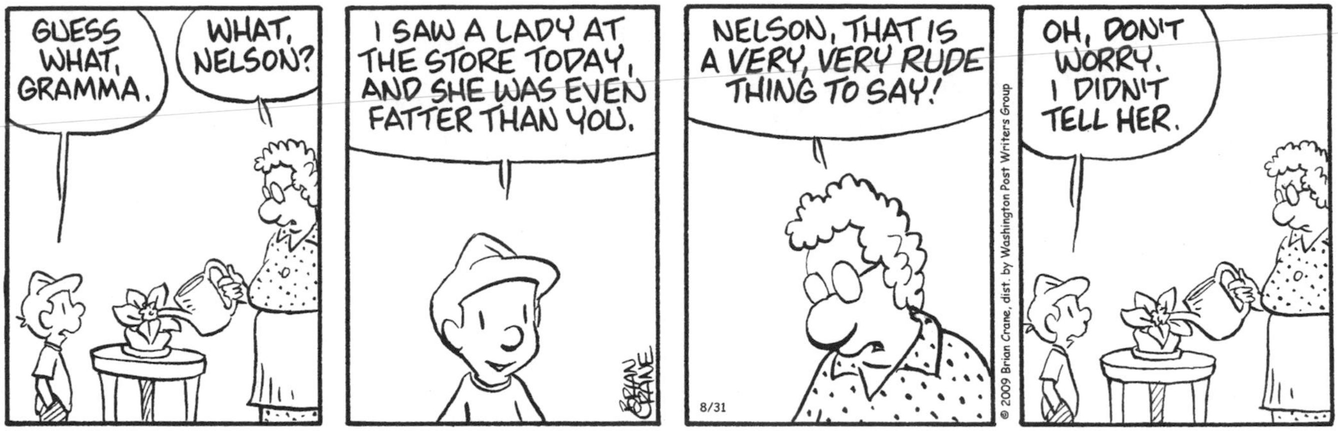
GUESS WHAT, GRAMMA.
WHAT, NELSON?
I SAW A LADY AT THE STORE TODAY, AND SHE WAS EVEN FATTER THAN YOU.
BRIAN CRANE
NELSON, THAT IS A VERY, VERY RUDE THING TO SAY!
8/31
OH, DON'T WORRY. I DIDN'T TELL HER.

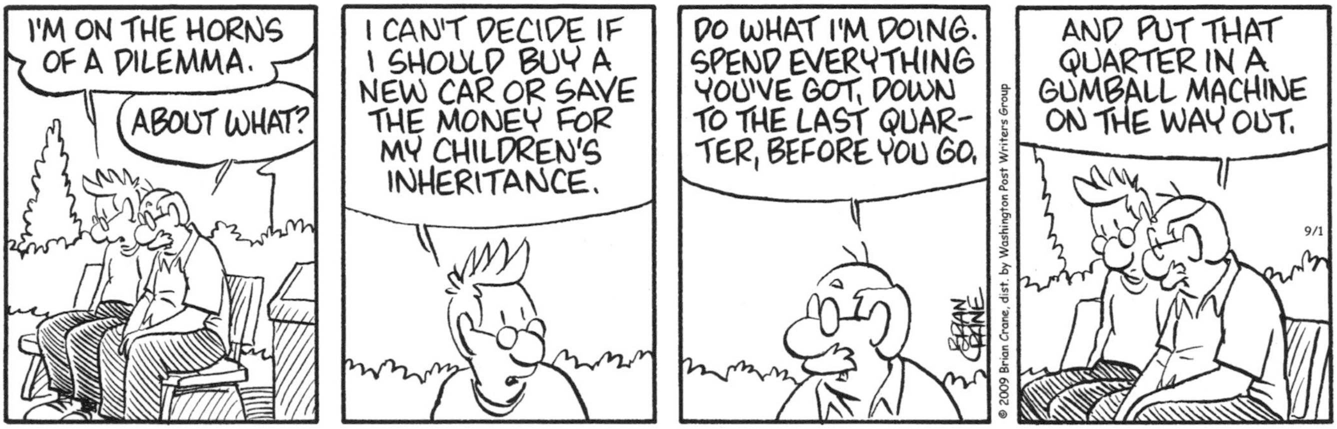
I'M ON THE HORNS OF A DILEMMA.
ABOUT WHAT?
I CAN'T DECIDE IF I SHOULD BUY A NEW CAR OR SAVE THE MONEY FOR MY CHILDREN'S INHERITANCE.
DO WHAT I'M DOING. SPEND EVERYTHING YOU'VE GOT, DOWN TO THE LAST QUARTER, BEFORE YOU GO.
BRIAN CRANE
AND PUT THAT QUARTER IN A GUMBALL MACHINE ON THE WAY OUT.
9/1

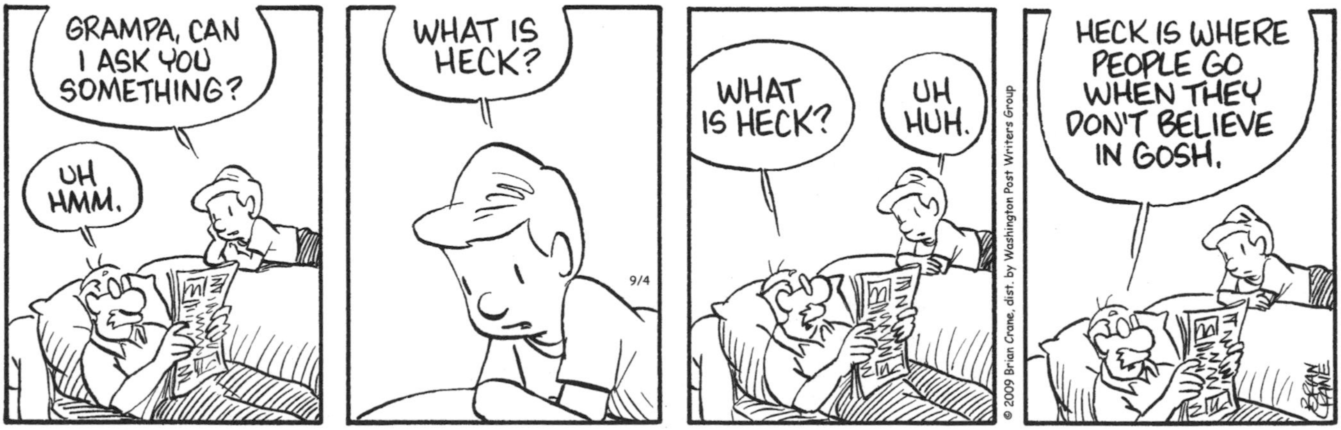
GRAMPA, CAN I ASK YOU SOMETHING?
UH HMM.
WHAT IS HECK?
9/4
WHAT IS HECK?
UH HUH.
HECK IS WHERE PEOPLE GO WHEN THEY DON'T BELIEVE IN GOSH.
BRIAN CRANE

SundayPickles

PICKLES
by BRIAN CRANE
ACK!! WHERE'S THE REMOTE?!!
I DON'T KNOW. I THOUGHT YOU HAD IT.
NO! NO! I DON'T HAVE IT!!
NOOO!!
DON'T LISTEN! LA! LA! LA! LA! LA! LA! LA!
HEY!
BRIAN CRANE
8/2
© 2009 Brian Crane, dist. by Washington Post Writers Group
I WISH THEY'D STOP ADVERTISING THOSE TYPES OF PRODUCTS ON TV!!

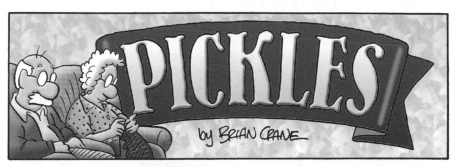

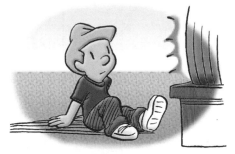

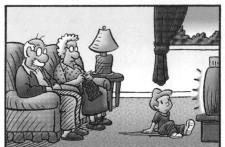

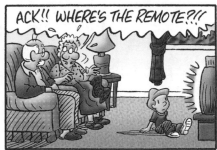

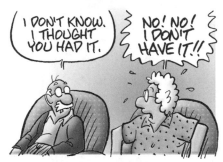

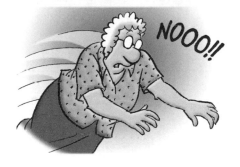

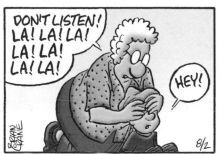

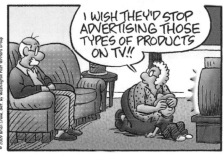

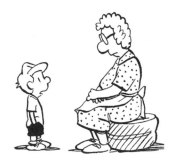

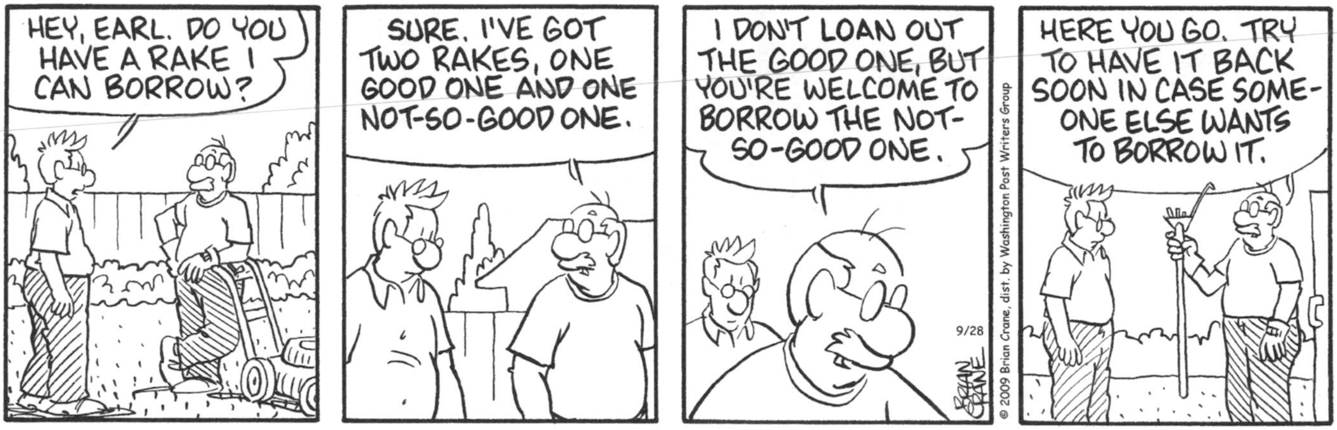
HEY, EARL. DO YOU HAVE A RAKE I CAN BORROW?
SURE. I'VE GOT TWO RAKES, ONE GOOD ONE AND ONE NOT-SO-GOOD ONE.
I DON'T LOAN OUT THE GOOD ONE, BUT YOU'RE WELCOME TO BORROW THE NOT-SO-GOOD ONE.
9/28
BRIAN CRANE
© 2009 Brian Crane, dist. by Washington Post Writers Group
HERE YOU GO. TRY TO HAVE IT BACK SOON IN CASE SOMEONE ELSE WANTS TO BORROW IT.

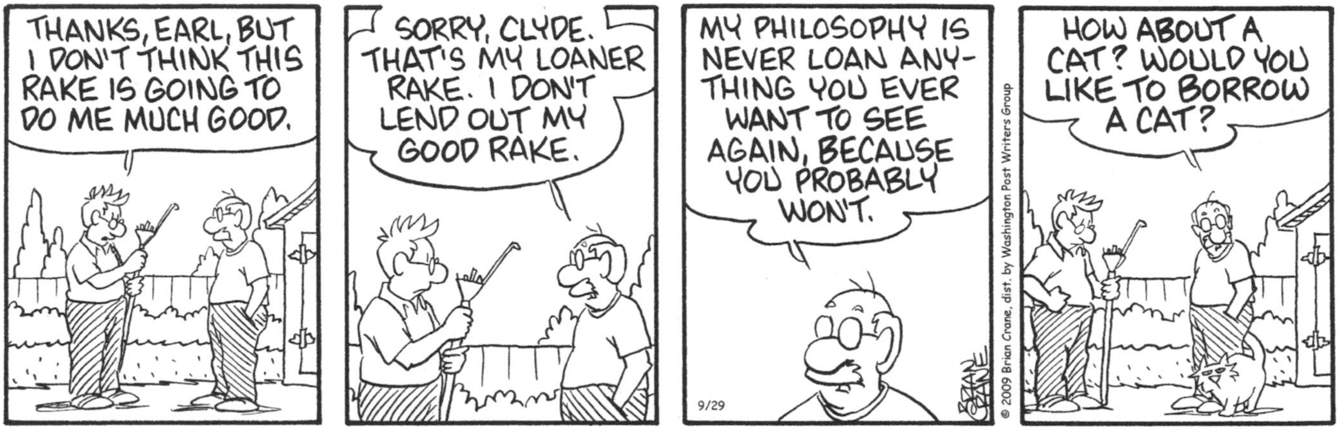
THANKS, EARL, BUT I DON'T THINK THIS RAKE IS GOING TO DO ME MUCH GOOD.
SORRY, CLYDE. THAT'S MY LOANER RAKE. I DON'T LEND OUT MY GOOD RAKE.
MY PHILOSOPHY IS NEVER LOAN ANYTHING YOU EVER WANT TO SEE AGAIN, BECAUSE YOU PROBABLY WON'T.
9/29
BRIAN CRANE
© 2009 Brian Crane, dist. by Washington Post Writers Group
HOW ABOUT A CAT? WOULD YOU LIKE TO BORROW A CAT?

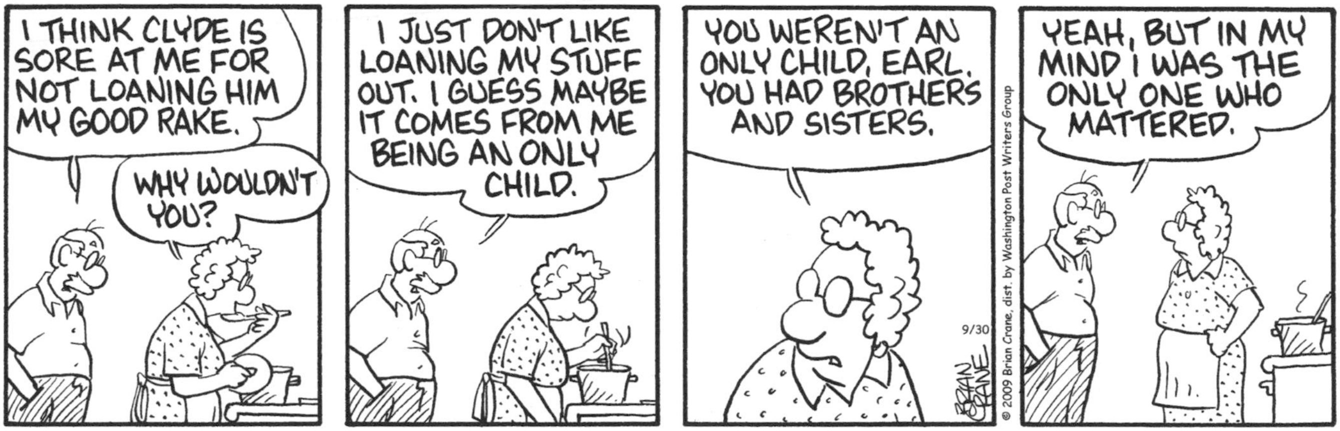
I THINK CLYDE IS SORE AT ME FOR NOT LOANING HIM MY GOOD RAKE.
WHY WOULDN'T YOU?
I JUST DON'T LIKE LOANING MY STUFF OUT. I GUESS MAYBE IT COMES FROM ME BEING AN ONLY CHILD.
YOU WEREN'T AN ONLY CHILD, EARL. YOU HAD BROTHERS AND SISTERS.
9/30
BRIAN CRANE
© 2009 Brian Crane, dist. by Washington Post Writers Group
YEAH, BUT IN MY MIND I WAS THE ONLY ONE WHO MATTERED.

SundayPickles

by Brian Crane

RATS WITH FURRY TAILS, THAT'S WHAT THEY ARE!

I'M GOING OUT TO BUY SOME SQUIRREL TRAPS.

WHAT FOR?

OUR BACKYARD IS BEING TAKEN OVER BY SQUIRRELS! THAT'S WHAT FOR! YESTERDAY AFTERNOON I COUNTED 32 OF THOSE RASCALS OVER A PERIOD OF TWO HOURS!

HOW DO YOU KNOW IT WASN'T ONE SQUIRREL YOU COUNTED 32 TIMES? OR MAYBE TWO SQUIRRELS YOU COUNTED 16 TIMES?

WELL... I... UMM...

MAYBE YOU SHOULD JUST RELAX WHILE I MAKE YOU SOME COOKIES.

MAYBE YOU SHOULD STOP FEEDING THE SQUIRRELS, MOM.

NO WAY.

10/4

© 2009 Brian Crane, dist. by Washington Post Writers Group

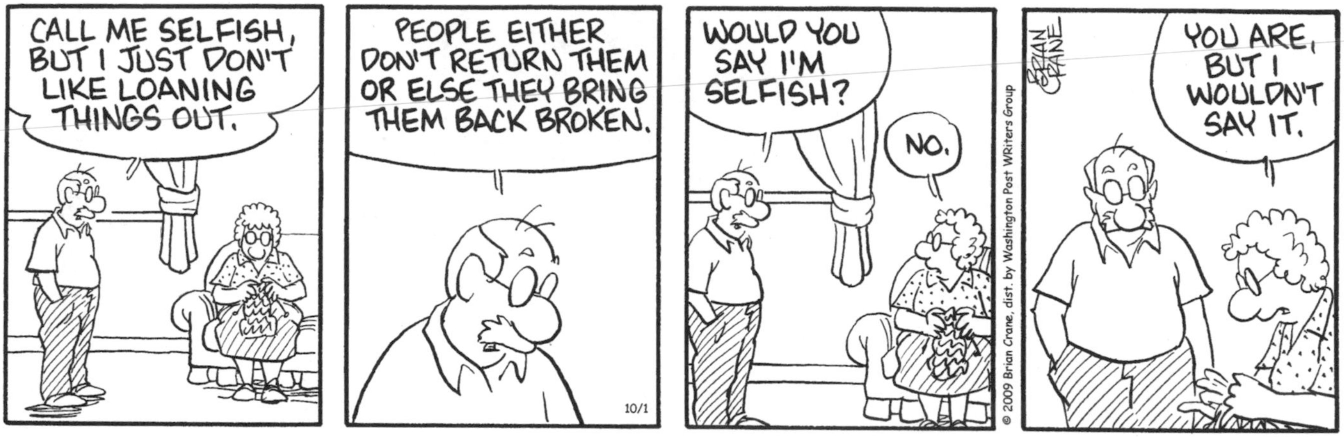
CALL ME SELFISH, BUT I JUST DON'T LIKE LOANING THINGS OUT.
PEOPLE EITHER DON'T RETURN THEM OR ELSE THEY BRING THEM BACK BROKEN.
10/1
WOULD YOU SAY I'M SELFISH?
NO.
© 2009 Brian Crane, dist. by Washington Post Writers Group
BRIAN CRANE
YOU ARE, BUT I WOULDN'T SAY IT.

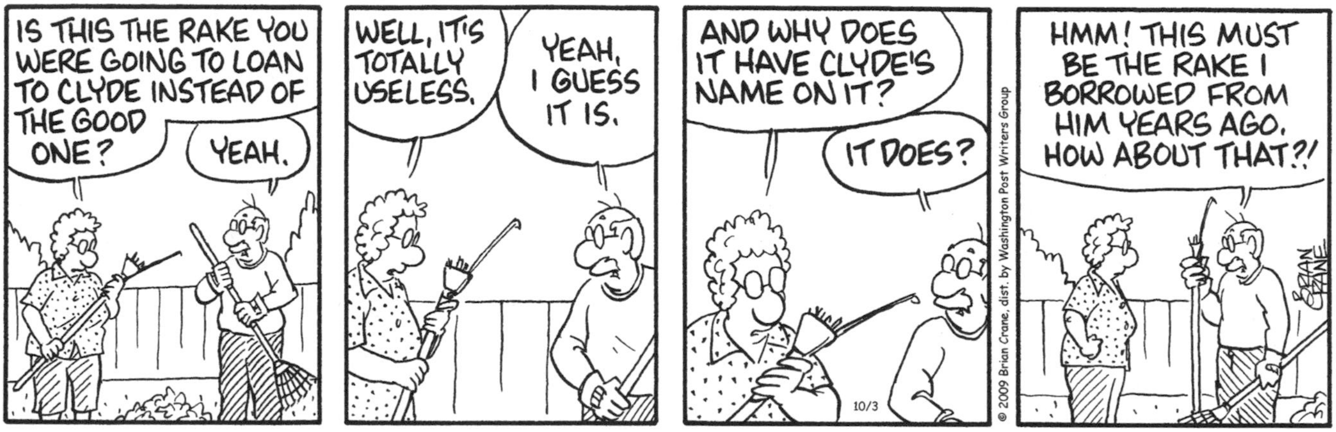
IS THIS THE RAKE YOU WERE GOING TO LOAN TO CLYDE INSTEAD OF THE GOOD ONE?
YEAH.
WELL, IT'S TOTALLY USELESS.
YEAH, I GUESS IT IS.
AND WHY DOES IT HAVE CLYDE'S NAME ON IT?
IT DOES?
10/3
© 2009 Brian Crane, dist. by Washington Post Writers Group
HMM! THIS MUST BE THE RAKE I BORROWED FROM HIM YEARS AGO. HOW ABOUT THAT?!
BRIAN CRANE

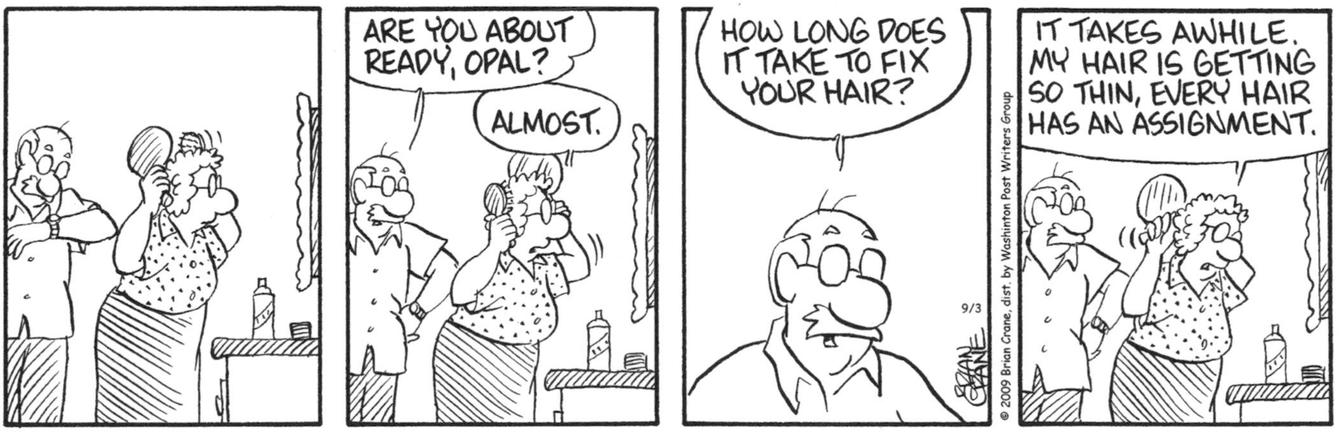
ARE YOU ABOUT READY, OPAL?
ALMOST.
HOW LONG DOES IT TAKE TO FIX YOUR HAIR?
9/3
BRIAN CRANE
© 2009 Brian Crane, dist. by Washington Post Writers Group
IT TAKES AWHILE. MY HAIR IS GETTING SO THIN, EVERY HAIR HAS AN ASSIGNMENT.

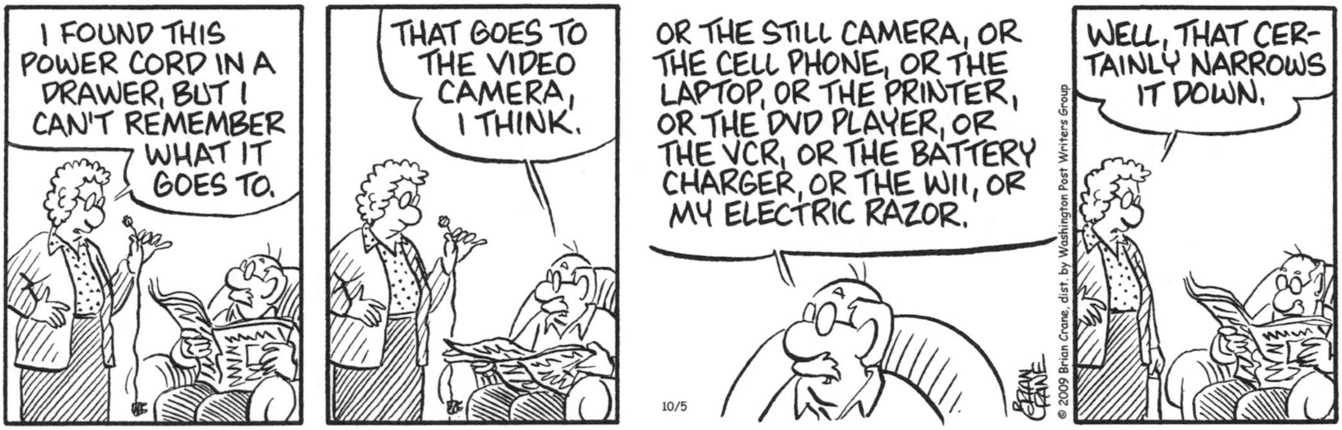
I FOUND THIS POWER CORD IN A DRAWER, BUT I CAN'T REMEMBER WHAT IT GOES TO.
THAT GOES TO THE VIDEO CAMERA, I THINK.
OR THE STILL CAMERA, OR THE CELL PHONE, OR THE LAPTOP, OR THE PRINTER, OR THE DVD PLAYER, OR THE VCR, OR THE BATTERY CHARGER, OR THE WII, OR MY ELECTRIC RAZOR.
10/5
BRIAN CRANE
© 2009 Brian Crane, dist. by Washington Post Writers Group
WELL, THAT CERTAINLY NARROWS IT DOWN.

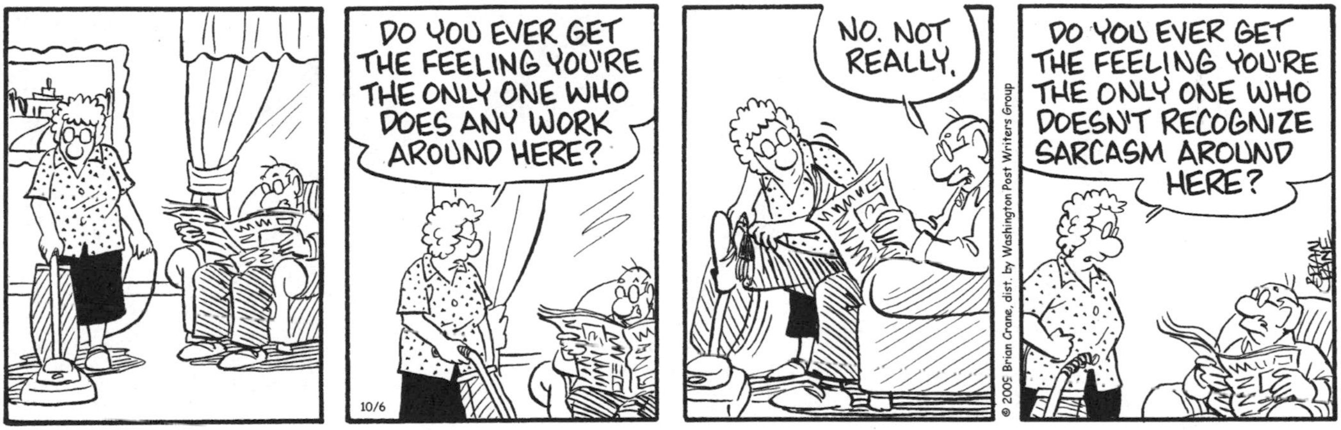
DO YOU EVER GET THE FEELING YOU'RE THE ONLY ONE WHO DOES ANY WORK AROUND HERE?
10/6
NO. NOT REALLY.
© 2009 Brian Crane, dist. by Washington Post Writers Group
DO YOU EVER GET THE FEELING YOU'RE THE ONLY ONE WHO DOESN'T RECOGNIZE SARCASM AROUND HERE?
BRIAN CRANE

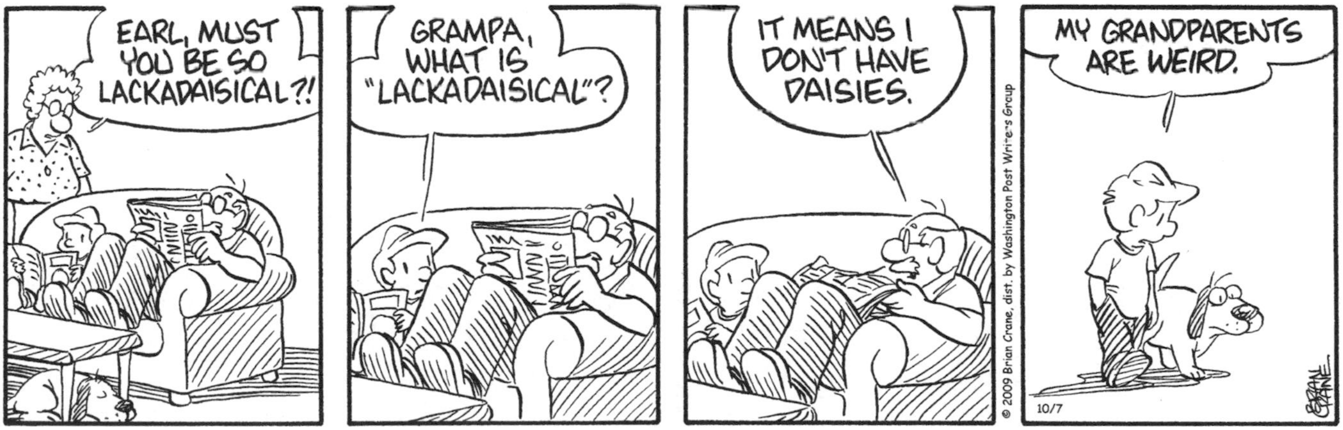
EARL, MUST YOU BE SO LACKADAISICAL?!
GRAMPA, WHAT IS "LACKADAISICAL"?
IT MEANS I DON'T HAVE DAISIES.
© 2009 Brian Crane, dist. by Washington Post Writers Group
MY GRANDPARENTS ARE WEIRD.
10/7
BRIAN CRANE

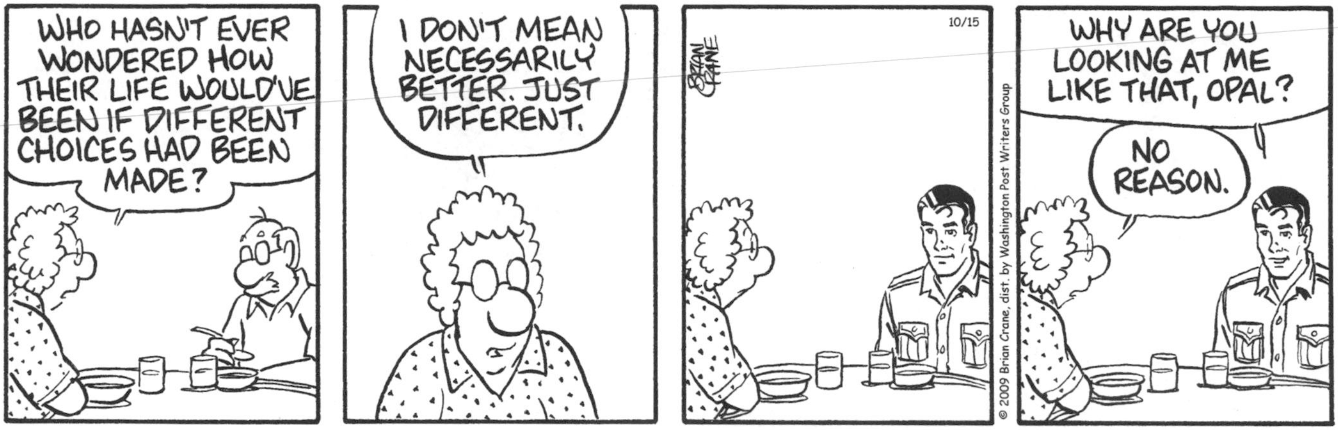
WHO HASN'T EVER WONDERED HOW THEIR LIFE WOULD'VE BEEN IF DIFFERENT CHOICES HAD BEEN MADE?
I DON'T MEAN NECESSARILY BETTER. JUST DIFFERENT.
10/15
WHY ARE YOU LOOKING AT ME LIKE THAT, OPAL?
NO REASON.
© 2009 Brian Crane, dist. by Washington Post Writers Group

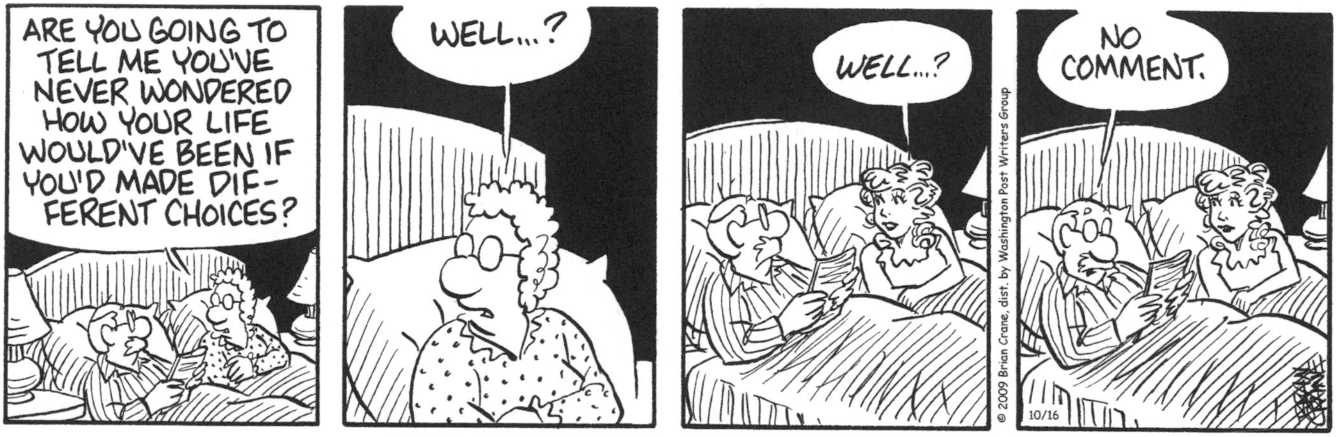
ARE YOU GOING TO TELL ME YOU'VE NEVER WONDERED HOW YOUR LIFE WOULD'VE BEEN IF YOU'D MADE DIF-FERENT CHOICES?
WELL...?
WELL...?
NO COMMENT.
10/16
© 2009 Brian Crane, dist. by Washington Post Writers Group

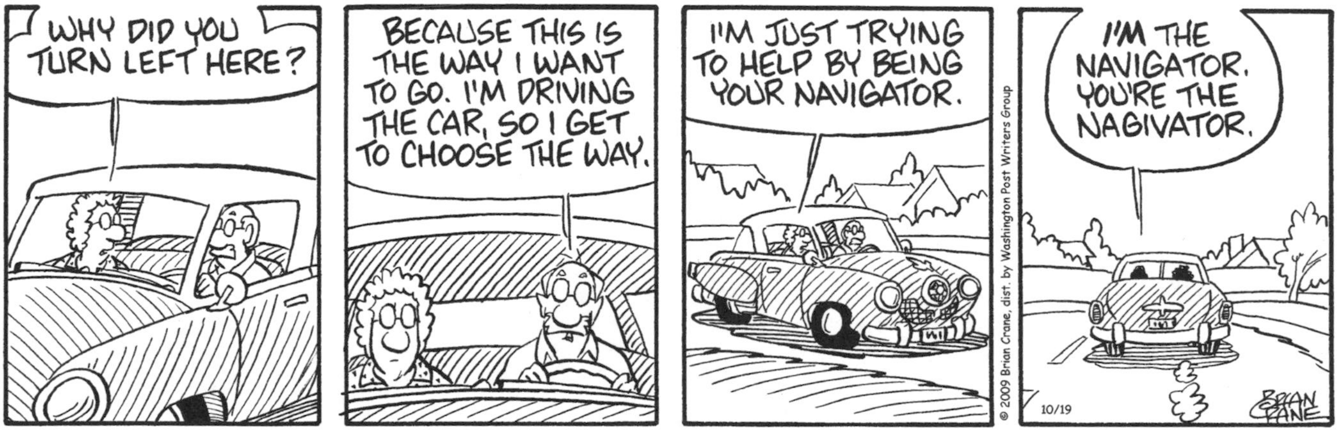
WHY DID YOU TURN LEFT HERE?
BECAUSE THIS IS THE WAY I WANT TO GO. I'M DRIVING THE CAR, SO I GET TO CHOOSE THE WAY.
I'M JUST TRYING TO HELP BY BEING YOUR NAVIGATOR.
I'M THE NAVIGATOR. YOU'RE THE NAGIVATOR.
10/19
BRIAN CRANE
© 2009 Brian Crane, dist. by Washington Post Writers Group

SundayPickles

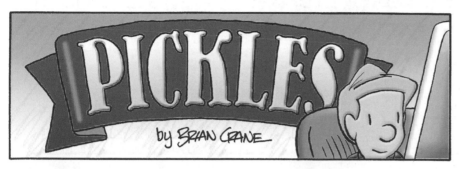

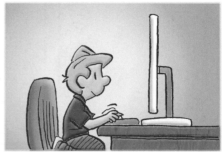

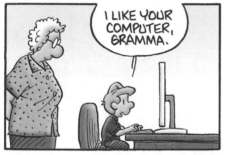

PICKLES
by BRIAN CRANE
I LIKE YOUR COMPUTER, GRAMMA.
YOU DO?
UH HUH.
IT HAS A BIG SCREEN AND IT'S REALLY FAST.
I HOPE I CAN GET ONE LIKE THIS SOMEDAY.
TELL YOU WHAT... YOU CAN HAVE THIS ONE WHEN I DIE.
10/25 BRIAN CRANE
© 2009 Brian Crane, dist. by Washington Post Writers Group.
REALLY? WHEN WILL THAT BE?

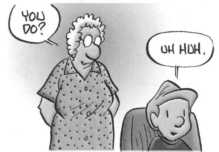

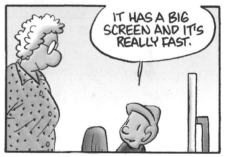

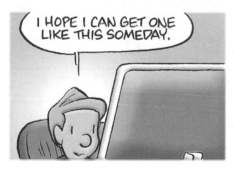

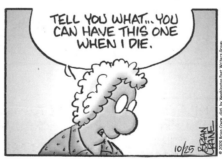

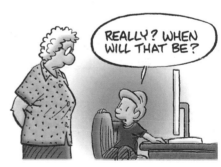

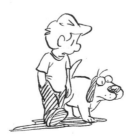

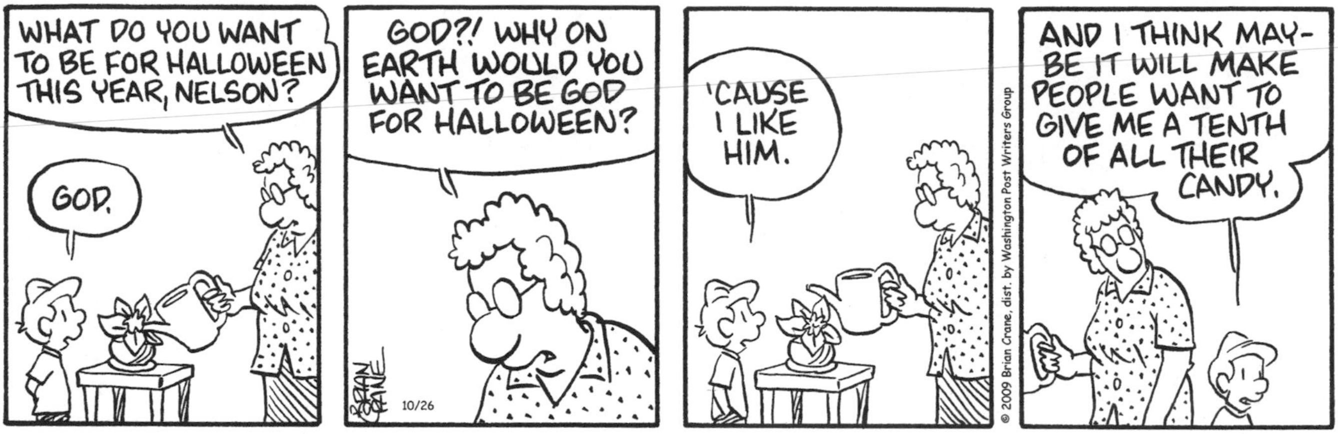
WHAT DO YOU WANT TO BE FOR HALLOWEEN THIS YEAR, NELSON?
GOD.
GOD?! WHY ON EARTH WOULD YOU WANT TO BE GOD FOR HALLOWEEN?
10/26
'CAUSE I LIKE HIM.
© 2009 Brian Crane, dist. by Washington Post Writers Group
AND I THINK MAY-BE IT WILL MAKE PEOPLE WANT TO GIVE ME A TENTH OF ALL THEIR CANDY.

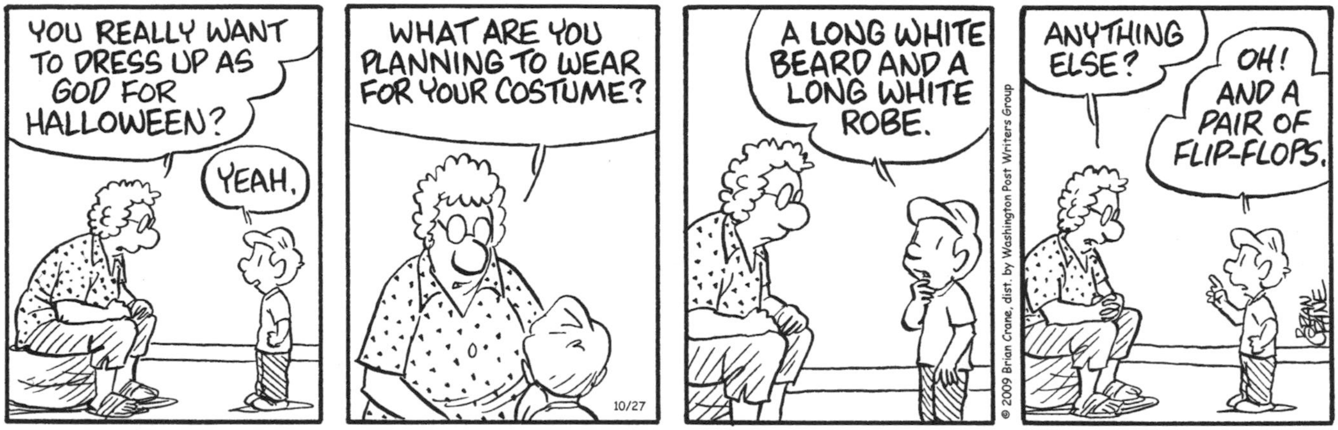
YOU REALLY WANT TO DRESS UP AS GOD FOR HALLOWEEN?
YEAH.
WHAT ARE YOU PLANNING TO WEAR FOR YOUR COSTUME?
10/27
A LONG WHITE BEARD AND A LONG WHITE ROBE.
© 2009 Brian Crane, dist. by Washington Post Writers Group
ANYTHING ELSE?
OH! AND A PAIR OF FLIP-FLOPS.

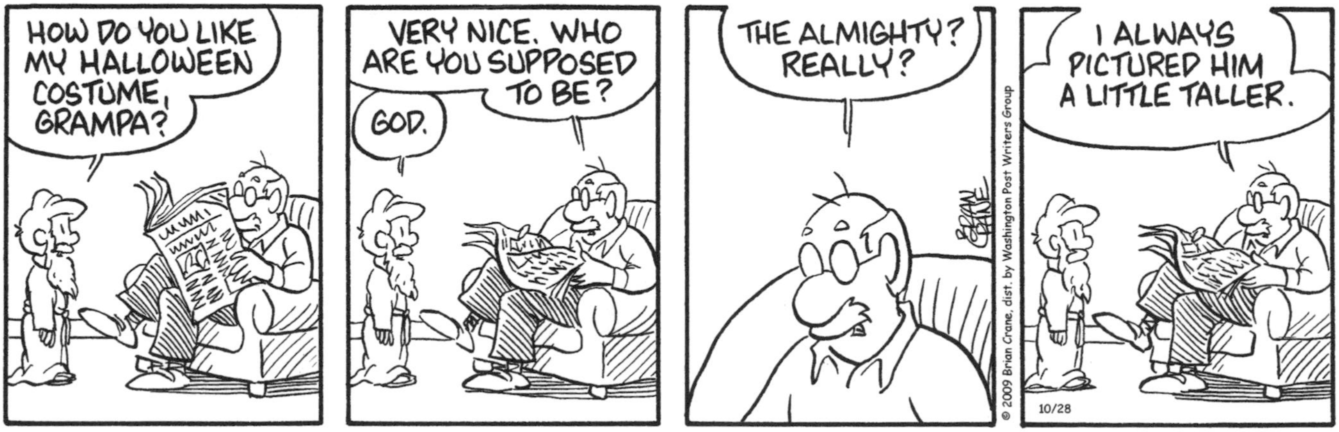
HOW DO YOU LIKE MY HALLOWEEN COSTUME, GRAMPA?
VERY NICE. WHO ARE YOU SUPPOSED TO BE?
GOD.
THE ALMIGHTY? REALLY?
© 2009 Brian Crane, dist. by Washington Post Writers Group
I ALWAYS PICTURED HIM A LITTLE TALLER.
10/28

SundayPickles

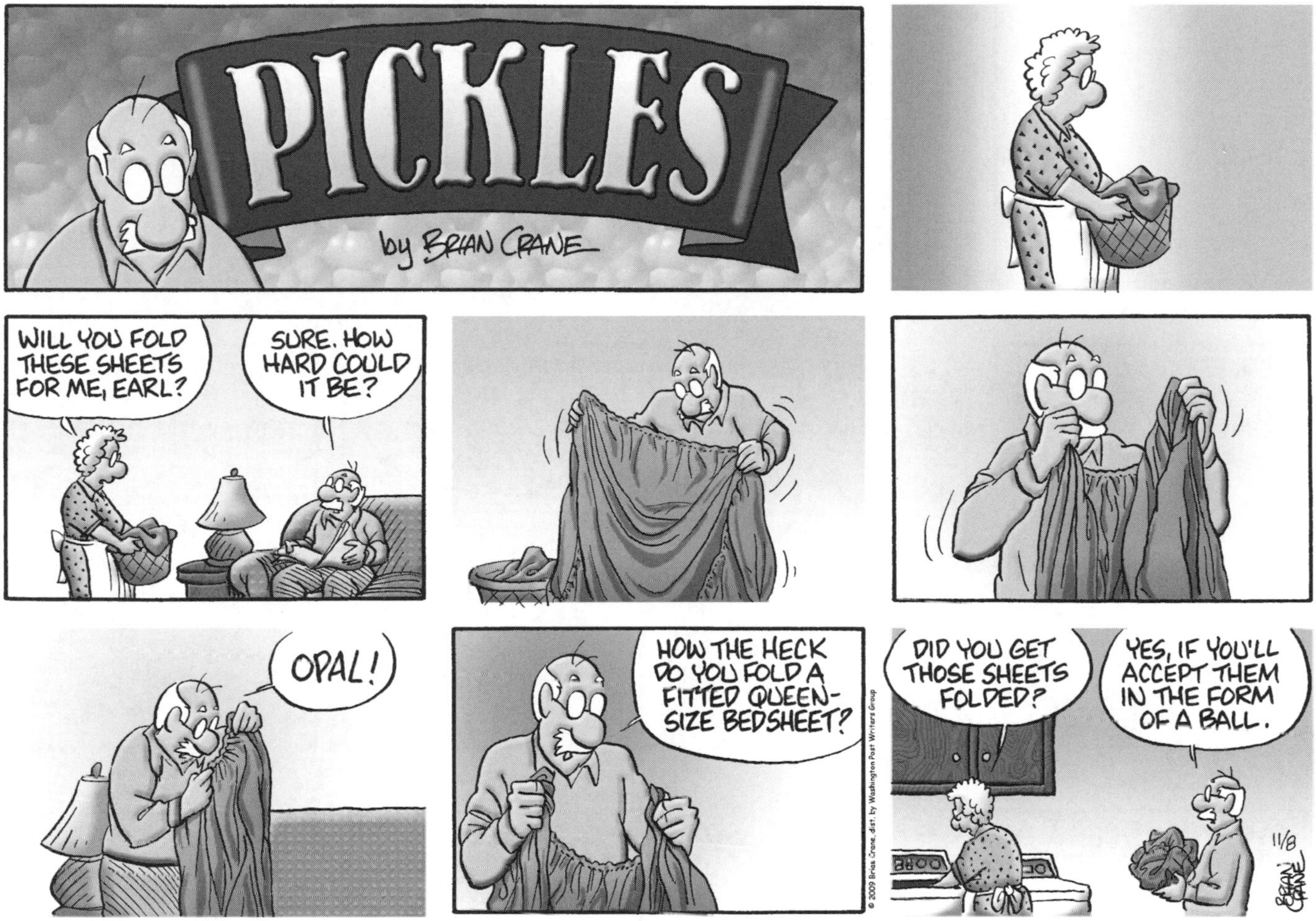
PICKLES
by BRIAN CRANE
WILL YOU FOLD THESE SHEETS FOR ME, EARL?
SURE. HOW HARD COULD IT BE?
OPAL!
HOW THE HECK DO YOU FOLD A FITTED QUEEN-SIZE BEDSHEET?
© 2009 Brian Crane, dist. by Washington Post Writers Group
DID YOU GET THOSE SHEETS FOLDED?
YES, IF YOU'LL ACCEPT THEM IN THE FORM OF A BALL.
11/8
BRIAN CRANE

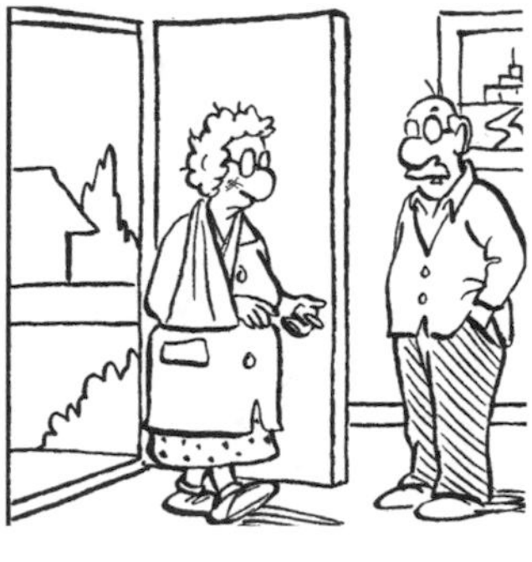

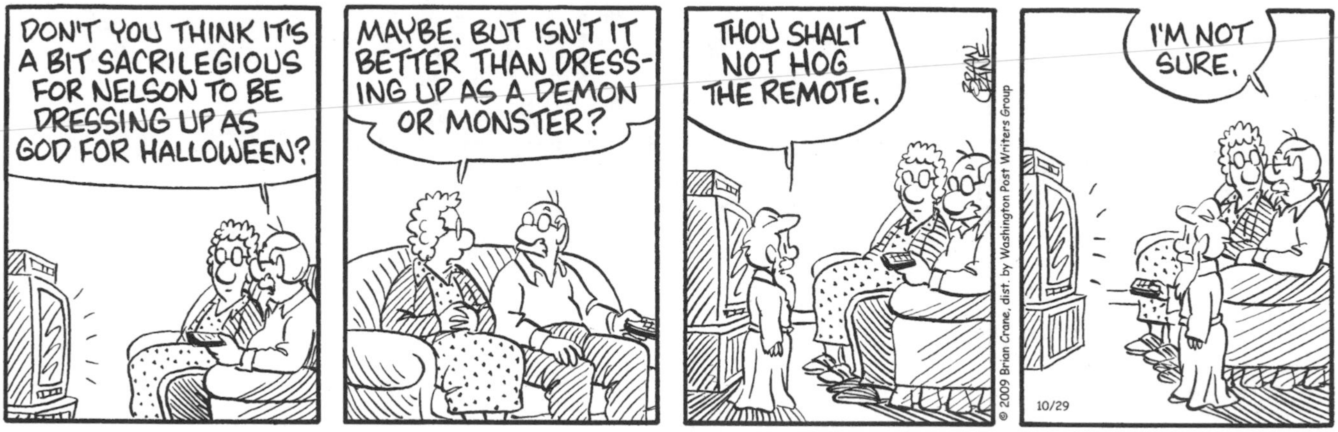
DON'T YOU THINK IT'S A BIT SACRILEGIOUS FOR NELSON TO BE DRESSING UP AS GOD FOR HALLOWEEN?
MAYBE. BUT ISN'T IT BETTER THAN DRESSING UP AS A DEMON OR MONSTER?
THOU SHALT NOT HOG THE REMOTE.
I'M NOT SURE.
BRIAN CRANE
© 2009 Brian Crane, dist. by Washington Post Writers Group
10/29

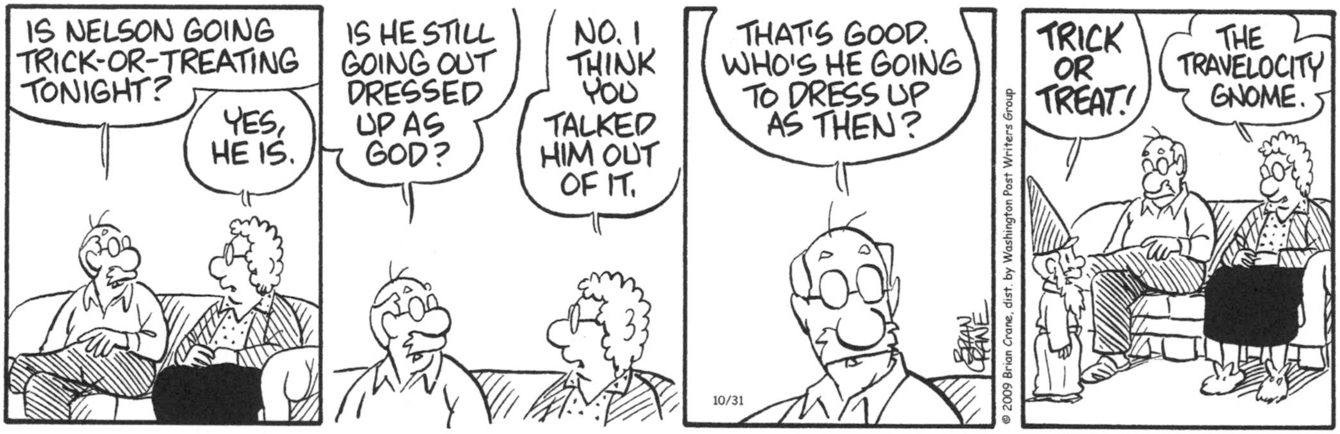
IS NELSON GOING TRICK-OR-TREATING TONIGHT?
YES, HE IS.
IS HE STILL GOING OUT DRESSED UP AS GOD?
NO. I THINK YOU TALKED HIM OUT OF IT.
THAT'S GOOD. WHO'S HE GOING TO DRESS UP AS THEN?
10/31
BRIAN CRANE
© 2009 Brian Crane, dist. by Washington Post Writers Group
TRICK OR TREAT!
THE TRAVELOCITY GNOME.

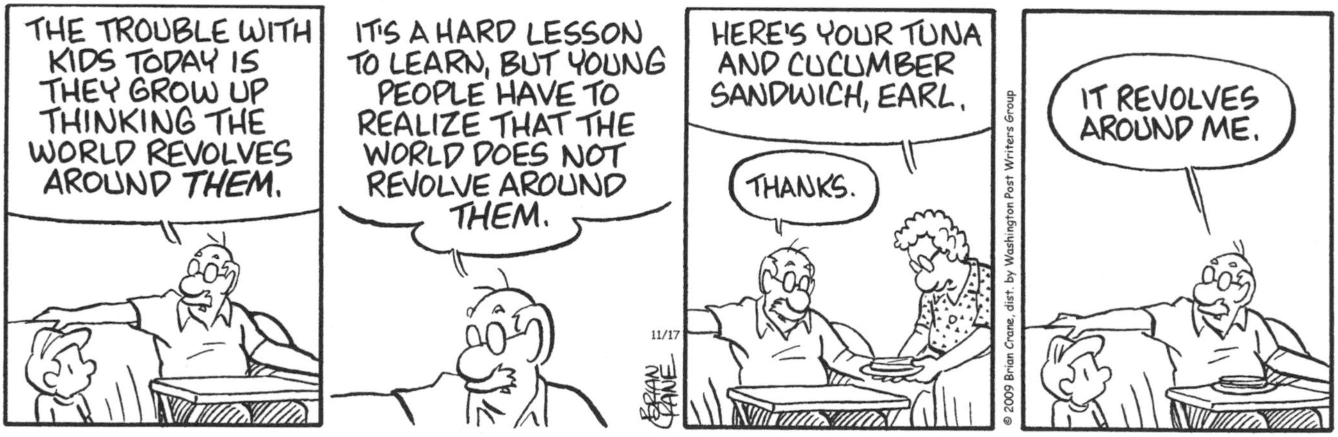
THE TROUBLE WITH KIDS TODAY IS THEY GROW UP THINKING THE WORLD REVOLVES AROUND THEM.
IT'S A HARD LESSON TO LEARN, BUT YOUNG PEOPLE HAVE TO REALIZE THAT THE WORLD DOES NOT REVOLVE AROUND THEM.
11/17
BRIAN CRANE
HERE'S YOUR TUNA AND CUCUMBER SANDWICH, EARL.
THANKS.
© 2009 Brian Crane, dist. by Washington Post Writers Group
IT REVOLVES AROUND ME.

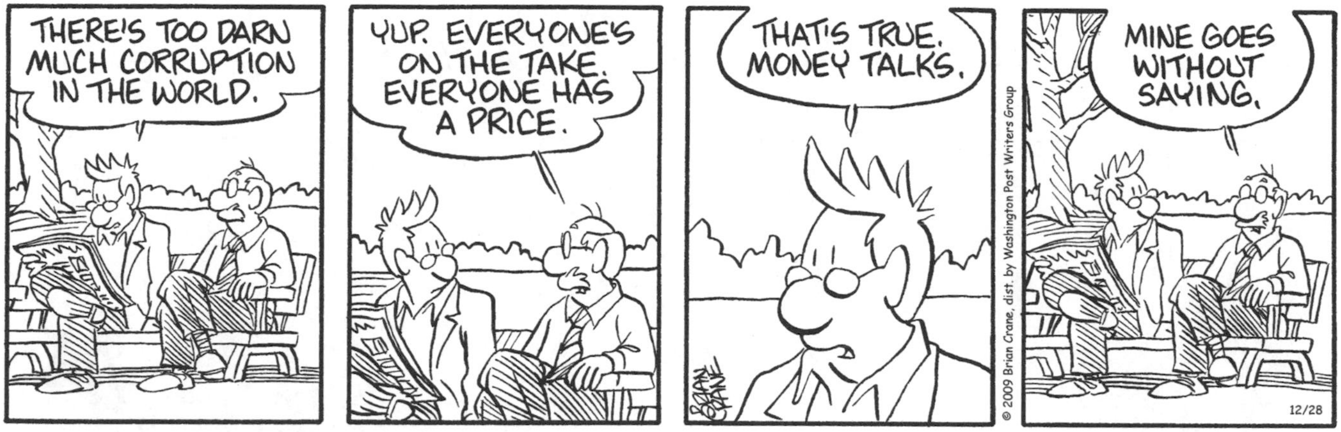
THERE'S TOO DARN MUCH CORRUPTION IN THE WORLD.
YUP. EVERYONE'S ON THE TAKE. EVERYONE HAS A PRICE.
THAT'S TRUE. MONEY TALKS.
© 2009 Brian Crane, dist. by Washington Post Writers Group
MINE GOES WITHOUT SAYING.
12/28

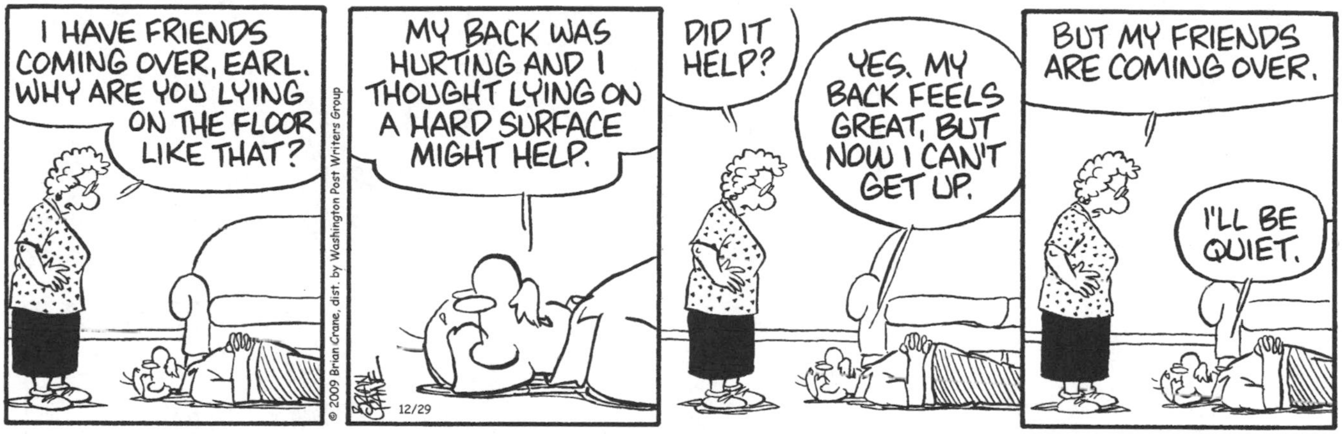
I HAVE FRIENDS COMING OVER, EARL. WHY ARE YOU LYING ON THE FLOOR LIKE THAT?
© 2009 Brian Crane, dist. by Washington Post Writers Group
MY BACK WAS HURTING AND I THOUGHT LYING ON A HARD SURFACE MIGHT HELP.
12/29
DID IT HELP?
YES. MY BACK FEELS GREAT, BUT NOW I CAN'T GET UP.
BUT MY FRIENDS ARE COMING OVER.
I'LL BE QUIET.

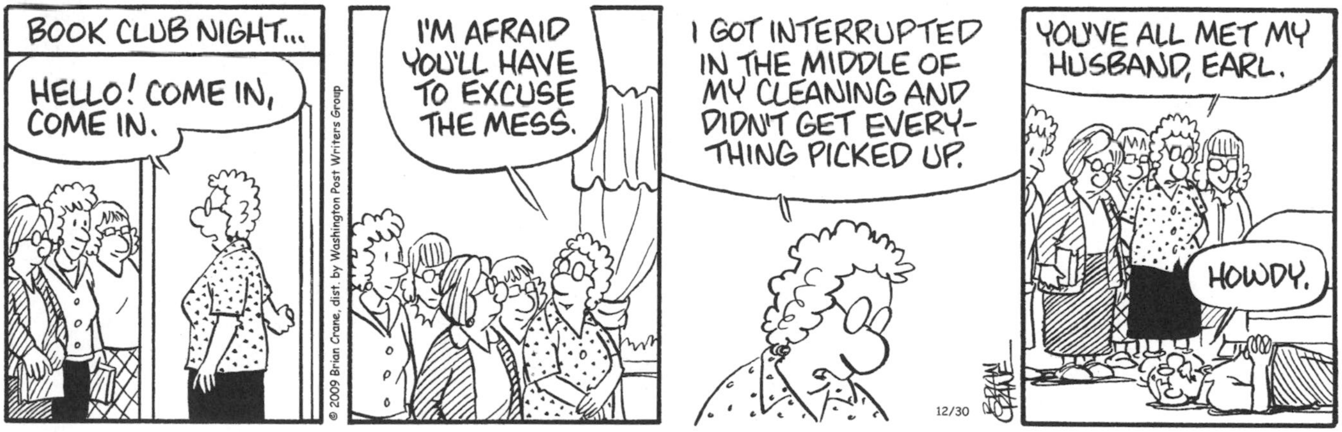
BOOK CLUB NIGHT...
HELLO! COME IN, COME IN.
© 2009 Brian Crane, dist. by Washington Post Writers Group
I'M AFRAID YOU'LL HAVE TO EXCUSE THE MESS.
I GOT INTERRUPTED IN THE MIDDLE OF MY CLEANING AND DIDN'T GET EVERYTHING PICKED UP.
12/30
YOU'VE ALL MET MY HUSBAND, EARL.
HOWDY.

SundayPickles

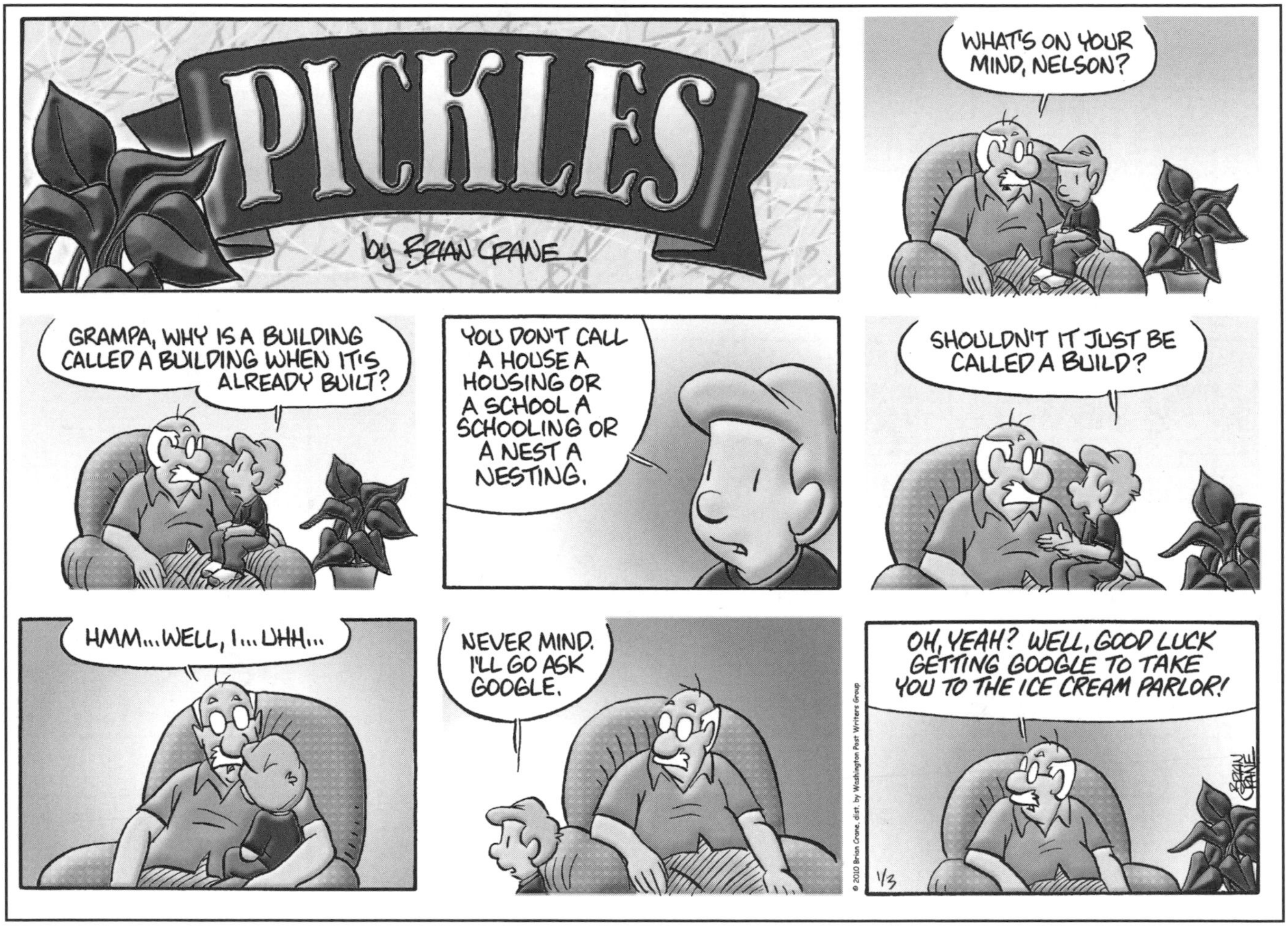
PICKLES
by BRIAN CRANE
WHAT'S ON YOUR MIND, NELSON?
GRAMPA, WHY IS A BUILDING CALLED A BUILDING WHEN IT'S ALREADY BUILT?
YOU DON'T CALL A HOUSE A HOUSING OR A SCHOOL A SCHOOLING OR A NEST A NESTING.
SHOULDN'T IT JUST BE CALLED A BUILD?
HMM... WELL, I... UHH...
NEVER MIND. I'LL GO ASK GOOGLE.
© 2010 Brian Crane, dist. by Washington Post Writers Group
OH, YEAH? WELL, GOOD LUCK GETTING GOOGLE TO TAKE YOU TO THE ICE CREAM PARLOR!
BRIAN CRANE
1/3

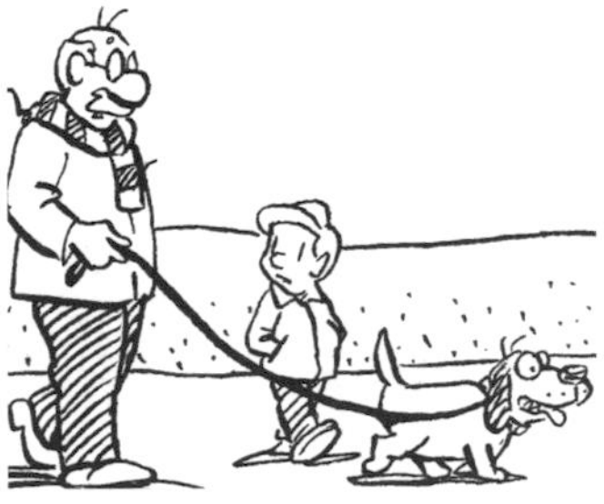

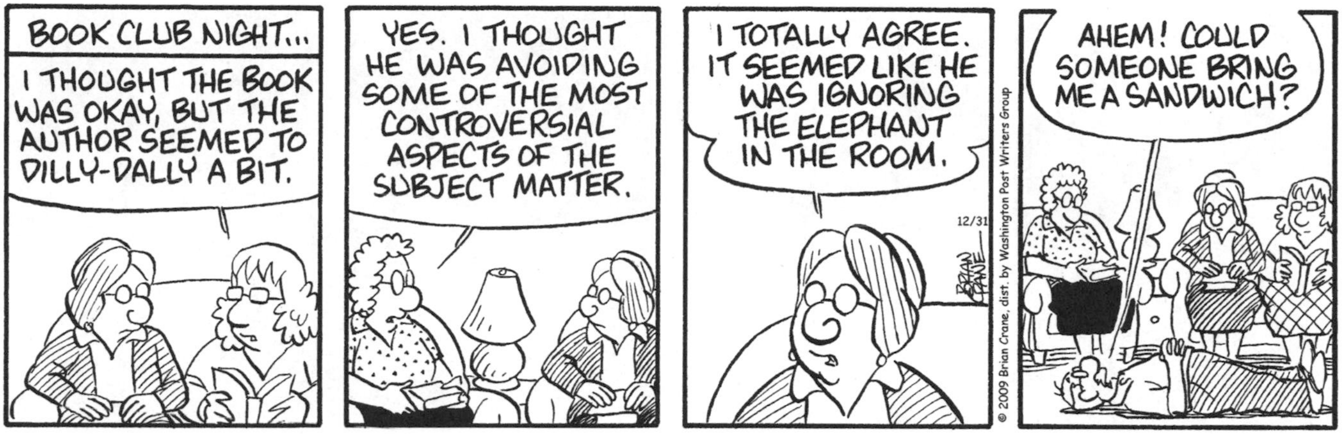
BOOK CLUB NIGHT...
I THOUGHT THE BOOK WAS OKAY, BUT THE AUTHOR SEEMED TO DILLY-DALLY A BIT.
YES. I THOUGHT HE WAS AVOIDING SOME OF THE MOST CONTROVERSIAL ASPECTS OF THE SUBJECT MATTER.
I TOTALLY AGREE. IT SEEMED LIKE HE WAS IGNORING THE ELEPHANT IN THE ROOM.
AHEM! COULD SOMEONE BRING ME A SANDWICH?
12/31
© 2009 Brian Crane, dist. by Washington Post Writers Group

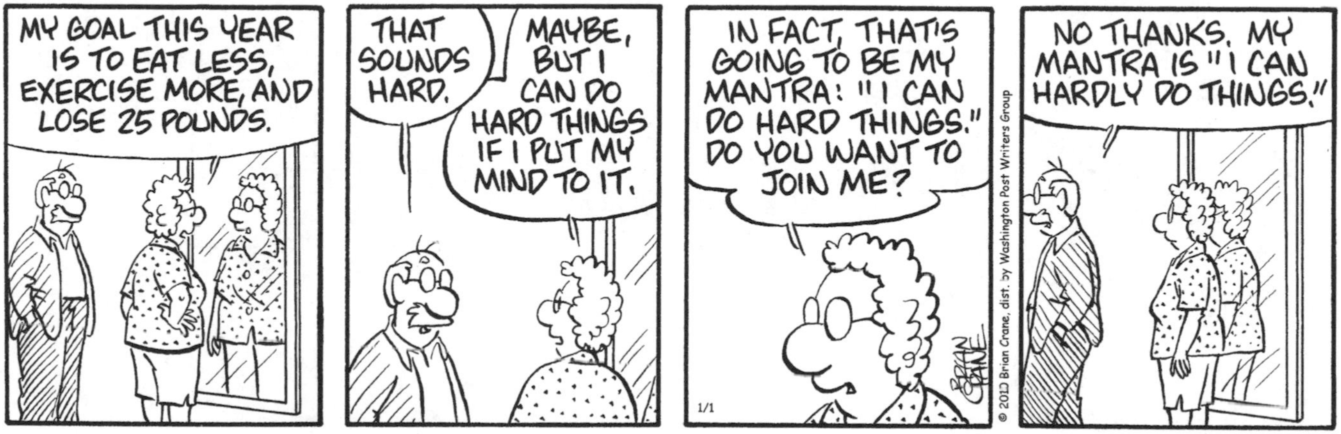
MY GOAL THIS YEAR IS TO EAT LESS, EXERCISE MORE, AND LOSE 25 POUNDS.
THAT SOUNDS HARD.
MAYBE, BUT I CAN DO HARD THINGS IF I PUT MY MIND TO IT.
IN FACT, THAT'S GOING TO BE MY MANTRA: "I CAN DO HARD THINGS." DO YOU WANT TO JOIN ME?
NO THANKS. MY MANTRA IS "I CAN HARDLY DO THINGS."
1/1
© 2010 Brian Crane, dist. by Washington Post Writers Group

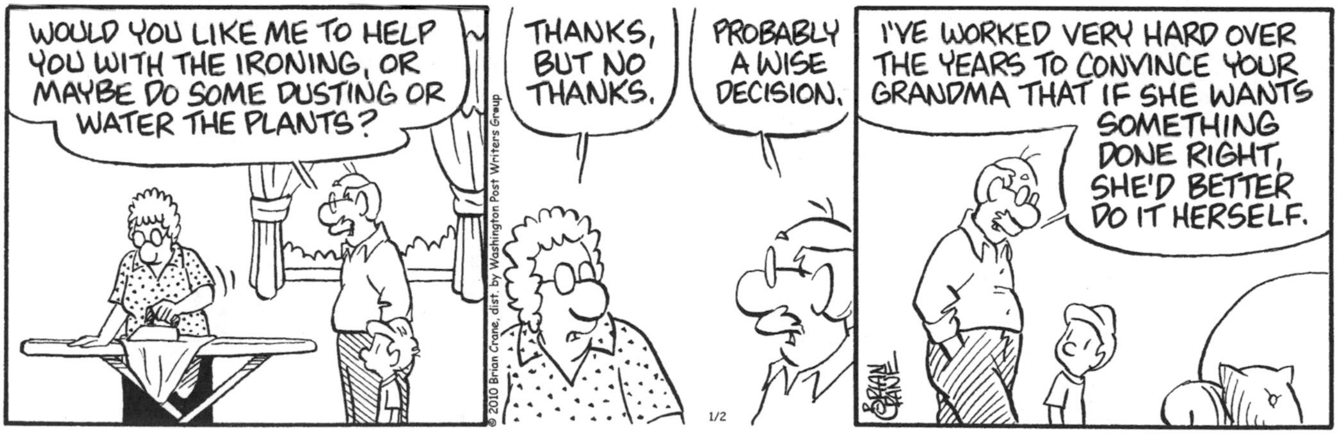
WOULD YOU LIKE ME TO HELP YOU WITH THE IRONING, OR MAYBE DO SOME DUSTING OR WATER THE PLANTS?
THANKS, BUT NO THANKS.
PROBABLY A WISE DECISION.
I'VE WORKED VERY HARD OVER THE YEARS TO CONVINCE YOUR GRANDMA THAT IF SHE WANTS SOMETHING DONE RIGHT, SHE'D BETTER DO IT HERSELF.
1/2
© 2010 Brian Crane, dist. by Washington Post Writers Group

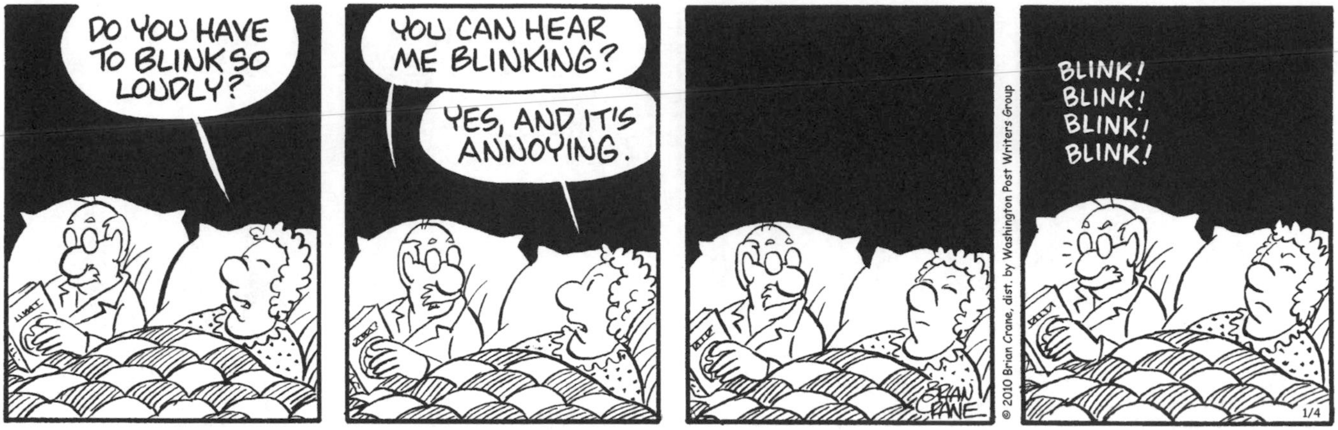
DO YOU HAVE TO BLINK SO LOUDLY?
YOU CAN HEAR ME BLINKING?
YES, AND IT'S ANNOYING.
BLINK! BLINK! BLINK! BLINK!
1/4

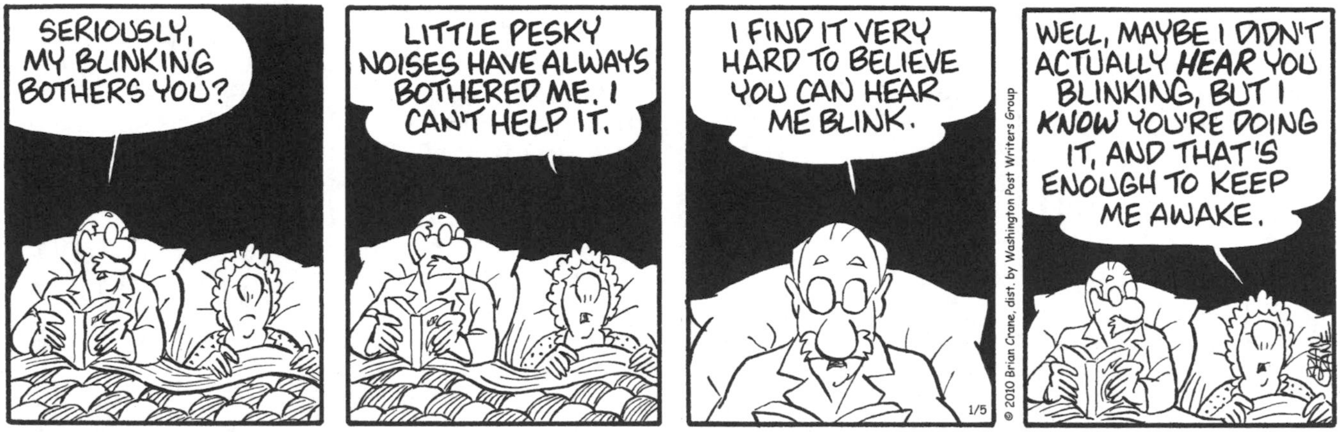
SERIOUSLY, MY BLINKING BOTHERS YOU?
LITTLE PESKY NOISES HAVE ALWAYS BOTHERED ME. I CAN'T HELP IT.
I FIND IT VERY HARD TO BELIEVE YOU CAN HEAR ME BLINK.
1/5
WELL, MAYBE I DIDN'T ACTUALLY **HEAR** YOU BLINKING, BUT I **KNOW** YOU'RE DOING IT, AND THAT'S ENOUGH TO KEEP ME AWAKE.

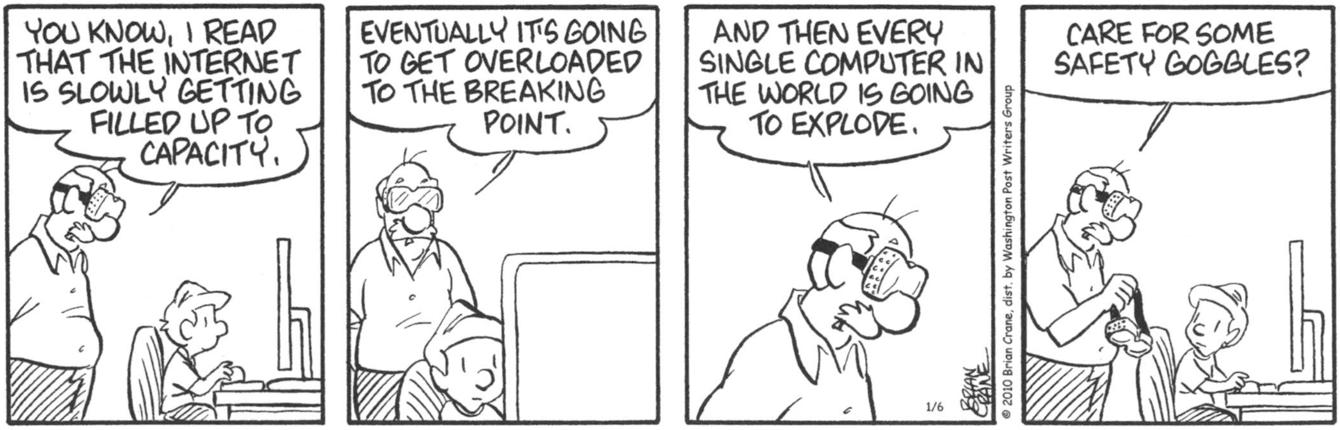
YOU KNOW, I READ THAT THE INTERNET IS SLOWLY GETTING FILLED UP TO CAPACITY.
EVENTUALLY IT'S GOING TO GET OVERLOADED TO THE BREAKING POINT.
AND THEN EVERY SINGLE COMPUTER IN THE WORLD IS GOING TO EXPLODE.
1/6
CARE FOR SOME SAFETY GOGGLES?

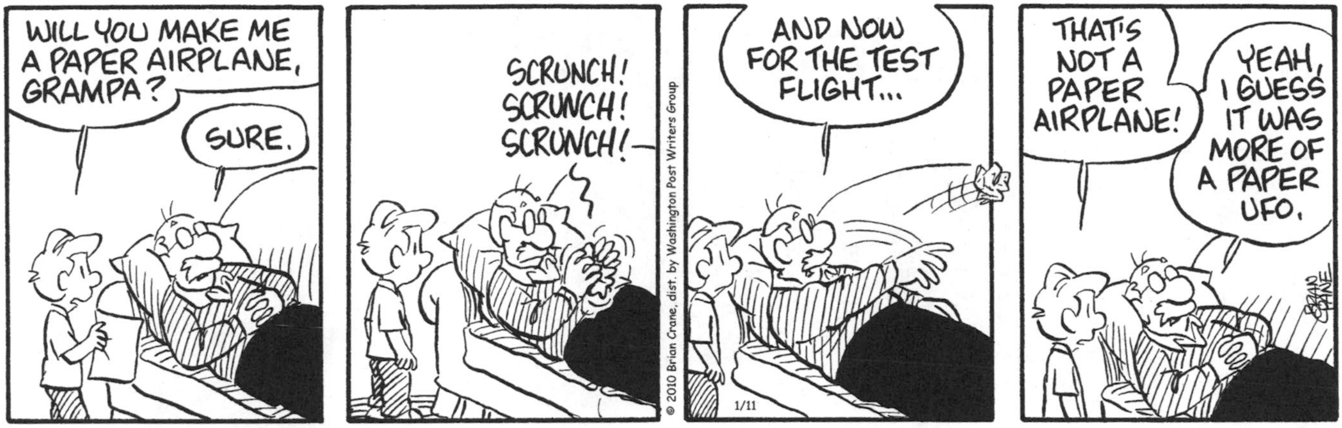
WILL YOU MAKE ME A PAPER AIRPLANE, GRAMPA?
SURE.
SCRUNCH! SCRUNCH! SCRUNCH!
© 2010 Brian Crane, dist. by Washington Post Writers Group
AND NOW FOR THE TEST FLIGHT...
1/11
THAT'S NOT A PAPER AIRPLANE!
YEAH, I GUESS IT WAS MORE OF A PAPER UFO.
BRIAN CRANE

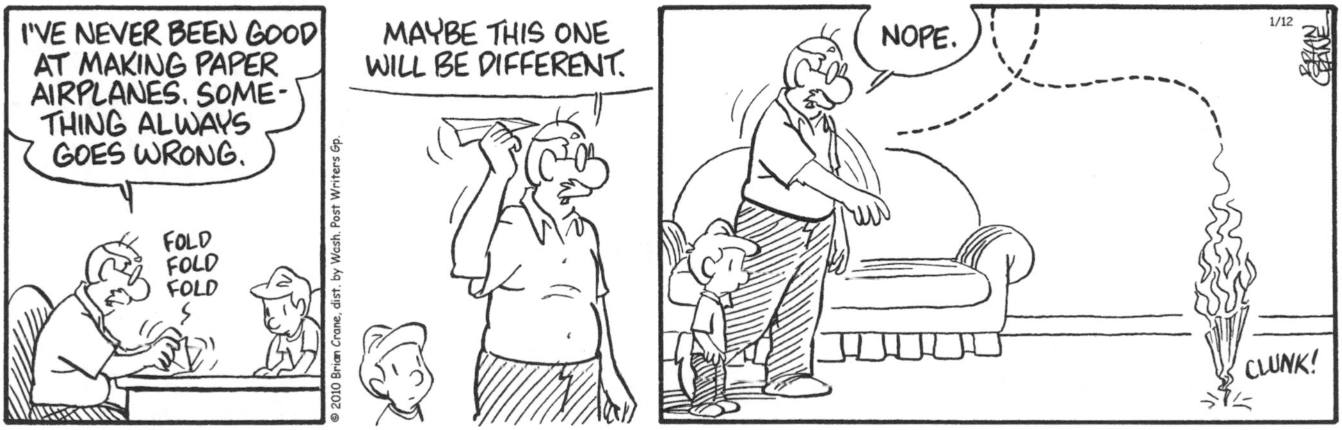
I'VE NEVER BEEN GOOD AT MAKING PAPER AIRPLANES. SOMETHING ALWAYS GOES WRONG.
FOLD FOLD FOLD
© 2010 Brian Crane, dist. by Wash. Post Writers Gp.
MAYBE THIS ONE WILL BE DIFFERENT.
NOPE.
1/12
CLUNK!
BRIAN CRANE

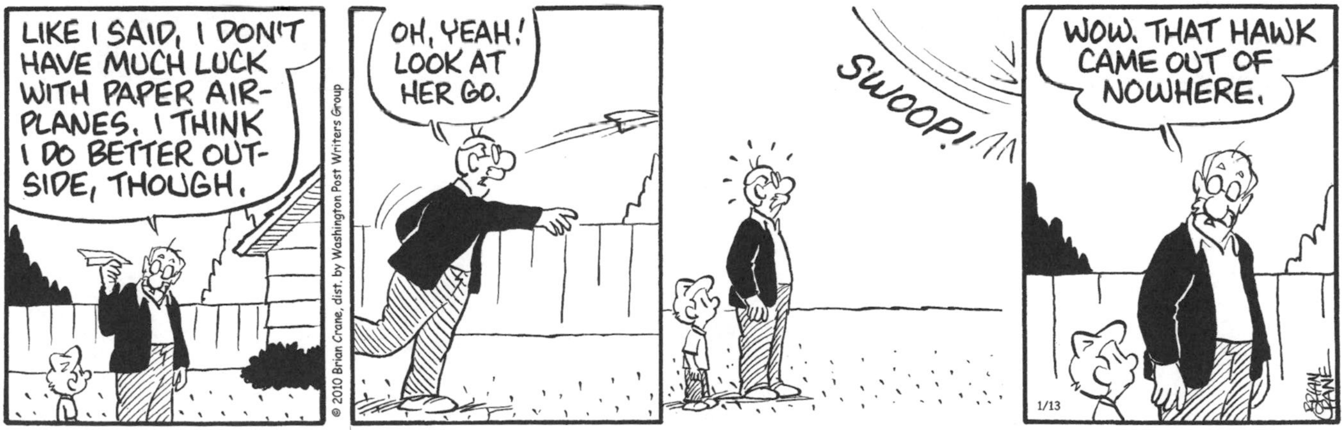
LIKE I SAID, I DON'T HAVE MUCH LUCK WITH PAPER AIRPLANES. I THINK I DO BETTER OUTSIDE, THOUGH.
© 2010 Brian Crane, dist. by Washington Post Writers Group
OH, YEAH! LOOK AT HER GO.
SWOOP!
WOW. THAT HAWK CAME OUT OF NOWHERE.
1/13
BRIAN CRANE

Sunday Pickles

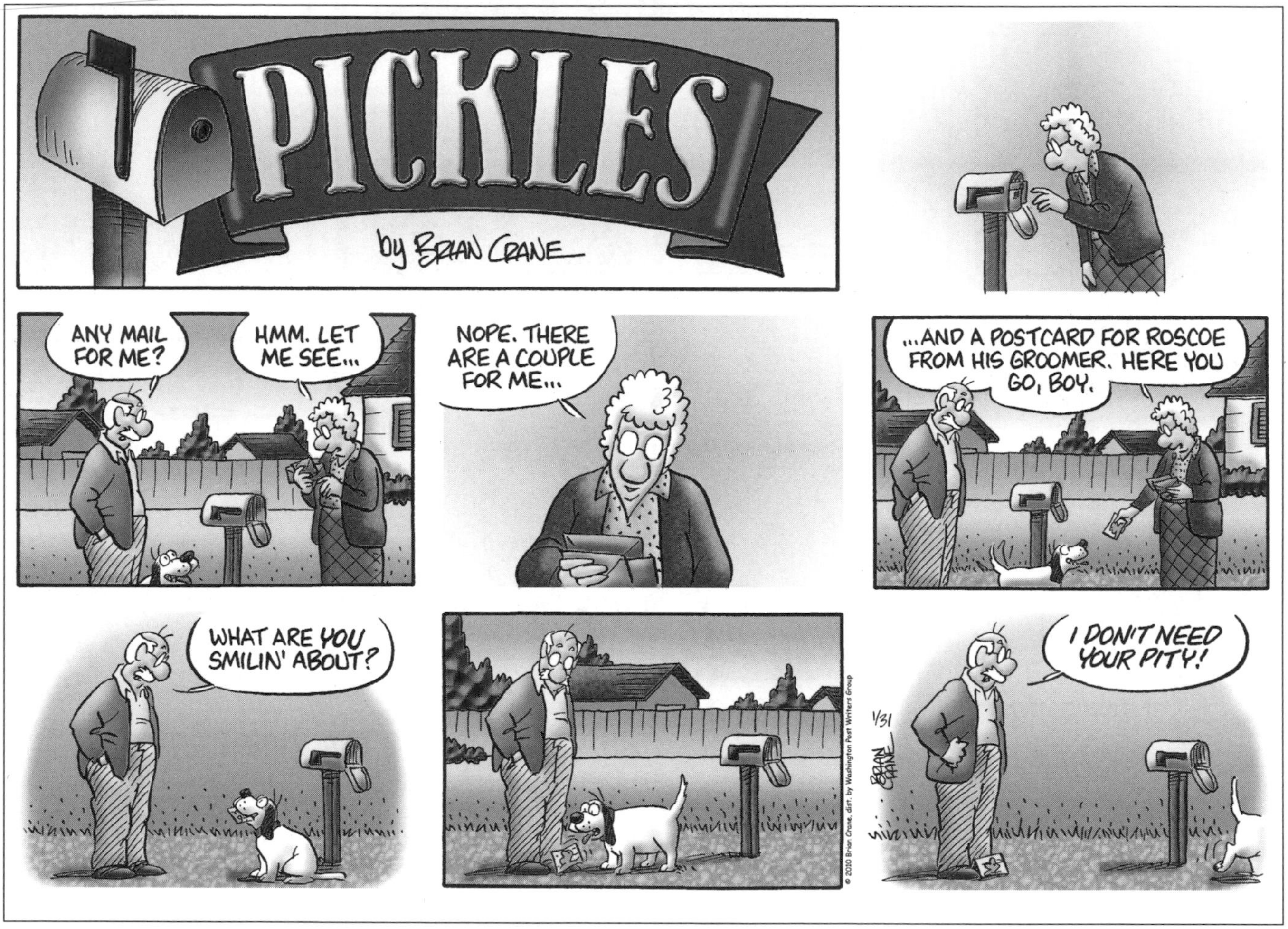
PICKLES
by BRIAN CRANE
ANY MAIL FOR ME?
HMM. LET ME SEE...
NOPE. THERE ARE A COUPLE FOR ME...
...AND A POSTCARD FOR ROSCOE FROM HIS GROOMER. HERE YOU GO, BOY.
WHAT ARE YOU SMILIN' ABOUT?
© 2010 Brian Crane, dist. by Washington Post Writers Group
1/31
I DON'T NEED YOUR PITY!

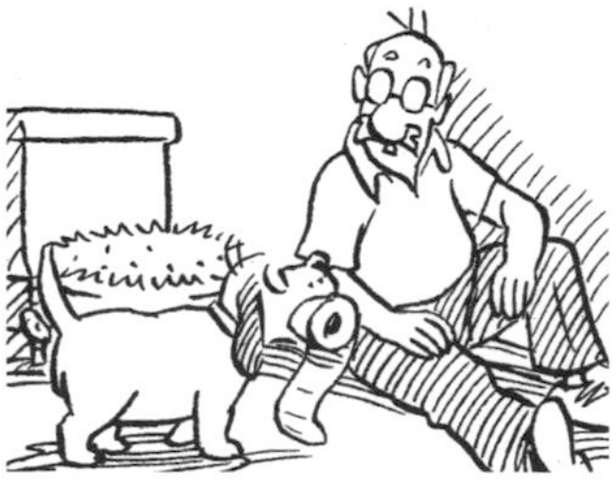

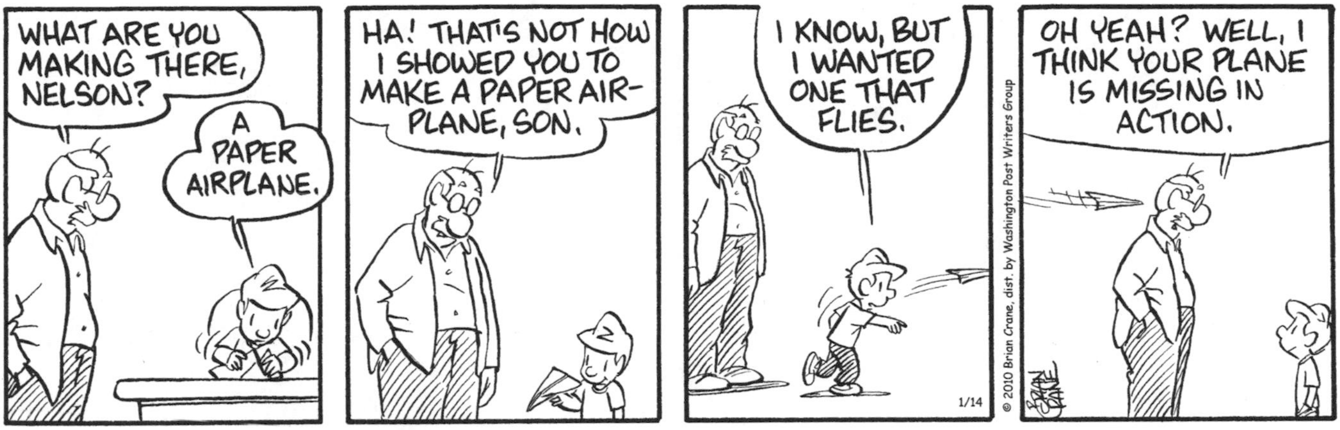
WHAT ARE YOU MAKING THERE, NELSON?
A PAPER AIRPLANE.
HA! THAT'S NOT HOW I SHOWED YOU TO MAKE A PAPER AIR-PLANE, SON.
I KNOW, BUT I WANTED ONE THAT FLIES.
1/14
OH YEAH? WELL, I THINK YOUR PLANE IS MISSING IN ACTION.
BRIAN CRANE

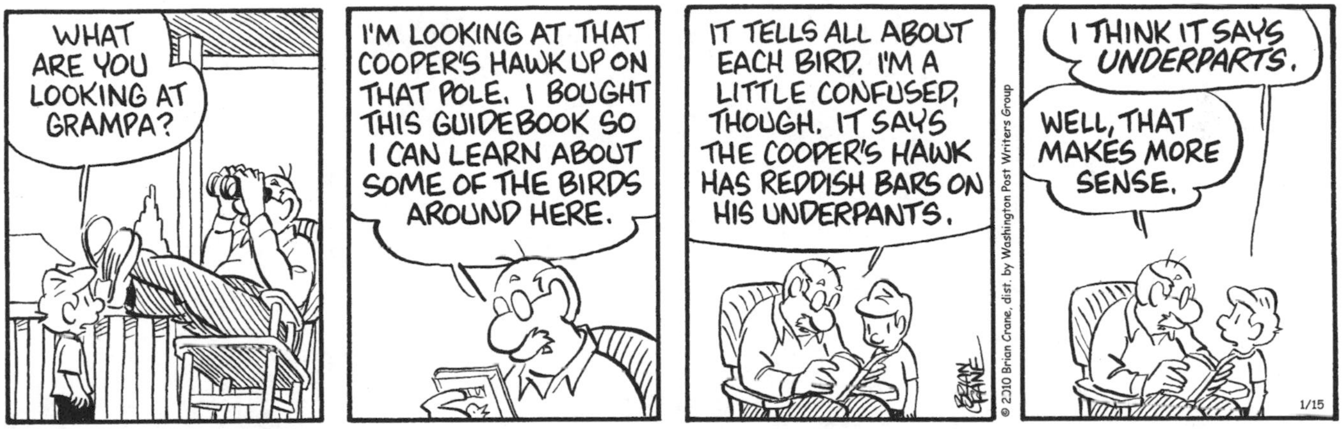
WHAT ARE YOU LOOKING AT GRAMPA?
I'M LOOKING AT THAT COOPER'S HAWK UP ON THAT POLE. I BOUGHT THIS GUIDEBOOK SO I CAN LEARN ABOUT SOME OF THE BIRDS AROUND HERE.
IT TELLS ALL ABOUT EACH BIRD. I'M A LITTLE CONFUSED, THOUGH. IT SAYS THE COOPER'S HAWK HAS REDDISH BARS ON HIS UNDERPANTS.
BRIAN CRANE
I THINK IT SAYS *UNDERPARTS*.
WELL, THAT MAKES MORE SENSE.
1/15

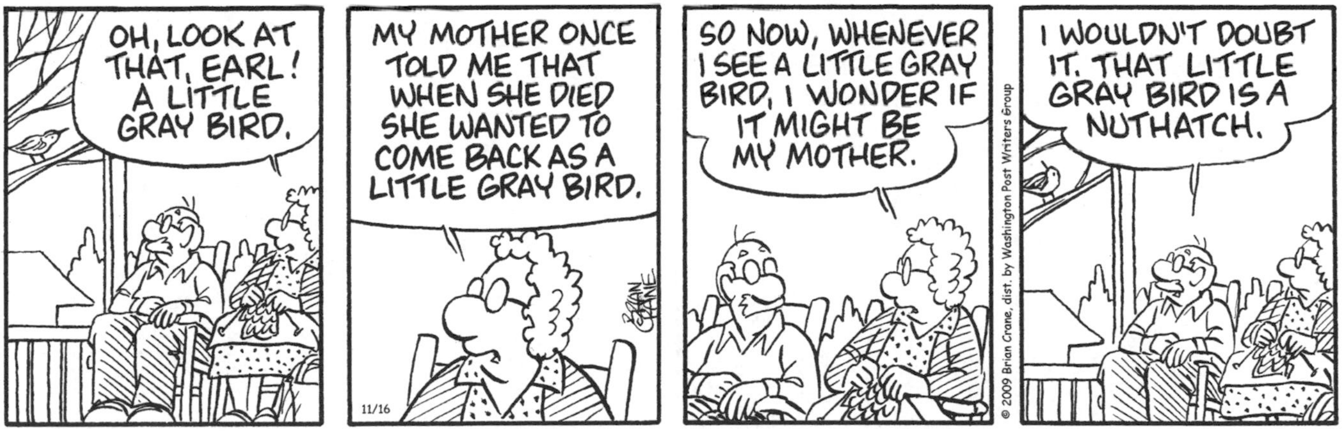
OH, LOOK AT THAT, EARL! A LITTLE GRAY BIRD.
MY MOTHER ONCE TOLD ME THAT WHEN SHE DIED SHE WANTED TO COME BACK AS A LITTLE GRAY BIRD.
BRIAN CRANE
11/16
SO NOW, WHENEVER I SEE A LITTLE GRAY BIRD, I WONDER IF IT MIGHT BE MY MOTHER.
I WOULDN'T DOUBT IT. THAT LITTLE GRAY BIRD IS A NUTHATCH.

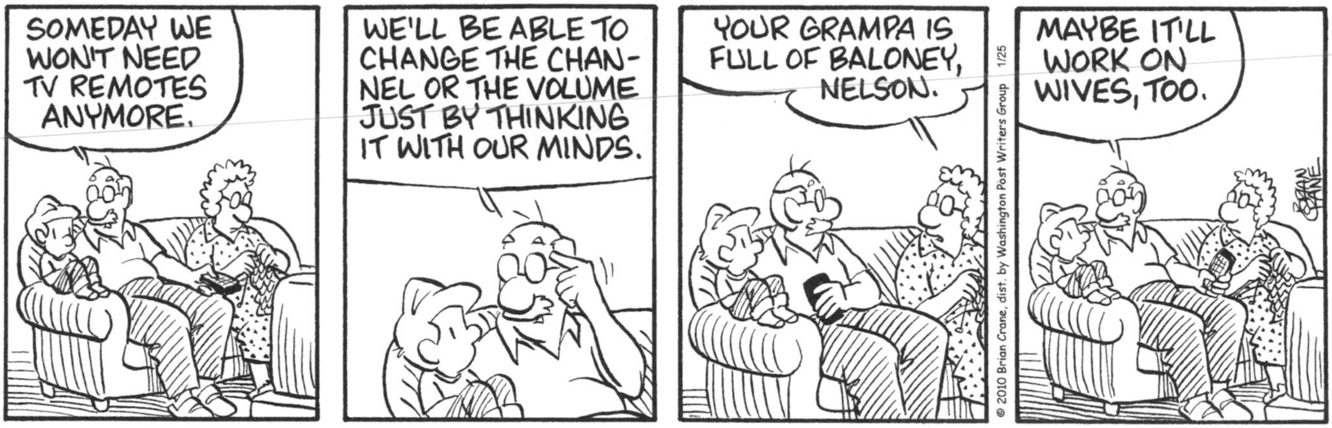
SOMEDAY WE WON'T NEED TV REMOTES ANYMORE.
WE'LL BE ABLE TO CHANGE THE CHANNEL OR THE VOLUME JUST BY THINKING IT WITH OUR MINDS.
YOUR GRAMPA IS FULL OF BALONEY, NELSON.
MAYBE IT'LL WORK ON WIVES, TOO.
BRIAN CRANE
© 2010 Brian Crane, dist. by Washington Post Writers Group 1/25

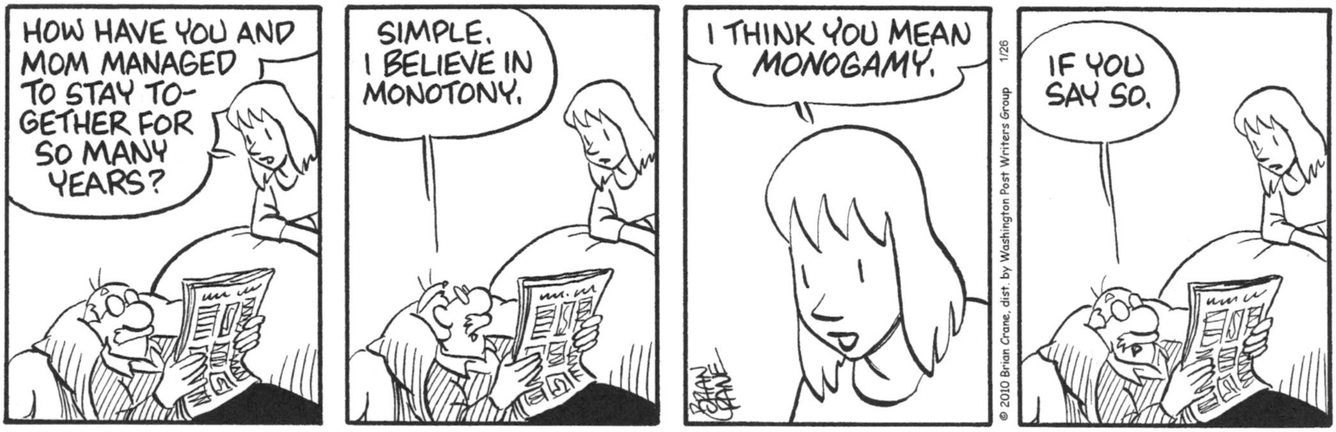
HOW HAVE YOU AND MOM MANAGED TO STAY TOGETHER FOR SO MANY YEARS?
SIMPLE. I BELIEVE IN MONOTONY.
I THINK YOU MEAN *MONOGAMY*.
IF YOU SAY SO.
BRIAN CRANE
© 2010 Brian Crane, dist. by Washington Post Writers Group 1/26

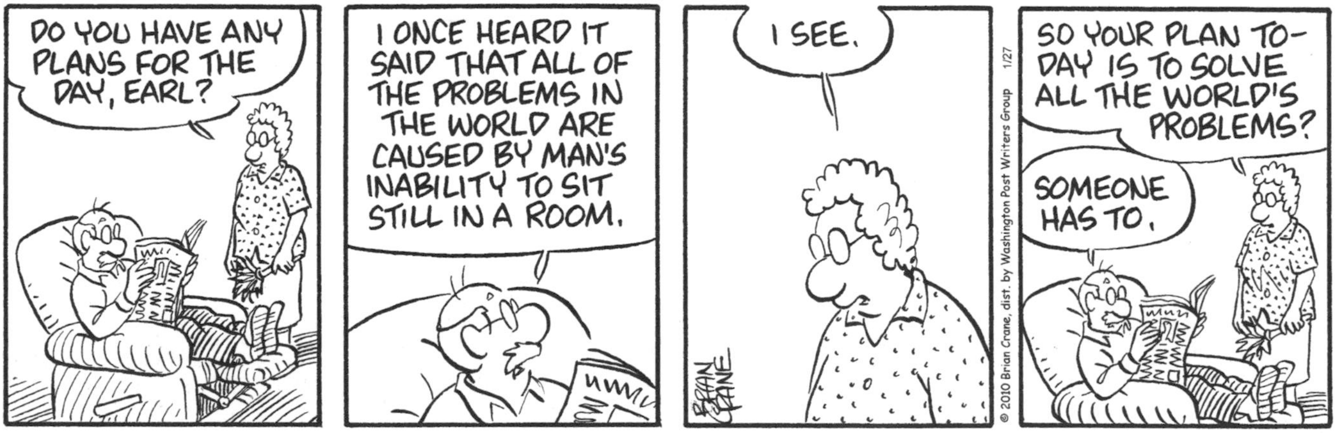
DO YOU HAVE ANY PLANS FOR THE DAY, EARL?
I ONCE HEARD IT SAID THAT ALL OF THE PROBLEMS IN THE WORLD ARE CAUSED BY MAN'S INABILITY TO SIT STILL IN A ROOM.
I SEE.
SO YOUR PLAN TODAY IS TO SOLVE ALL THE WORLD'S PROBLEMS?
SOMEONE HAS TO.
BRIAN CRANE
© 2010 Brian Crane, dist. by Washington Post Writers Group 1/27

SundayPickles

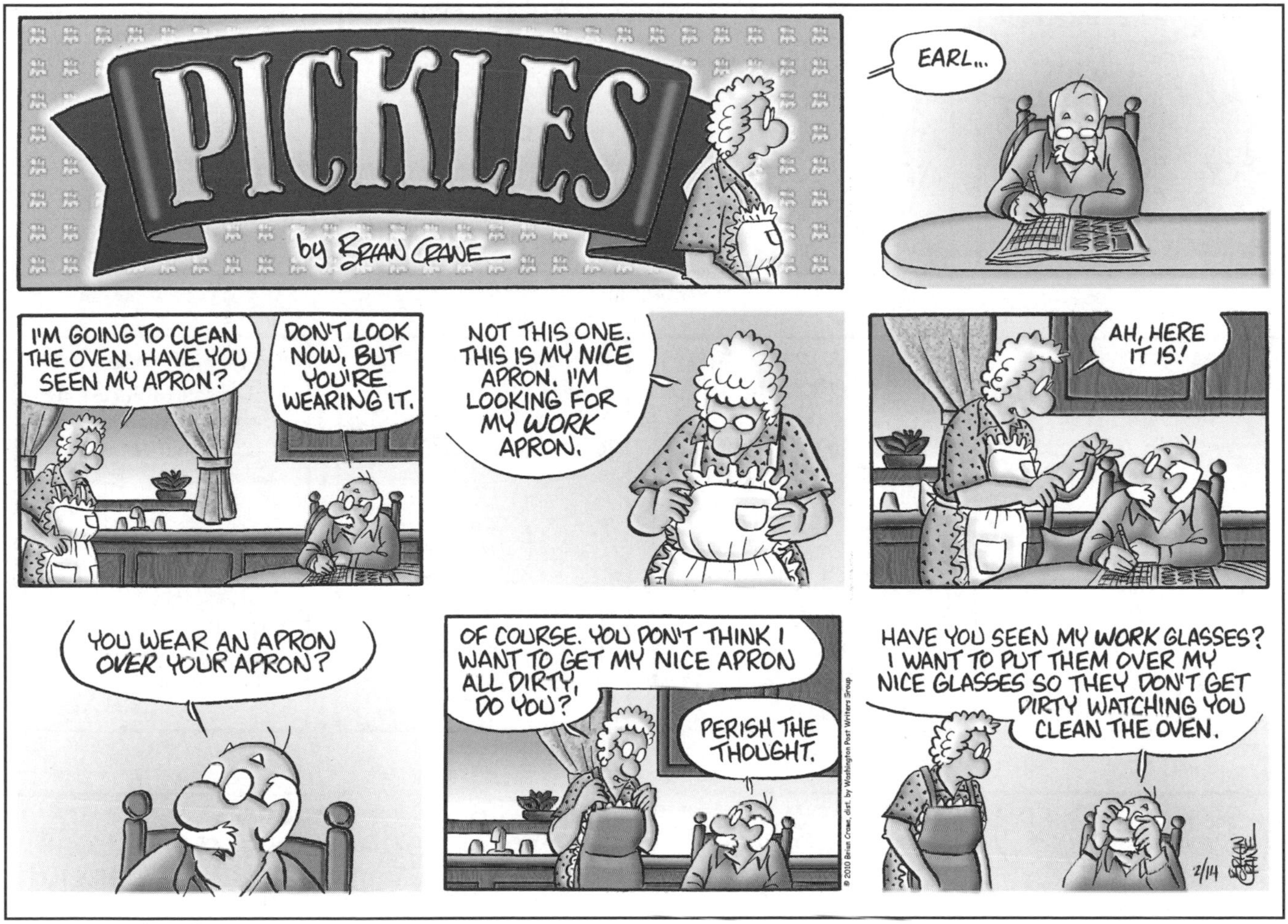
PICKLES
by BRIAN CRANE
EARL...
I'M GOING TO CLEAN THE OVEN. HAVE YOU SEEN MY APRON?
DON'T LOOK NOW, BUT YOU'RE WEARING IT.
NOT THIS ONE. THIS IS MY NICE APRON. I'M LOOKING FOR MY WORK APRON.
AH, HERE IT IS!
YOU WEAR AN APRON OVER YOUR APRON?
OF COURSE. YOU DON'T THINK I WANT TO GET MY NICE APRON ALL DIRTY, DO YOU?
PERISH THE THOUGHT.
© 2010 Brian Crane, dist. by Washington Post Writers Group
HAVE YOU SEEN MY WORK GLASSES? I WANT TO PUT THEM OVER MY NICE GLASSES SO THEY DON'T GET DIRTY WATCHING YOU CLEAN THE OVEN.
2/14
BRIAN CRANE

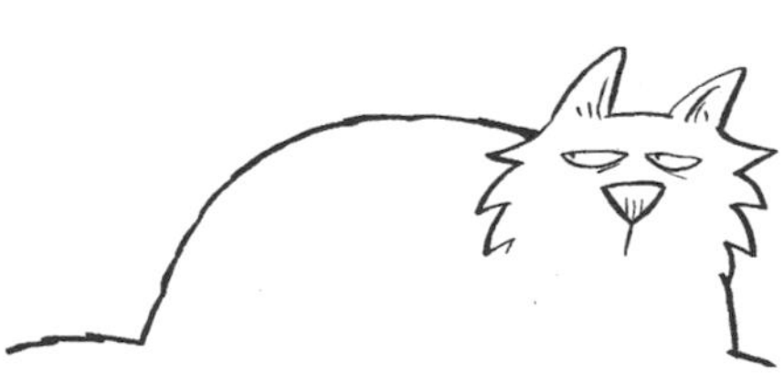

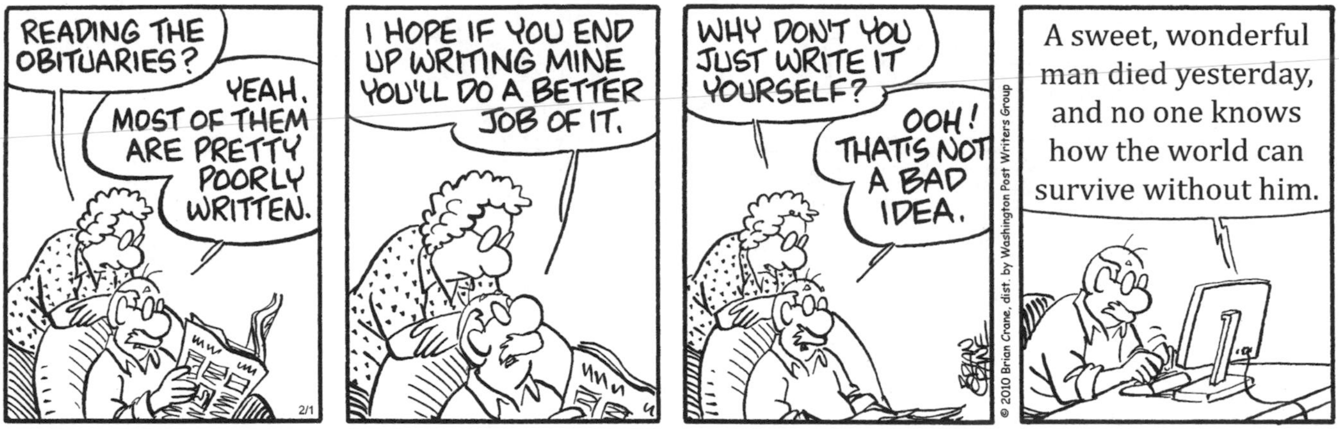
READING THE OBITUARIES?
YEAH. MOST OF THEM ARE PRETTY POORLY WRITTEN.
I HOPE IF YOU END UP WRITING MINE YOU'LL DO A BETTER JOB OF IT.
WHY DON'T YOU JUST WRITE IT YOURSELF?
OOH! THAT'S NOT A BAD IDEA.
© 2010 Brian Crane, dist. by Washington Post Writers Group
A sweet, wonderful man died yesterday, and no one knows how the world can survive without him.
2/1

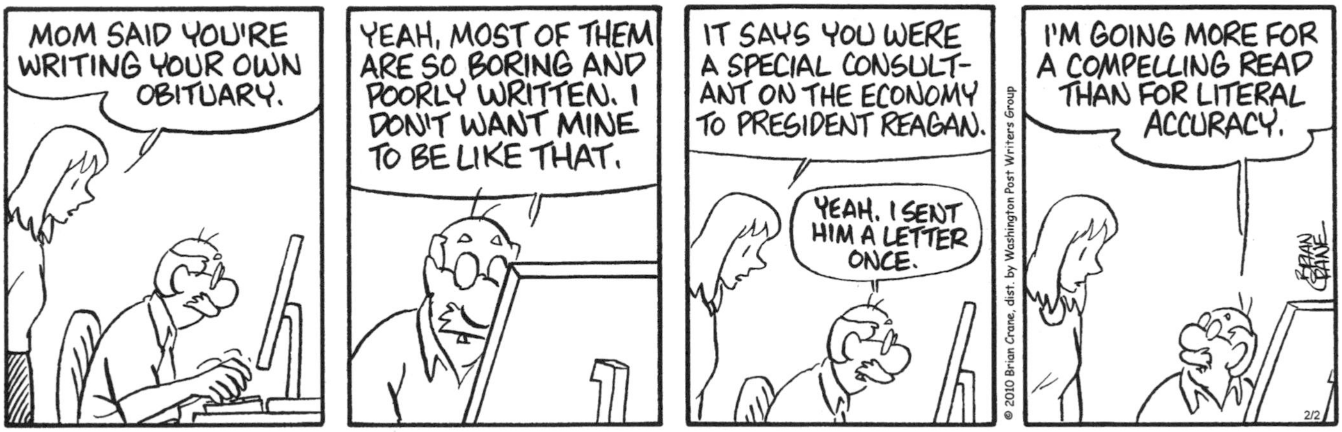
MOM SAID YOU'RE WRITING YOUR OWN OBITUARY.
YEAH, MOST OF THEM ARE SO BORING AND POORLY WRITTEN. I DON'T WANT MINE TO BE LIKE THAT.
IT SAYS YOU WERE A SPECIAL CONSULTANT ON THE ECONOMY TO PRESIDENT REAGAN.
YEAH. I SENT HIM A LETTER ONCE.
© 2010 Brian Crane, dist. by Washington Post Writers Group
I'M GOING MORE FOR A COMPELLING READ THAN FOR LITERAL ACCURACY.
2/2

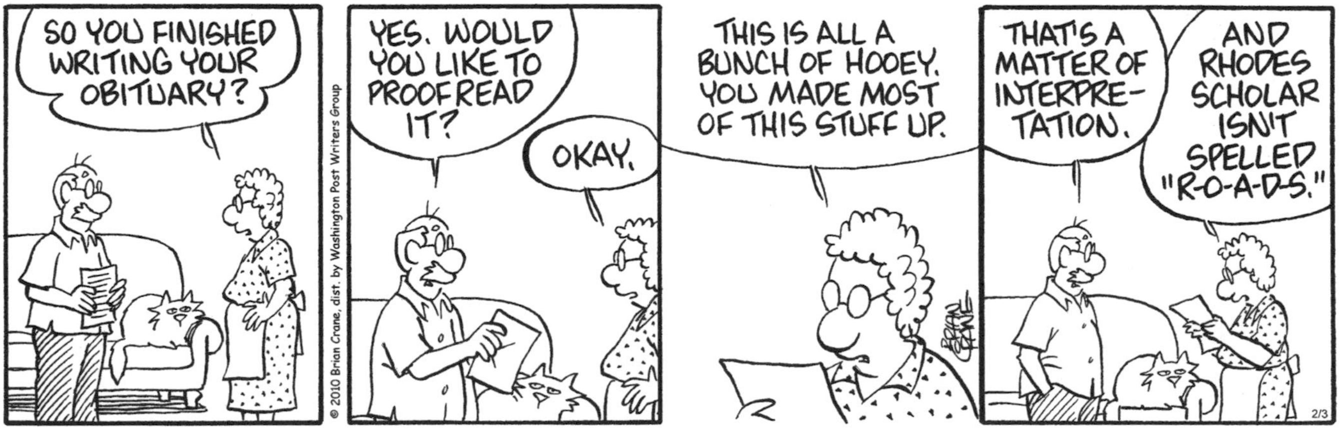
SO YOU FINISHED WRITING YOUR OBITUARY?
© 2010 Brian Crane, dist. by Washington Post Writers Group
YES. WOULD YOU LIKE TO PROOFREAD IT?
OKAY.
THIS IS ALL A BUNCH OF HOOEY. YOU MADE MOST OF THIS STUFF UP.
THAT'S A MATTER OF INTERPRETATION.
AND RHODES SCHOLAR ISN'T SPELLED "R-O-A-D-S."
2/3

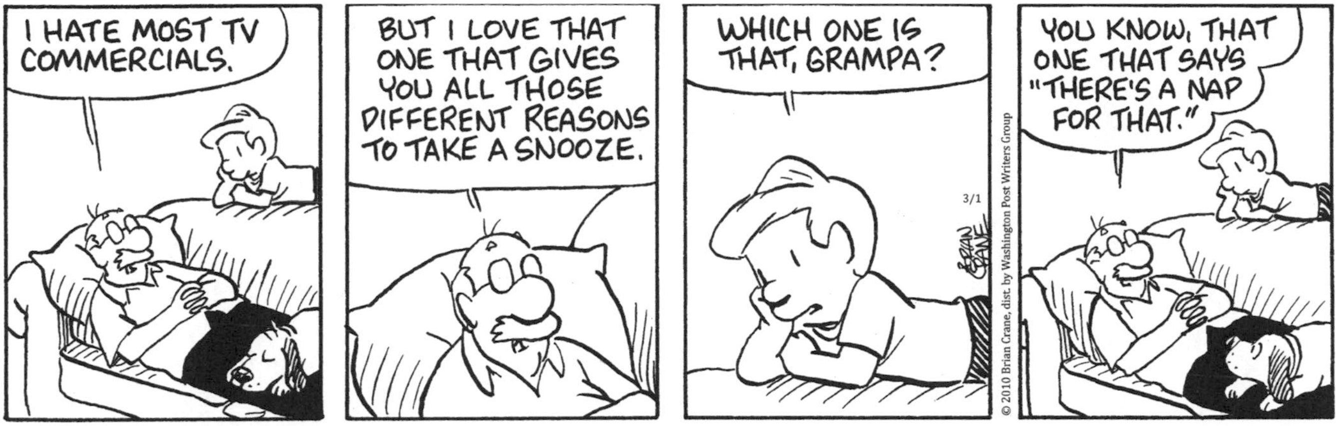
I HATE MOST TV COMMERCIALS.
BUT I LOVE THAT ONE THAT GIVES YOU ALL THOSE DIFFERENT REASONS TO TAKE A SNOOZE.
WHICH ONE IS THAT, GRAMPA?
3/1
YOU KNOW, THAT ONE THAT SAYS "THERE'S A NAP FOR THAT."
© 2010 Brian Crane, dist. by Washington Post Writers Group

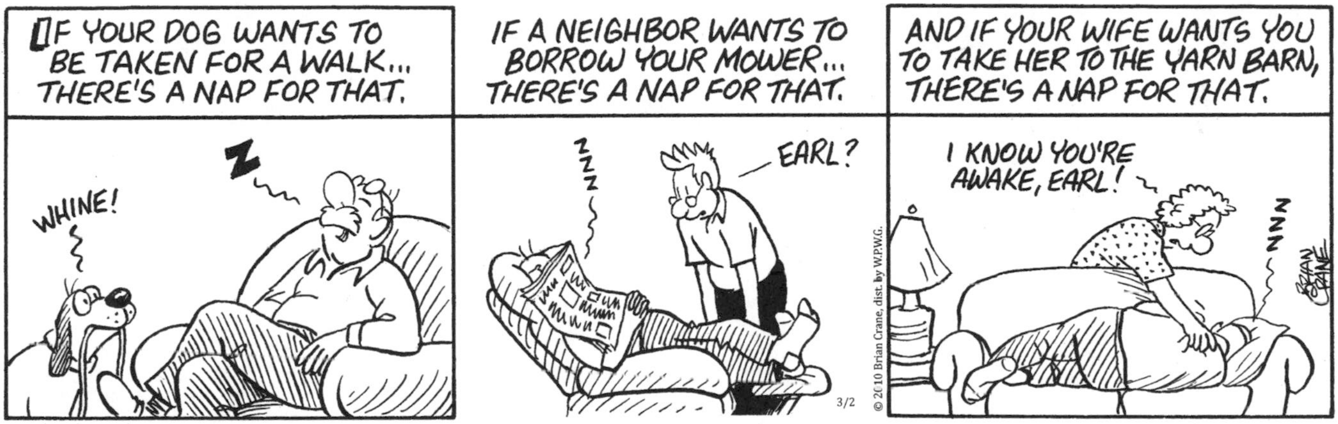
IF YOUR DOG WANTS TO BE TAKEN FOR A WALK... THERE'S A NAP FOR THAT.
WHINE!
Z
IF A NEIGHBOR WANTS TO BORROW YOUR MOWER... THERE'S A NAP FOR THAT.
ZZZ
EARL?
3/2
© 2010 Brian Crane, dist. by W.P.W.G.
AND IF YOUR WIFE WANTS YOU TO TAKE HER TO THE YARN BARN, THERE'S A NAP FOR THAT.
I KNOW YOU'RE AWAKE, EARL!
ZZZ

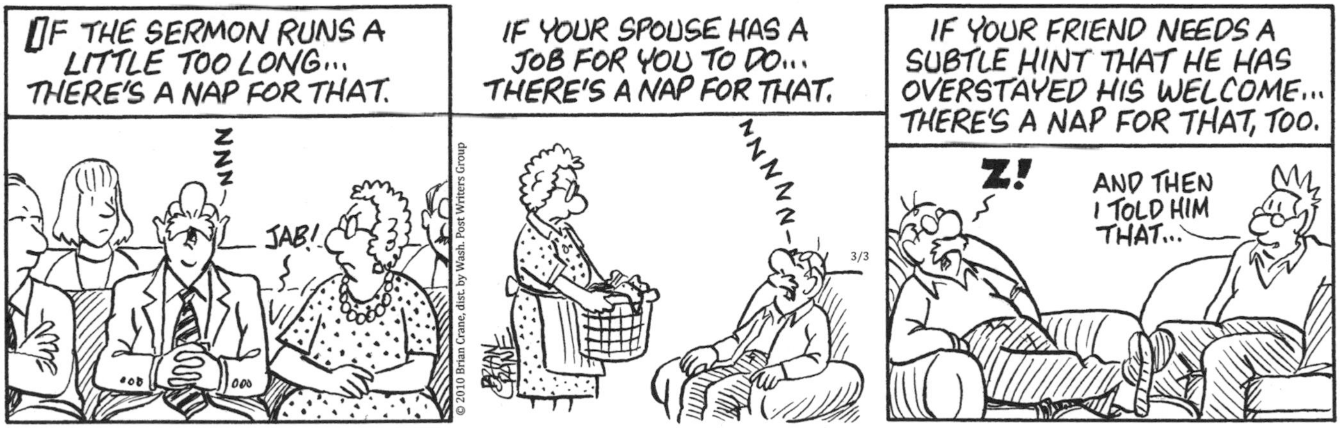
IF THE SERMON RUNS A LITTLE TOO LONG... THERE'S A NAP FOR THAT.
ZZZ
JAB!
© 2010 Brian Crane, dist. by Wash. Post Writers Group
IF YOUR SPOUSE HAS A JOB FOR YOU TO DO... THERE'S A NAP FOR THAT.
ZZZZZ
3/3
IF YOUR FRIEND NEEDS A SUBTLE HINT THAT HE HAS OVERSTAYED HIS WELCOME... THERE'S A NAP FOR THAT, TOO.
Z!
AND THEN I TOLD HIM THAT...